Kimberly's Capital Punishment

Richard Milward was born in Middlesbrough in 1984, where he now lives and works. His debut, *Apples*, was published in 2007, and his second novel, *Ten Storey Love Song*, in 2009, both to huge critical acclaim. He graduated from Byam Shaw at Central St Martins in 2008 with a Fine Art degree, and is currently working on his next novel.

by the same author

Apples

Ten Storey Love Song

Kimberly's Capital Punishment
Richard Milward

faber and faber

First published in 2012
by Faber and Faber Limited
Bloomsbury House
74–77 Great Russell Street
London WC1B 3DA

Typeset by Faber and Faber Limited
Printed in the UK by CPI Group (UK) Ltd, Croydon, CR0 4YY

A CIP record for this book
is available from the British Library

Limited Edition ISBN 978–0–571–28345–3
Trade Paperback ISBN 978–0–571–28898–4

FSC
www.fsc.org
MIX
Paper from
responsible sources
FSC® C101712

10 9 8 7 6 5 4 3 2 1

One day it will have to be officially admitted that what we have christened reality is an even greater illusion than the world of dreams.

Salvador Dalí

Oh, outcast of all outcasts most abandoned!—to the earth art thou not forever dead? to its honors, to its flowers, to its golden aspirations?—and a cloud, dense, dismal, and limitless, does it not hang eternally between thy hopes and heavens?

Edgar Allan Poe, 'William Wilson' (1839)

Part 1) Kimberly Clark

I found the eyeball fifteen minutes before I found the rest of him. I stood there in shock for a while, wondering which poor soul had lost it, then I smirked, thinking they'd have quite a bit of trouble finding it again.

The eyeball winked, I think. I bent down with my hands on my knees, to have a closer look. I staggered backwards. Eyeballs are miles bigger than you imagine, what with them being blocked off by the sockets most of the time, and I shivered at it. The stalk was disgusting, like a dog-eared umbilical cord. I wished Stevie was around to show him, although he wasn't that keen on the eyeball in *Demolition Man*, and I doubted he'd be keen on this one either.

You wouldn't expect to find an eyeball in the middle of a clearing, in the middle of a common, in the middle of the Capital, but, then again, you wouldn't expect to find a three-wheeled pushchair, an unopened bottle of Glen's Vodka, a yo-yo with the string missing, or a purple carrot either. The common was a tip, especially the muddy bit me and the eyeball were standing in. I trod about on the spot, cracking twigs, then carried on looking for Stevie. I was growing thirsty. I think I was cultivating a sore throat too, and I dreamed of orange juice as I bounded through the trees. In fact, the sun reminded me of a giant orange, slowly being squeezed on the horizon as it began to set. I licked the air. It was getting a little chilly, and I felt a little silly having only come out in the dotty cardigan.

Stevie loved running away from things. He loved it so much, he did it for a living. Me and him moved to the Capital so he could pursue a career in athletics or, more specifically, the 200m sprint, which is the ideal activity for fast-footed, impatient people

1

who only like to participate in sports for twenty or thirty seconds at a time. Stevie's legs were like a leopard's, with freckles all over them. We used to shave them together at bathtime, causing tiny hairy rafts to set sail in the seafoam, and in the early days I took pride in treating his athlete's foot for him, as well as all his other athlete's body parts. He was an incredible sprinter, often coming home from his 'meets' with more gold, silver and bronze necklaces than I've got in my entire jewellery box. I was proud of him, but it could be annoying at times, the way he couldn't stand five minutes in a park or recreation ground without running off. Stevie was a shy boy – I think he enjoyed the peace and quiet of jogging about, with only his thoughts for company. The loneliness of the short-distance runner.

Or perhaps he'd already seen the eyeball, and got frightened.

I started waddling like a penguin, going down a steep bit. I was incredibly thirsty by this point, and feeling less and less impressed with Stevie. It was about half past four: time for him to take me to the pub and buy me an orange juice, I thought. I grumbled as I stepped in some wet mud. The whole place was dead. Perhaps it was that time of day when no one goes to the common, or perhaps it's just one of those commons no one ever goes to, no matter what time of day it is. I decided to suck on a Strepsil, dishing a lemon one out of my Medicine Bag.

I could've given Stevie a ring but, unfortunately, like a lot of men, he's a sufferer of a severe socially debilitating disorder known as telephonophobia: the irrational fear of speaking to people on the blower. He didn't have a phone. He hated talking to people as it was, let alone when they weren't even present. I'm not sure what came first – his hatred of social interaction, or his st-st-st-stutter.

I sighed, accidentally spitting out the Strepsil. The trees were looking more like burned witches' fingers, the further I went. A

2

lot of the Capital is haunted, due to the oldness of the place and the many executions and murders that have gone on. Gulping, I decided to make my way back to the eyeball, just in case it had seen which way my boyfriend went. Tripping over roots and four-pack plastic rings, I followed the elms back up to the clearing where the eye lived. I scampered carefully round the three-wheeled pushchair and the vodka bottle on tip-toes, hoping not to tread on it accidentally.

'Stevie?!' I yelled at the wood. It made my tonsils hurt. I was about to give up on him and head back home in a huff when I spotted something winking at me from under the leaves, and I caught the eye of the eyeball again. Kneeling down, I saw the iris was glittery, like some kind of reflector you might put on your bike. The pupil had changed its focus – it seemed to be staring at something down the mound now, and I frog-hopped on the balls of my feet to get a better view. Lining my two eyes up with the one in the mud, I followed its gaze over the yo-yo; through the legs of the pushchair; underneath some fallen branches; then out across the children's adventure playground, fifty-odd feet away. Squinting, I could just make out the empty swings, zip-line, bouncy hippos, and a man hanging from the top rung of the climbing frame. I jumped up with fright. Usually when you climb a climbing frame, you hang with your arms above your head, gripping the rungs like a monkey, but this young fellow somehow had the knack of hanging from it with his arms by his sides. He'd tied his shoelaces around his neck, attached himself to the top rung, and let himself drop. He was dead, by the look of it.

My throat was so sore, I couldn't get a scream out. I was paralysed – in fact, the whole area of woodland was suddenly still and quiet, except for my heart clattering in my ribcage. After ten seconds of shock, I coughed and wiped my face. All I wanted was for Stevie to be there, to have someone to hug, and cry on. I spun

3

around, desperately calling his name. After about ten seconds of doing that, finally I clocked him, lingering some fifty-odd feet away. I sprinted towards him, with my arms outstretched. I burst into tears, grabbing him. He didn't grab me back. He just swayed a bit, hanging there from the top rung of the climbing frame. With his arms by his sides. And one eye missing.

⊙

I couldn't save Stevie in time:

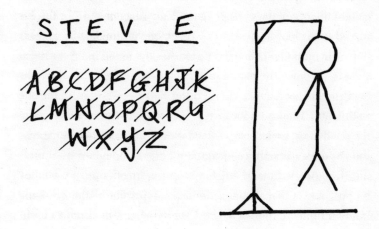

When Stevie was alive, he had white-gold hair, two magnificent silver eyes, two ears slightly too big for his head, a little stubble, a button nose, muscly arms and legs, thin lips, freckles, one earring, a few popped spots, and a penchant for wearing Lycra cycling shorts.

When Stevie was dead, he had a big blue face, white-gold hair, one magnificent silver eye, one bloodied eye-socket, two

4

grey ears slightly too big for his head, a little dribble, a button nose, dangly arms and legs, purple lips, freckles, one earring, a few popped blood vessels, and a penchant for wearing four pairs of shoelaces round his neck.

⊙

And now for a short paragraph about Stevie's famous silver eyes:

When I first met Stevie in the Southern Cross pub in Marton-in-Middlesbrough, the first thing that drew me to him was his eyes. It's a well-known fact that humans are naturally drawn to each other's eyes, but Stevie's were special. Like quite a few folk in Teesside, Stevie was of Scandinavian descent. And, while he shared many physical attributes with the Vikings (like height, and near-transparent hair), it was the low amounts of melanin in his iris stroma that made my legs go to jelly that evening in the Cross. His eyes were like crystal balls – as soon as I looked into them, I knew he was the one. They were beautiful; the irises speckled with various shades of grey, like moon maps. Stevie wasn't conventionally good-looking (and, to be honest, it's hard to fully trust a man who shaves his legs more often than you), but his eyes were the main attraction for me over the years. Unfortunately for Stevie, the low melanin count meant he couldn't stare at bright objects (so we seldom went on summer holidays, and never went out on Bonfire Night, or New Year's Eve), but at least he wasn't albino. Red eyes would have been a turn-off.

And now for a short lesson in ornithology:

Unlike Stevie, the magpie, *Pica pica*, loves staring at (and collecting) bright objects. They're a pest. Famously one of the most sinister birds around, magpies enjoy devouring helpless insects; swaggering about like tiny, tuxedoed gangsters; harassing cats and other birds; and stealing jewellery from your mam's dressing-table. Apparently it's the males that go mad for all your

5

sparkly things, in an attempt to attract females during mating season (the bird equivalent of your boyfriend buying you a nice brooch in the hope of getting you into bed). However, despite all their glamour, magpies will always be associated with death and sorrow. According to folklore, they all go around with Satan's blood in their beaks and, when Jesus was crucified, they didn't cry, and couldn't even be bothered wearing full black mourning gear. They didn't mourn Stevie's death either; in fact, I was convinced I could hear a group of them cackling in the woodland. And I couldn't help feeling that, while Stevie was hanging there on the kids' climbing frame, one of the little bastards (one for sorrow . . . surely not five for silver?) must've burst out of the sky and peck-peck-peck-peck-pecked his beautiful, bright right eye out. I just hope to God Stevie was already dead by the time they got to him.

Ironically, Stevie always used to bang on about hating 'the Magpies', but I think he meant Newcastle United, not the birds.

⊙

The Necropolitan Police agreed it was suicide, which was kind of them. I think it was Stevie's Joy Division T-shirt that swayed it. It was the creamy *Closer* one – the one with the dead bloke on it, and the woman having a good old mourn.

I was still in shock when the police turned up, after shakily tapping 999 into my Sony Ericsson. While it was my first ever first-hand experience of death, for them it must've been fairly routine, turning up to the scene of a suicide to find a person bawling their eyes out. I couldn't watch when they untangled Stevie from the climbing frame. His body made a horrid thud as it hit the soft play bark. They hoisted him onto a trolley and wheeled him into the ambulance, covering his big blue face with a sheet because he was much too depressing to look at.

I didn't have a tissue, so my fingers were sadly synchronised-swimming in a pool of tears. One of the younger policemen wasn't sure whether to put his arm around me, but he stayed with me as the ambulance trundled off the common. They didn't even bother putting on the siren – Stevie was definitely, definitely dead, they said. I felt cold and hollow. The young policeman said I should go home and get some rest, and they'd be in touch in a few days when they knew some more. I sobbed and nodded. I wondered what more there was to know. Perhaps there was a chance he might come back to life, after a quick go on their defibrillators.

My cardigan cuffs were drenched now in snot and saltwater, and I shivered all my little hairs on end as I slumped away from the disaster spot. I had that horrible, sudden sinking feeling of being completely and utterly alone on the planet.

Skirting the clearing where the eyeball had been, I watched the clouds churn into gruesome faces, and all of them were Stevie's. I hoped he'd made it into Heaven alright. I stumbled down the path, with the whole landscape swaying either side of me. The tears were easing now, leaving me with just an empty, panicky feeling, with blurred edges. Before long, I remembered how thirsty I'd been, so I pointed myself towards the shops, trudging zombie-fashion past brokeLads and the New Capital Kebab. The streets began to get peppered with not only raindrops, but people too, and seeing all those unfamiliar faces just made me feel even colder and more alone. I felt the tears brewing again in my skull, so I pressed on down Turnpike Lane with my head lowered, hoping not to spill them on anyone.

The first pub I came to was a Wetherspoon's. It was a typically vast affair, with football news on the telly, and a mute Polish person serving behind the bar. It appeared to be Unhappy Hour. I was in no mood to smile, but I managed to muster up a 'Please' and a 'Thanks' when I ordered my orange juice. I took it back to an empty table. I sat down with my back to everybody.

As I stared at the grain in the tabletop, Stevie's blue face kept fl-fl-flickering between the whites of my eyes and the black of the backs of my eyelids. I figured the image would haunt me for many years to come. I saw him hanging off the fancy lampshades, and hanging off the edge of the bar. I saw him hanging off the bowls of sauce sachets. I saw him hanging off an old patron's nose. Sniffing, I couldn't help hanging more tears off my eyelashes, and dropping them one by one into my orange juice, creating a sour, salty cocktail. I was glad I'd turned away from the folk in the pub – I didn't want any attention from the loud, annoying bloke with the seal-like whiskers, or the fellow honk honk honking with laughter on his own in the corner, or the mute Pole.

It didn't feel right sitting in a pub without my Stevie, even though typically he'd be staring over my shoulder at the football news and not talking. It made my whole body convulse, to think I had to go home that night and wake up without him for the rest of my life, and do something about his dirty washing, and his CDs, and his MFC programmes, and Tuesday's uneaten Margherita he was saving. I sipped more salty orange. I guessed I'd have to give all his clothes to a charity shop, but that made me feel even sicker, imagining someone else going round in his sweatshirts and cycling shorts, pretending to be Stevie. I wondered what the police would do with the Nike trainers, off-white socks, shellsuit bottoms, Calvin Classics boxers, creamy *Closer* T-shirt, and jade green parka he had on when he killed himself. I wondered if they'd bury him in them. Or burn them.

I cried a bit more. I'd stopped wearing make-up around that time, so I wasn't turning my face into a vast Expressionist painting, for example, *The Scream*. When I came to the end of the orange juice and tears, I carried on sitting there in silence, watching the last dregs of juice crawl back to the bottom of the glass. A

8

lot of police cars were zooming around outside with their sirens on, puncturing the silence, and I wondered if they'd stuffed Stevie into the lockers yet at the morgue. It made me want to vomit, the idea that once someone dies, there's nothing you can do to ever see or speak to them again. I wish I could've undone Stevie's shoelaces and brought him back to life with them like a puppet but, sadly, he was irreversibly suffocated and brain-dead.

I got up from the table. I took my glass back to the bar. I headed out onto Green Lanes. I watched a bird crashing into a cloud.

Once I was back out in public, I did my best to suppress the rest of the tears. As I slumped towards the bus stop, every step made my heart and gut ache. In a way, I looked forward to getting back to the flat and flooding it with projectile crying.

Perhaps the saddest thing about Stevie dying was me having to spread even more sadness by letting everyone know about it; or perhaps the saddest thing was me having to sleep alone that night in the bed that was too big even for the two of us. I stood in the bus shelter, squashed next to some strangers. I hated myself, and I decided I might as well go back to the flat and kill myself too – because the saddest thing about Stevie dying was having to live with the knowledge it wasn't Stevie's fault.

It was mine.

◎

While there was nothing particularly bad about Stevie per se, after four years of hardcore commitment I was desperate to get rid of him. Weirdly, it was all the things that made him a good boyfriend (like pampering me incessantly, or pledging his undying allegiance to me, or cuddling me non-stop in front of strangers) that drove me away from him.

At least twice a day, Stevie would stutter: 'I l-l-love you, I want want want to be with you for e-e-e-ever and ever.'

9

And I would say back: 'Ah yes, I feel the same, Stevie.'
Meanwhile, my brain would be elsewhere, plotting our escape.
I have a wicked old brain.

⊙

I was born to the sound of cackling witches on the thirty-first of
October. The year was 1984, or so I was told. I don't remember
the actual birth. I still feel about eighteen so, for all I know, the
year might've been 1989. Technically, I'm twenty-three, though.

On the sixteenth of June 2003, I accidentally walked into the
cross-hairs of Stevie's silver eyes in the Southern Cross pub, and
we threw countless shots of tequila down our necks, and ended
up jumping up and down on each other round his mam's house
on Captain Cook's Crescent. An orgasm popped its head out from
between my legs, for the first time in the company of someone
else. Then, in the following months, orgasms were a regular fix-
ture round Stevie's mam's house. Four strenuous years later there
were precious little orgasms for Stevie or Kimberly in their poxy
one-bedroom flat above a halal butcher's, in the south of Tottenham, in the north of the Capital. Stevie joined a prestigious
athletics club and went out running every other evening while
I stayed at home joining up the dot-to-dots in my bumper puzzle book. I was beginning to lead the boring, soulless life of a
half-dead housewife. During this period, I probably felt about
sixty-five.

The worst thing about being in a rock-steady relationship is
the indifference you begin to feel towards your partner. If someone keeps telling you they're going to stick by you for ever and
ever, you feel less and less need to impress them, or dress well,
or even do your hair in the morning. On the whole, there was
nothing scary about coming home each day to a ready-made cup
of tea and a pair of men's lips; it's just I stopped paying attention

to what those lips had to say to me. Plus, the idea of slowly rotting and dying in the arms of an average-looking, stuttering lover made me want to lemon-squeeze my own head. After four years of going out with someone, you stop enjoying yourself in nightclubs, you stop showering every day, and you stop having ravenous rabbit sex. I think the scientific term is 'overfamiliarity'.

Understandably, Stevie loved me very much. I was outgoing, quick-witted, and I was famous for possessing the Guillotine: a platinum-blonde bob so straight and sharp it could roll heads. However, I was also a melodramatic hypochondriac (or so people reckon – in fact, I'm just a normal person who happens to get ill all the time), and there were certain things about Stevie that gave me irritable bowel syndrome. For example, the secret to Stevie's sprinting success was this: to achieve that perfect, aggressive acceleration round the track, Stevie would imagine I'd just been raped, and he was chasing after my assailant. It made watching him compete somewhat disturbing. After enduring his first four sweaty, pink-faced victories, I decided to just stay at home and listen to him on local radio instead. My irritable bowels were soothed.

Occasionally, at less important meets, he'd imagine a young hunk getting off with me in a nightclub, and charging after him to give him a good old pounding in the head. Meanwhile, back at the halal butcher's, I'd sit around doing the puzzle book, imagining a young hunk getting off with me in a nightclub, and charging after him to give him a good old pounding in bed. My feelings for Stevie were faltering, like a ship's compass veering off-course towards sunnier climes. I wanted to feel young and happy again. And this was how I managed it:

I decided to be a horrible person.

⊙

One of humanity's favourite pastimes is destroying things. For example, the other day I was wandering past the Dutch Pub on the High Road, when I was greeted by a giant swastika someone had etched into the freshly squirted concrete. And next to the swastika: a pair of comedy breasts.

Is everyone born nasty? I've often wondered why people like to slash brand-new bus seats; or badmouth you; or key your car; or break the legs off your Barbie dolls. Perhaps it's got something to do with the original rebel without a clue, Oedipus – the Greek fellow who was destined from birth to kill his father and fuck his mother. Or perhaps it's more to do with getting a boost up the food chain. Bully or be bullied.

Around the time I turned fourteen, people at school began to comment on my 'evil eyes'. Some people are blessed with beautiful, soft, symmetrical eyes (like Stevie), while others (me) are cursed with slightly upturned, cat-like, 'evil' eyes, set beneath Draculaesque, upside-down-V eyebrows. Once I discovered the delights of tweezers and make-up, I managed to exorcise my demonic peepers with certain eyeshadows, but I still think people act suspicious around me.

Part of the reason I invested in the Guillotine was to detract people's attention from my devil eyes. I must stress, though, I'm not actually evil. When I first decided to be horrible to my boyfriend, it was more of an experiment than a malicious attack on the person I robotically said 'I love you' to every night before lights out. It wasn't revenge – Stevie hadn't done anything wrong. It was just unnerving to think he loved me so intensely, so unconditionally, that the only escape route would involve me falsely reciprocating his love, or breaking his heart into millions of whimpering pieces. Stevie was soft and cuddly, but incredibly suffocating: a bit like a pillow, if you smother someone to death with it.

12

Humans are famously never satisfied with anything. In fact, I think it's my constant search for perfection in men that makes me a terrible lover. The other man's grass is always greener, after all, and the other man's cheekbones are always in slightly better accordance with da Vinci's Golden Ratio, I find.

On top of all that, if you put two grown-ups in a 'serious' relationship, for some unknown reason they sometimes start speaking to each other like toddlers. Instead of trying to entertain each other with wisdom and wisecracks, they give each other pet names, and just giggle and gurgle gobbledygook all day. At first it's endearing. Four years down the line, it's more like torturous regression.

I didn't want to be a helpless toddler any more. I missed the single life, where you don't have to do someone else's washing; be a victim to someone's crap sexual fantasies; or sit in silence with a man screaming at twenty-two millionaires doing their Saturday jobs. I hated sport. During those long, tiresome evenings, pretending to be interested in televised kabaddi, I'd whisk myself off in my head to a fruity, forbidden land of discos, handsome strangers, swapped phone numbers and swapped bodily fluids. It was a Tuesday night – I was being hypnotised by Tottenham Hot Sperm vs Arsenumb on the box – when I first pondered how I'd get rid of Stevie. Stupidly, I'd been nice to him and agreed to go down the Dutch Pub to watch the football, but that was all going to change. Sipping a pint of flat Coke, I concocted a list of subtle – yet sinister – schemes to wean Stevie off poor, lifeless Kimberly. It started with an accidental kick under the table to Stevie's left shin. It ended with him strangled to death by four pairs of shoelaces. And what follows are all the intermediary bits.

For someone who went running every day and regularly drank Lucozade, Stevie was lazy. I think, in a way, he prided himself on being on the brink of Olympic-sized fame, and expected some sort of special treatment from me. While Stevie did cook our tea every night (the fun part), I was made to do all the washing-up (the dull part), and it was also my job to do the laundry, make the bed, and rearrange the living space after we'd had a 'party' (me and Stevie drinking booze in front of the telly, rather than eating tuna and cucumber sandwiches in front of the telly).

I love cleanliness, but I hate doing the actual cleaning. I have an intense fear of touching germs, dust and old food stains, which makes it difficult for me to be happy on buses, or in doctors' waiting rooms, or down on the Subterranean Ghost Train. Once, I bought an ex-library copy of *Hamlet* off a tramp, but I could only bear to read it after disinfecting each page with a mild Dettol wipe.

Oh, summer. August is not only the time of year when the sun's at its fullest – and bugs and bacteria are at their happiest – but it also heralds the arrival of the annual Amateur Athletics Association Championships. Last year, Stevie spent every day in the lead-up to the event revolving round the track at his club close to White Hart Lane, while I stayed at home doing the chores and being bored. I'd just been up the hill to get some shopping, and I was soaking wet with sweat as I sat there chomping on my Somerfield's Worst™ Lasagne-for-One.

When the last of the pasta had gone down the chute, I chucked the tub to one side and sighed. To spite Stevie, I'd started leaving dirty dishes all around the flat. However, since he'd been out training so much, he was yet to recognise it as a malicious act of bad will. He probably just thought I was forgetful, or ill again.

14

After two weeks of rampant mould growth, it was me who became aggravated by the plates. I felt sick, being stared out by all the shigella and salmonella bugs as I wandered from room to room. I couldn't bear it any longer. I put on Marigolds and a nose-peg and gave the flat a summer-clean, cursing myself. It was lonely up there above the butcher's, and so far my wicked scheme to turn Stevie against me was proving fruitless. I made a mental note: dirty plates annoy me far more than they do my boyfriend.

With all the washing-up done and all the dust dusted, I felt on a bit of a roll with the cleaning, as you do. Stevie's first heat for the AAAs was in a couple of days, and he prided himself on having the brightest, whitest, nicest athletics kit on the running track. He reckoned his kit could blind the other competitors, and help him on his way to victory. Sorting through the snowy mountain of dirty whites in the bedroom, I picked out Stevie's best sprinting vest, shorts, socks and boxers; a couple of my white dog-eared knickers; a white dressing gown I wasn't keen on; and last Chrimbo's red mittens, with the holly motif. My heart pounded childishly as I stuffed everything into the washing machine's tummy, then set it on forty degrees and went back through to watch some telly. I had to bite my tongue to stop the neighbours thinking I was laughing at *Loose Women*.

Two days later I was wobbling with excitement on a fold-down seat in a grandiose sports arena in Birmingham. The sun was at its peak, like the star on a huge invisible Christmas tree, and I peered through insectoid sunglasses as the runners jogged confidently out of the tunnel.

It was time for the 200m dash. My belly gurgled as the competitors lined up in their pristine whites and slightly off-whites, with numbers Sellotaped across their chests. I spotted Stevie straight away and gave him a big daft wave. He just ignored me, though. For some reason, he looked a bit sheepish, hopping about on the spot in his pretty bubblegum-pink sprinting outfit. I laughed hysterically behind very serious, shut lips.

When the man with the golden moustache fired the starting pistol, all the bright white runners – and the silly one in pink – galloped full-pelt towards the finishing line. Everyone was cheering and jeering. I could hardly watch. By the look on Stevie's face, I don't think he was imagining me being raped this time. He was probably imagining me being murdered. But, whatever was going through the boy's head, unfortunately Stevie didn't manage to qualify for the finals of the AAAs.

Kimberly Clark in . . . the Mystery of the Three Periods

I have a special talent: I can have three periods in one month, if I want.

After the racing-whites incident, things between me and Stevie began to go beautifully downhill. It's strange – I'd spent the first years of our relationship trying to suss out what made him smile, and what made his cock fire white javelins, only to find what I really wanted was for him to frown, and for his cock to do the Fosbury Flop. There's no easier way to frustrate a man than to deprive him of sex.

Men are ravenous, horny beasts, but women can be beastly too. Even after four years of the same old sex-by-numbers, me and Stevie still managed to have it away three or four times a week, discounting the week I got the painters in, of course. We were very particular about not having bright red sex.

For a whole two days after Stevie's upset on the running track, he lazed about the flat grumbling to himself, making a lot of pink noise. I saw much more of him than usual, but talked to him much less. Since I was the humble owner of an inferiority

16

complex, I was usually the first to apologise after an argument but, by this time, it was too much of a thrill to watch our relationship fall apart, so I kept my mouth shut.

However, I must stress, I didn't want to kill the lad. Yes, true love requires you to occasionally want to kill your partner, but that doesn't mean you actually want them to die permanently. I didn't want Stevie to hate me, just dislike me intensely for a few weeks and realise I'm not quite as perfect as he thought I was. It was always my hope for us to stay friends after all the cruelty – I imagined going to more of his meets, once he'd started imagining a different girlfriend getting raped. In fact, I was looking forward to Stevie having a new bird, and perhaps going for cocktails with her, and chattering about all his bad points. I imagined I'd get on well with her – as long as she wasn't better looking than me.

After the full two days of not talking to each other, I decided to break the silence by having loud foghorn sex with Stevie in the other room. It was to be our final shag. Even while I was bouncing up and down on his pelvis, bracing myself for the soggy bit, I knew I was being too nice to him. So I decided to bite him. But that only spurred him on more – suddenly, Stevie was grinning wildly, his legs vibrating like a huge, fleshy tuning-fork. I was enjoying it too, but only enjoying it in the way you enjoy watching your favourite film over and over again: you know all the action and dialogue off by heart, and I felt like fast-forwarding to the bit where Stevie and Kimberly topple off each other with wiped organs and go back to sleep. *Fin.*

I slept till eleven the next morning. I didn't have a job back then – Stevie was the sole breadwinner, what with his flashy sponsorship deals and full Lottery funding. After the cock-up at the AAAs, Stevie began to fret about money – he kept saying his career was going down the toilet. I mentioned to him a career is actually an abstract concept and can't physically fit down any drainage system (especially not in our tiny Victorian flat), and he started grumbling again. I smiled at his back, glad to be an annoying cow.

Soon, Stevie realised the only pleasure I was capable of giving him was through the ancient art of coitus. Over the following weeks, Stevie stayed at home while his fit friends jetted off to Osaka to train with the national sprinting team, and he spent at least ten minutes every hour trying to stroke me, kiss me and fish-hook me into his bed. I just yawned, though, or actually said the words, 'Naw, naw, I'm too tired.' Or I'd make out I was coming down with the flu, or hay fever, or food poisoning, or meningitis, or myxomatosis. 'Th-th-there's nothing even wr-wr-wr-wrong with y-you,' Stevie would plead. So I'd go into the bathroom and stick my fingers down my throat, then bring him in and show him the frothy sick in the toilet. And I'd forget to flush, or brush my teeth.

It was a constant juggling act, dunking Stevie deeper and deeper into depression, then quickly hoisting him back out before he realised I was being sadistic on purpose. The cruelty had to appear natural if the plan was going to work.

⊙

One day in mid-September, me and Stevie decided to go for a stroll round our local recreation ground, Downhills Park, where all the winding tarmac paths go magically downhill, like in an M. C. Escher drawing.

Me and Stevie got all the way down down down to the BMX circuit without saying a word to each other, before my boyfriend finally bit the bullet and piped up with this premeditated, serious speech:

'Eh, K-Kim, I was g-g-going to ask, er, like, do do do you think we're going d-downhill?'

'Er, yeah,' I answered, though I wasn't sure if he was referring to our relationship, or just the park. Stevie huff-huffed, skidding down a steep bit, and carried on:

'N-naw, but but but seriously, I feel like you're g-going off me. I mean, I st-st-still love you and all that, it's s-sound, we're not not splitting up, I think it's j-j-j-j-just the s-sex and that. It's like you k-keep making up excuses. I dunno, I I I I know you get d-dead ill all the time, but but but I j-just want things back to how it was. I p-proper love you.'

So, I agreed to have more sex with Stevie, just to sh-shut him up, and we walked on down down down towards the pond with slightly jauntier footsteps. But, of course, I had another trick up my sleeve. Or rather, up my fallopian tubes. I looked up at the bright blue food-dye sky and smiled, thinking about menstruation.

When I was eleven, I was the only girl in my class who cried when we found out we had to bloody our knickers once a month, for nothing. I've always been afraid of haemoglobin, and I thought I was going to pass out. I blame not having any sisters – I was clueless. Those insolent bints Stacey Garrick and Marie O'Shea had apparently conjured up six periods between them already, but I bet it was just too much beetroot in their diets.

With such an initial fear of the old 'Japanese flag', it's strange to think twelve years later I'd gladly wave three of those flags in one month. Once I'd been going out with Stevie half a year (and had him thoroughly checked out at the doc's), I started taking the Pill; the contraceptive one. Straight away it cleared up the latex rash I seemed to be harbouring in my pants but, on the flipside, it gave me bad skin and bad dreams. One involved a skeleton with syphilitic bumps on its skull, gyrating and thrusting its pelvis in a battleship-grey apartment. I think the dream meant I didn't fancy an STD. As soon as Stevie came back from the doctor's with a clean bill of sexual health, the bad dreams softened.

19

Aside from the nightmares, the Pill made my periods less messy, made my boobs bigger, and made my overall temperament slightly grumpier. It's a clever old thing. The Pill also turns your reproductive system into a kind of cuckoo clock except, instead of a cuckoo, it pings a stinking period out of your womb every twenty-eight days, on the dot. After munching one pill a day for twenty-one days, you stop taking it for a week (the 'placebo week', where you get dead moody and listen to Placebo), during which you have your 'withdrawal bleed' (or 'phantom period', as I like to call it), then, seven days later, you start munching on a new pack of pills again. This process goes on as long as you keep taking your prescription, like your ovaries have turned themselves into very slow egg-timers, except it just so happens they don't release any eggs.

Like any medication, the Pill can be exploited to sinister effect. If, for example, your boyfriend doesn't like having sex with you when you're on your period, and you want to have as many periods as possible in one month, so he'll become frustrated and ultimately not love you any more, here's my advice: After your latest 'phantom period', start taking the pills in a new packet, as normal. Say, if you take your first Pill on a Monday, keep taking it on Tuesday and Wednesday and Thursday, then stop. This makes your womb frown and scratch its chin, fooling it into thinking it's the 'placebo week' again, and it spits out whatever menstrual tissue you've got left up there. It should certainly be browny-red and sludgy enough to keep your boyfriend's bits away from you for another week. Then, repeat as required.

Stevie was tetchy that week. He kept stalking round the flat like a starving wildcat. I humoured him, blaming the onslaught of blood on 'breakthrough bleeding' or 'spotting', or the moon's position in the sky, or the bad feng shui of the flat. Meanwhile, my womb would be gently cackling inside me, with a bloody

20

nose. I cackled too, curled up on the sofa with two hot-water bottles pressed to my front and back. Poor Kimberly. Poor Stevie. I could've carried on forcing periods for the rest of the year as well but, sadly, after the fifth week running, I ran out of sanitary towels.

Kimberly Clark and . . . the Hamster from Hell!

Meet my hamster. Be careful, though – he might bite your hand off.

I bought Lucifer to keep me company on the lonely, lasagne-flavoured evenings in that flat. At the shop, JG Thomas & Sons, he seemed like a good-natured fellow, cowering in the sawdust before doing a sprint for me and Stevie on his blue wheel (which Stevie appreciated) but, once we got him back to Tottenham, he soon turned out to be a vicious, bloodthirsty beast. I think he's got psychological problems. By the time we got Lucifer off the 41 and into the flat, he'd already chewed through both ends of his cardboard lodgings, and got started on the palms of Stevie's hands.

Like Stevie, Lucifer's got very little melanin in his irises. In fact, he's albino. Lucifer got the name partly because of the red eyes, and partly because he leaves a Habitrail of destruction everywhere he goes. Once we got him into his cage – kitted out with swings and roundabouts, a so-called 'Mush-Room' to sleep in and a brand-new blue wheel – all Lucifer wanted to do was vandalise it. Me and Stevie tried our best to calm him down, gently lowering our hands into Hell to give him a stroke, but Lucifer was hell-bent on decapitating us. We spent the first week or so with our fingers in plasters.

By the time Lucifer was eight months old, he'd almost chewed an escape route out of the cage. In a way, I could see parallels between myself and the hamster – while Lucifer had a nice roof over his head and all the love and attention he needed, he must've felt suffocated by the same old scenery, and the ultimate lack of freedom. At times I'd sit in front of his cage, as if looking into a strange mirror, wishing I could let him roam the flat, although he definitely couldn't be trusted around Stevie's scratchable medallions. He was the only hamster I'd heard growl in my life, but I loved him. Sometimes I felt I had more in common with that hamster than I did with my own boyfriend.

I like hamsters. Stevie liked football. His only gripe with footy was our television not showing many of the games due to its lack of Sky, and season tickets being so expensive (and Middlesbrough being so far away, and so hopeless). This meant Stevie spent a lot of time down the local pubs – like the Dutch Pub, the Fountain, the Lord Parmo – despite not being a big drinker. Usually, he'd just sit in the corner with a poncey fruit juice, eyes fixed on Sky Sports or Setanta, avoiding the glances of all the hard-looking black and Polish patrons. Sometimes I'd join him, if I fancied being bored in slightly different environs to the flat. Otherwise, I'd just stay at home, contemplating taking up knitting, or stamp collecting, or murder.

One of the best days of Stevie's life was when they announced Middlesbrough were to play Sheffield United on terrestrial telly, in the FA Cup fifth round. It was my idea of Hell.

The day before the big match, Stevie had to go running in his pink outfit at the Data Connection Open, and he demanded I go to Tesco for some supplies: cheese footballs, chicken legs, Doritos, fizzy pop, fresh orange, one can of Carlsberg lager, and a four-pack of Smirnoff Ice for me. I ambled aimlessly round the aisles. I hate supermarkets. Not only do you have to manoeuvre round annoying kids, mams, and sociopathic males in the white glare of twelve or so aisles, but you also have to carry your shopping all the way home, with only two feeble arms. I had to wait fifteen minutes for a bus, with the shopping getting heavier and heavier as the bags filled up with rain. Then, the bus was absolutely rammed and steamy, and I felt flu-ridden and homicidal by the time I squelched back up the stairs to Flat D.

I splashed down on the sofa, then slowly evaporated once I'd pulled my shoes and socks off and turned up the heating. Round about four, Stevie came back from his Open in good spirits; or, at least, his footsteps sounded chirpy as he bounded across the carpet. Not that I was listening. Twiddling my thumbs, I was tucked up in bed next-door, in the dark, dreaming up revenge for my soaking. My first idea was to leave the shopping bags on the breakfast bar, instead of unpacking them. Yes! Imagine Stevie's face, waking up to a lukewarm can of Carlsberg! I groaned. I decided to mull it over a bit longer.

At about sundown, Stevie joined me in bed. He said he was shattered after such a s-s-successful spot of sprinting, but I think he was just looking for an excuse to put his naked body next to mine, in a socially acceptable place to harass me.

It was my first week in a while without a period, and Stevie 'Mmmmm'ed, as he clamped his clammy arms around me. He tried to kiss my ears, neck and back, but I stiffened and said, 'Naw, Stevie. I'm too tired. I'm in bed, aren't I?'

Stevie grunted sadly. We turned out the lights. It was only about seven but, since Stevie was apparently so shattered after such a s-s-successful spot of sprinting, he had to force himself to sleep, so as not to lose face. I revelled in his twisting and turning.

By eleven, Stevie had managed to black himself out. I put on the dotty cardigan and crept out of the bedroom, quietly moving my tiptoes in time with Stevie's bellowing breaths, so as not to rouse him. He'd gone and left the curtains open in the living space – the whole place was doused in this lovely, fake blue moonlight.

I felt shy when the double-decker 243 rumbled past, but none of the stony passengers caught my eye as I stood there in semi-nakedness. I whizzed the curtains shut. Then, I shuffled towards the TV, which was sleeping soundly on standby, next to the flowering cactus and Lucifer's cage. Lucifer had been condemned to live in the living space by Stevie, who complained about strange noises and insomnia after Lucifer's trial run in our bedroom.

I turned on the lamp, which had a shade patterned with diamonds and what looked like Hula Hoops. My shadow jumped across to the opposite side of the room, from where it watched as I switched the TV off at the wall and uncoiled the power cable. I dangled the cable into Lucifer's cage, then flick-flicked on the bars, to get him interested. Lucifer was in his favourite spot under the Mush-Room, and he smiled when he saw the telly cable. He knew what to do. I switched the lamp off again and left him to it, creeping back into bed with even lighter footsteps.

The next morning, Stevie awoke – very groggy – at 10.30 a.m. He'd managed to oversleep twice his usual amount (fourteen hours, as opposed to his usually strict seven), and he looked grotesque as he got dressed in his worst clothes. My intestines were squirming about with excitement, knitting themselves into gooey, gruesome plaits. Stevie kept rabbiting on about how much he was looking forward to the football. I had to suppress the giggles, sticking my head into the pillow.

I didn't want to miss his reaction to the cable having magically found its way into Lucifer's cage, so I hopped out of bed fast, and whipped on my worst clothes as well. We wandered into the living space with very bad fashion sense and grey mannequin faces. Stevie wanted to put the telly on early for an hour of pre-match babble, and I chewed my gums ecstatically as he pressed the POWER button, and frowned. For a second we saw the BBC host, then the power cable fizzed unspectacularly, and the picture

24

sputtered out. Lucifer squeaked, panicking, thinking his house was being struck by a tiny shard of lightning. Fortunately, he survived. But, even better than that, Stevie's silver eyeballs turned scarlet, and they didn't get to watch the football, and they cast venomous glances through Lucifer's bars, while he worked his way through his one horrible, lukewarm can of Carlsberg.

As punishment, I foolishly agreed to go to the Lord Parmo to watch the highlights on Sky. Stevie didn't speak. I kept shouting, 'Come on, England!' at the top of my voice, just to make it worse. Stevie carried on sulking, staring straight ahead with a soft drink in one hand, as Boro and Sheffield United treated us to a fine display of footballing prowess. It ended up 0–0.

Stevie was devastated and, as the days went on, I watched with glee as he became more and more detached and unhappy. For some reason, he still didn't dump me, though. I felt like a wicked witch, but Stevie continued to spend most nights trying to get his hairy broom between that witch's legs. But those legs weren't interested. Those legs were beginning to drift elsewhere.

Kimberly Clark in . . . the Adventure of One Man's Tongue Going Where It Shouldn't Go

Every day, people see actors on TV pretending to be human – acquiring lovers through scripted seduction techniques; getting hitched; then being unfaithful; having a jolly good, inconsequential shag, and a great old laugh together – and it makes you want to be unfaithful too.

In the Capital Zoo, there's a plaque celebrating the fact female Patagonian maras are monogamous. Beavers are monogamous too, as well as penguins, gibbons, black vultures, shingleback skinks, and dik-diks. I think this is because they don't watch the soaps.

25

After months of cruelty towards Stevie, it turned out I was the one suffering the most. The more Stevie put up with my relentless nastiness, the more pathetic he seemed to me. Any normal man would've called off the relationship by now, although there was always the chance I wasn't being obvious enough. Or, there was always the chance Stevie was being far too good a boyfriend, sticking by me through thick and thin, regardless of my idiocy. He was a tricky bastard.

For the next few weeks, I pulled out all the stops: borrowing his depressive CDs and not putting them back in the right cases; taping over the video where Middlesbrough FC win the Carling Cup; masticating violently at teatime; smashing his favourite mug accidentally against the kitchen wall. But still he kept stressing: 'I l-l-love you, I want want want to be with you for e-e-e-ever.'

It's always surprised me how much aggravation one person can tolerate. Just for fun, I tried to go a whole week in the flat without speaking – feigning laryngitis again – but, instead of annoyance, I got nothing but sympathy from Stevie, and many Lemsips. Perhaps he could see our love affair dangling precariously off a cliff-edge, and he was trying with all his might to reel us back in. We tug-of-warred through winter.

Although I hated Stevie bringing me to the Capital, it did make cheating on him anonymously very easy. During the early days of being horrid to him, I thought I could refrain from kissing someone else until we'd officially broken up, but I hadn't counted on Stevie being so hard to shake off. Perhaps every year we'd been together was like an iron claw stuck into our hearts, and it was proving very difficult to prise all four claws out without leaving behind a lot of rust and tetanus.

On the twenty-second of February, Stevie had a plus-one for this swanky dinner do at his old athletics club in Teesside but, conveniently, I'd already agreed to go out with my Promiscuous

Pal Polly from Southampton (I wish she was from Portsmouth for the sake of alliteration, but unfortunately she's not). I used to work with Polly down Pizza Express when I first moved to the Capital, and before I left the job to become a professional parasite we'd agreed to meet at least once a month for wine and a whinge. Stevie was usually alright about his girlfriend going out without him, but he was desperate not to go to the swanky dinner thing on his own, and I forced him into having an argument with me.

Me and Polly left the flat in an exaggerated huff, stealing Stevie's jade green parka so he'd be freezing cold in the North East. The parka swamped me as we swaggered down the High Road, caked in make-up. It was typical of Polly to be near-naked on a Friday night, but this particular evening I gave her a run for her money, in my tightest tights and turquoise bustier. I was like a tiny, rude Russian doll underneath all the furry Siberian apparel. We tapped out a *lozhki*-like rhythm in our heels, laughing at the night.

One thing I've always hated about the Capital is the tarmac has the audacity to tell you what to do, so we had to LOOK LEFT as we came to the Ghost Train station. Luckily, though, it meant we didn't get run over by the grey Ford Mondeo blasting over the junction. We clattered down the steps into Seven Sisters, underneath the barely discernible Seven Sisters constellation, and I straightened the Guillotine with my fingertips in one of the circular mirrors.

We drank Smirnoff Ices on the Subterranean Ghost Train. It's called the Ghost Train because it transports silent, ghostly lost souls round and round the city. Me and Polly were the only ones making a bit of noise. The train itself was making a hell of a racket, so we had no choice but to scream at each other, and you could tell we were annoying the ghosts.

27

I explained to Polly all my troubles with Stevie. She didn't understand commitment, though – my Promiscuous Pal Polly was a semi-famous maneater in the Capital. She was the type of lady who uses her sexuality as a weapon, mesmerising men with her bottomless cleavage before dragging them helplessly into the nearest available bed or bin alley. In fact, for the whole of spring 2006, Polly used her sexuality as a gonorrhoea dispenser, swallowing up and crippling poor men and boys in its fiery wake.

In 2007, Polly had a microchip installed in her left arm, to stop her from getting pregnant, and she's also double-jointed. She's a bionic shagging machine. Enter at your peril.

At Piccadilly Circus we jumped off the Ghost Train with mouths overflowing with fizz, swaying along to the honking city rhythms. Our club of choice in those days was somewhere called China White – the swankiest club ever named after smack, I think – where overpaid men buy overpriced drinks for under-dressed girls like me and Polly. It was about half nine by the time we got through the lavish entrance, hobbling past the water feature and the pretentious pebbles and all that. Suddenly, I was roasting in the jade green parka. I checked it into the cloakroom, imagining Stevie shivering at his athletics do, with a big blue face. I looked forward to the massive row the morning after.

My Promiscuous Pal Polly received a Polaroid camera from one of her male slaves for Christmas. She had to buy a new handbag to accommodate it, and now she never goes anywhere without it. For posterity, Polly took a picture of me and her redoing our make-up in the lasses' bogs, prior to us getting mortalled and disgusting. Then, we tottered onto the dancefloor, trying to be the most over-the-top ones in there. Straight away, Polly had two eligible bachelors closing in on her, like sperms round a scrambled egg. One of them had a square face; the other's was more triangular. Polly made them buy us some drinks, then we all danced together in an awkward, perfumed circle.

In the past, I spent the nights in China White watching Polly swap saliva with suited blokes, from a vantage point in amongst the palm trees. I used to pride myself on being faithful to Stevie. The fact that loads of men pestered me made me feel happy to have Stevie, since he wasn't the type of man who pestered strange girls in nightclubs for sex. However, he was the type of man who preferred to single out one strange girl in a flat above a halal butcher's and pester her for sex incessantly instead.

The drinks made me whip one hand round the Square-Faced Bachelor's waist, and the other one round the top of his bottom. Oh, evil evil temptation. The drinks made me stare at his square face like a goon, until he kissed me. Then, all of a sudden, I felt a chemical reaction in my stomach, like when the teacher lights magnesium and it gives off this incredible snowball-white blast, and you have to look at it through bluey-purple glass so as not to go blind. I looked at the Square-Faced Bachelor through bluey-purple disco lights. My Promiscuous Pal Polly was already licking the Triangle-Faced Bachelor's mush, right up his hypotenuse, when she spotted me getting off with Square-Face. She squeaked with delight, and couldn't resist firing the Polaroid at us. Me and my new male friend laughed. Surprisingly, he had a laugh like a stellated dodecahedron: spiky and painful.

Me and Square-Face only spoke to each other in the names of drinks for the rest of the night, but we kept trying to accidentally bump into each other again and again, and have lots more passionate, hush-hush snogs. It felt incredible to kiss someone new; our lips like four pink slugs sumo-wrestling. Suddenly there was regret, and suddenly there was absolute joy. The one time Stevie joined us at China White, he grumbled about money and ended up drinking tap water. I chuckled in every tooth and carried on kissing the stranger.

At the end of the night, the bachelors wanted to come home with us, but that was simply out of the question. In the bitter lemon streetlights, the boys were beginning to look ugly. Me and Polly sucked their tongues goodbye, then marched off to an out-of-the-way bus stop. We jumped on the 73, which is shaped like a gigantic eel on wheels, chomping its way through the centre of the Capital.

We wobbled in our seats, wanting more alcohol. At first we were hardly talking (so depressing it was, travelling on public transport after midnight), but then Polly whipped out the fifteen square photos she'd taken, and we laughed at them, one by one. In some of them I looked good-looking, and in some of them Square-Face looked good-looking, and in some of the later ones neither of us looked good-looking at all. We were like Siamese twins, joined at the tongue. I took the most raunchy example (the one with the four slugs playing skip-rope with our saliva), and slid it into the parka's secret inside pocket. In that drunken state, I had the queer idea of posting Stevie the photo, should he dump me particularly heavy-handedly – if he dumped me at all, that is. 'REVENGE', I would scribble on it, and cackle hysterically.

After the laughter, me and Polly slumped to sleep the rest of the way home, taking it in turns to open an eyelid to make sure we got off after Tesco but well before Tottenham McDonald's.

We awoke the following afternoon, like a pair of tasteless cushions, on the sofa. Stevie was in a foul mood but he still made us cups of tea, and Polly left around four, with a pale face and limbs. I had my tail between my legs all day, despite not quite getting a tail between my legs the night before. I felt genuinely sorry for Stevie all of a sudden, or perhaps it was just self-pity. Stevie seemed to have had a rubbish time at the athletics do, although he didn't want to talk about it. He looked glum all day, like he could see I'd been unfaithful in his crystal-ball eyes. I couldn't resist giving him a modest squeeze for a minute or two, but it seemed like he didn't want to be touched. My hangover was cursing me for my terrible behaviour, and my heart was banging desperately, unsure what was happening to it. All I could think about was how much I was hurting Stevie, and the hurt was catching. I had so many bad thoughts, black holes and blinding aches racing through my skull, I completely forgot to take the Polaroid out of his parka.

That evening, I decided I wanted to be nice to Stevie again, and stay with him. He obviously cared about me tremendous amounts, and I cared about him too. Unfaithfulness is overrated. I realised cheaters are just the sad, insecure bastards of the world; the ones always seeking validation from others; the ones who just aren't sure if they're good-looking, or funny, or interesting any more. The ones daft enough to risk infinite comfort for a fleeting flash of fresh flesh.

And with singlehood, there's always the risk you'll find yourself in a no-man's-land, desperately scouring the streets and nightspots for someone only vaguely comparable to the lovely lover you lost.

The next morning, we woke up at opposite ends of the bed. Stevie still seemed down – I tried my best to cheer him up with smiles, soft drinks, and strokes to the arms and chest. It was selfish and pointless to treat him so badly – we obviously weren't going to split up as easily as I thought, and I wasn't even sure if I wanted us to any more.

After an afternoon breakfast of cheese footballs and Doritos, we headed down the common to kick some leaves and enjoy the grey weather. It was chilly out, so Stevie slung on the jade green parka. I didn't want to overdo the niceness (and appear weird, or guilty),

31

so I just linked arms with him and stared out the bus window as we slid along West Green Road. I smiled softly, sandwiched between Stevie and the translucent reflection of him in the bus window. I wondered how I'd feel if Stevie had locked lips with a random square-faced lady. I felt bloated with guilt. I felt like an idiot.

It was nearing sunset when we got out onto the common. The two of us were practically mutes, wandering about aimlessly, flattening a path of grass between the elms. I shivered once or twice in the dotty cardigan. Stevie didn't half look cosy in the parka. When we got to the public bogs, I went in to try and cough up a bit of leftover hangover, and I had a long wee in the porcelain cubicle, watching my breath. I washed my hands as best I could in three stingy blasts of hot water, then I smiled at the hand-towel dispenser. It looked back at me, open-mouthed.

I felt better waltzing back out onto the common. I strode past an arrogant, swaggering magpie, indulging my lungs in the sweeping blasts of fresh air. When I got back onto the flattened grass track, I realised someone was missing. Stevie appeared to have gone off on one of his impromptu jogs, or else it was hide-and-seek. I sniffed and tottered off into the man-made wood, where the trees were all bent in aerobic poses. I took a tissue out of my Medicine Bag, and fired alcoholic snot at it. Posting the soggy Kleenex up my sleeve, I penetrated further into the wood, keeping an eye out for my boyfriend. I weighed up the possibility of us having an al fresco roll in the thicket.

I broke out into a canter as I went up an incline, making twigs yelp and squeak underfoot. There was a bit of a clearing up ahead, with a few tree-stumps, scrawny bushes and piles of mud – the perfect spot for a private smooch. The perfect spot to repledge my allegiance to my boyfriend.

I took a few deep breaths, with my hands on my knees, giggling at how unfit I was. Then I stiffened, and gasped, balancing one elbow on this knackered old three-wheeled pushchair.

Something was winking at me from under one of the bushes.

⊙

If you haven't noticed already, I appear to have been named after a toilet-tissue dispenser. My dad, the late Barry Clark, was the caretaker at my old primary school for twenty-five years and twenty-five days, at which point his heart decided to stop working. As the story goes, he used to enjoy the sweet serenity working three hours a day at the school after lights out, with all the kids gone – just him, his mop, and his daft, dithering thoughts. He used to tell the mop disgusting jokes on his way round the corridors, making the wet mop screech, probably with laughter. It was my dad's dream to be a stand-up comedian, but his comedy was awful – he used to be famous for his fat jokes, until he got older and fat himself, so the jokes fell flat. Barry probably would've died on stage, if he hadn't died in the Year Three girls' toilets with the mop clutched tightly in his rigor-mortised fist, like a microphone.

At work, Barry was an obsessive cleaner. I think he saw himself as a Ramboesque vigilante, saving innocent kids from evil, malignant germs. He used to give me pencils he found down the backs of dusty drawers and desks, and leftover cleaning products. He also gave me the hypochondria, I think.

Whenever I sign my name, I like to imagine my dad refilling the Kimberly-Clark containers in the toilets, smiling at that simple, satisfying name embossed in the plastic. Now I go to certain pubs and restaurants specifically to try out their Kimberly-Clarks. Now I have such dry hands, I think I'm getting eczema on them.

But at least I'm not called Armitage Shanks.

⊙

From an early age, I've had an unhealthy obsession with death. I blame it on growing up in a town full of ghosts, graveyards and old-age pensioners. Though I was born in a giant factory called Middlesbrough, my mam and dad took me home a couple of days later, to an obscure little place down the A171 called Guisborough.

Guisborough is very old. The 'ancient capital of Cleveland' used to have a cattle market back in days of yore, and it's hardly changed. In the daytime you still get a pleasant market selling veg, stinking fish and cheapo cassettes, then, at night, the mad cows start roaming about again; usually on a Friday or Saturday. The place is like a senile werewolf except, instead of fur and fleas, it's covered in cobbles and dithering old ladies.

There's only one secondary school and, to walk there, you've got to tackle the haunted graveyard round the back of St Nick's. You can hear the dead bodies groaning when it comes to home time; all the kids acting daft, disturbing the peace and rampaging round the headstones. Footballs roll about like severed heads. Crisp packets are laid down like cheese-and-onion-flavoured wreaths.

Aside from the crispy condom me and O'Shea found in Year Nine, by far the scariest thing in the cemetery is the infamous Black Monk's grave. There used to be a monastery out the back of the graveyard, which Henry VIII burned down for fun a long time ago. Rumour has it the Black Monk (I'm not sure if he's got black skin – if so, he's one of the only black people in Guisborough) comes out once a year to inspect the ruins.

The Black Monk's grave is in the centre of the graveyard, all sinister and overgrown, with an anti-dancing fence around it. I've had plenty of nightmares about it. As the story goes, if you're brave and nifty enough to dance on top of the Black Monk's grave, you'll come to a swift, watery demise. In other words, watch your back at bathtime; don't play on the banks of the beck; don't jump in any puddles.

I've seen many zany individuals dance on that grave over the years (including our science teacher, Mr Levington, who had a red nose, and did it for a bet on Red Nose Day), but all of them survived. All except for Daniel Brady, who treated the Black Monk to a fine bit of Saturday Night Fever on the last day of term in Year Ten. Apparently he went missing a couple of years back, scuba-diving off the west coast of Australia. Despite the shark bites in his chest and his lopped-off leg, I blame the Black Monk.

So, every school day for me was tinged with mild doom. That's what spending a lot of time around corpses does to you. And, as if that wasn't enough, as soon as you get onto the High Street, you come into contact with all the painfully slow old codgers moping about the market. I think they're attracted to Guisborough for its *Coronation Street*-style houses and the view of the hills, rather than the nightmarish, orgiastic nightlife. It used to make me sad, seeing them all weary and lonely in the many pubs and bakeries, or fingering dog toys on the stalls, despite not having a dog with them. They're practically corpses themselves. You can see the bones.

For someone with such a morbid preoccupation with death, I've got surprisingly good posture. However, hanging around with people who are dead – or on the very edge of death – can be bad for the spirit, and I'm ashamed to say I went through a black-fingernailed Goth phase in my early teens. I used to haunt my mam and dad at mealtimes; this pale, sinister presence that wouldn't speak, but would now and then throw plates around. However, by the time I grew up and met Stevie Wallace in the Southern Cross, I was wearing bright clothes again, and the world seemed to hum with all sorts of rose-tinted, romantic possibilities. Until lots of people around me died, that is.

⊙

When Mag Clark died, me and my dad went through hell trying to convict the owner of a J-reg Volvo estate.

When Barry Clark died, the primary school had a minute's silence to honour him, but none of the kids knew who he was, and some of them made silly noises, and it all ended in laughter.

When Stevie Wallace died, I decided I might as well go back to the flat and kill myself too. I finished the glass of orange and tears, and walked to the bus stop in silence. Inside the dotty cardigan, all my organs were just frozen meat. Momentarily, a little girl on a blinding pink bicycle caught my attention, but then the thought of Stevie being hung flung itself back into my head, and the beauty of the world collapsed again. The image was like a mouldy carrot on a rope, leading me onto the 41, constantly pulling at my heartstrings. My lips wobbled tragically. The bells kept going off on the bus, and they were funeral bells.

I got off at the lane named after black boys. I fancied a walk before dying, and I moved at the pace of a snowman through Downhills Park, where Stevie first confronted me about being a horrible, cold-hearted person. As I walked, I rolled more tears, perhaps subliminally hoping some kind soul might take pity on me and talk me out of the suicide. However, everyone went out of their way to avoid the manic, miserable woman, crossing over the fields with their heads dipped. I slid onwards, down down down down down.

It was dark by the time I got to the halal butcher's. I did the trick with the door, to get it open. Winter was in full swing, and all the trees and doorways in the Capital had shrunk and warped. You had to yank the door firmly towards yourself before attempting to turn the key, and I grimaced at the strain. At least it was the last time I'd ever have to do it.

When I got upstairs, I had to decide how I wanted to kill myself. Hanging looked a terribly painful way to go, and there was a chance I'd survive if I threw myself out of the third-storey window, and I definitely didn't want to do the trick with the door again. I began the projectile crying. I wondered if the halal lads downstairs fancied ritually slashing my jugular.

I was gradually filling the flat with tears; soon the carpet felt soggy underfoot. After five minutes, a tide was forming, with its own currents, waves and sealife, and before long I found myself paddling in saltwater, up to my ankles. I figured drowning was as good a way as any to kill yourself, and it felt appropriate, choking on my own sour rainfall. But then, just as the water level was creeping up towards my calves, the tears dried up. Humans are only capable of a certain amount of projectile crying, even in times of massive despair. So, I decided to go for a rummage in the fridge. There was one unopened Carlsberg in Stevie's compartment, and five Smirnoff Ices in mine. I gathered up the Smirnoffs, then waded through to the bedroom, where various cushions, stockings and magazines were darting about like manta rays and octopuses. I changed into my nicest underwear – the satin pink affairs with dainty black bows. I was not going to die in disgusting, discoloured granny pants.

Back in the living space, Lucifer's cage was floating about like a space-age Noah's Ark. I remembered to give him four or five days' worth of pellets and coloured cornflakes, just in case it took a while for the Necropolitan Police to find my decomposing body. I figured he'd have ample water, though.

I sat down on the sofa-raft and sighed. To inspire a suitable mindset for suicide, I recalled all the horrible things I'd done to Stevie over the last few months, gulping the Smirnoff Ice as quickly as I could. I wondered what happens to you after the last gasp. How long was Stevie in agony before all his pain receptors packed in? Was Stevie already up in Heaven shagging supermodels? Or is death just a big, black, rotten void? It was a scary prospect. In the olden days, they reckoned death was just like being asleep and dreaming – a break from that other bloody nightmare: life.

But I'd need more than just Smirnoff Ice if I was going to top myself successfully. I paddled back through to the kitchen, where a sea cucumber was floating about – or was it just a normal cucumber? I fished it out of the tears and slung it back into the fridge. I started crying again, because I'd never eat another tuna and cucumber sandwich. They were mine and Stevie's favourites.

After slamming the fridge door shut, I went over to my Medicine Bag, which was full of vitamin supplements, tissues and lozenges, as well as many packs of Panadol. I gathered up the paracetamol, then sploshed back through to the bedroom and laid down on the blue gingham bedcover.

I started unpopping the pills, and popping them one by one into my mouth, sending them down the hatch on a lemon-flavoured waterfall. After the fourth Smirnoff Ice and the ninth painkiller, sure enough the drowsiness took hold. My heart was racing while my head swam, and I curled myself round the bottom of the bedframe, like a limpet stuck to a burning Viking longboat. My skull hurt, despite the painkillers, but I treated it as punishment for me punishing my boyfriend. In fact, I punched myself in the temples a few times to encourage irreparable brain damage. More tears flowed.

As soon as I felt sufficiently depressed and hateful, I swallowed four more Panadol and tried to carry on drinking the Ice, but after three more sips the bottle fell from my hand and into the ocean below. If there was a message to be found in that bottle, it consisted of only vodka, lemonade, and tears. I wasn't one for writing suicide notes. Instead, I'd just created one final, saddest cocktail of all.

My head sank into the soggy pillow and, though my heart was still beating, I felt my organs shutting down, killing me softly on the bedcovers. They say a heroin overdose is the most relaxing way to die – and I probably could've got my hands on some up the High Road, although I didn't want to risk being stabbed or shot, of course – but, under the circumstances, Smirnoff and Panadol seemed a reasonable alternative.

I think I coughed up some sick. I can't remember. For the rest of the evening, a mysterious opaque curtain was drawn around my brain. I shifted to and fro on the blue gingham, struggling to keep my eyes open. Then, all of a sudden, there were red sparkles. Then, there were purple sparkles. Then, there were black sparkles.

⊙

Unfortunately, I woke up the next morning. Obviously four Smirnoff Ices and thirteen Panadol isn't enough to kill yourself, and I felt stupid. I had a hangover the size of Mount Everest growing on the side of my brain. I considered taking more Panadol to combat the pain, then decided against it.

My eyes felt like I'd been crying shards of glass, and my bones felt soft. My belly groaned. I'd been asleep almost sixteen hours. There was still a veil of sadness, but it was much blurrier and nondescript compared to the previous night.

The ocean of tears appeared to have evaporated, though it was still faintly damp underfoot. As I walked across the carpet, my legs kept getting tangled up and knotted. The rest of my body was twisted and creased as well, since I'd foolishly decided to die in my clothes. I had a long stretch and a yawn.

Outside, the sky was like two pieces of slate rubbing against each other, conjuring up heaps of rain, lightning and pathetic fallacy. I moped into the kitchen with a dark cumulonimbus over my head, and rain streaming down my face. It took ages to make a tuna and cucumber sandwich, and in the end I couldn't stomach eating it. Depression had shrunk my stomach to the size of a dormouse's shower-cap.

I spent the rest of the afternoon trying to kill myself again, but the attempts were halfhearted. I used the sharp cucumber knife on my wrists, but I didn't have the guts to cut deep enough into my radial artery: the M1 of the circulatory system. I pulled the shoelaces out of Stevie's red Reeboks and twisted them round my neck, then stood precariously on the sofa arm and tied the other end round the curtain-rail. I was too scared to jump off, though. I stood there on the sofa arm for twenty-five minutes, before sighing and untying myself. Later on, I poured myself a mug of bleach, but then I quickly poured it back again.

I wasn't cut out for killing myself, I don't think. It was more my style to just wallow in self-pity, so I spent the rest of the week in bed, grinding out the days unenthusiastically, pretending to be glad to be alive. I developed a severe case of lethargy – by Tuesday I couldn't even be bothered walking to the toilet, so I weed in a saucepan under the bed. The flat soon began to smell, and I contracted bed sores from the musty mattress. The Guillotine quickly went rusty (not ginger), and the only exercise I got was rolling from one side of the bed to the other, which was actually quite a distance now Stevie was gone.

To keep the demonic depression at bay, I got myself a job as a part-time self-harmer. I substituted the radial artery for the more fleshy, child-safe biceps, slicing thin lines with the cucumber knife, playing noughts-and-crosses with myself. It became a morbid, sickly-sweet treat to slash my arms open like clockwork every day at sunrise and again at sunset, resulting in aaaaaaahh two minutes of relief, then straight back to the sadness. It felt like a more sensible punishment for killing Stevie than taking my own life as well. After all, I thought, two suicides in one week was going a bit overboard.

40

Cutting yourself is suicide for fannies.

Luckily, no one called round the flat during this horrendous period. I was worried about the landlord turning up and demanding rent, only to find his tenant dead and his tenant's girlfriend in bed, looking like death, with a piss-pot between her legs. I was eating only tuna and cucumber at this point, and wasn't passing solids very often, thank God. The telly cable was still fried, so I just watched the changing of light and weather through the single-glazed window.

I had no idea what I was going to do with myself. By the end of that week, I'd gone so long without speaking, I thought my mouth might scab over. My arms were tiger-printed with scabs, too – and my legs. To illustrate just how much I was cutting myself up, I decided to cut up the following bit of text for you (in any case, it was far too depressing in its original format):

Oh, woe! Do you ever get that f, I decided to focus on the smash your own face in? For sombad bloated blue face. After absolutely obsessed with suffercrosses on my weedy biceps, things, humans love to suffer asures of cutting oneself. Of crisis, instead of just gettoff whole sections of my smiling, they prefer to sit arothe notice-board and imagining the sweet feeling of feel that lovely lovely through their skulls. Oh, if onny darts. Or a notice-board. Of my brain that was making me tions across the gingham bed, strength power-tool! Living aloumber knife, and did twelve more intense, like painting ovet to work on demolishing my thick sloppy indigo. Of all theeeling you just want to about on the whole planet Earthe reason, humans are most depressing – Stevie's big ing. Along with destroying fifty-odd games of noughts-and-t least once a day. In times my arms became dead to the pleaing on with their lives and for a bit I considered cutting und with wet eyeballs, arms and legs, pinning them to thrusting sharpened pencils throwing darts at them, just toly I could hack out the part pain again. But I didn't have asad, with an industrial-instead, I just did twelve rotane makes sadness so much picked up the trusty crusty cucr sun-bleached sky blue with rotations back again. Then I se possible things to think scabs.

CUT TO:

INT. KIMBERLY'S BEDROOM – UPSTAIRS AT THE HALAL BUTCHER'S – DAY/NIGHT

EXTREME CLOSE-UP of KIMBERLY's sleeping head. Her eyelids are shut, dancing to REM. As if by magic, her dead, tiny father, BARRY CLARK, falls from the ceiling, into her earhole. He wears wings and a stainless-steel halo.

> BARRY CLARK
> (in her ear)
> And now for some comic relief: What's twelve inches long, stiff, has a purple head, and makes a woman scream at night?
> > (beat)
> A cot death!

Kimberly wakes up with a start.

⊙

On the seventh day of depression, I woke up to find the flat full of water again. I couldn't remember crying in my sleep. I turned over in the bed to find all my tuna and cucumber plates, socks, dirty tissues, and the full piss-pot floating in murky one-inch-deep water. I groaned.

I hadn't cried in a couple of days, I hadn't showered, and I hadn't done the washing-up, or turned on any taps either. I wriggled my way up the headboard, staring at the grey water with eyes like rusty marbles. It took about ten minutes to realise it was the ceiling that was crying. Or, rather, a water pipe had decided to burst upstairs, springing a leak in my dingy lair.

I supposed it was time to get in touch with the landlord. I levered myself out of bed, cringing as I felt the leakage splash up my ankles. I grabbed the disgusting piss-pot, plodded through to the bathroom and poured it down the toilet. Despite washing out the saucepan three times in the sink, there was still some yellow residue left behind. I slammed it in the cupboard, and figured I'd never make sauce again. I never made it anyway.

I looked a state. My flesh was the colour of a tuna and cucumber sandwich, cut into thousands of triangles. Back in the bedroom, I found a knee-length jumper which covered my sins, though the frolicking bunnies on the front didn't match my emotions.

I tried to avoid getting dripped on the head as I searched for the Post-it note with the landlord's number on it. I realised it hadn't been a dark cloud above my head all this time – it was a leaking ceiling. I felt ever-so-slightly better, making the bed for the first time in a week. I knew I had to make a good impression on the landlord, since I didn't fancy being kicked out of the flat. I plumped up the pillows and cleared my throat, preparing to speak for the first time in a week. Then, I dialled his number.

Once I got off the phone, I went and sluiced round a white blob of toothpaste. I massaged talcum powder into my well-oiled platinum hair and put on new trousers. I let Lucifer the hamster set sail underneath the bed, out of sight. I blew him a warm south-westerly with my hairdryer.

The landlord arrived half an hour later. He seemed pleasant enough. He couldn't speak brilliant English, but he understood

I was Stevie's girlfriend, and he nodded kindly and compassionately when I explained what had happened to my boy. I had to do the impression of being hung, mind you, with tears frosting my eyelids.

I asked politely if I was allowed to stay in the flat, and he nodded again and said he'd suspend the rent a week or so, to help me get my feet back on the ground. Wherever he came from, the landlord believed in mourning the dead properly. However, rather than letting me stew, he couldn't resist sharing his views on ghosts with me, despite my pained expression and unenthusiastic grumbles. Mr Henry was brought up believing in ghosts – and he knew everything there was to know about different cultures' attitudes towards them.

Despite his bad English, Mr Henry was a talker. With no hint of irony – and no tact, as it seemed at the time – Mr Henry filled the silence with a tale about this temple in Rajasthan which was occupied by around 20,000 sacred black rats. The rats were treated like royalty – for instance, offered gifts of coconut milk, sweets and garlands – because the local Hindus believed they were their reincarnated ancestors. Mr Henry concluded, straight -faced, 'So, you know, your boyfriend he is probably still here with you. But not that there is any rats in this flat . . .'

After his speech, Mr Henry made it clear the rent would be £515 a month, and my guts tightened. The landlord wanted me to give details of a guarantor, but I explained to him my parents were dead as well, and I got more sympathy and nodding of the head. Luckily, I didn't have to do the impressions of a car crash and a cardiac arrest. I picked crumbs off my jumper while the landlord fished some papers out of his briefcase-cum-toolbox. I drew the logo of Kimberly-Clark for him on the bottom of our old tenancy agreement. Then I flopped back down onto the sofa arm and stared into my lap.

Once the contractual formalities were out of the way, Mr Henry said his goodbyes and scuttled up to the boiler room. He bashed around with the pipes for five or ten minutes until the ceiling agreed to stop crying. And then, as if by magic, the sun popped its head into the flat, to try and dry my carpet. I spent the rest of the afternoon with weary shoulders, tipping bucket after bucket of grey water down the plughole. By the end of it, the bath had a crab-coloured scumline round the sides and, potentially, I had cholera. My flat smelled of a sweaty octopus's eight armpits. I went downstairs to the Turkish-Polish-English supermarket to buy knock-off Glade air-freshener, and some fresh fruit and veg.

While it was tempting to go back to bed and start the gloom all over again, I soon remembered the £515 I had to conjure up by the beginning of March. There was also Stevie's funeral to think about, and my ticket up to Middlesbrough, to pay my last respects to the boy I loved and killed.

It was time not to be lazing about in bed all day, wasting away. It was time to resign my post as a part-time self-harmer, and get myself a proper job.

⊙

First things first: prospective employers will not recruit any-one with a greasy, rusty hairdo. It felt weird jumping in the bath after a week of wall-to-wall waterworks, and I left my own crab-coloured scumline behind in the tub. I often wonder how baths manage to get so filthy – I always presumed they were self-cleaning. After pulling the plug out, I massaged some Schwarz-kopf Absolute Platinum into my roots, and sharpened the Guillotine with my nail scissors.

Swanning about in a plastic bonnet, I felt noticeably happier being clean again. Next came spring-cleaning the flat. Once the floors had dried out completely, I gave the carpet a once-over with Shake n' Vac, turning the living space into a snowy, citrus-scented wonderland before sucking it all away into the hoover.

Before long, I felt more positive about running the flat independently. To keep my mind off Stevie (and keep the cucumber knife away from my flesh), I tried to surround myself with living things, like lilies and more flowering cacti, and I kept Lucifer's cage well stocked with food. He'd put on a bit of weight after I'd given him four days' worth in one go, but over the weeks he ran off the calories on his blue wheel. Lucifer was now officially the best sprinter in the flat.

I didn't feel as lonely that week. Being stuck indoors quickly made me tire of my own company, but it was nice having the plants and pets to tend to. The only difficult part was I wished I still had a man around to tend to as well. Despite me desperately wanting to get rid of him, I missed Stevie unbearably. Absence makes the heart grow fonder, after all, and being dead is about as absent as you can get.

So, I tried to rebuild him. I went back down to the Turkish-Polish-English supermarket and bought four bananas, one pear, one apple, some glacé cherries and a punnet of raspberries. Loitering around the cold meats section, I gathered up a couple of chicken legs, sausages, some Danish back bacon, chipolatas, then went next door to buy liver and minced beef from the halal butcher's. I took the bags upstairs and spread out all the ingredients for reanimation on the crummy breakfast bar. I laid a metre-long sheet of clingfilm across the work surface, then set to work, arranging the foodstuffs into two small effigies of Stevie. Fruity Stevie had bananas for arms and legs; a pear torso; blushing raspberry genitalia; a Golden Delicious head; and two glazed cherry eyeballs, pinned on with cocktail sticks. I smiled at him. He didn't smile back. For realism, I plucked out his right eye, and gave it a chew. Then, I got on with Meaty Stevie, making him a body of back bacon; sausage arms; chicken legs; chipolata genitalia; a head of liver, with frizzy minced-beef hair; and mini-meatball eyes. This time, I decided not to eat his raw eyeball. I chucked it in the bin instead.

After washing my hands thoroughly with Carex, I stood for a good ten minutes, nattering away to the Stevies. The good thing was I didn't have to speak to the effigies like babies. I felt I could get to the bottom of matters with them – they were very good listeners. However, when I asked if they knew of any job vacancies in the borough of Haringey, they were stumped. Meaty Stevie appeared to yawn, a small crack in the liver drooping open.

I slumped back through to the living space, feeling wrong in the head. I think, more than anything, I wanted to see the Stevies decomposing, as a gruesome reminder never to be nasty to any more boyfriends. I imagined the real Stevie in the morgue fridge, trying his best not to perish before his big send-off.

Thankfully, the North Capital Coroner ruled that Stevie had taken his own life under non-suspicious circumstances so, from a legal point of view at least, my guilty conscience was off the hook. Still, I felt sick. It was time to get out and raise some capital. I blew hundreds more gluey tears into my sixteenth Kleenex of the day, and changed into something more formal than the bunny jumper. I strengthened the Guillotine with hairspray, then picked up my handbag, my Medicine Bag, and my scarlet rain-coat, and made another sad dash out of the flat.

☉

I never want to die. I don't smoke, because it makes you die. I don't do drugs either, because they make you die as well. I do, however, carry round a bag filled with pills, cough mixture, throat lozenges, antiseptic wipes, and a flask of Lemsip Max Strength. It makes me feel immortal.

One of the main attractions of the Capital was its abundance of jobs, but it's the Capital's overabundance of competitive parasites that makes finding those jobs near enough impossible. It was frustrating when we first moved down, spending a week crawling round the pubs in exasperation, me asking, 'Vacancies?' and them answering, 'No no *nein* naw no *non* nay.' I spent the first two months on the dole, but it made me feel degraded; then one day me and Stevie were having a 'romantic' dinner down Pizza Express (actually, we weren't talking – Stevie was upset about some tennis match or other, and I had the flu), when I spotted the magic words WAITRESS WANTED. It was a good job. I only quit because Stevie grew rich off his Lottery funding six months later, but then for some reason I started being nasty to him, and he stopped winning races, and his funding was cut, and it all backfired on me.

I didn't want to go crawling back to Pizza Express, though. In any case, that branch was all the way down in Hammersmith, and it involved travelling on the infamous Subterranean Love Train twice a day. If you fancy a huge, sweaty orgy with your clothes on, take a trip on the Subterranean Love Train. It's a bit like the Ghost Train, except at rush-hour. The other week, I had an erotic encounter on the train with an elderly gent – both of us breathing hot passion into each other's necks, rocking rampantly back and forth, brushing wet flesh, his groin pushed up against my backside – but then the bastard didn't even say goodbye to me afterwards, let alone ask for my number. The chauvinist!*

---

* As an aside, the Love Train sees a hell of a lot of action in one day. In an independent scientific study conducted in the 2000s, countless sperm cells (from various men's bollocks) were found – still alive, but gasping for breath – wriggling on the Love Train's handrails. That's right, ladies: not only are the Love Train's lovehandles filthier than your boyfriend's cock on a bad day; they're worse than all your past boyfriends', friends', and bosses' cocks put together.

So, instead of subjecting myself to the dirty gyrations of the Love Train, I decided to stay local in my search for employment. I buttoned up my scarlet raincoat, then did the trick with the door and wandered out onto the wide, wonky pavements of Tottenham.

Apparently, South Tottenham is the most multicultural place in Britain, like a whole world map folded into a paper aeroplane and flown down the High Road at high speed. That afternoon, the place looked mostly African. I paced swiftly down the slope to the internet caff, which isn't a caff at all, unless you like nibbling wires and hard drives. I put my elbows down on the counter and asked the man behind it if he'd photocopy my CV for me. He poked his printer angrily with his finger until it coughed out ten copies, and he charged me a pound for the privilege. I frowned at him instead of saying 'Thank you', then stormed back out onto the High Road and decided to head for the pubs . . .

The Swan is a pub famous for appearing on the front of Capital buses – for example the 149, which goes to Tottenham Swan. It's an old, rickety affair, and all the Afro-Caribbean patrons turned to stare at me when I entered, like a Blaxploitation OK Corral. I felt like a swan – calm on the surface, but quivering down below. I decided to swan off, before the barman spotted me and demanded a CV.

The Dutch Pub doesn't have anything noticeably Dutch about it, except for all the red, white and blue outside, although that's this nation's colours as well. You might expect some Edam cheese, or windmills, or tulips, but all the Dutch Pub has to offer is loud pop music, and odd people boozing away on their tods. The barman at the Dutch Pub wasn't Dutch but he was amicable, so I stayed for a Smirnoff Ice, to be sociable. Once I'd mustered enough Dutch courage, I caught his eye for the umpteenth time and asked him about a job. He just shook his head and said, 'Sorry,' in plain English.

The Golden Stool used to be called the Mitre, but for some reason the new owners renamed it after 24-carat faeces. The place is more a hall of mirrors than a normal public house, which can make it disorientating after a few drinks and a nibble of their spicy Ghanaian grub. I watched five thousand reflected Kimberlys get rejected by five thousand reflected barmaids, and left the Stool feeling like shit.

Further into Tottenham, the Lord Parmo has the feel of a lucky-horseshoe-shaped living room but, as it turned out, I didn't have any luck in there, either.

I refused to try the kebab shops.

It'd started to rain by the time I got to the Fountain. I took shelter with another Smirnoff Ice for half an hour, feeling more like a mermaid than a barmaid, drenched through. And, despite my best efforts, I couldn't seduce the manager into giving me a job. I slithered sheepishly back out onto West Green Road, like a fish out of fucking water.

The Ristorante di Fantasia is an Italian establishment, situated on Philip Lane between the church and the AUND ETT, where you get your clothes washed. Inside, the décor looks like the place belongs in 1920s Little Italy, but the signage outside reckons it was opened in 2005. The place is awash with clichés and falsities: an inept violinist serenades the diners; plastic roses wilt in vases; and they've even drilled bullet holes into the wall behind table 13. The Ristorante has an impressive five Food Hygiene Stars but, if you look closely, three can be peeled off the certificate with a sharp fingernail.

'What can I do you for?' asked the round man by the cash desk. I explained I had CVs and I wanted a job. I shuffled on the tiles, underneath a water-spoiled photograph of a leaning tower of pizza.

'You are very looking-good lady,' remarked the round man, but I wasn't sure what that had to do with it. He tugged a MENU out of the MENU-holder, passed it to me, and explained that, if I could memorise all the dishes by Friday and wear 'more better clothes', the job was mine. He didn't even want a CV. I felt like I'd wasted a pound now, but from somewhere deep in my dark soul I managed to smile at him.

I spent the next two days mesmerised by the menu. I tried to get Meaty Stevie and Fruity Stevie to help test me on it, but they just stared up at the kitchen ceiling with slack jaws. Nevertheless, I had the knack of it by the weekend. At night, the dishes invaded my dreams, becoming a sort of culinary concrete poem in my sleepy brain-pipes:

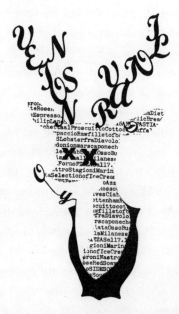

That Friday, I sat with the round man (whose actual name was Paolo: a round name) in the back of the restaurant, while he tested me on prices, ingredients and 'Vegetarian yes?' or 'Vegetarian no?' Paolo had a scar on his left cheek, and I wondered if it was from an accident in the kitchen, or punishment from the Mafia for crimes against cuisine. He kept trying to make me laugh because I was a very looking-good lady, and that made me laugh. I got the job.

I started that night. It was strange being suddenly plunged into a new occupation – I felt like a gymnast: balancing plates, bending over backwards, tentatively tiptoeing between the tables. Like any job, the first day was the toughest, and the longest. Paolo rushed me off my feet, it being so busy on Friday nights, and only two of us waitressing. The other one was called Nina: another very looking-good lady, though she didn't have very good English. I think she was from Romania. I don't think she liked me much. She kept huffing and puffing whenever I stalled at the till, or nudged into her on the way round the tight window tables, or splashed béchamel sauce on her blouse.

The violinist turned up at about seven, although there weren't many loved-up diners. It was mostly groups of fat Italian men, spending for ever on each course; discussing business in a hushed foreign tongue; laughing; and making daft comments about the poor waitresses. Me and Nina got a lot of attention, thanks to us being female, and under the age of twenty-five. Plus, the uniform involved a plunging neckline. I could see it was practical, though – the blouse kept you cool when the kitchens fired up, and won you lots of tips. Saying that, Paolo's queer idea was to split the tips three ways, between me, Nina and himself – the stingy bastard. He had breasts himself, but I didn't see him wearing a plunging neckline.

At the end of the night, I was shattered. The balls of my feet were throbbing, but there was definitely that satisfaction of having earned an honest crust. Paolo gave me and Nina some crusts of stale garlic bread and £40 cash in hand, which seemed reasonable enough for six hours' work. I spent £2 of it on the bus home, so killing were my ankles, and I had a long shower, to get rid of the stink of Italy. I frothed myself up with the Imperial

Leather Japanese Spa shower cream, the one that gives you a *satori* every time you squirt it. Each *satori* revealed to me the same thing: how much I wished I was in an actual Japanese spa, being rubbed down by gorgeous male geishas, not standing in my mouldy bathtub.

I dried myself to the murky sound of cars going past the window with the curtains shut. Every muscle in my body felt stiff, like one night waitressing was equal to doing a decathlon with a ball and chain round your ankle. To be fair, I must've walked about five miles over the imitation Roman mosaic during the course of the evening. I experienced my loveliest sleep in ages, despite waking up sporadically to serve customers, count money and subconsciously twist the pepper-grinder. By the second night, I felt like I'd been sprinting on a flaming hamster wheel. Then, by the third night, I had enough money to return to the North East, to watch some people dig a hole, and throw my boyfriend into it.

☉

Stevie had his revenge. It was freezing at the funeral. The Capital's always at least two or three degrees warmer than the North (due to its toxic climate, caused by pollution, overpopulation, and its slightly closer proximity to the equator) and, stupidly, I'd gone back in only a light black jacket, black skirt and black tights.

I recognised a lot of people, like Stevie's crying mam and dad, his crying aunties and uncles, and his lad mates trying to put on brave faces. Stevie was there too, dressed in a wooden box. I stood by his side for a bit, and I wanted to tell him I was sorry, but I didn't think he could hear me through all that shining pine.

There was a lot of standing up involved throughout the service. My feet were still aching from my first week at the Ristorante di Fantasia, and every time we settled down on the pews we had to stand up again and pay yet more respects and say 'Amen' over

53

and over again. It was a typical Catholic affair, with plenty of cathartic howling and long-winded prayers. There was a particularly poignant moment when Joy Division's 'The Eternal' came through the church PA, which was the song Stevie had chosen to go out to. It was one of the more miserable numbers from that album *Closer* he had emblazoned on his chest the day he died. I'd prefer something a little more upbeat at my funeral – something like 'Celebration' by Kool & the Gang, or 'I Will Survive'.

Outside, we huddled about, shivering, while they lowered Stevie into the ground. The priest seemed fairly convinced Stevie was going to Heaven, the way he was preaching. I wasn't sure how much I believed in Heaven. It was a nice idea, your soul floating off to enjoy the heady delights of Cloud 9, but, more than likely, death's just a vacant black void, where the most excitement you get is putrefaction.

I imagined Stevie being fed grapes by girls better looking than me, on a pink, fluffed-up cloud, and I grimaced. Still, it was a nicer idea than him being fed on by maggots. I rolled my first tear of the afternoon, like an invisible snail making a trail down my left cheek.

Foolishly, I'd forgotten to buy any flowers to put on Stevie's grave, which read:

STEVEN ANTHONY WALLACE

1.4.1984 – 23.2.2008

YOU WILL NEVER BE FORGOTTEN

KEEP ON RUNNING

REST IN PEACE

Soon, the snot and tears were going haywire, giving me a salty Vaseline moustache. There was an ice-cold body going down there into the dark earth, just because I'd been selfish and kissed a man with a square mouth one night in the Capital. The grave itself was like a huge square mouth, chewing up my boyfriend in a second square mouth: the coffin. I appeared to be in such distress, I got cuddled by various Wallace family members, and the fact I'd forgotten to buy any flowers went unnoticed.

I was well and truly getting away with murder.

⊙

The wake was at four o'clock in the Dorman's Club, just a short walk from the graveyard. Mrs Wallace had booked out the top room and put on a marvellous spread; all the food laid out with little grave-markers attached, with PRAWN and MILD CHED-DAR and TUNA epitaphs. Everyone tried to get drunk instead of being silent and depressed, although, of course, most ended up doing both. They had to put down WARNING! SLIPPERY SURFACE! signs by half five, the floor was so drenched.

Cleverly, the DJ played cheery disco music. I steered clear of the Smirnoff Ices, instead slurping back gin and tonics courtesy of Stevie's dad, and I danced with him too. It was halfhearted shuffle-dancing, though; the way you tend to dance when you've just killed your dancing partner's son.

All the people there were typical Middlesbrough, as in far too friendly and loud. Having been horrible for the past few months, I found it all a bit overwhelming. Once the drinks had been flowing a good while, strangers I recognised and strangers I didn't recognise kept coming over to give their condolences. It turned out Stevie had been singing my praises all over town, and I had to dam the tears because everyone was under the impression I was a wonderful girlfriend.

'Oh, Stevie loved you so much, love,' they said.

'You've got a heart of gold, you,' they said.

'It must be so hard for you, darl,' they said. 'Stevie was an idiot doing that to you. Selfish, in a way.'

55

'You've lost your accent, you,' they said.

As the wake went on, yet more people turned up, to pay their respects, and add to the puddles. I didn't recognise many of Stevie's athletics mates, apart from Tel the bog-eyed hurdler, and Natalie the fat pentathlete. Natalie had the potential to be a great sportswoman, if only she didn't keep getting pregnant by a string of different sportsmen. She must've been one of Stevie's closest clubmates, because her puddle was by far the biggest. I decided to avoid her.

I was maudlin by nine. I went to sit on my own in the corner, nervous I'd inadvertently spurt something out about the attack of the red mittens, or the three periods, or the hamster, or the tongue. It was weird being back in Teesside. In the Capital, it was easy enough to be anonymous, and I could hide under the blue gingham covers and pretend none of this horror had happened. But, up in the Dorman's, I was face-to-face with the sad results of my selfishness, like watching a live, updated re-enactment of Goya's *Disasters of War*. All's well in love and war – except when you change your fucking loyalty, that is.

'Ey up,' two voices said in stereo, as I was mid-munch through a chipolata. I glanced up cautiously.

It was a gruesome two-headed monster. No, pardon me – on second glance, it was only Shaun and Sean, Stevie's two best pals.

'Aw, hi, lads,' I chomped.

Shaun and Sean were born minutes apart from each other in Middlesbrough Parkside Hospital in 1981 – to different parents – and have been forced into friendship ever since. Growing up in neighbouring semis in Billingham, then studying the same medical degree and finding work together in funeral care, the boys have been practically inseparable for over twenty-six years. Nowadays, it's debatable if they still even like each other – they seem to spend every waking moment slagging each other off, and embarrassing each other. They're the type of lads who pass off intense cruelty as 'harmless banter', though they're nothing but charming towards other people.

It took my bleary eyes a second or two to focus. There's this daft thing Geordies and Mackems like to say about 'smog monsters' from Teesside – that they've got two heads and twelve toes from living so close to mammoth chemical plants – and Shaun and Sean don't help dispel the myth. They're like Siamese twins. The only irony is they look nothing like each other – Shaun's tall and skinny with hair like a crow's left wing; Sean's short and stubby, and his T-shirts are always too tight. Sean also has a habit of staring, like both his eyes are lazy.

Being around them is like listening to domestic abuse in Dolby surround-sound:

SHAUN	KIMBERLY	SEAN
Ey up		Ey up
	Aw, hi, lads	
		How you doing? Alright?
	Ah, well, yeah, you know	
You've lost your accent, you		
		Keeping your head up?
	Yeah	
Fucking mad. Absolutely mad		
		Aye, but you won't want to talk about it
	Nah, well	
		Still in the Capital?
	Yeah, are youse?	
		Yeah. The Bush
Shepherd's Bush		
		Fuck off, she knows
Where are you, like?		
	Me? Tottenham	
Ah, fucking Sperms		
		Aye, they fucking, 1–1
1–0, you prick		
		Fuck off, 1–1. Luke Young gone and eq—
Anyway, what you doing down there?		

57

            Me? Just this waitressing
                    thing

                                        How is it?

        It's alright, yeah

                                        I'm behind this bar now.
                                        The funeral care didn—

Fucking gar bar

                                        Fucking *gar bar*?

Fucking gay bar, then

                                        Is it fuck

He comes home with
loads of lads' numbers

                    Ha, hm

                                        Naw, do I fuck. Fuck off!
                                        He's a fuckin—

    Eh?

                                        Fucking . . . David
                                        Hasselhoff here

                    Ha, hm

                                        Daft lifeguard, he is

    Tit

                                        Anyway, we should all
                                        go for a drink down
                                        there, then

                With me?

                                        Yeah, yeah, like

    Aye

                Mmm, that'd be nice,
                lads

I left the two-headed monster to its bickering, sloping back over to the bar for another gin. It's strange how there comes a point when best friends (or boyfriends and girlfriends) stop trying to impress each other; instead, being blunt, mildly bitter and revelling in each other's misfortunes, just because they've been spending far too much quality time together.

Apparently, arguing is healthy, and you only argue with people you love, or people who remind you too much of yourself – hence, there's no point falling in love with someone unless you're willing to hate them now and then, too. Love is a fluffy, swaddling straitjacket; a bagful of kittens sent down a river; a sugar-coated bullet to the groin. Love is certainly lovely, but you build up a tolerance to it.

Perhaps it was inevitable I'd start being nasty to Stevie. Perhaps it was fate. That's what I told myself anyway, guzzling down more and more gin until the room started to spin spin spin into a black and white whirr, and then blacked out completely.

⊙

'Cup of tea, love?!'

I didn't recognise the voice. I didn't recognise the room either. Worryingly, it had photographs of Shaun and Sean plastered all over the plaster. Panicking, I scoured my pounding memory banks for clues, or misty images of me treating the two-headed monster to a sympathetic, gin-soaked spit-roasting session but, thankfully, the records came up blank.

'Er, yeah, ta!' I shouted anyway. Only fools turn down free tea. Taking another glance round the room, I was glad to see no funerary urns, cocktail shakers, or Speedos. Instead, I blinked at the photos of other ex-Newlands students; the cuddly-toy mascots; the workbooks; the trophies of gold and silver runners poised for ever on plastic turf, going nowhere. I picked and flicked a crumb of sleep out of my left eye, just as Stevie's mam came bursting into the bedroom, armed with a steaming cup of tea.

'Morning, pet. Here we are, love,' she said, placing the cup on Stevie's dresser. 'Ooh, your head must be killing.'

I smiled, meaning, 'Yes, it is, thanks.'

I hardly recognised Stevie's room from the lair of sportswear me and him used to mope around in, years back. Obviously Mr and Mrs Wallace – like all mams and dads – couldn't resist tidying the place once Stevie flew the nest. Sitting up in bed, I picked more sleep out of my eyes, and spotted myself in some of the photos – as a tourist in the Capital, or dressed as a skeleton on my twenty-first birthday, or in a loving, long-lost embrace with Stevie.

'As if I ended up here,' I said, with an exaggerated look of hangover on my face. Mrs Wallace smiled, her own petite hangover wrapped up in her soft dressing gown and slippers.

'Oh, don't worry, love, me and Tone were happy to bring you back. Anyhow, Martin'll be here in half an hour. You were better off coming back here,' said Mrs Wallace.

Martin Sawyer, the family lawyer, was set to read Stevie's will at noon. It was typical of Stevie to write a will at his age – I bet he even bought himself a calligraphy pen. I wondered if he liked me enough to leave me something. All I wanted was his jade green parka – I imagined the Necropolitan Police dusting it for fingerprints, and finding all these square-shaped, square-faced bachelor fingerprints.

It turned out they didn't bury Stevie in the clothes he'd died in. Instead, his parents forked out for a Marks & Spencer suit. As I sipped my tea, I imagined all the dapper skeletons lurking underground like a malnourished, rat-eaten Rat Pack.

After the tea, Mrs Wallace left me to get dressed, and I felt depressed putting on yesterday's boozy clothes. As I pushed my legs back into the black tights I shuddered, wondering whose job it was to put the suit on Stevie's corpse. When Shaun and Sean started up their funeral home, they used to show me and Stevie films on their phones of their workmates mucking about with the corpses – like making them feel each other up, or talk with daft spazzy accents, or do the electric boogaloo. It increased my desperation not to die a million-fold.

Downstairs, the lounge was absolutely spotless, except for the navy blue spots on the wallpaper. Old people love cleaning. I felt bad sitting on the new sofa in my stinking, gin-spiked clothes, but standing up didn't seem appropriate either. Martin Sawyer, the family lawyer, came round at twelve on the dot, and we had to drink more cups of boiling tea while he readied his papers.

60

Jade green parka jade green parka jade green parka, I repeated to myself. *Burn the evidence burn the evidence burn the evidence.*

The reading of the will was less formal than I'd imagined – Martin was clearly a good friend of the family and, while he retained the stock sympathetic face required at times of mourning, he cracked a few jokes as well.

I just wanted to get it over with, and get back down to the Capital. It felt uncomfortable, being back in Teesside – and even less comfortable being back in Stevie's pad, drinking tea with his mam and dad. The reading of the will was the last formality in the mourning process – the last abstract, origami nail in Stevie's coffin. After all this, there'd be some sort of closure, I thought, and I could flee south and be alone again, with everybody. I needed to be surrounded by people who've never even heard of Stevie Wallace.

The will was surprisingly straightforward. I'd imagined Stevie might divide his record collection into categories for family and friends, according to taste and disposition; or for him to distribute his wardrobe and remaining money round numerous different charities. If that was so, I'd be straight round Scope the next morning to buy back the jade green parka – hopefully with the Polaroid of me and Square-Face still there, untouched, in the secret inside pocket. Nowadays, whenever I hear a police siren, I get the shakes. But surely you can't be arrested just for cheating on your boyfriend?

I listened to Martin reading the will, with my toes crossed. This was the gist of it:

Mr and Mrs Wallace would receive the contents of Stevie's trophy cabinet.

The slums of Africa would receive the contents of Stevie's wardrobe.

Kimberly Clark would receive the contents of Stevie's bank account – a whopping £7,777.77 – for being 'my one true love', in the words of Martin Sawyer, although I think it was supposed to be Stevie speaking. My face reddened with equal parts joy and despair.

The rest of Stevie's possessions were to be auctioned off, and the money given to his charity of choice, United Through Sport.

Straight away, Mr and Mrs Wallace got wittering about building a holy shrine for Stevie in his bedroom, with all his medals and certificates. We all had a cuddle. Even Martin gave me a kiss on the cheek, more as a 'sorry for the loss' rather than a 'congratulations on the gain'. He took my bank details all the same, and explained someone would be round the flat to pick up the trophies and everything else in the next week or so. I'd have to tidy.

It was time to retreat back to the Capital. Mr Wallace seemed intent on buying me one last gin down the Southern Cross, but I lied and said I had a shift that evening at the Ristorante, hotfooting it out onto Captain Cook's Crescent with Mr Sawyer. It was strange being on Stevie's snaking street again – me and him had had many happy voyages down it over the years. And this was to be my last.

I felt a little queasy, hugging everyone goodbye again. Martin offered me a lift to the station, and we sat together in the front, with the rain causing interference on the windows. As we sallied forth, Martin told me a few stories about Stevie as a nipper, playing football with his son, and one about his son doing well now on a computing course at Teesside. I had to pretend to be interested. While we sped forward, all I could think about was getting back to the flat. I looked forward to seeing Lucifer, and the two Stevies, and the 243 bus that says 'Hello' at my window every eight to ten minutes, Monday to Friday. I looked forward to telling them all about the money.

☉

Meaty Stevie and Fruity Stevie appeared to have been fighting while I'd been away. Fruity Stevie had bruises down his yellow arms and legs, and his red cherry eyeball had turned black. Meaty Stevie wasn't bruised at all, but you could tell there'd been some retaliation because his skin was red raw, and a bit scabby round the edges. I tutted at them, tearing the clingfilm down the middle and sliding them to opposite ends of the worktop. I incarcerated them under two glass mixing bowls.

Neither protested.

⊙

One weird thing about Stevie was he only ever listened to music by people who'd killed themselves.

On my next day off (a Tuesday), a pair of removal men came round to remove Stevie's clothes and trophies, and more or less half my memories of him. All I had left were his CDs, some sports paraphernalia, and a spare house key on his silver AAA keyring. And all his money.

The removal men turned their noses up at the two mouldy effigies in the kitchen, and refused a mug of Lemsip Max Strength, but they didn't turn their noses up at Stevie's bad fashion sense. Stevie's empty wardrobe gaped open like yet another square mouth. I tried my best to plug the orifice, stuffing Stevie's records into the compartments where his boxers and socks used to live, and listening to the odd one as I went. Work the day before had been murder (I annoyed Nina by stepping on her toes, and I annoyed Paolo for doing some sums wrong, and they annoyed me too, by being annoyed at me), so the moody, blue music mirrored my emotions quite well.

To the sound of Nirvana, Elliott Smith, INXS, the Manics, and the manic cars outside, I wondered if it was possible to kill yourself just because of the music you listen to. I refused to put on the *Closer* album, just in case it had voodoo powers, causing its listeners to attach shoelaces to their necks and fall off a climbing frame. It eyed me up from between *Unknown Pleasures* and *Still*, while I shimmied about, halfheartedly shaking my bottom to the harmonica part of 'Suicide Blonde'.

Some of the songs were more miserable than others. Richey Edwards out of the Manic Street Preachers wrote lyrics about abortions and mausoleums, while Nirvana now and then sang about moist vaginas and Mexican seafood. Generally, though, the theme was suffering.

My ears were suffering by about three. I decided I needed some fresh air. Also, I wanted to find out why Kurt, Ian, Elliott, Richey, Michael and friends had topped themselves. Was it because they listened to depressing music? Or was it because their wives and girlfriends depressed them?

I did the trick with the door, and stomped up the High Road with period pain grinding my insides, like a hedgehog doing stretches in my womb. I popped a couple of ibuprofen out of the Medicine Bag. It felt sickly brushing shoulders with the obnoxious, raucous schoolkids piling out of the fried-chicken shops and yapping at each other. For some reason, the kids of the Capital speak with queer Cockney-Yank accents, and wear baggy sports-smocks – it must be all that gangsta rap they listen to, piping out of their phones like shady, subliminal Linguaphone. That afternoon, Tottenham looked like a watered-down wannabe Compton or Bronx, or a shoestring-budget Kriss Kross video. I didn't fancy a cameo.

It was a relief to get through the door of the internet caff. I put 50p on the counter, then slumped down at computer number 8. The guy behind the counter had far too much forehead and not enough chin. I could feel him watching me, in between mouthfuls of his steaming curry. I rubbed my womb and ignored him. After checking my empty email inboxes, I did some research on the dead members of Stevie's favourite groups, and I was saddened to find most of them had kicked the bucket because of girls. I kicked the bottom of the computer desk, lightly.

I felt like a wicked witch again. A nasty piece of work. To add to the effect, just then the sky darkened, and the heavens opened. Over the top of the monitor, I watched shards of lightning pin-pricking the far-off estates. The kids of the Capital yapped louder, shutting their chip boxes and running for cover.

Planet Earth has enjoyed a rich history of nastiness. In the olden days – long before the world's first nice person, Jesus Christ – there used to be these tyrannous, gruesome creatures called dinosaurs roaming about. These so-called 'terrible lizards' would still be around today, wreaking havoc at our supermarkets, garden centres and beach holidays, if it wasn't for a freak explosion that occurred just before the Ice Age, killing them all off. Sadly, though, it didn't take long for new tyrannous, gruesome creatures called humans to colonise and conquer the Earth's surface.

I wondered if the world was due another freak explosion. While it was nerve-wracking being in a small room filled with electrical equipment during an electrical storm, I had eighteen mins remaining on the PC I didn't want to waste. The gaps between flashes and rumbles were getting slimmer and slimmer, so I decided to write my will, just in case. I brought up Microsoft Word and picked the fanciest, most formal, flowery font I could find. I typed:

The Last Will and Testament of Kimberly Clark

To whom it may concern. Providing I've still got my looks, don't burn me. Embalm me please – I would like an open casket, and would like to look my best. Then bury me in an airtight, watertight coffin – the most expensive you can find, please. Keep my organs where they should be (I did think about getting a donor card, but I don't want to look like a doner kebab once the doctors have finished with me). Don't let anyone muck about with me at the funeral parlour, e.g. treating me like a puppet. Play 'Celebration' by Kool & the Gang at the service. Make sure everyone's well fed. Give all my money to the Samaritans, or another charity dealing with suicidals. There is a hamster in Flat D above a halal butcher's on Tottenham High Road that desperately needs feeding. Thank you. Hopefully I will have had a good life by the time you read this. Farewell.

I double-clicked PRINT, but nothing happened. I clicked PRINT again, and again, and again, and again, giving the printer icon a miniature heart-massage with the cursor. Still no reaction. I glanced across at the guy behind the counter, but he was too engrossed in his curry to notice my plight. The hush of the internet caff made me shy, so I just clicked PRINT again, instead of complaining. Still nothing happened.

'Print print print . . . I've gone and pressed print, but why's it not fecking printing?' the chubby Irishman beside me blurted out, obviously having the same trouble.

The guy behind the counter looked as gormless as the open-mouthed printer. He put his dinner to one side, then twiddled the wires in the back of the Epson halfheartedly and sighed through his nose.

My neighbour clearly didn't like being sighed at – especially with only three mins remaining on his PC.

''Ere, black boy, why's it not print?' he snapped, getting up from his spinning chair.

Ah, racism – the last bastion for the ignorant and indignant. I cringed, with my eyes down at my keyboard, sensing danger. Round about me, everyone else became suddenly transfixed by their own keyboards.

66

'What did you call me?' grunted the guy with the curry.

'Black boy,' coughed the Irishman, striding up to the desk. 'Well, you wouldn't want me calling you *white boy*.'

To keep myself busy, I glanced across at his frozen monitor. Of all the things, the irate Irishman was trying to print out a clip-art image of a smiling woolly monkey, wearing a fez and juggling peanuts, with the words SMITH FAIRYTALE FUNLAND in a large speech bubble.

'You leave now, you leave,' said the guy behind the counter, heroically/foolishly standing his ground. The only weapon he had at his disposal was a tepid punnet of lamb madras, whereas the Irishman had biceps like triceratops' legs, and some fairly nasty insults, to boot:

'I've already paid, you fecking grandmotherfecker,' he replied, getting right in his face. Despite the brilliant insult, my heartstrings sagged sadly for the internet fellow. It must be an awful job, looking after slow, petulant, fickle, self-centred, mute computers. Not to mention slow, petulant, fickle, self-centred, vocal customers. 'No, you leave. You no talk to me like that,' he said.

'You fecking nigging grandmotherfecker,' I think the Irishman said next, though there was a bus going past. Then, a loud drum-roll of thunder.

Round the caff, everyone kept the act up, pretending to be more interested in the internet than in the insults. I wished the lightning would strike us down, after all. I hated the idea of it hitting an innocent family household (perhaps halfway through the little one blowing out their birthday candles), when it could hit this internet caff, full of selfish, ignorant scumbags.

At least, next to these bastards, I didn't feel like a witch any more. Yes, I was a chronically bad girlfriend, but I realised there's more tyrannous, gruesome creatures than me roaming the

Earth – it's just that they don't have unstable, suicidal partners, that's all.

Perhaps I was a good person, underneath it all. I wasn't sure.

I decided to put it down to fate. If the lightning killed us, I'd accept my lot (probably reborn as a slug), and suffer my sins graciously. If we survived, I'd start my life afresh, and be as nice as possible to everyone and everything, from then on.

I waited for something to happen, while the thunder drowned out the arguing. I picked fluff off my raincoat, and straightened the Guillotine with my fingertips. I wasn't going to die looking ropey. It worried me that my will hadn't printed out, although, thankfully, it was still frozen on the screen in front of me. Hopefully it'd still be legible in the instance of an electric attack. Hopefully the Microsoft screensaver wouldn't kick in before the ambulancemen got to me.

With the lightning more or less overhead, I tried to convince myself I'd enjoyed a good innings. I could recall about five or six times I'd been overwhelmingly happy, and about fifteen times I'd been uncontrollably upset. As the flashes and rumbles got closer and closer together, I felt sick, imagining us all turning into crispy charcoal and bubbling fat – and the world not being any worse off for it. I prayed for a quick, painless death. But, more than that, I prayed for a second chance.

What I got was silence.

Through the window, I saw the lightning moving on, pointing out distant landmarks in the Capital while the thunder grumbled, having trouble keeping up. I breathed relief into my fists, feeling suddenly ecstatic. Round the room, everyone was still tap-tapping obliviously at their keyboards, like the last pitter-patters of the storm.

In my belly, I felt something shift. I was going to be a nice person. From then on, there would be no more cruelty. Nina's toes wouldn't have to fear coming into work with her; my land-lord wouldn't have to worry about his flat flooding again; and no future boyfriends would be coaxed into suicide after spending too much quality time with me. And I told myself: if I ever find true love again, I'm going to keep hold of it.

Looking about the caff, I tried to conjure up some empathy for my fellow customers. Maybe they weren't ignorant scumbags, after all – maybe they were just trying to keep their heads down and survive, in a town that's not well known for its community spirit. Over by the counter, the Irishman and the internet man were still bickering, only with less enthusiasm and conviction, now the creative insults had run dry.

I wondered if I could employ some forcible kindness to ease the tension. I weighed up my people skills. In the end, though, I didn't have to step in. It could've been the storm passing, or it could've been fate again but, just then, the printer kicked back into life, spitting out six copies of my will, and one sheet with a smiling woolly monkey on it, wearing a fez.

'Eh, eh, who are these?' the internet fellow announced, trying to sidestep the argument. He fanned out my six wills, and wafted them.

Embarrassed, I got up out of my spinning chair. I didn't want anyone to laugh at my last rites but, fortunately, they were typed in an almost illegible font, and being wafted, too. I smiled at the internet bloke, just to be nice, then removed my purse and said, 'Thanks, love. Er, here, I'll pay for his too.'

I placed a pound on the counter, to cover the seven printed sheets (including the monkey), plus a generous 30p tip for my long-foreheaded, chinless friend.

'No, no,' the internet fellow protested, meaning, 'Thank you.'

'Cheers, like,' the Irishman said to me, with a furrowed brow, meaning, 'Have you got fecking brain damage?'

69

Thrown by my nice gesture, the chubby Paddy rolled up his woolly monkey picture and stormed back out of the caff without saying anything else. Me and the internet fellow watched him disappear, trudging between the puddles. My friend took a shy mouthful of cold curry.

'Thank you,' he said, also meaning, 'Thank you.'

'Don't worry. He was an idiot,' I said, which wasn't particularly nice of me, but it was the truth, at least. 'Are you alright?'

The internet fellow nodded, no doubt appreciating his crap job a bit more, now the Irishman was gone. I decided to make it even better for him.

'Here, here's my number, if you ever want a . . . friend, or anything,' I said, scribbling my Sony Ericsson digits onto his napkin. Then, I gave him a winning smile, posted my six sheets of A4 into my handbag and sauntered out of his shop.

The internet fellow dribbled a little sauce, all merry and confused. As I slipped past the window, I waved, and I could tell I'd made his day. He didn't dare wipe his chin with the napkin.

⊙

I don't have a complete heart of stone, you know.

While I've always found humans a bit on the unbearable side, I've got a real soft spot for nature, and the flashes of beauty it fires at you throughout the year: for instance, plaintive winter nights when the moon's gloomy face reflects your own, like a huge, distant shaving mirror; or the double rainbow me and Stevie rode past on the FirstCapitalConnect in spring 2006; or that fleeting whiff of ozone I sniffed up last summer, blessing me with the gift of time travel, sending me hurtling back to my first ever kiss, on a wet and windy Wednesday night outside Marton Country Club.

I find it strange how people get annoyed when it rains. Alright, so you get drenched and the bus is always packed and steamy, but what people don't realise is the rain transforms the street into a never-ending silver mirror, reflecting the sky. Birds nest in the paving slabs. Planes go down the drain.

I think the most beautiful thing I've ever seen are the stars, especially when you go up the hills in North Yorkshire and you're away from the pollution, and you can see simultaneously into the future and into the past. Often I'd go up there on my lonesome, taking the track up the back of Guisborough, and sitting for hours up one of the evergreen Christmas trees, tucked under the blankety blank night sky. The tree would cuddle me and keep me warm, pointing out every single star and constellation with its branches – including some that haven't even been named yet. So I'd name them after me.

Another – less conventional – sight of natural beauty is my current bathroom in Tottenham. In the weeks following Stevie's death, I noticed the inside of the bathtub gradually turning from white to coral pink, as if by magic. Every day it got pinker, like a huge porcelain poppy, with dainty black seeds in the middle. I scraped a sample of the pink out of the bath with my tweezers, popped it in my handbag, then went down to the indoor market to build myself an outfit coordinated to the tub. However, days later, the poppy seeds had sprouted – turning the coral pink to a sickly, mouldy black. It took four days to scrub the porcelain white again, and the day after that I took my coral pink dress, shoes and hairgrips back to the market, to get my money back.

There's so much effortless beauty in the world, in all manner of guises, it's a wonder I've spent so much of my time on Earth in a foul mood. I often wonder who the happiest people are – probably Buddhist monks, since the whole point of being one is to look after each other, keep your karma on the good side, and keep your mouth shut. I imagined my karma levels were a bit

71

ropey at the minute, but that was going to change. I wanted to go to Heaven/Nirvana/Valhalla desperately, if it was still possible. I wanted to see more beautiful sights.

It was high time for some random acts of kindness, I thought.

Kimberly Clark gets . . . the Seal of Approval

It seemed daunting at first, unadulterated altruism. It's just not a very natural human trait, is it? Nowadays, people seem to prefer being scornful and slanderous – to earn brownie points and respect from their so-called pals – though they won't look very clever in years to come, being whipped by Beelzebub and his minions in Hell.

I spent most of Thursday morning disguising my pesky, evil eyes with turquoise shadow, practising different styles of smiles in the mirror, and putting on a good bra, for the sake of pleasing the boys. My dad used to say the most powerful people in the world are beautiful, kind, intelligent women, since other women will respect you, and men will bend over backwards to help you, whatever your needs. Therefore it had to be the Wonderbra.

All morning, the sun played peekaboo with me from between the altocumulus clouds. To be nice to the flat, I opened the sash windows to air it out, then went round picking up knickers, plastic bags and receipts, and stuffing them in the appropriate places. After the tidy-round, I pulled the bunny jumper and scarlet raincoat over the Wonderbra, and tugged on fresh jeans. I straightened the Guillotine with the ceramic ghds. To be nice to my landlord and his insurance company, I remembered to slide the sash windows shut again and switch off the straighteners. The flat let out a lovely sigh of relief, also known as air displacement. In a way, houses are a lot like human bodies, what with their central heating respiratory systems, glass eyes, flapping mouths, AC/DC nervous systems, fatty insulation and vital organs (boiler, oven, fridge-freezer, waste disposal). They even age the same way, leaning over at funny angles, and their skin slowly cracking. In human terms, my building must've been about eighty-odd.

I wrote a shopping list of beauty products on the back of a Kleenex, then snuck down the spinal-column stairs and out into the brisk afternoon. I used Stevie's spare key on the tricky door, for old time's sake, then headed west towards Wood Green Shopping City. It was quite a trek, but the walk seemed pleasant enough, without my usual, nagging hatred for humankind. I bought chips from the lonely looking lad at MFC Chicken, just to be nice, and threw them away to the squirrels and pigeons, also to be nice.

I was nervous about going up to Shopping City, because it meant walking past the common for the first time since Stevie hung himself. My pulses thumped as the adventure playground came into view in the distance. The garish primary colours seemed unbearably cheerful for a suicide spot. I picked my fingernails into bloody ruins.

As usual, the play area was empty, except for two little girls scrambling along the climbing frame, enjoying themselves. I'm not sure what made me stop by the railings to watch them. Maybe I was looking for closure, or perhaps it was exhaustion. Nevertheless, the girls looked happy, swinging from the same rung Stevie had swung from only a month or so before. They looked like twins, though one had her blonde hair in a sharp bob, while the other had a plaited ponytail. I think the one with the Guillotine was smiling the hardest.

Before long, the girls spotted me staring at them, and they became instantly shy, dropping onto the soft play bark with a horrid thud.

'Ey up!' I said, smiling at them.

The girls just stared back, confused. They probably didn't even know what an 'Ey up' was.

With cheeks blazing, I set off again, striding past the Subterranean Ghost Train station, with brokeLads and New Capital Kebab on my left. While I'd never forget the image of Stevie's big blue face, it felt good to have another – happier – image of the climbing frame, to superimpose over the heartbreaking one. I could hear the twins giggling again behind me, and I giggled too, into the collar of the raincoat.

Despite the kindness being a bit forced and sickly sweet, I felt like a changed woman. I swear the Capital seemed more colourful, like someone had been at it with their felt-tips. Everyone I passed appeared to be smiling – either that, or they were screwing their faces up at the strobing sun. I chased my shadow towards Shopping City, which loomed up ahead like a dull, halfhearted Las Vegas. I shimmied between the shoppers.

In the Capital, there are three varieties of mugger: the tramp, the criminal and the charity worker. Most vocal of the three is the charity worker. While warning you of their presence with their bright, oversized fleeces, charity workers have the ability to pinpoint – and fleece – weaklings in crowds of people with hawk-like precision.

I've never been a fan of speaking to strangers, let alone strangers whose job it is to politely pester you into parting with your pennies. When I spotted the charity worker up ahead with its ginger dreadlocks and fluorescent yellow fleece, my heart's initial reaction was to play dead. But then I remembered the altruism again, and it was actually a strange treat when the charity worker picked me out of the hundreds of dour faces and said, 'Hello! You're wearing red! I'm wearing yellow! How are you?! Can I have a quick chat?!'

To the charity worker's surprise, I stopped in my tracks, and said back to it, 'Hello! Yeah, I'm fine! Go on!'

A bit stumped, the charity worker fumbled with its clipboard, scratched its dreadlocks and stumbled over a snigger. I felt bad for fazing it. All the charity worker could think to do was hand me a leaflet covered with pictures of butchered seals.

'Ugh,' I said, a bit confused.

'Erm, erm,' the charity worker said, getting back its composure, 'I'm collecting for a, er, anti-sealing campaign. For just two pounds a month, you can help put an end to innocent seals being slaughtered for, er, their pelts and fur.'

'Sound,' I said. I couldn't get my Maestro card out quick enough. Hummmming, I wrote my details onto one of its sheets, feeling my heart swelling. Once I'd filled out the application, the charity worker gave me a hug, though I think the hug was scripted. Breathing in the worker's dank jungle hair, I spotted on the bottom of its clipboard: FINALLY, WHY NOT GIVE THEM A HUG, OR SAY 'HAVE A LOVELY DAY!'

Nevertheless, I let the charity worker grope me for as long as it fancied.

'Have a lovely day!' it said, waving me off. I just laughed.

As I waltzed further into Shopping City, I looked up at the loaded clouds and put my hood up. I couldn't believe it'd taken me this long to learn the pleasures of being selfless. I imagined the seals clapping their flippers together, just for me. I let the clouds dribble on me, and I didn't feel at all fluey. Whether a placebo or not, the altruism was working wonders for my hypochondria.

However, two steps later, I was surprised to find myself surrounded by four or five other charity workers, all waving their clipboards at me and trying to rip my arms off.

☉

By three o'clock I had seven new direct debits set up. After all that strenuous form-filling, it was time for a breather. Paolo didn't want me at the Ristorante di Fantasia till half six, so I spent an hour sipping the cheapest coffee off the Marks & Sparks menu, with a carrier full of cosmetics between my knees. I turned the Clarins anti-ageing-cream bottle over in my hands, contemplating immortality.

I got halfway through the instruction booklet when, suddenly, I found myself spasming uncontrollably. I was vibrating. Pre-1990s, this might've meant an epileptic seizure, but in this day and age it's more likely just a phone call.

I tugged the humming Sony Ericsson out of my damp jeans.

'Hello?' I said.

'Ey up, Kimberly,' the phone said back. It was either Shaun or Sean – I couldn't tell without looking at them. Inside, my heart flinched, and I considered feigning signal problems, but then I remembered the pesky altruism again.

It turned out the two-headed monster had caught wind of my windfall at Stevie's will-reading, and wondered if I fancied a pint or two, to 'toast my success'. It was still only early, so I agreed to meet them for a quick one at this Danish pub down Holloway. I had a funny feeling they wanted more from me than just a pint of froth but, nevertheless, I decided to be nice, and set off from Marks's with my prejudices behind me. And four more charity workers behind me, too – tailing me all the way to the Subterranean Ghost Train station, still flap-flap-flapping their pens and clipboards.

Kimberly Clark in . . . the Taming of the Shrewd Two-Headed
  Monster

This was my first real test: being nice to two truly putrid people.

I took the Ghost Train down to Holloway. I was tempted to make conversation with some of the stony passengers, but I didn't want to frighten them. People are so paranoid in the Capital. I think it's that feeling of being trapped underground with total strangers, in one of the world's most dangerous cities – with not much oxygen – that makes people a little nervy.

I decided to be nice and kept my mouth shut.

On Holloway Road, I walked away from the dangling sun, weaving in and out of the charging pedestrians and limping pigeons, trying not to get in anyone's way. This only resulted in me getting in everyone's way, though. It's not easy being nice – I had to keep a constant tape-loop of SMILE! SMILE! SMILE! SMILE! SMILE! spinning round and round my head but, whenever someone went past with an angry face – or shoulder-barged me, or sneezed near me – the tape kept getting jammed, or ruckled, and it was starting to wear thin.

I got to the Copenhagen ten minutes late but, after two breathless laps round the bar, I realised Shaun and Sean were late too. I ordered a Smirnoff Ice, perching myself on one of the high stools. As I poured out my drink, the tumbler turned into a miniature fantasy planetarium, with thousands of tiny, spinning comet bubbles, and larger ice-cube meteorites. I sucked it up, into a black hole.

Waiting for people always makes me nervous – especially when you're not overly keen on who you're waiting for. I'd got halfway through the Smirnoff when the double-doors swung open, and in they came. Sean was dressed in his trademark tight T-shirt, while Shaun appeared to have swept his floppy fringe-wing back with grease, or rain.

77

SHAUN	KIMBERLY	SEAN
Ey up		Ey up, Kimberly
	Hiya, lads	
Soz we're late, he fucking los—		
		Well, you were fucking rushing
	What's that?	
		Ah, the bookies
Fucking pathetic		
		Aye, and you cleaned up, eh
I've got money for a pint		
	No, no, I'll get youse a drink	
		Aw
Ta		
	What youse having?	
		Er, pint of Carling please
Stella. Not that piss		
	Just nip to the ladies first, lads	

I used the pub's Kimberly-Clark facilities, then strolled back to the bar for the lads' pints. They were a funny old pair. Like a lot of boys I knew from the North East, the pull of the betting shop had failed to loosen its grip round their necks and wallets. All those shops ever seemed to do was stir up false hope and disappointment. I preferred shops such as Topshop or New Look, which, to be fair though, had their own disappointments, if you happened to be larger than a size 12.

I placed the drinks down in front of the two-headed monster, hoping the fizzy bubbles might perk the boys up a bit.

SHAUN	KIMBERLY	SEAN
	There we are	
Nice one		Nice one, cheers
	So, how youse getting on?	
		Not bad. How about you?
I bet you're alright!		
	Hm?	

78

Fucking, what was it,
seven grand?

Er, yeah, yeah. It's mad

Mint, that. Nice to get
settled

Yeah, I suppose

See, cos we were gonna
ask

Yeah, we were gonna, er

Yeah, naw. *I'll* ask

Go on, lads, spit it out

Ha

Well, see, we're not
happy in our jobs much

I am. He's not

Fuck off

Just sayi—

Well, like, we're
thinking of setting up a
new business

Down here

Funerals again

Like, cos it was daft
what happened up there

Aye, cos we've got the
skills

But we're totally
strapped

Like, we've got the
business cards

Just not the business

Simultaneously, Shaun and Sean rummaged through their
trousers, and removed a deck of business cards. The stock was
cheap and nasty, almost like copier paper. Sean fanned his out,
and I plucked one from the pile. It read: SS FUNERALS – KIND
RELIABLE SERVICE, with their numbers and address underneath. I had to bite my lip. I wondered if they were aware of the
Schutzstaffel, the other SS. The other death squad. Shaun even
had a hairdo like Hitler.

Like, we'd pay you back

Hang on, we haven't
asked her yet

Aw, you want a borrow?

79

Yeah, er, please

Five grand would be a
springboard

You can tell he's a
fucking lifeguard

Piss off. We'll definitely
pay you back

Like, straight away

See, loads of people die
and that, down here

Shut up, she doesn't
fuckin—

Like, you'll definitely
get it back

You'll get it back

Deffos

Yeah, alright then

The monster's four eyes widened, almost in disbelief. To be fair, though, Shaun and Sean deserved the money as much as me – at least they'd been loyal to Stevie over the years. They might've ripped the piss out of him now and then, but they never would've pushed the poor soul to suicide – not even if business was slow at SS Funerals. Which, by the sound of it, it was.

Usually, when humans are asked for money, their initial reaction is to squirm and feel uneasy. I just felt numb, though, as I wrote out the cheques for £2,500 each. I mechanically handed the money over, like an ATM being daylight-robbed, but it was the right thing to do. I felt a bit of my guilt subside as I signed the dotted line.

That's unreal

Cheers, you're a star

God, that's amazing

And then came the unexpected ripple of joy. I flapped my legs under the bar, beaming. Even though funeral care seemed like a morbid career path, it was great to see Shaun and Sean happy for once. Finally, the bickering fell silent. I patted the lads on their shoulders, feeling like a beardless Jesus, rising slightly on my seat to beckon the barman for another drink.

'You couldn't write *me* out a cheque, could you, lovey?' spluttered this old codger who'd appeared on the opposite side of the bar. I laughed, just to make him happy.

'Ah, I wish I could,' I replied, genuinely disappointed not to have more charity money in the vaults. 'Here, though, what you drinking? I'll get you a pint.'

It's an expensive business, being generous. I plucked the last tenner out of my purse, then asked the barman for a pint's worth of Tetley's for the old man. My pockets (or, rather, the zip pocket in my handbag) were feeling considerably lighter but, in equal proportion, my heart felt a lot plumper. After slurping the froth off the top of his pint, the old man smiled all six of his teeth at me. As it happened, it wasn't your average smile of gratitude – it seemed more like a smile that said, 'Ha ha, I fucking got one over you there, you daft cow!'

I just smiled back sheepishly.

☉

Money's meant to be the root of all evil, but it can also be a route to happiness. Then again, I knew I had to be more careful about it. The wage at the Ristorante di Fantasia was enough to pay my rent and keep my head above water, but it was clear I'd need to conjure more pocket money if I was going to carry out endless good deeds.

On the packed Love Train back to Seven Sisters, I tried to think up ways to beg, borrow or steal more money, while thrusting my pelvis involuntarily in an old Asian man's face. He acted coy, pretending not to notice. Afterwards, I felt used, wandering down past Tesco with a layer of sweat down my back. However, when I got to the pistachio green door of the Ristorante, all the male customers seemed pleased to see me and the Wonderbra, but, instead of lust in their eyes, I saw shining pound coins.

'You on fire tonight,' Nina snarled as I dropped another couple of quid in my TIPS jar. Once I'd been working at the Ristorante a month or so, I plucked up the courage to question Paolo about the three-way tips split. I had a long speech planned – about how it was immoral (and probably illegal), him taking a cut out of mine and Nina's hard labour – but, in the end, I think it was the Wonderbra that swayed it. While I spoke, Paolo just stared into the dark, mysterious chasm between my breasts, purring, 'Oh, okay, baby.' He got us our very own TIPS jars from out the back: mine led a former life as a pesto jar; Nina's looked like a sardine can. Mine had £19.62 in it. Nina's had £1.30-ish.

'Here, Nina, have some for yours,' I said, scraping a few quid from table 2 into the sardine can. She shot me a look of sarcastic gratitude.

I don't know why she was so moody about it. It wasn't difficult making an impact in that place – all you had to do was keep smiling and not drop anything. I felt a bit like Anthea Turner on Prozac, with a huge watermelon grin even air hostesses might find over the top.

Being nice in the Ristorante di Fantasia made the nights go so much quicker. Compared to Nina – plodding about in her high heels, with a face like a clenched fist – I found myself enjoying the customers' company more, racing about like a mother hen, laughing at their bad jokes, phoning taxis for those too intoxi-cated to move/speak.

Some of the customers needed mothering more than others. One of the sweetest characters in the restaurant is Malcolm, a boy with Down's syndrome, who sometimes sits in the corner with his dad, and with his Velcro undone. His dad runs this homeless hostel in Shepherd's Bush, and he makes his son help out with cleaning up the drunks' drinks and other menial bits (it's a 'wethouse', which means the homeless folk are allowed to get lashed), in order to 'integrate' Malcolm into normal society. I don't know who's weirder – Malcolm or Malcolm's dad. I guessed a homeless hostel was nothing like normal society – and even the Ristorante had its quirks.

The clientele in the Ristorante di Fantasia was made up largely of large males. Therefore, the most foolproof technique to earn tips was to combine the contents of my bra with the napes of these men's necks. If you're skilled and subtle enough to stroke a man's neck with your bosoms, and make him think he's the only one you're doing it to, the money should roll in.

Though Tottenham has its fair share of hot-blooded, wide-mouthed young males, it's not very often you see them in the Ristorante di Fantasia. Perhaps going for an Italian isn't the sort of thing lads do together on their evenings off, especially when there's a perfectly good pub over the road. However, drinking booze can create an almost bottomless hunger in many folk, and sometimes, after eleven, we get a few drunken stragglers from chucking-out time.

We shut at twelve. Usually, by this time, no sane person would enjoy serving food to rowdy pub-rejects, but (as long as they haven't pissed all their money down the pub urinals) there's potential for plenty of tips. The other night I was listlessly disinfecting the wine lists when this bunch of butch boys came bumbling into the restaurant. They were like a six-pack of lager: shiny, round, full of booze, frothing at the mouth, and with brand names plastered all over them.

'Table for six?' I said, through six coats of lipstick.

'Yeah, darlin',' the six-pack chorused, spraying me with fizz. I pushed tables 1 and 2 together, so they could sit by the window and ogle passers-by.

They ordered all the meaty dishes, because they were meaty boys. I figured it'd be hard work trying to rub all their necks with my knockers, but I managed to give one of the lads' heads a slight tit-wank as I laid down new cutlery. Suddenly, he became all happy and bashful. It's funny – it only takes a little affection from a vaguely good-looking girl to turn a boy's bravado to mulch. I allowed all the boys' eyes into my blouse while I handed out the food, and I allowed all their tips into my pesto jar. Six pounds sterling in shrapnel! As the lads put their coats back on, the Ristorante di Fantasia was silent, except for the shuffle of shellsuit fabric. Malcolm and his dad were the only ones still eating, over on unlucky table 13. It's unlucky for two reasons: it has a habit of tilting violently without warning, and it's closest to the toilets.

With every tilt, Malcolm coughed sauce from his nostrils. After the tenth tilt, Malcolm's dad slammed down his cutlery and stormed off to the gents. I think he resented having a son with Down's syndrome, as if it proved his genes weren't quite up to scratch. Nowadays, you can get a 'combined' pregnancy test, to tell if your kid's going to be a mongoloid or not, so you've got enough time to murder them while they're still in your belly, if you're that way inclined. Fortunately, Malcolm seemed too doe-eyed to notice (or care about) his dad's resentment. When I looked over, he was more interested in keeping his spaghetti on his fork.

Meanwhile, back on tables 1 and 2, the lads had successfully put on their coats, and were edging towards the door. On their way out, they all cooed, 'Later, darlin',' to my cleavage, each of them desperately hoping to go home with it. My cleavage just stared back though, knackered. I was ready to call it a night myself, and tot up my tips, when I heard a grunt behind me: 'Kimberly.'

The grunt came from Malcolm. His mouth had bolognese around it, like fluorescent orange lipstick. He flashed me a droopy grin and announced, 'You're my friend.'

Despite sometimes suffering from temper tantrums, people with Down's syndrome can also be overwhelmingly affectionate. Instead of hardened, boring adult minds, their brains seem soft and untarnished by cynicism. I wanted to give Malcolm a hug, but my blouse was clean on that morning. And it was white. So, I just smiled instead, from a safe distance.

Unfortunately, the lads in the shellsuits hadn't quite made it through the exit yet, and they were itching to ridicule someone. While copious amounts of alcohol can – like Down's syndrome – turn your brain into that of a child's, the lads clearly thought they were superior to Malcolm, and one of them hooted, 'Mate, mate, mate, you've got no chance, mate!'

Malcolm stared back with the eyes of a lost teddybear. I could see the anger boiling in his oversized head, as he looked round for his dad, then back to his plate, then back to me and the lads. I shot them my own look of venom, hoping my eyes still looked evil under the eyeshadow, just this once. Then, I scampered over to table 13, grabbed Malcolm's saucy face, and planted a lingering kiss on his forehead.

Malcolm looked stunned. A crumb of minced beef clung to his quivering bottom lip, like a first-time rock climber.

'Of course he's got a chance,' I snapped, glaring at the lads again. 'We're going out on Monday, aren't we, Malcolm?'

Malcolm nodded, completely confused. The six lads snorted and shook their heads, also confused. They had nothing more to say, stepping shamefully back out onto Philip Lane. Once they got well past the Lord Parmo, they let rip a snippet of laughter but, fortuitously, Malcolm suffered from something called 'glue ear', so he didn't quite catch it, I don't think. Instead, he gazed up at me with his shimmering moony eyes, and grunted, 'Squeeze me.'

I couldn't resist. I didn't even like that blouse, anyway. I squeezed the living daylights out of him.

And the next day, I came to work wearing orange.

⊙

Even though it says NOW WASH YOUR HANDS above the sink, Paolo thinks I'm strange because, every time I touch raw onion, or garlic, or any stain, I have to wash my hands. Surely, though, there was a good reason he'd forged three Food Hygiene Stars – and I wasn't going to risk dysentery to find out. It's not the best workplace for a melodramatic hypochondriac. During quiet moments in the Ristorante I imagined all the pathogens cavorting on Paolo's worktops; writhing against each other in a kind of greasy conga; chewing up filth; multiplying; farting out toxins; going up my nose, and into my bloodstream.

But everyone's got their quirks. Paolo, for instance, keeps a photo of Marilyn Monroe in his wallet, which has a similar effect on him. He removes it about once a week, taking it into the bathroom for about five minutes before coming back out all out of puff, with a red face and glassy eyes. Then, he washes his hands thoroughly. It's like it's sacred or something: a magic picture of Jesus or the Madonna. But Madonna's a different celebrity altogether. It's Marilyn Monroe he likes.

⊙

Squawk! Squeak! Splutter!

In the Capital, the lowest forms of street dweller are pigeons, rats, and the homeless. You often see them hanging about together in alleyways or doorways, or prowling around with their heads down, looking for snacks or miracles. I used to see them as vermin, but now I see them more like fleshy/furry/feathery vacuum cleaners, tidying up all the leftover food and debris the posh people don't want.

My favourite tramp in the borough of Haringey is an Irish

Catholic called Donald. I know he's called Donald, because his speech is always the same: 'Hello, missus, my name is Donald. I'm not on drugs, I don't drink – I just need one ninety-nine for a cheeseburger and chips.'

For someone who eats only cheeseburgers and chips, Donald's frighteningly skinny. I've always been dubious about homeless people's stories. Donald smells like his internal organs have been replaced with distillery instruments, and he's got scars like a Union Jack across his face, which suggests a life spent in dodgier places than your local Burger King. He's a charmer, though – in fact, his manners are impeccable, like he found them in a bag out the back of a finishing school.

Donald once told me he's got a daughter called Kimberly, but I saw him the other day telling someone his daughter's called Nicola, and some time before that his daughter was called Stacey, and another time she was Rose, and Mary-Ann, and Joanne, and she's even been called Anastasia once. Perhaps he's just highly fertile, though.

That Sunday, I indulged myself in another gigantic lie-in, tunnelling through dream after dream like a hound down a rabbit hole. I emerged around two o'clock with soily sleep in my eyes, and I was barely casting a shadow as I walked up to the big Sainsbury's near White Hart Lane. I got a few bits for my tea (working alongside food had made me less enthusiastic about cooking at home – hence, my basket had in it tuna, mayonnaise, bread, butter, and a cucumber) but, more importantly, I magically turned my heavy tips from brown and silver shrapnel into crisp ten-pound notes at the Coinstar. The previous night's slog had earned me £33.87. I was tempted to press the DONATE TO CHARITY button, but the idea of my money being guzzled up by a bleeping machine made me feel empty. I figured my small change might make a much bigger change if I just gave it to people myself.

What's the point in being generous if you can't see what good it's doing? What's the point in being selfless when you don't get anything out of it yourself?

Yawning, I carried the raw materials for tuna and cucumber sarnies back towards the bus stop. I was still in a daze – pondering whether I was developing an ear infection, or if it was just the way I'd been sleeping – when I heard loudly through the good ear: 'Hello, missus, my name is Donald. I'm not on drugs, I don't drink – I just need one ninety-nine for a cheeseburger and chips.'

I blinked. The Guillotine was getting a bit long – in fact, it was coming close to beheading me. I flicked it out of the way, then plucked the crispest tenner from my purse and handed it over to Donald. Next thing I know, he's all over me:

'Oh, you're an angel. Are you sure? God bless you, God bless you,' he squawked, before launching into a string of violent coughs.

'Do you want a Soother?' I asked, carefully putting down the shopping, though it still managed to keel over on the pavement.

'Hghm?' Donald said.

'A Hall's Soother. Just for your cough? I've got loads.'

I dipped into my Medicine Bag and took out a couple of honey and lemons for him. He coughed 'Thanks' at me. Then, he took my hand and planted a dry kiss on it. I laughed. I made a mental note to buy more wet-wipes.

Round about, people were staring at us, instead of staring at the bus routes, or the ground. Some of them even tutted or kissed their teeth, because they hated people without roofs. People without roofs are a menace to those with roofs; always wanting what they can't have. Donald didn't seem that dangerous, though, tottering off, trying his luck with one of the old dears further down the red bench: 'Hello, missus, my name is Donald . . .'

I smiled as he staggered off down a street which also had a

name: Percival. I dragged the Sainsbury's bag between my calves and clicked my neck from side to side, finally waking up to the sun-struck afternoon. I felt supreme, soaking up the vitamin D, not to mention all the other vitamins already in my system. Everyone carried on staring at me, though, like I was lower even than the pigeons, rats, and the homeless.

It was only when I got on the 149 that I realised Donald had tottered past six or seven takeaways between the bus stop and Percival Street, all with the same shining slogan stuck in their windows: CHEESEBURGER AND CHIPS!! £1.99!! All the shops stared at me too, with frowning awnings.

And that's when I realised both Donald and the bus had taken me for a fucking ride.

⊙

I was late for my date with Malcolm.

It was his idea to meet me at Tower Bridge at 1 p.m. – one of the furthest tourist attractions from the halal butcher's. I thought I had time to nip into town beforehand – for the wet-wipes, and a new dress – but I got waylaid, fannying about in a cheerful trance, trying to help everyone out, despite their stony faces.

Kindness slows you down. Rather than steaming through the throngs of shoppers like a snowplough, I sedately slalomed between them, like a weekend skier. I still had fifteen quid's worth of tips from the Ristorante, one fifth of which I spent on Mr *'Big Issue* please'. I helped tourists with directions in a language they didn't understand, and I lost twenty minutes looking for somewhere to recycle all the gaudy fliers and handouts I'd amassed after one hectic wrong turn down Oxford Street.

Some people don't understand good nature – they see it as a sign of weakness, or they're suspicious you want something bigger in return. Or, they tease you for being 'too good', what-

89

ever that is. At Tower Hill I helped this lady with her pram, up the ninety-seven steps outside the Ghost Train station, and she actually got her purse out and tried to lumber me with money. I was nice, though, and threw it back in her face.

I wish I could swap my old, world-weary brain with a toddler's. Kids have such a carefree outlook on life, because they've hardly even heard of death, let alone come across it. I remember seeing a dead person on telly when I was about four, but my mam said he'd just gone to sleep. God knows how he could sleep with all that red stuff coming out of his skull, though.

I was instantly suspicious of my parents from then on. They tell you all sorts of lies: your pet stick insect didn't run away, she's dead; that man's not asleep, he's dead; Father Christmas (fortunately) isn't dead, but (unfortunately) he was never alive in the first place.

I strolled across the grandiose bridge, beneath the sky-blue walkway where prostitutes used to operate a kind of Mile High Club round the end of the nineteenth century. It took me for ever to get over the river, not just because of all the tourists, but because I ended up taking their photos for them. I had to think up what 'Cheese!' was in different languages, though part of the fun was getting it wrong:

'Fromage frais!' I said, to the ones who looked French.

'Quark!' I said, to the ones who looked German.

'Smile!' I said, to the ones I'd class as Other/Unknown.

The more I made them laugh, the better the photos. The Japs were the best – giggling constantly and putting up peace-fingers, like miniature, much cuter Yokos. I wondered if they'd go home and tell their family and friends everyone's lovely in England.

As it turned out, though, Malcolm was in a foul mood when I turned up, ten minutes late. I spotted him sitting on the grass with his dad, to the west of the bridge, by City Hall. People with

Down's syndrome are born with long faces but, that afternoon, Malcolm's was longer than usual. Him and his dad seemed to be having some kind of dispute.

I smoothed out my new dress and adopted a jauntier strut. When Malcolm saw me he leapt from the grass and gave me a huge cuddle, unsmoothing the dress again.

'You're late,' Malcolm stated. I put my hands together in a sorry/praying position, glancing at Malcolm's dad, whose eyes were on the river. I wasn't sure whether to give him a hug too, or shake his hand, so I just stood awkwardly, pretending to admire the view I'd already taken twenty-seven photographs of.

'How long do you want with him?' Malcolm's dad asked me, hopefully not meaning to sound like Malcolm's pimp.

'Er, I'm free all afternoon. I don't mind,' I replied, with some bonus nervous laughter. 'How are you doing, Malcolm?'

'Fine,' he answered, stamping round a pigeon.

'Do you want me to stay and watch?' Malcolm's dad asked, hopefully not meaning to sound like a peeping tom.

'No!' Malcolm shouted, clearly going through a teenage-like phase of stubborn parent-hating, only fifteen years too late. Malcolm was thirty-one.

'Naw, naw, it's fine,' I said.

Nevertheless, Malcolm's dad kept glancing over his shoulder as he waddled off towards the Ghost Train, leaving me and Malcolm to sit back down on the manicured lawn. I scooped the dress between my knees, trying to sit ladylike.

'What have you been up to today?' I asked.

'Been at the Wethouse,' he replied. At first, I had to squint to make out exactly what he was saying, though I soon got the hang of it. It was quite a choppy way of speaking, with 'w's where the 'r's should be.

'How was it?' I asked.

'Good.'

Even though it sounded like an aquatic adventure emporium, the Wethouse was in fact a dismal place, from what Malcolm's dad had told me. Apparently, you get used to the loutish behaviour of the hammered homeless folk, but you never quite get used to cleaning up their many spillages. Malcolm's dad wanted to install en suites. Or, rather, he wanted to de-install himself and Malcolm from the Wethouse, and become a hotelier instead.

'Everyone likes me there,' Malcolm added with a straight face. I could imagine him being a hit at the hostel – there was a directness and dreaminess to him which drunks could probably relate to.

I ran my fingers through the AstroTurf-perfect grass, enjoying my afternoon off. For about a minute everything was quiet, except for Malcolm's daysnoring. Daysnoring is an affliction caused by having your mouth wide open while your eyes are also wide open. It made Malcolm sound a little like Darth Vader, or a faulty submarine sonar.

'Do you want an ice cream?' I asked, nodding towards the pink van.

'Yes,' Malcolm snapped, as if it was obvious.

I wasn't looking forward to the masticating. Malcolm leapt to attention again, then pretended to trip a few times on his way down the giant granite steps to the van. I scurried after him. It felt strange entertaining a bloke for the first time since Stevie's death, though it wasn't exactly a date – I felt more like Malcolm's parent or carer than a potential girlfriend, grabbing for his hand as he careened along the riverside. I was just trying to make the boyman feel happy.

'Er, two Mini Milks, please,' I said to the vendor, going for the cheap option. I swapped a pound for the lollies, then tore the wrapping off both and passed the white, worse-tasting one to Malcolm.

'Fankoo,' Malcolm said, which is the only phonetic represen-
tation of his speech you're going to get.

'You're welcome,' I replied.

We sat down on one of the benches, out of the way of the seagull
muck. Malcolm wanted to carry on holding my hand, which made
life difficult when his Mini Milk decided to start dribbling.

'Ooh,' was all I could think to say, watching the spunky lolly
drool down the back of his hand.

All around us, the Capital was acting like it was summertime:
men strutting about with bare, goosepimpled chests; women
wearing sunglasses the size of flies' eyes; flowers wriggling out of
the ground; the sun licking at our lollies. It was only early April.

Fortunately, I had the wet-wipes. Once we'd finished the Mini
Milks, I spring-cleaned my fingers while Malcolm licked his,
like five more fat ice lollies. Despite the temper on him, there
were so many endearing things about Malcolm: for starters, he'd
never accuse me of being 'too good'; he held my hand like we'd
been friends since birth; he was full of life (despite the short life
expectancy); he had a beautiful, elastic smile; and Velcro on his
shoes.

I was relieved about the Velcro. I didn't want to find him hanging from Tower Bridge by his shoelaces after one date with Kimberly Clark.

'Do you like the Capital, then?' I asked, though I regretted the
'then' bit. There was no need to threaten the lad.

'Yes, I like the Wethouse, and the trains, and the gulls,' Malcolm replied, playing with his hands. I couldn't tell if he'd said
'gulls' or 'girls'. Despite his directness, a lot of what Malcolm
said was wide open to interpretation. I decided to play it safe,
and replied, 'Yeah.'

I leaned over him to lob the dirty wet-wipes and lollysticks
in the bin. Sometimes it's difficult finding a bin in the Capital,

since terrorists like to keep their bombs in them – and terrorists tend to favour the same hotspots as tourists. Fortunately, though, I came away with all my limbs intact.

'See that boat?' I said, for the sake of it, pointing to one.

'Yes,' Malcolm replied. 'Can you squeeze me?'

Malcolm was a man who knew what he wanted. Compared to Stevie – who always pussyfooted around the subject of sex and intimacy, despite wanting both desperately – Malcolm wasn't afraid to cut to the chase. He would make an incredible businessman, if only he was allowed to wear a white collar.

Malcolm's collar was orange.

Sliding my free arm under Malcolm's armpit, I gave him an enthusiastic-but-platonic squeeze. Malcolm groaned, squeezing back. Malcolm's arms were much bulkier than my limp lady-limbs, and I found myself gasping for breath the more he cuddled me, but they were joyful gasps. He was like a six-year-old on steroids. I grinned as he cushioned me then crushed me with his bosoms; my brain going all dreamy and soft.

'Do you love me?' Malcolm grunted, just as the grey river started running pink.

'Yeah, of course,' I replied, just to be nice. I did love him, but more in the way someone loves a fluffy puppy or a strawberry Mini Milk – you don't actually want to marry them. In general, men who say 'I love you' on a first date are dangerous. They will either cling to you like an insecure leech, or they will murder you in the most unimaginable manner.

I glanced up at Malcolm with squashed eyes. His own eyes didn't seem particularly murderous, but he was certainly clinging to my arm quite firmly. Then again, Malcolm wasn't a leech – despite his 'special needs', he'd successfully avoided going into care his whole life. While he was lucky to have his dad at hand, apparently his mam upped and left after one too many nervous

94

breakdowns – or one too many circulation-cutting squeezes. Or perhaps it was Malcolm's dad's fault.

'Right, er, ha, that's it for now,' I wheezed, as nicely as possible. It was bad enough getting the daysnoring down my eardrum.

Grudgingly, Malcolm stopped suffocating me. He left one arm round my shoulder as we turned towards the river again. In fairness, he seemed more interested in me than the gulls, though it was hard to tell exactly what he was looking at, with those crossed eyes. I shifted on the bench.

'What do you fancy doing, love?' I asked, regretting the word 'love' that time.

'Take you somewhere,' Malcolm stated. He pulled at his thumbs for a few seconds, then bullfrogged off the bench. I swung my handbag and Medicine Bag back onto my shoulder and followed him along the bank of the Thames, towards Bermondsey. If it was meant to be a romantic stroll, Malcolm's idea of chivalry meant dragging me about by my left wrist: up steps, across roads with red men guarding them, and into an estate of sterile-looking prefabs. Each block was the colour of sour milk, and every window had shut net curtains.

'You've got to meet someone,' Malcolm snapped. By the looks of the estate, it was a series of care homes: slightly off-key-looking characters lurked about the gardens while sterner-looking adults paced about with ID badges and bunches of keys. The place had the feel of a psychiatric Center Parcs, only with fewer bicycles and restaurants and slightly more dribble.

Before we got to the right door, Malcolm stopped to watch a lad with cerebral palsy struggling to get up the kerb in his electric wheelchair. The kerb must've been cut by cowboys – the lad couldn't even get up the tapered lip. A wave of sickness swept over me. Even worse was Malcolm's reaction:

'Idiot,' he cat-called, with a clowny grin. Instead of helping the lad, Malcolm did a kind of dance, sticking two fingers up and swinging his hips, like a drugged-up football hooligan.

'Behave!' I yelped as Malcolm picked up a handful of gravel from one of the gardens and chucked it at the boy. Thankfully, Malcolm was a bad shot. The gravel clashed off the tarmac, two or three metres short of the buzzing, churning wheelchair.

'Are you alright?' I shouted. The lad's head spasmed from left to right – I couldn't tell if that was a 'yes' or a 'no'.

Fortunately, one of the care workers was coming to his rescue. A youngish woman, resplendent in aquamarine nylon, grabbed the handles of the wheelchair and manoeuvred him roughly back onto the pavement. She didn't make eye contact with me, so I didn't bother saying, 'Sorry.' I felt like clipping Malcolm round his glue-ear, but I didn't fancy a faceful of gravel either.

Malcolm kept grinning as we slipped past the halfhearted rhododendrons and dog-eared lawns. I wondered if he wanted me to laugh along with him, like any good girl on a first date. I followed him in silence down the path, just to make a point.

'Malcolm, why did you do that?' I asked eventually, feeling like his social worker.

'I don't like him,' was Malcolm's reply. And he left it at that.

I stuck my bottom lip out and stared hard at the ground. And now for a confession:

Rather than simply being nice to Malcolm, I'd positioned myself close to him with an ulterior motive, which had backfired. Foolishly, I'd assumed all disabled folk had great personalities (to compensate for their bargain-bin bodies), and I thought Malcolm's good nature might rub off on me.

As it turned out, Malcolm was a bit of a bastard. Or, rather, he was just the same as everyone else. I reluctantly held his hand as he led me up one of the driveways with doe eyes, just to be nice nice nice nice nice nice . . .

'Squeeze me,' Malcolm urged, after ringing number 25's keypad. I slid my left arm under a fold of hip, just above his jean seam. We watched a blurry face materialise behind the frosted pane in the door, then become crystal clear as the whole thing swung open. The face looked like it'd been cheerful once upon a time, but had had the cheerfulness sucked out of it over the course of adulthood, leaving behind just empty laughter-lines and crows' feet.

'Alright, Malcolm,' the face said, with a local accent.

'Hello, Barbara. Get Jessie?' Malcolm requested, leaving out his 'please's and 'fankoo's. When was his reign of terror going to end?

'Two ticks,' said Barbara, swanning off.

I chewed my lip and asked, 'Who's this Jessie?'

'Wait,' said Malcolm.

I waited. I rolled my eyes, for the benefit of no one.

I listened to Malcolm daysnoring for half a minute or so before a young, plump girl finally emerged from the stairway and came down to greet us. She was the absolute spit of Malcolm. At first, I thought they must be brother and sister, but then I realised it was just that she had Down's syndrome too.

Jessie was ever so pleased to see Malcolm. Her face widened in hysterical bliss, and she flung her arms around his neck. Ever the gentleman, Malcolm just grunted, leaving his arms by his sides, while the girl kissed and smothered him. I felt uncomfortable, stepping to one side.

It took a few more kisses before Jessie realised Malcolm wasn't quite so pleased to see her. She loosened her grip; her face set in a lost, half-smiling expression.

'We're not getting married any more,' Malcolm announced, deadpan. 'She's my new girlfriend.'

My cheeks burned and my heart sank as Malcolm motioned at me, and flippantly at that. I tried to protest, 'No, n—'

'We're in love,' Malcolm added.

'No, but w—'

Jessie's moon-eyes wettened. She made the sound of a dialling tone for a few seconds, before bursting into almighty bawling. She seemed almost too scared to look at me, instead firing her anger at Malcolm, screaming the contents of a shook-up Scrabble bag at him:

'Akajskwjliksybakgwitfqaytfdtksafzajd!' she screamed, scoring at least 115 points by my reckoning.

'Fuck off,' Malcolm stated, as charming as ever.

I was speechless. Had I any history of care work – or any people skills whatsoever – I might've been able to calm the situation. As it stood, my brain drew blank after blank. I was welded to the spot.

I realised, by being nice to Malcolm, I might have inadvertently ruined young Jessie's short life. I backed away, down the driveway. I hugged myself sadly. Then again, perhaps I'd done Jessie a favour – she was too good for Malcolm, after all. And, all things considered, I guessed I was too good, too.

⊙

Men, men, men. If you remember, the whole point of being cruel to Stevie was to allow me the freedom to date random men again, and to feel young and happy once more. I promise I'm not a tart, but perhaps it might not come as such a surprise that, by the end of the week, I was seeing seven different men from the restaurant: one for each day of the week.

I was just trying to be friendly.

To be both good-looking and amicable is a dangerous weapon. All around me, men were falling head over heels in lusty piles, as if I was wearing chloroform instead of the jasmine Japanese Spa stuff.

I had seven new men drooling over me by Sunday, and I just didn't have the heart to shake any of them off. I assigned each one a day to ravish me.* I saw it as doing them a favour. As far as I knew, they weren't aware of each other's existence – all they were probably bothered about was attaching a semi-pretty young girl to their arms. Most of these fellows seemed incapable of acquiring a ladyfriend, you see. That was the beauty of it: I was lending myself to boys in dire need of a woman's company. A female philandering philanthropist.

This was how the rest of the week panned out:

Mr Tuesday was the violinist at the Ristorante di Fantasia, and he worked there Tuesdays, Fridays and Saturdays. There were only four people dining when he turned up that first Tuesday, and they tried to ignore him as he came shuffling up to their tables, waggly-hipped, with the violin shrieking obscenities at them. I felt sorry for him. His eyes were always gloomy, with blue-grey irises that clashed with his Mediterranean complexion. Mr Tuesday's violin was this battered old thing with one of the strings always out of tune and, while he could conjure up the odd appealing arpeggio, on the whole he was useless. The violin used to attack him, sawing at his neck with its splintered body and grating his fingers with its cheesewire. Paolo only let him play at the Ristorante because he was a friend of a friend of a second cousin. That Tuesday night, after all the customers had left and I was about to load the sink with the last few dishes, Mr Tuesday slumped down next to the cash desk, bubbling with affected woe and exhaustion. There was an awkward silence. It was obvious he wanted to talk, but I pretended not to be good at

* Malcolm became 'Mr Monday'. I'd intended never to speak to him again after what happened at Jessie's, but a couple of days later Malcolm's dad left me a note at the Ristorante di Fantasia, thanking me for showing his son 'such a marvellous time'. So, I crumbled.

reading body language, busying myself with the pots. I put on the radio to kill the silence, but that just killed Mr Tuesday – the First Movement from Rimsky-Korsakov's *Scheherazade* sprang to life from the speakers, mocking Mr Tuesday with its swirling, sugar-spun strings. Rubbing his bald spot, he explained to me how he felt worthless and inferior whenever we listened to Classic FM. So, I switched it over to Heart, but it turned out he felt worthless and inferior to the strings on Westlife's 'Home' as well. So, I switched it off at the socket. Usually, by the end of a shift, I'm in no mood to look at anyone, let alone talk to them, but there was something strangely soothing about listening to Mr Tuesday. His voice had a nicer tone than his violin, anyhow. While I carried on with the dishes, Mr Tuesday told me how he got married by the lakes of Lombardy, but it went tits-up and, when he moved to Britain, he took up the violin to fill the void left by the divorce. He named the violin after his ex-wife, Maria, but it couldn't replace the embraces and caresses of a lover. In fact, all he got from the violin was callouses. He told me about the envy and exasperation he got from ruining couples' nights at the Ristorante, and he reckoned the violin was cursed, causing him to play badly and be alone – just him and the instrument – the rest of his life. Mr Tuesday blinked his dewy blue-greys at me. 'Maybe you just weren't meant to be with her,' I offered. After I finished the last of the plates, I took Maria by her neck and – in a fit of puckish, pugnacious clarity – smashed her crash-clung-clash against the kitchen wall. Maria screamed out in the key of C, weeping splinters. 'Oh hell, hell, hell,' Mr Tuesday murmured, a bit taken aback. I told him not to worry, and said I'd replace the violin. Not in the sense of buying him a new one, you understand, but in the sense of becoming Mr Tuesday's inamorata. I gave him a full-bodied hug, and our hearts beat out a rhythm much more beautiful than anything on that radio.

100

Mr Wednesday was a wanker. He was one of those people who wears expensive suits because it's like the fabric's made of actual banknotes, showing how much money you've got. He was good-looking, in his way, if you discounted the hair, the nose, the ears, and the chin. He also had a face full of freckles, which he tried to hide behind last season's designer stubble. Mr Wednesday's favourite dishes were the ones with the biggest price tags attached – for instance, the Lobster fra Diavolo £15.50. This particular Wednesday he arrived around eight o'clock, and proceeded to pester me between each of his courses to go on a date with him. I figured no one was likely to go out with such a creep, so I let him buy me some cocktails after work. He expected sex afterwards, mind you. I shrivelled inside. I figured no one was likely to go at it with such a creep, so I let him dry-hump me later on a park bench, sighing semi-erotically while he carved a tiny hole in the front of my work trousers. I felt sad and empty, like a hollowed-out lobster, except much, much, much, much cheaper.

Mr Thursday never tipped, but I let him off because he had three daughters and no wife. I felt an affinity with him because his partner was dead, although it wasn't Mr Thursday who killed her. He often came to the Ristorante to self-consciously say 'Hello' to Paolo and sip a cappuccino – usually around the half-six mark, when he finishes at Wickes. I was off that Thursday, but went in to collect my wages, and caught Mr Thursday gazing at me as I gathered up some dishes Nina had missed. 'Hello,' he said to me, self-consciously. I gave him a noncommittal, day-off smile. I didn't want to reel in any more men (after all, my privates were still stinging after the previous night's friction), but it seemed like Mr Thursday wanted some company. Or, rather, he wanted some advice. While I waited for Paolo to get out of the bathroom with Marilyn, Mr Thursday said to my back, 'When did you start wearing make-up?' I spun on my Primark flats. 'I've always worn make-up,' I replied curtly, not sure what he was getting at. 'No, no,' he went on, 'I'm wondering about my daughter. She's only seven, see.' As soon as Mr Thursday mentioned he had three little girls, I felt a surge of soppy emotion. I squeezed myself into the fixed seat opposite Mr Thursday and listened as he poured his heart out about his little treasures. 'I just don't know anything about seven-year-old girls,' was the gist of it. I didn't know much about seven-year-old girls, either. I had no desire to wear make-up until I was fifteen, and even then it was jet-black lipstick and deadly-nightshade nail polish. Nevertheless, I agreed to pop round to Mr Thursday's pad, to meet the girls and donate a few comedy-colour lipsticks from the bottom of my dresser. I had such weak-kneed admiration for him raising three kids on his own, and such sympathy for him being so skint. His wife had died in a cycling accident – someone opened a car door on her, in rush-hour. I took extra-special care crossing the road, as me and Mr Thursday headed up to his. He lived up seven flights of stairs, in a not-very-spacious council flat. I had to admit, the Capital looked beautiful from afar, shining and whining at us beneath each balcony, then twinkling and winking at us for miles and miles across the horizon, once we got to the top. As we marched down the concrete corridor, one of the flat doors creaked open, and a woman's face appeared. 'Ah, Charlie!' she said, grinning. 'How are you? Ha ha! They're just watching the Beebies. I gave them toast. But Number One's saying she's hungry. Ha ha! I tell her to wait.' Mr Thursday laughed, patting his neighbour on her blouse shoulder. 'Ah, ha, cheers, Mod,' he said, carrying on down the corridor. Modupe Sowunmi was a buoyant, buxom black lady who seemed to laugh at absolutely anything. I wondered what her trick was. I giggled politely as we passed her door. It sounded manic inside Modupe's flat – apparently, she had five kids of her own, but she didn't mind keeping an eye on Mr Thursday's while he worked. He paid her back by doing odd jobs round hers, like tarting up the young Sowunmis' bedrooms, or donating things the youngest Thursday had grown out of. I couldn't wait to meet the girls. 'This is a treat,' I cooed, as Mr Thursday undid his front door. 'Yeah,' he replied, 'we don't get many visitors.' We stepped into the hallway, which stank of baby lotion and custard. At first, I supposed they didn't get many visitors because of the seven flights of stairs, but then I realised it was more likely because of the Thursday girls. There were spills and frilly frocks thrown willy-nilly about the flat, and three yapping voices coming from the other room. They all had brash, squeaky Tottenham accents, no doubt stolen from the Sowunmis. I cringed, privately. Mr Thursday was much more softly spoken, with one of those nondescript Northern accents even I couldn't place. I wanted to hug him. I wondered how old he was. Mr Thursday had shiny white hair, which made you think he was a dinosaur, although his sperms certainly weren't extinct. When we stepped into the living room, the girls became suddenly quiet, thanks to the strange lady standing in their house. They evil-eyed me from behind their toys. I tried not to evil-eye them back, though it was difficult, what with my permanently evil eyes. 'Hel-looo,' I purred, realising I'd hardly spoken to anyone under the age of ten before, even when I was under the age of ten myself. It was like a miniature Mexican stand-off – the smallest of the girls even had a plastic pistol in her hand. I didn't stay very long. 'They're just not that used to strangers,' Mr Thursday explained afterwards, walking me back down the corridor while I picked the last of the Plasticine out of the Guillotine. 'Ah, it's fine, seriously,' I said, even more in awe of him raising those three bastards on his own. For a bit, we stood on the balcony, peer-ing down at the streetlights masquerading as stars the Thursday girls had probably never even seen before. We gave each other a modest squeeze goodnight, and Mr Thursday was too much of a gentleman to turn it into a proper kiss. 'So, what do you want to do? Do you wanna do this again?' he asked, shoegazing now. 'Yeah, definitely,' I replied, and not just to be nice. I did want to see him again. I just hoped Modupe was up for more babysitting. Or, even better: adoption.

Mr Friday was a sports fan. Apparently, he used to play basketball with Paolo back in Italy, and now he looked like one. Perhaps that was his dream – not to be a professional basketball player, but to be the basketball itself. He first bounced into my life on a blue-skied Friday afternoon. While a lot of businesses treat their employees to 'casual Friday', Paolo enforced 'formal/flamboyant Friday' with an iron fist – me and Nina had to wear our shortest, tightest skirts and our highest heels, to cater for the wild-eyed weekend punters. I was a bit embarrassed, getting my English legs out, like two white rugby posts on a scorching Sports Day. Because of the legs, Mr Friday was eyeing me up greedily – I think he wanted to get in between them, despite being a basketball, not a rugby ball. I always gave him extra portions of his Milanese osso buco – I wanted to help him on his quest to become perfectly spherical. He even shaved his head – a ball on top of a ball. All Mr Friday ever talked about was sports, in this clipped Italo-Cockney accent he'd developed. He wanted to take me ice skating one evening and, although he was desperately unattractive, part of me wanted to see how a huge snowball would cope on the ice. I courted him for comedy value. I agreed to meet him the following Friday, at an old ice-hockey rink in the north-west of the Capital. I felt self-conscious on the Ghost Train, clad in a white leotard, with a diaphanous skirt over the top. Mr Friday kept kissing me, pretending it was an Italian custom. He was unbearable. The funny part was he kept landing on his arse as he shuffled round the ramshackle rink, but the unfunny part was he kept getting in a strop about it, blaming me, or kicking off at the other skaters. He wasn't impressed by my slinky rink skills – he kept grabbing for me, and grappling me to the ground. By the end of it, my bottom half was covered in bruises. People kept gawping at us, trying to suss out what the relationship was. Despite all the shame and sore bits, Mr Friday wanted to see me again. I tried to make out I was snowed under for the next couple of weeks, but I could sense Mr Friday's heart growing heavier inside his chest, and I didn't want the poor sod to have a cardiac arrest. After all, it was probably my fault his arteries were clogged, after overfeeding him the osso buco. So, I agreed to watch the Champions League with him in a fortnight's time. And I even agreed to buy myself a Milan top.

Mr Saturday wasn't from the Ristorante di Fantasia. He was from a different eatery altogether: the internet caff. The next night, I was tucked up in bed, being lulled to sleep by the life-weary lilt of Elliott Smith, when, suddenly, I found myself spasming uncontrollably. I was vibrating. I didn't panic, though – it wasn't delirium tremens, or the onset of motor neurone disease; it was my second phone call in seventeen days. It'd taken almost a month for Mr Saturday to get in touch, and I hardly recognised his voice, because I'd hardly heard it before. He was from Ghana, and his English wasn't great. It didn't help that he was mumbling, either. I wondered if he suffered from telephonophobia, like Stevie. I held my knees up to the chest of my PJs, and felt my tummy squirm, when Mr Saturday slurred, 'Eh . . . hello, hello . . . I phone for the . . . I pay for the sex . . . the sex with you now?' Lo and behold, Mr Saturday thought I was a prostitute. The poor sod obviously thought it was impossible a seductive siren like me would give him my phone number without wanting something sinister in return. At first, my instinct was to hang up the phone – like any normal lady – but I decided not to be horrible, and instead explained: 'Naw, naw, I thought you might just want a drink, or . . . a bite to eat, or . . . something.' Mr Saturday paused. 'No, no,' he murmured, 'just the sex . . . I pay you for the sex . . . please . . . I really want. Please.' I looked up at my headache-inducing Artex, grinding my teeth. Fifty minutes later, thirty pounds was inside my purse and Mr Saturday's penis was inside a blue condom, inside me, inside his bedroom, inside the internet caff. For some reason, he wanted to keep the lights off – probably to stop the folk on the 243 peering in at us – but he might as well have been having a blindfolded wank. I shut my eyelids and dreamed of Stevie. With the right amount of mind power, you can tolerate almost anything – from fish-hooking, to 'playful' strangulation, to the piledriver position. Annoyingly, though, I think the bruises I had on my buttocks from ice skating added to the impression I was a prostitute. Mr Saturday must've been a fan of watching internet S&M after hours at the caff – he clung to my jugular with one hand while he bucked me, using the other to smack right where I'd slapped off the ice the day before. It was agonising. I bit into his duvet, which tasted like second-hand boxer shorts. I kept my eyes shut and kept my gob shut. I didn't even want to accept his money, but Mr Saturday insisted I keep it, once he'd finished up and pulled off the blue condom with a *shhhleppp*. I spotted specks of blood on my side of the latex, and I definitely wasn't on my period. Once he was dressed, Mr Saturday phoned for a takeaway from his friend's chicken place, then explained he wanted me out of his flat before the food turned up. The closest he got to chivalry was mumbling, 'Goodbye,' before locking the door behind me. Tears fell off my eyelashes as I hobbled back to the halal butcher's. The journey took longer than usual – I felt like I needed a hip replacement. I probably needed a lobotomy. When I finally got back to the safety of Flat D, a Ghost Train must've been going underneath the building, because Elliott Smith appeared to be shaking his head at me, on the cover of *Either/Or*.

Mr Sunday restored my faith in men. It was hard work the next day, trying to put on a brave face and be sweet to the customers, when what I really wanted was Paolo to dispose of us all in a freak chip-pan fire. Undoubtedly, I'd made a few men in Tottenham temporarily happy, but I was beginning to doubt my own happiness. It's a wonder the altruism gene hasn't been phased out of humanity (like us growing out of our gills, 300 million years ago), the way people exploit and bully those who are good- natured. Thankfully, I spotted the gene in action that afternoon, when Mr Sunday turned up to the Ristorante with someone else's nan. Mr Sunday volunteered at the old folk's home on alternate weekends, taking the old dears out to stretch their legs, or spin the cobwebs out of their wheelchairs. The nans all loved him, especially when he took them for 'proper coffee' at the Ristorante di Fantasia. It wasn't proper coffee, mind you – it came out of a jar with a Sainsbury's Basics label on. 'What can I get you?' I asked Mr Sunday, giving him my most genuine smile of the day. Mr Sunday ate at the Ristorante most nights – he was either an awful cook, or awfully rich. 'T   c fe , p eas ,' Mr Sunday replied, far too quiet for a half-full restaurant. While Mr Sunday was a handsome chap, his good looks were let down by his intense, almost offensive shyness. 'Say again? Something with peas?' I went, poised with my pen. 'Two coffees, please,' Mr Sunday repeated, far too loudly this time. 'The proper stuff,' his companion added, which I ignored. When I came back with the drinks, Mr Sunday was engrossed in this pamphlet about the ancient Egyptians. He didn't seem the greatest company for the old dear but, then again, she was someone else's nan, not his own nan. As I put down the coffees, I brushed up against Mr Sunday, peering over his shoulder at the papyrus drawings of

Osiris, Ra, the Great Devourer, and all them lot. 'Do you like the Egyptians?' I asked, practically in his earhole. Mr Sunday stiffened, nodded, and managed an 'Mm!' I'm a big fan of the Egyptians myself, what with them taking extra-special care of their dead bodies, despite breaking their noses in, and hacking their brains up. The Egyptians didn't think the brain was important, though – in fact, they gouged out the rest of your vital organs with poking-sticks, leaving just the heart. To them, the heart made all the important decisions in your body, like whether to feel happy or sad, or whether to take someone else's nan out for a proper coffee. When one of your Egyptians dies, they do the 'weighing of the heart' procedure: if your heart's as light as the 'feather of truth', they reckon you must've been a good person, and you're allowed to become a god in the afterlife. That afternoon, my heart felt pretty heavy. I asked Mr Sunday, 'Do they have Egyptians in the Capital? The dead ones, I mean . . . the . . . *ancient* ones?' Mr Sunday sniggered nervously, and replied, 'In the British Museum.' I didn't want to embarrass him in front of someone else's nan, so I left Mr Sunday a secret note with the bill, more or less inviting myself to the museum with him the following Sunday. We met on the giant, Hellenic steps. Mr Sunday walked like a mannequin on wheels, with his arms by his sides, and he had that terrible habit some lads get on first dates, where they can't stop asking, 'Are you alright? Are you alright? You okay? Are you still alright?' By the time we got into the ancient Egyptians, I was more than alright. Mr Sunday was in his element up there, reeling off all these facts and figures, and stories about the gods. Apparently, scarab beetles symbolised evil turning to good – a bit like yours truly, except I didn't have the four extra legs, or the ball of shit. We looked at these tiny mummified cats, tiny crocodiles, and tiny humans (back then, everyone was tiny), and he explained they preserved the bodies so the person's soul (or the Ba and Ka, if you're from Egypt) could visit in the nighttime – and they sometimes did the 'opening of the mouth' ceremony, so the corpse could talk and eat again. I shivered, imagining all the brown, crispy mummies creaking back to life after hours at the museum, all confused about waking up in a glass cabinet in the Capital, instead of the pyramid they went to bed in. Then, without warning, I felt all panicky and upset, and I had to stride out of the Egyptians and into the Greeks, and I had to hold on to Heracles' sandal to stop myself from crying. I hoped Stevie was getting on alright, wherever his soul had sailed off to. I wished there was some way of conducting a makeshift 'opening of the mouth' ceremony for him, so I could say, 'Sorry,' and he could say, 'Ah, don't don't be daft K-Kim, it's alright, n-no no hard f-feelings.' But Stevie was probably just a puddle in a Marks & Spencer suit now, and I wasn't sure even the Egyptians had any magic spells to get puddles to talk. I sniffed, clutching Heracles' big toe, even though Heracles was telling me quite sternly PLEASE DO NOT TOUCH. I wished there was some way of bringing Stevie back to life. It's sad that, when you split up with someone, all you can do is compare your subsequent lovers to the one you lost – and they never seem to match up. For a second I contemplated murdering Mr Monday, Tuesday, Wednesday, Thursday, Friday, Saturday and Sunday, and using their different attributes (childishness, blue-grey irises, freckles, white hair, sports fanaticism, telephonophobia, shyness) to construct a Stevie doppelgänger. When Mr Sunday came dashing into the Greeks to check I was alright (again), I was this close to wrenching Heracles' spear out of the statue's grasp and sinking it into Mr Sunday's chest.

But that wouldn't be very nice, now, would it?

⊙

The Capital famously suffers from severe overcrowding and, suddenly, so did my life.

I think it's the overcrowding that makes everyone so paranoid. Whenever you're walking around the Capital, you've always got that nagging feeling you're being followed – because you are. You can guarantee there's always a stranger just a few paces behind you, breathing down your neck.

One afternoon I was minding my own business, rolling a black dungball down down down to the recycling point at Downhills Park, when a voice said behind me:

'Hello, missus, my name is Donald. I'm not on drugs, I don't drink – I just need one ninety-nine for a cheeseburger and chips.'

Donald still wasn't looking any fatter. I blinked at him through my insectoid sunglasses. I must've given Donald enough money for a dozen cheeseburgers and thousands of chips over the past couple of months, and yet he still looked frighteningly skinny. I was desperate to find out the secret to his full-fat, slim-fast diet – perhaps it was all the walking he did.

I gave him an over-the-top smile. Donald just stared back at me. He never seemed to recognise me, despite us being on first-name terms. Like a lot of tramps in the Capital, Donald had this hazy, glazed look about him, which I've seen before in people on analgesic drugs, as well as people who've just devoured a large McDonald's. The jury was still out as to whether Donald was being honest with me about the drugs, drink, and burgers.

Tips were still rolling in nicely at the Ristorante – especially on Mondays, when Malcolm/Mr Monday came in with his dad; or on Wednesdays, when Mr Wednesday came in for lobster and a leer; or on Fridays, when Mr Friday popped in for his osso buco. As I opened my purse, finally Donald smiled too, showing off what could only be described as the onset of scurvy. It was like someone had gone round his teeth with a black fineliner.

110

''Ere though,' I said, mid-donation, 'do you not fancy something better than cheeseburgers and that?'

Donald's smile faltered. I swapped hands with the balled-up binbags, and suggested, 'See, I could sort you out some dinner at this restaurant I work at. Do you eat Italian?'

'I . . . don't know if I could shtomach . . .' Donald slurred, before launching into a violent coughing fit.

'Don't be daft. It's on me,' I said, dishing a Hall's Soother out of my Medicine Bag for him, as an appetiser.

Donald didn't know what to say – he was that grateful. I slung my dungbags into the correct recycling bin, then we walked together, shoulder-to-shoulder, away from the park. With the spring sun springing in and out from between the branches, our shadows kept tailing us then hiding, like a pair of shoddy detectives. I was feeling pretty peckish myself, so we decided to outrun our shadows altogether, power-walking down Philip Lane, towards the Ristorante di Fantasia.

'You don't have to do this, darling,' Donald said, but I politely ignored him. He made a sad slurping sound with his Soother.

'I'm just an old bastard,' he added.

The more Donald talked, the more teeth I realised he had missing. And the further we walked, the more obvious it was he had a size-10 Hi-Tech trainer on one foot, and a size-14 snakeskin loafer on the other. As it turned out, Donald hadn't owned a matching pair of shoes for years – he had to make do with stealing odd footwear off the racks outside shops. But, even so, something must have attracted him to the flamboyant loafer.

We stopped outside the pistachio green door. I wasn't overly keen on going into the Ristorante on my afternoons off, since it reminded me too much of hard work. Plus, I was so nice nowadays, I couldn't resist straightening the BUONGIORNO mat, collecting glasses, and wiping down a few of the tables. The last one I wiped down, me and Donald sat down at with a crunch. The cutlery jumped.

'Kimmy, Kimmy . . . this is another of your fancy man, no?' Paolo guffawed, the greasy twat.* Admittedly, it must've looked a bit iffy to Paolo, now I was dating half a dozen of his customers – some people mistake kindness for weakness, or empty-headedness, or dirty-mindedness.

'Have whatever you want,' I said to Donald.

'Oh . . . mm . . .' Donald mumbled, as he stared blankly at the menu, 'I don't think I can eat . . . I don't eat . . . mebbie I'll just drink . . . you know . . .'

'I thought you didn't drink?' I said. I tried to slam the menu shut – like you would your bedroom door after a petty argument – but the menu was made of paper, not wood. Donald glanced at me, equally disheartened, like he genuinely did want to eat, but just couldn't.

'My stomach's shrunk,' he offered, by way of apology.

I picked up my menu again. I couldn't be annoyed at him for long. I understood a lot of homeless folk only stay alive thanks to a steady drip of alcohol, rather than three square meals a day. The withdrawal from booze must far outweigh any hunger pains and, in any case, food soaks up the magical, mind-numbing properties of alcohol. As soon as they stop drinking, that's when alcoholics start dying. It's like anyone else on the planet: as soon as they stop working, that's when workers start dying. As soon as they stop running, that's when runners start dying.

I just hoped Donald hadn't lied about the drugs as well.

I took a couple of Kalms tablets out of my Medicine Bag and downed them with a swig of table water. Then, I looked up at Donald and suggested, 'Well . . . what say, er . . . I can take you out on the lash, if you want?'

* Pardon the insult.

Donald flashed more teeth at me or, at least, he flashed the gaps where they should've been. I ordered us a handful of limoncellos, prompting the odd dirty wink and unrepeatable hand gesture from Paolo. I ignored him. I thought the citrus might improve Donald's scurvy, and the alcohol definitely improved his spirits. He wheezed at me, 'You're a dying breed, a dying breed . . .'

'Ah no,' I said, blushing a bit. After the face-tingling shots, I settled the bill with Paolo, then led Donald to the next Mecca for wreckheads: the Turkish-Cypriot off-licence a couple of doors down.

I don't know if it was the lemon shots or just the sight of more booze, but Donald began acting like a child when we got inside the off-licence. I tried not to act like his mother, watching him load a basket greedily with packs of Polish Warzone lager, and a 35cl bottle of Glen's, the 'exciting vodka'. Donald certainly looked excited as he hauled them over to the counter. I decided to push the boat out, and bought myself four 6% Babychams, instead of my usual 5.5% Smirnoff Ices.

After the off-licence, Donald led me down to Lawrence Road, stopping now and again to inspect specks on the pavement. Just past the gypsy car park, we came to this battered, battleship-grey unit, which was home to creeping weeds, creaking stairwells, and an overabundance of cotton reels – and it was Donald's home, too. Lo and behold, Donald had a roof after all. He squatted on floor six, in a spacious, open-plan dwelling, with no mod cons or floorboards. My brain squealed as we manoeuvred up the stairs, past wet newspapers with toadstools erupting out of the centre pages, and many empty Warzone cans. Donald had already polished off his first one before we'd even made it to the first-floor landing.

'This rich lot are squatting on, er, third,' he explained as we creaked our way up the steps. 'What do you call the cunts? *Artists*.'

I was exhausted by the time we got to the sixth floor, especially after lugging the Babycham about. Donald kicked open his front door and told me to make myself comfortable, with no hint of irony. The door looked like it needed a deworming tablet, but I didn't have any in my Medicine Bag. I let out a violent cough. My lungs felt suddenly tight, like they'd also sprouted mushrooms.

Donald's lodgings were filled with the skeletons of sewing machines and the smell of waterlogged underlay, which had been stripped away from the wood beams and rolled into a corner. Donald kicked a few rusty sleeping bags to one side, then pointed at something for me to sit down on. It looked like a sofa.

'It's new, that is,' he stated. I strained a smile, gingerly lowering myself down onto the sofa arm.

To my right, I noticed a seven-piece tea service, perfectly arranged on a scratched silver platter. It looked like half-decent china, like a selection of misshapes from the Royal Albert factory, patterned with trilliums and trimmed in gold round the rims. Only a few bits were cracked.

'Do you have many people round for tea?' I asked, not sure if I was trying to be funny.

'No, no. They're all dead,' Donald replied matter-of-factly. And he left it at that.

A shiver went through me. I uncapped the Babycham and glanced about the room with slitted eyelids, like someone watching a horror film through their fingers. I was worried the place might give me bronchitis, or send me into anaphylactic shock. I surreptitiously took a slurp of Benylin before getting stuck into the sparkling perry. As we sat there in silence – and in darkness – I wanted to ask Donald if he was alright, but I didn't want him to think we were on an awkward first date.

In the end, I said nothing. Before long, Donald had found some candles, but they were difficult to light in such dank conditions. When they finally ignited, the next thing I noticed was the shitting-and-pissing bucket in the far corner, then all the white tablets strewn about underfoot. They didn't look like anything I had in the Medicine Bag – some were embossed with a Nike swoosh while others were light green, with 'Shrek II' stamped on.

'What are they?' I asked, with pill-envy.

Donald wiped his lips and muttered, 'Ecstasy, they reckon.'

I tried to look disappointed, but I wasn't sure how visible my facial expressions were in the half-light. Donald squinted back at me blankly.

'So, like, when you say, er, "Hello, my name is Donald, blah blah, I'm not on drugs, I don't drink," it's all just a . . . a fib?' I asked, choosing the more friendly 'fib' over 'lie', so I wouldn't end up with my decapitated head in the shitting-and-pissing bucket.

'I'm not on drugs,' Donald snapped back. 'I've got a rat problem.'

'Eh?'

'I got given these pills from a friend,' Donald explained, 'but I don't take it. I don't touch them. They're all cut with rat poison, are they not? And I've got a rat problem.'

In the dim light, it was hard to tell if Donald was joking or not. On the upside, I couldn't see any rats. I took another glug of sweet perry and turned my attention back to his sleeping quarters. Next to a bug-bitten mattress there were a few old photographs of a handsome footballer in red, and I kept glancing at Donald, then the footballer, then Donald, then the footballer.

'Is that you?' I asked.

Donald coughed a bit of Warzone back into the black can.

'Eh? No, no! It's George Best, that ish,' he slurred. 'A fine footballer; fine, fine man . . .'

I blushed, scratching my wrists. I wished I'd paid more attention to Stevie's dull football chatter. I imagined him glaring down at me

115

from the clouds, and tutting – for all sorts of different reasons.

For a few uncomfortable minutes, me and Donald sat in silence again while I thought up a better question. I was torn between one about the weather, or one about his tea-set, or one about his white snakeskin loafer. In the end, though, I plumped for: 'So, what were you, then, if you weren't a footballer? Jobs-wise?'

Donald cackled, with a twinkle in his eye. The cackle turned into a cough, before he finally composed himself and answered, 'I was a gravedigger.'

'Fucking hell,' I said, smiling, using the vocabulary of tramps. I don't usually swear, if you haven't already fucking noticed – I was just getting drunk. I took another long slug of Babycham, then asked, 'How was it?'

'Oh. Dead muddy,' Donald said with a smirk, starting on his third Warzone. 'It was alright, but it makes you think, doesn't it. You know what I mean? It made me think. Like, I mean, everyone's going to die, aren't they?'

Suddenly, Donald was speaking my language. I could keep myself occupied for hours, contemplating my own death. Hugging the perry bottle, I asked him, 'So, what do you think happens when you die?'

'What? What do you mean? As in rot?'

'Naw, I mean . . . the afterlife . . . or whatever you think.'

Donald pondered that one for a while, taking mouthful after mouthful of lager, before replying, 'Christ. Well, no one knows for sure, do they. That's the only, er . . . that's the only thing they know for sure, isn't it. I mean, I've seen tons of dead bodies – rotten ones – but, like, they're all lifeless . . . but they keep their character. Like, the, the soul's still there . . . and other bits and pieces.'

For some reason, Donald laughed again. No doubt he was mortalled. To be polite, I nodded along with him, but I decided not to mention Stevie.

'But, see, tons of folk believe in the, some sort of, er, afterlife,' Donald went on, 'and these are fellas – you know, the Aztecs, Mexicans, Buddhas, Egypt, er, the Norwegians, and all them fuckers – they never could've shared notes . . . so there's something in it . . . there could be something in it . . . afterlife, and all that . . . they never could've shared notes . . . but how would they know?'

I sipped more drink while Donald got more and more excitable. Veins strained through his forehead as he launched into another rant: 'Unless it's all a fucking ploy . . . unless some cunt invented Heaven and all that, just to make everyone behave themselves on Earth . . . naw, but death though . . . everyone's too scared about it . . . everyone's too scared about *living*, cos they're too scared about dying . . . and, like, it's just natural, it's just natural. Death's just . . . it's just as natural as living, except just without all the talking and the arguing and the hassle . . . all that fucking *hassle* . . . fuck death . . . fuck it . . .'

Donald was beginning to lose me. I shifted uneasily on the sofa arm.

Once he settled down, Donald went to sit on the edge of one of the knackered sewing machines. He turned his head, to have a discreet burp, then he went on, 'Well, anyway, go on . . . what do you *want* to happen when you die?'

'I don't know,' I said to my chest. 'That's the worst thing about it, like: the unknown.'

I shuddered, to illustrate the point. Then I added, 'I just hope . . . it works out alright. For everyone.'

'Fuck everyone,' Donald gurgled, gradually beginning to gyrate as he perched on the old Brother machine. 'Don't worry about it . . . I fuck death up the arse, me! I fuck it right up the arse!'

I gulped, not so sure me and Donald were on the same page any more. Soon, Donald was thrusting his pelvis round the room;

117

laughing; describing in great detail what he was going to do to death, should he get his hands on it. I strained a smile, sitting with my hands in my lap. I didn't know where to look.

After almost a minute of eye-watering crotch-rotation, I think Donald cottoned on I was feeling uncomfortable, and he slumped back down on the sewing machine. He panted, 'I'm sure you'll be alright, petal . . . you'll get to Heaven . . . been an angel tonight . . . getting me the drink . . . I mean, like, so long as you haven't been a complete bastard, or killed anyone, you'll go straight there . . . straight to Heaven. That's my reckoning . . .'

The more Donald talked, the smaller my heart shrank. And my face sank. I felt instantly miserable, finishing off the last drops of flat perry. I decided it was time to leave.

As I rose from the sofa, my shoulders felt heavy, like I was carrying the whole weight of Stevie's coffin on my back. I realised then I had little chance of a happy afterlife. I was a complete bastard and a boyfriend-killer, and I was going to Hell.

On my way out, I dithered a bit, unsure how to say goodbye to Donald. However, by then his eyes looked like penny-slits, so I just patted him gently on the shoulder and left the last bottle of Babycham by his side. Donald held my hand, coughed violently and mumbled, 'I'll treasure it, I'll treasure it . . . we'll have it another time . . . don't go . . . cheerio . . . angel . . . angel . . . I'll treasure it . . .'

I felt like a devil, though, leaving Donald to doze on the mouldy machine. Tiptoeing from beam to beam, I covered my mouth, spotting the odd beady rat's eye peeking at me from the shadows. I kicked one of the Nike pills towards them, then marched off, back down the corridor. I thought about taking the lift, but it smelled like a latrine, and the mechanisms looked life-threatening. So, I took the stairs instead:

118

I
AM
NOT
THAT
HAPPY
TAKING
RICKETY
HORRIBLE
ELEVATORS

Back out on Lawrence Road, it was a relief to fill my lungs with fresh air again. I glanced up at Donald's dark windows, and shuddered. I thoroughly wet-wiped my fingers, then walked onwards, away from the gloom. It was high time for some more random acts of kindness, I thought. Either that, or some sort of transcendental religious salvation, before it was too late.

⊙

'Excuse me,' I said to the fellow in the Foyles T-shirt, 'can you point me towards your DEATH section, please?'

He raised an eyebrow and laughed. I tried to smile reassuringly, with extra dimples. I'd already spent twenty minutes in the shop, searching for a book about Mexican attitudes to death (which are meant to be dead positive, full of celebrations, dancing and skull-shaped sweeties), but I could only find books on how to cook burritos.

'What exactly are you after?' the Foyles fellow asked. His skull was disproportionately large compared to the rest of his body, probably to accommodate all the long words he'd accrued in his lifetime.

'Er,' I said, 'something like . . . the afterlife. Like, *The Road to the Good Afterlife*, but I dunno if that's a book. Like, like, *How to*

119

Be Good and Not Go to Hell . . . except I'm not into the Christian side of it. I'm not after the Bible or anything.'

We laughed together, although I wasn't joking. The Foyles fellow must've thought I was weird but, in a city populated by ten million people, you can rest assured you're never the single maddest person in any one square mile. For example, out of the bookshop window I could see a woman wheeling a baguette in a buggy, instead of a baby. I could also see a mentally ill deaf person making sign language to himself – unless it was just an actor from the Phoenix Theatre, practising jazz hands.

After much exaggerated 'flirty' chin-stroking, my Foyles friend finally had a brainwave. Smiling blissfully at his mammoth intelligence, the boy led me to the Eastern Philosophy section, and pointed out something called the *Tibetan Book of the Dead*. The publishers had spent a lot of money making the cover emanate metallic red, giving it the quality of a very holy tome. I flicked through it, marvelling at all the ancient poetry and jazzy drawings of cheery, chubby Buddhas, as well as other ones with fangs, breathing fire. I respected a religion that employed psychedelic artists to paint their death scenes.

In a way, I didn't feel so frightened about snuffing it any more. Each page of the book was peppered with words like 'inspiration' and 'enlightenment' and 'peace' and 'bliss'. By the looks of it, the only distressing word in the book was the price tag (£12.99!), but I bought it anyway. I wasn't intending on going home and shaving my head and putting on a tangerine nappy, but I felt noticeably more content as I waltzed back out onto Charing Cross Road, with the book swinging by my side like a lucky charm. I was ready to fuck death up the arse, me!

There was even a section of the book entitled 'Natural Liberation of Fear through the Ritual Deception of Death', which sounded right up my street. I wondered if I could deceive death

120

completely, and live for ever. After what I'd done to Stevie, I was resigned to the fact I was probably destined for Hell, but there was always a chance I could rebalance my karma, if only I could hold death off long enough. I unzipped my Medicine Bag, and took out three multivitamin tablets. With my mouth overflowing with chemical orange fizz, I snuck into Soho Square and sat down in the lotus position, on the grass.

The sun slowly craned its neck over a cloud, then over my shoulder, reading the text with me. Its rays were so bright, the pages became fluorescent. Squinting, I swung my eyes from left to right to left to right, skim-reading. A lot of the Buddhist terminology – like most religious terminology – went over my head: at first it seemed the only way to 'avert death' was to get this god Mahākarunika to do it for you. But I persevered, letting the text march into my brain like a band of disoriented Hare Krishnas.

It was a funny old read. There was a whole section devoted to recognising the signs of 'remote death', 'near death' and 'extremely near death' and, as my eyes hoovered up the text, my heart began to droop. All the weird demons, wolfheads and three-eyed wrathful deities from picture 9 marched into my brain, hot on the heels of the Hare Krishnas.

There should've been a warning on the front: NOT SUITABLE FOR HYPOCHONDRIACS. I never realised there were so many signs to let you know you're on your way out. Rather than being sent on a 'blissful journey towards a high state of being' – like the blurb reckoned – I sat there quaking in the middle of the square, more afraid of death than ever before.

Some of the signs of impending death were strange (like not making a sound when you snap your fingers, or not being able to see the tip of your own tongue), and some of the rituals to avert them were even weirder. For instance, should you have protruding anklebones, the only way to save yourself from dying within the month is to attach a dog's tail between your legs, defecate in a pile and eat three mouthfuls of it. The book was barking mad.

Out of curiosity, I snapped my fingers. Despite the noisy traffic, I definitely heard something click.

Then, I stuck my tongue out. Boys have often complimented me on the length of my tongue – I caught a glimpse of it too; no bother.

I turned the page, feeling a little better. But I didn't dare look at my anklebones.

⊙

It was my day off the following Wednesday. Coincidentally, it was my seven fancy men's day off as well, and they all wanted to see me. I didn't want to be nasty and blow any of them off, so I spent the day desperately rushing from date to date to date to date to date to date to date. Like so:

> Mongoloid Mr Monday met me
> Round the 7.30 a.m. mark on
> Markfield recreation ground and, completely
> Out of the blue, said he
> Needed squeezing again. But not like that
> Day I squeezed him by Tower Bridge.
> Against all the odds, he
> Yanked out his elastic penis and
> Made me squeeze that instead. I grimaced,
> Relieving him in his trackie bottoms, listening
> To the daysnoring growing gradually heavier,
> Until it was time to meet Mr Tuesday at the
> Employment agency. I felt bad now for
> Smashing his violin. He seemed even more
> Depressed, and his eyes were even bluer

122

As he perused the job vacancies. Bogies
Yo-yoed out of his nose, while he
Moaned about missing Maria, and I wasn't
Really attracted to him any more.
When I met Mr Wednesday – dressed in an
Emporio Armani vest and slacks – I
Didn't expect him to stuff a fifty-pound
Note in my bra and drag me into the
Empty gents at Searcy's, demanding rough
Sex, and one of his thumbs up my
Dirt-pipe. I held back the tears through dinner.
At least I had more money for Donald,
Yet I felt like a manky old prostitute.
My bum-hole was a red-
Raw bullet-hole and, when I found Mr
Thursday lingering outside his
High-rise home, my fresh-on daisy
Underwear felt itchy with blood. A
Rushed cappuccino round the corner didn't
Serve to clear my head, and I
Ducked out of going upstairs with him, on
Account of his daughters turning up in
Yellowed school uniforms, and glaring at me.
Milan beckoned. Before the match, I
Remembered to buy the football top
From JD Sports in Wood Green, but I
Realised – once I got to the pub –
I'd bought Internazionale instead of
Dumpy Mr Friday's dear beloved
AC. He went absolutely ballistic,
Yelling at me in front of his mates. I
Made a quick getaway. I went for a

Refund at JD, then power-walked back to
South Tottenham. Suddenly, I was spasming.
As per usual, it was only a
Telephone call. Mr Saturday wanted to
Undress me again and shag me
Rotten in his rotten, pitch-
Dark bedroom. Again, the blood in my knickers
Added to the impression I was a whore, and I
Yowled as he forced entry into
My privates. Afterwards, I didn't dare
Report him to the police. Instead, I
Staggered over to the old folk's home, to
Unwind with Mr Sunday and someone else's
Nan, but the pleasantries and tea-
Drinking were ruined by the constant, nagging
Assumption I'd contracted HIV or a
Young child off the previous bastard.

Get me to a nunnery!

All this philanthropy was taking its toll on my health and safe-ty. I wasn't even sure if any of these men respected me – with some of them I felt more like a voodoo doll, letting them stick their pricks in me more as a means of them venting their anger and frustration, rather than them actually caring about me.

The more saintly I was, the more my seven weekly lovers seemed tuned to the seven deadly sins: greedy, very-special-needy Mr Monday; envious failure Mr Tuesday; proud, pomp-ous, Prosecco-quaffing Mr Wednesday; lusty, highly fertile Mr Thursday; gluttonous, basketball-shaped Mr Friday; wrathful ladybeater Mr Saturday; slothful, softly spoken Mr Sunday.

A couple of the men (Mr Thursday, or good old Mr Sunday) seemed pleasant enough, but their good will was cancelled out

124

by some of the other men's bad willies. Men are hard work. As soon as you give them what they want, they get bored of you, or take liberties. I felt like a daft cow, making a bloody butterfly-painting in my knickers as I laid in bed that night with insomnia.

It was one of many nights of loneliness and depression. All I had for company were the two morning-after pills swimming in my stomach, and the men's eyes looking in at me from the top deck of the 243. It wasn't just my private organs that killed – my whole chest ached, every time I thought of my weekly lovers. I had no idea how I was going to get rid of them. Of course, there was always the possibility I could make them all hang themselves on a climbing frame by being incessantly horrible to them, but I didn't really want that.

Rather than killing more boyfriends, I just wished I could bring back to life the one I'd had in the first place. Grabbing my stomach, I sighed at the empty room, then slipped out from under the gingham bedcovers. I felt like a drowsy centipede, practically crawling across the carpet, doubled over with abdominal pain. I scrabbled through my Medicine Bag for a fresh pack of Panadol, then stumbled into the unlit kitchen for a glass of water.

I found the glass alright, draining casually on the worktop, but when it came to finding the water, my heart rate quickly quadrupled. The glass slipped from my hand, and clatter-shattered across the lino. I stared in disbelief at the horrors that lay before me on the marble-effect melamine.

Although I'd been thinking about Stevie non-stop for the last few months, I'd forgotten all about Meaty Stevie and Fruity Stevie. Fruity Stevie looked half-dead under his glass mixing bowl: his arms and legs leaking purple banana-pus; his head oxidised to a crisp; and his torso half-eaten by mould. Meaty Stevie, on the other hand, looked very much alive, sitting upright on his magic carpet of clingfilm, with bright green chest hair, and

125

maggoty teeth falling out of his mouth. Glaring at me through the dark, with his mad meatball eye, Meaty Stevie screamed, 'Die! Die! Die!'

All I could do was carry on staring, panic-stricken, as Meaty Stevie hauled the Tefal igloo off himself and crawled towards me along the plastic worktop. I felt the insides of my cheeks leak. Then, in a moment of inspiration, I leapt for the light switch. As soon as the bulb sprang to life, I saw Meaty Stevie was back on the clingfilm, under his glass mixing bowl, playing dead again. I swallowed back a gobful of saliva. I still didn't trust the old pile of meat, so I gave him and Fruity Stevie an impromptu burial in the dustbin, tying up the binliner, then carrying them out into the hallway, playing Chopin's Funeral March in my head.

Back under the safety of my gingham bedcovers, I noticed the pain easing in my abdomen, although there was still a seven-way tug-of-war going on with my heartstrings. I hid my head under both pillows. My first experiment to reanimate Stevie had failed miserably, but I still wanted him back. I tried to instigate a makeshift seance in my head, to no avail.

'Stevie, love, move amongst us, move amongst us,' I whispered, feeling idiotic.

I chewed my lip, still unable to sleep. I didn't have the heart to split up with any of my weekly lovers (the lads were insecure enough as it was), and I didn't want to dampen their love with cruelty, either (they were probably prone to suicide, too). But I had to get rid of them somehow.

I stayed awake, until I came up with this solution: perhaps I could test their dedication to breaking point, by feigning mental illness and setting them a stupid task.

The next morning, I parcelled up seven athletics bibs, seven pairs of Lycra shorts and seven bottles of peroxide, and posted them to my seven special men, with a note:

HI. I'VE GOT PROBLEMS. IF YOU EVER WANT TO BE WITH ME AGAIN, DYE YOUR HAIR AND WEAR THESE. LOVE FROM KIMBERLY

x x x x x x x

The first half of the *Tibetan Book of the Dead* kept me on track to becoming a good-natured person, while the second half kept me on track to becoming a paranoid wreck. I refused to sleep too near to it, but always picked it up robotically first thing in the morning, for a gander.

I had a good long stare at the tip of my tongue in the bathroom mirror, then went through and made a cup of Best-in. I still didn't dare look at my anklebones.

Once the coffee had reassembled the jumbled Lego blocks in my skull, I headed downstairs for a sip of fresh air before work. My legs felt stiff and heavy as I plodded down the steps, and it was frustrating having to do the trick with the door, which was also stiff and heavy. I stubbed my toe, yanking it towards myself a bit too aggressively once I'd got it open.

Instead of grumbling, I decided to do something about the door, once and for all. I counted my pennies and headed down to the local builders' merchant to buy a wood plane (£9.55 excl. VAT). I carried it back to the flat, then attacked the bottom of the front door, watching in awe as the spirals and curls of wood waterfalled onto the doorstep. At one point I got a bit carried away – like when I accidentally grate too much Parmesan on people's pasta – and I had to stop myself from shredding the door completely.

Soon enough, it was good and loose. No longer would me and my neighbours have to do the annoying trick with the door. I chucked the wood plane next to the pile of shoes in the hallway, then opened and closed and opened and closed and opened and closed the front door, smiling serenely. The hinges squeaked with gratitude.

I waltzed/limped away from the flat, picking sawdust out of my fingernails. I was all set for a grand day in the Capital when, just then, a mammoth halal van pulled up alongside me, ready to drop off the morning's corpses. The stench of dead flesh and disinfectant swept up my nostrils as they pulled open the back door, revealing fifteen or twenty hung, drawn and quartered cows. I gagged, quickening my pace.

Now might be a good time to mention I'd turned vegetarian. After being tormented by Meaty Stevie the night before, I'd vowed never to put another dead body in my mouth. It was all well and good being nice to humans but, as religious folk might tell you, being nasty to any of God's creatures probably won't inspire St Peter to let you into Heaven.

I power-walked away from the van, watching out for ants and ladybirds underfoot. Vegetarianism has endless benefits: it reduces the amount of bounties put on animals' heads; improves your skin; saves you time umming and ahhing over menus; and I liked the idea of spring-cleaning my intestines with easily digestible plant matter and fresh fruit juices.

I got to the Ristorante di Fantasia just before eleven. Paolo was gobbling a bit of breakfast – coffee, with open sarnies of speck and mozzarella – and my stomach turned over. I put my raincoat on the rail and washed the rest of the sawdust out from under my nails. While Paolo wasn't watching, I wanted to swing open the refrigerators and let all the frozen carcasses run free, up the A10, away from the city. But I guessed it wouldn't be good for business, so I went round adjusting and readjusting the cutlery instead.

There's something that happens around noon in the Capital

called 'lunchtime', which we don't have up North, and it causes people to come flocking to the Ristorante with howling stomachs. Before long, the place was quite packed, and I became suddenly hyperactive, busying myself with the orders rather than the feng shui of the soup spoons. For the first twenty minutes nobody ordered meat, but I knew the truce couldn't last for ever.

At about half past, a man with thick eyebrows and pretty Persian cheekbones sat down firmly at table 16, making the plastic flowers wobble. He was one of the more unadventurous men of the Ristorante: he always sat at 16, he always wore denim, and he even had a 'usual'. This man's usual was venison ravioli. I pretended to be busy, polishing the coffee cups in the kitchen, dreading going over for his order. In the end, I tried to distract him from his normal thought processes, pressing my Wonderbra against his left ear, but it didn't sway him. I scribbled a reindeer on my notepad, with its eyes crossed out, and stalked sadly back through to the kitchen. I stood about, kicking my heels and looking glum, while I waited for Paolo to come out of the toilet with Norma Jean. He smiled at me sheepishly, red-faced, then gradually the smile turned into a straight line.

'Well? What is order?' he snapped.

I didn't have the heart to tell the truth. I picked at a loose thread on my blouse, and answered, 'What's the, er . . . veggie equivalent of venison again?'

'There is no equillavent.'

I looked at my feet, which were still jiggling underneath me.

'Customer wants vegetarian ravioli? I can do this,' Paolo said, though he didn't look impressed.

I nodded, coquettishly. Paolo sighed, then stormed off to get the meat substitute out of the back of the freezer.

Twenty minutes later, a miserable-looking tofu ravioli was sitting on the counter, awaiting service. I carried it over to table 16, feeling twitchy but gallant enough, stroking the Persian bloke's neck with my bosoms again, praying he didn't have the heart (or the language) to make a complaint.

Once I put his plate down, I scurried off to bother the other diners, though I couldn't help catching his reflection in the freshly wiped windows. His eyes followed me round the tables – it was hard to tell if he was angry or not, with those thick, permanently knitted eyebrows.

I couldn't stand it any longer. I sent the next few orders through to Paolo, then made my way back to the Persian's table, to ask if everything was alright. As I paced across the mosaics, I had a speech planned about animal rights, inhumane butchery, and how nice his denim was.

As it turned out, though, he didn't want to talk about the venison. What he wanted to talk about did have horns, mind you – but only the type of horn you keep in your trousers. With eyebrows still firmly knitted, Mr No Tomorrow – as he shall now be known – tugged my blouse sleeve towards him and, in hushed tones, said, 'I hear you do intercourse for free?'

'Sorry?'

'Intercourse.'

I nearly spat out my tongue. Despite being ashamed about saying 'intercourse' out loud, Mr No Tomorrow clearly wasn't shy.

'I wasn't going to . . . eh . . . ask you about the you know,' he went on, 'but your things,' pointing at my Wonderbra with his knife, 'you are rubbing me for three weeks now. So I heard you are part-time prostitute?'

I made a face. I wasn't sure whether to be offended or not. Holding his gaze, I explained I wasn't a part-time prostitute, as he so kindly put it – I just happened to be shagging quite a few different men at the minute, and they were giving me money for it.

130

Mr No Tomorrow raised one of those eyebrows.

'I'm desperate,' he pleaded. The daft thing was he was physical-ly very attractive – I just couldn't go on recruiting lovers, though. It wasn't my fault I was magnetic to the opposite sex, although I did consider not coming to work in the Wonderbra any more.

Curiously, Mr No Tomorrow added, 'I am not illegal citizen,' which meant he probably was. He certainly had an accent like an illegal citizen.

'Oh, don't worry,' I said instinctively. I bit my bottom lip (not provocatively). I didn't want to embarrass Mr No Tomorrow by subjecting him to rejection by a 'part-time prostitute', and I did appreciate him not booting off about the tofu. I just didn't have enough days in the week to satisfy him. And not enough perox-ide, either. Poking my dimples out, I rapped my fingernails on the tabletop, wondering how to let the Persian sex pest down gently.

And then it struck me. I knew someone who'd be absolutely perfect for him.

⊙

My Promiscuous Pal Polly from Southampton came striding across the pub forecourt, holding on to her pink minidress to stop the wind licking her thighs. Her hair was done in a sort of blonde beehive, and she made hoof-prints in the dirt as she gal-loped forwards in her heels.

She shrieked when she saw the bungee-jumping apparatus. I smiled at her, in a terrified manner.

'New hair?' I asked, trying to be feminine.

'Aw, yeah, yeah,' she replied, patting the beehive, also trying to be feminine.

The cumulus clouds had begun to spit, so me, Mr Sunday and Mr No Tomorrow were huddled with our drinks, under the brick

canopy of the pub. It turned out Mr No Tomorrow was adventur-
ous, after all – a sadist, in fact – and he'd arranged for us to do a
dual bungee-jump off a crane in Wood Green, just to 'break ice'.

I was more bothered about 'breaking neck'.

'Everyone'll see up my skirt,' Polly remarked, gesturing at the
empty car park.

Mr No Tomorrow laughed, because he fancied her. I was glad.
I wished he knew he didn't have to go through all this bungee
ice-breaking to coax Polly into bed, but he'd already paid for the
jump and we didn't want to disappoint.

Once we'd polished off our drinks, the four of us went up in
this creaking, yellow lift with SMITH FAIRYTALE FUNLAND
plastered on the side. I'd purposefully been nursing my Smirnoff,
despite Mr No Tomorrow snapping 'Drink up' every thirty seconds.

I was so nervous, I could've fired lightning from my fingertips.
It felt like a dress rehearsal for the afterlife; like we were ascend-
ing to Heaven, only to be turned down by the gatekeeper and
sent plummeting to a hellish red end on the car-park concrete. I
had pangs of vertigo – that perilous, sickly feeling you're going to
fall from a great, stupid height, and the worst thing about it was
I was actually willingly going to throw myself from a great, stupid height. The brain malfunctions, spewing all sorts of confused
signals round your system, trying to eject itself from your skull.

I clutched Mr Sunday's hand, like it could somehow counter-
act the cogs of the lift. He glanced at me, shivering in the crisp,
white athletics kit and shaking his crisp, white hairdo. I smiled
back at him, but it was a wobbly smile. Me and Mr Sunday had
been getting on well – he knew a lot about women (since he spent
most of his free time with gangs of old ones), and he'd come out of
his shell more since those first terse exchanges in the Ristorante
di Fantasia. He was a professional carer, and that's what set him

132

apart from the other barbarians: he seemed to have evolved a bit further. Life, for many men, is just about stuffing food and drink into their mouths, and stuffing their penises into females. Mr Sunday, on the other hand, looked after ladies for a living, and I imagined he'd look after me too, should we grow old together.

'I only came out for a quiet pint,' he mumbled, staring at the Capital expanding beneath us. Polly giggled, keeping her thighs tight together. There was a bit of a crowd forming, after all.

Polly and Mr No Tomorrow were the first to jump that afternoon – they'd hardly even said 'Hello' to each other before they were bound together with a rubber band and chucked off the top of the crane. My guts unravelled as I watched them turn to screaming specks then screaming humans again then specks again then humans again then specks then humans then specks humans specks humans specks humans specks.

I wondered why some people get a thrill off terrifying near-death experiences, such as rollercoasters and GHB abuse. Humans are odd and foolish in that way. Even people who manage to stay calm during air travel are mad as well, putting all their faith in these gigantic, metal bird-machines that don't even flap their wings. Humans were not made for the sky.

I gulped and looked down at Polly and Mr No Tomorrow being released from the elastic band. They seemed to be in one piece, though it was hard to tell from so high up. I glanced again at Mr Sunday, and we squeezed each other's hands tighter, forming a sweaty lagoon between them. We watched with white faces as the wobbly wire was winched back up the crane, while the gypsy instructor explained how to have a happy fall. I paid close attention.

We had to look into the distance, before dropping off the crane. The clouds looked grey, miserable and sorry for us. I kept whining, 'I don't think I can do it. I don't think I can do it.' In contrast, Mr Sunday was trying to come across as calm and collected, especially in front of the instructor, who didn't seem at all fazed by heights, let alone throwing himself off them.

We had to count '5-4-3-2-1', then hurl ourselves off the crane.

We counted '5-4-3-2-1', then we paused, then we squealed, then we hurled ourselves off the crane.

I probably gave Mr Sunday tinnitus from screaming so much. The ground flew at us at 150 miles an hour, like planet Earth was a giant football and someone was kicking it at us. They kicked it at us repeatedly for about thirty seconds, kicking softer and softer, until me and Mr Sunday finally landed on the surface of the football with a swift bump. I let out a gasp.

Instinctively, me and Mr Sunday laughed, hugged each other, and exclaimed empty lines like, 'God, fucking hell, that was fucking mint. Again! Again!' To be honest, though, I was glad to be untangled from the rope, and I knew I'd never do it again.

We walked dangly legged back towards the pub. Me and Mr Sunday were still the same shade as that grey and miserable sky. However, when we got back under the brick canopy, it was heart-warming to find Polly and Mr No Tomorrow kissing, with their hands in each other's waistbands.

In an abstract, elastic fashion, the bungee jump had served its purpose. We decided not to get another drink; instead, we walked back through the evergreen trees to the Ristorante di Fantasia, to get something to eat now our stomachs had settled. I thought Paolo might even throw in some free tofu ravioli, since he'd made a full batch of the stuff and no one ever ordered it.

Surviving the bungee jump made me happy to be alive – the Capital seemed to shine that little bit brighter, giving the dark clouds ruby crowns. And, for the first time since Stevie, I felt like I was falling in love again. There was a schoolgirlish excitement in the pit of my stomach, which I hadn't felt since the sixteenth of June 2003, in the Southern Cross.

After Stevie died, I was worried I might not recognise love the next time I came across it, but Mr Sunday seemed like a keeper. While he was a man of very few words, everything he said I agreed with. As we passed the huge wooden crucifix on West Green Road, Mr Sunday murmured, 'This has been great.'

I reached into his pocket, where his left hand was hiding.

'Don't know how you feel, but we could, like, make a go of this, if you want?' I said, which was a roundabout way of asking him to be my boyfriend.

'I . . . eh, that'd be amazing,' Mr Sunday replied, which was a roundabout way of saying, 'Yes, please!'

We stopped by the side of the road, to concentrate on a long kiss and a cuddle. We couldn't stop grinning. I kept pushing and pushing my body into his, to see how well we fitted together. Butterflies hatched in my belly. After a few minutes, I decided I'd best not suffocate another love of my life, so we parted and carried on up towards the Ristorante, swaying from paving slab to paving slab, giggling at nothing.

Up ahead, Polly and Mr No Tomorrow were giggling at nothing as well. Skipping over the crossings, we soon caught up with them and entered the Ristorante together. I was looking forward to turning Mr Sunday vegetarian, and perhaps even persuading Paolo to crack open the Prosecco.

After striding through the glass door, I got halfway through unbuttoning my raincoat when my face became tight with fear. The butterflies turned to butterfly knives.

Dotted around the restaurant, Mr Monday, Tuesday, Wednesday, Thursday, Friday and Saturday were sat, dressed in identical white athletics kits, with identical sullen expressions. Some of the men (Mr Monday, Friday and Saturday) had on the full kit, while others had gone for just the bib, or just the shorts and socks. For some reason, Mr Wednesday had complemented his bib with a pair of stockbrokers' braces, despite not being a stockbroker (I think he worked for T-Mobile). Him and Mr Monday were the only ones to dabble in the peroxide: Mr Wednesday had fashioned an unfashionable blond quiff, while Malcolm's coverage was patchy, like he'd been caught under a drizzle of acid rain.

All twelve eyes locked onto mine. I tried to hide behind the Guillotine, dreading an altercation. I dithered about the entrance for a bit, like a frightened fawn in the bright headlights of their athletics whites. Suddenly, I was no longer hungry.

When Mr Sunday saw his weekly rivals, he frowned as well, self-consciously picking at the seams of his Lycra shorts. I managed to get him seated with his back to the sporting sextet, but he looked rattled as he flicked through the menu. I sensed impending doom. The air felt charged with venom, like the build-up to a lightning storm, or a wrestling match.

'Is it the Capital Marathon or what?' Polly asked, sitting down.

'Ehm . . . naw, naw, I don't know,' I mumbled, picking my fingernails off. I asked Mr Sunday, 'Should we, er, have some proper coffee?'

'Mm,' he replied, distantly.

I kept my eyes on the Formica. I dreaded the next word. It happened to come from Mr Tuesday, the least sporty-looking of the lot. He dragged his chair up to our table and asked me in his soothing, timid tenor, 'Why are we all dressed like this?'

I stuck out my bottom lip and shook my head, feigning ignorance. I glanced at Mr Sunday and murmured, 'Are you even hungry? Maybe we should eat somewh—'

'Or maybe we should do some sexy-sexy *here*!' Mr Saturday goaded, clearly drunk on whatever his empty glasses used to have in them.

The Ghanaian clapped his hands on his table. Then, it all

went haywire. Despite having had sex at least three times in his life (hence the daughters), Mr Thursday disliked hearing a young girl spoken to in such lewd terms. I think he also disliked people from Ghana. 'Wog,' he muttered, behind his cappuccino. Mr Saturday shot up from table 13, which tilted violently in response.

'What did you call me?' he snapped, pointlessly pointing a finger in Mr Thursday's direction. It was like a re-run of my first encounter with Mr Saturday in the internet caff. I understood now why he had so much pent-up aggression: every time he made a mistake (whether in IT, or in gentlemanly etiquette), people scapegoated his skin. I felt daft now for sending him a bottle of bleach through the post.

'Well, leave her alone,' Mr Thursday said, ignoring the question. He kept the cappuccino held up to his face, as if it was insurance against being punched. Surely Mr Saturday wouldn't hit a white-haired man holding a piece of imitation porcelain – especially not one filled with hot coffee.

I kept staring coldly at the tabletop, though it was difficult to ignore the scene unfolding, especially when Mr Wednesday pulled his chair up to ours and wrapped an arm around my shoulder. I felt his red braces grate against my skin. He took an indignant glance at Mr Sunday, then chirruped in my ear, 'Someone's popular, ha ha ha ha!'

I wanted to disappear under the table. Although he never seemed like the aggressive type, Mr Sunday must've felt it his duty to protect me, and he said to Mr Wednesday, 'Do you mind getting off my girlfriend?'

My chest sank. The word 'girlfriend' was like the trigger of a starting pistol. All of a sudden, there was chaos in the Ristorante di Fantasia. Mr Saturday gurgled something along the lines of 'fucking fuckpig', referring to me, which didn't bode well with Mr Thursday, nor Mr Sunday. They leapt from their seats and tried to

137

frogmarch the drunk Ghanaian out of the establishment, yanking at his biceps. During the tussle, Mr Saturday fell head-last onto Mr Friday's table, who, until then, had been blithely tucking into a large portion of osso buco. Both the osso and the buco went flying. Now, if you remember, Mr Friday had a bit of a temper – especially if you happened to wear an Internazionale top, or deprive him of his food. His face went amber, like a basketball, and he cursed and flung Mr Saturday and Sunday back towards our table. 'What is going on?' Paolo snarled, watching in disbelief as his restaurant got rearranged. I just shook my head, trying not to incriminate myself. Mr Tuesday – who'd returned to the Ristorante with a brand-new violin, in an unsuccessful bid to get his job back – took my hand and tried to lead me out of the place before I got hurt. It was kind of him, but Mr Wednesday must've seen it as a thinly veiled kidnap attempt. He obviously fancied himself as a Sean Connery or Roger Moore character, pulling me to his breast. I hung limply in his grasp, feeling sick. 'Don't worry. I've got you, I've got you,' he said in my ear, pushing Mr Tuesday away with his elbow. I felt tears sprout in the roots of my eyelashes as Mr Saturday and Sunday carried on grappling with each other, shouting all sorts of unmentionables. Mr Wednesday couldn't resist sticking his boot in, for the sake of it. It seemed he wanted to establish a pecking order, with himself as alpha male, but he was pretty powerless when it came to being pelted with food by Mr Monday. A rock-hard chunk of ciabatta gave him a glancing blow on the side of the neck, causing him to panic unnecessarily. Daysnoring excitedly, Malcolm seemed to think beginning a food fight was the only way to disperse the violence. The rest of the loaf came next, thudding against the windowpane. No one dared give the disabled boy a clip round the ear, so they carried on focusing their wrath towards Mr Saturday, especially once he'd smashed the Peroni bottle open. He went at Mr Sunday and Wednesday with the jagged edge, opening up miniature shark bites on their hands and cheeks. Seeing red, Mr Friday took a swing at the three of them, like a father trying to discipline unruly triplets. Mr Monday carried on groaning, whale-like, in the corner, surrounded by breadcrumbs. Mr Saturday went down, taking Mr Sunday and table 3 with him, and cracking Mr Sunday's skull against the exposed brickwork. I shrieked. Mr Friday was about to put Mr Saturday's head through the front door when the young Ghanaian let out a wheeze and announced, 'Look . . . why we all fight over fucky prostitute?'

My heart rate tripled. I felt lightning in my fingertips again.

'You what?' Mr Sunday spat, with one hand pressed against his head. His fingers came away bloody.

'We don't really care about girl we all fucking for money?'

Mr Saturday's English left a lot to be desired, but it also left a queer silence in the Ristorante. The pots burbled away in the background, but everything else was quiet. I kept my eyes down. I wished there was some advice printed on the laminated menu or, better still, an ejector-seat button underneath the table. Or, even better: a bomb detonator.

'She wouldn't sleep with you,' Mr Sunday scoffed. I felt his eyes flick towards me, and he added, 'Would you?'

I lifted my shoulders sheepishly, which could only mean yes. I knew I had to talk, but I couldn't quite bring myself to say, 'I needed the money, for the greater good of society. And for this old tramp I know. With scurvy. And rats. And . . .'

All the friendly strands between me and the men were quickly unravelling. When you're unfaithful, it's incredible how fast your partner's love (or lust) can turn to hatred. Mr Sunday looked disgusted at me. Mr Saturday looked proud of himself. Mr Monday squeezed his hooded eyes shut. Mr Tuesday cradled his newly broken violin. Mr Wednesday cradled his newly broken nose. Mr Thursday

139

dabbed the cappuccino from his chinos. Mr Friday stomped back over to his ruined osso buco. Mr No Tomorrow smirked into the lapels of his denim jacket. Polly hobbled backwards onto the pavement. Finally, it was Paolo who broke the silence:

'You been using the place like brothel,' he coughed at me. 'You fired. You never come here again. You go now.'

I tried to say sorry to Paolo and to the magnificent seven, but there were too many of them to do each individual sorry any justice. Mr Sunday bobbed his head. He couldn't bear to look at me any longer. I wasn't sure what was worse: that I'd ruined his chances of settling down with a lover, or that I'd ruined mine. We certainly weren't going to be an item any more.

Sniffling, I got up from my seat and staggered out of the door. I said nothing more. Keeping my head hung, I strode off down Philip Lane, staring gormlessly at the weeds crawling out of the concrete.

I didn't wait for Polly or Mr No Tomorrow – instead, I headed straight back to the halal butcher's, panting, with tears fogging my vision. I wanted to drink five Smirnoff Ices and down fourteen Panadol. I wanted to do another bungee jump, only this time without the elastic band.

When I got to the High Road, I remembered how hungry I was. I wiped my face, then stumbled into the Turkish-Polish-English supermarket to buy my last-ever meal. It took me almost ten minutes to decide what I wanted.

After all, I couldn't go back to the Ristorante di Fantasia for the tofu ravioli.

⊙

After the half-eaten tuna and cucumber sandwich, I made a selection of petrol bombs. The ingredients of a Molotov cocktail are similar to the ingredients of a Cosmopolitan except, instead of vodka and Cointreau, I filled a Smirnoff Ice bottle with white spirit and, instead of the lime and cranberry juice, I doused a couple of tampons in nail polish remover and stuffed them into the neck of the bottle. In a way, I supposed it was more like a flaming sambuca.

I made four of them. The production line was a bit slow-going, what with me taking a break every two minutes to wail into my cushions. By the end of it, my fingers smelled like petrol pumps. I was almost tempted to throw the Molotov cocktails at my own face, there and then, just to get it over with. It gave me a sick thrill, the idea of my black, chargrilled skeleton appearing in the paper, with the headline: IDIOT IMMOLATES HERSELF.

Lucifer stared up at me, ruby-eyed, begging me not to do it. He had so much more to give – he hadn't even seen a female hamster yet, let alone felt one's sweet caresses.

I wiped my fingerprints on my new dress, then packed up the Molotov cocktails in a carrier bag and hung them on the door-knob. I supposed it wouldn't be fair, killing an innocent hamster, let alone all my innocent neighbours. My death deserved to be more symbolic than flash-frying above a halal butcher's.

I rummaged through some drawers for my battered old Disc-man, then took Joy Division's *Closer* from the pile in Stevie's wardrobe and slung both in the bag with the cocktails. I changed my underwear and redid my make-up. Then I locked the flat, out of habit, and set off downstairs, back towards the Ristorante di Fantasia.

Closer was the record I most closely associated with Stevie's death, and it would be the record most closely associated with the death of my seven Stevie wannabes, and me. I wanted 'The Eternal' ringing in my ears, as my skin turned from gooseflesh to roast beef.

Luckily, I didn't have to stall to do the trick with the door – it was still good and loose. As I power-walked back towards Philip Lane, I felt devoid of emotion: the perfect mindset to commit a mass murder. All that mattered to me was getting to the Ristorante as quickly as possible, to put me and my weekly exes out of our misery. It would be a fitting revenge for seven men gang-raping my good nature. And I was going to go down with my rusty old ship. If you can't beat them, join them. If you can't make seven men happy by dating them and letting them have sex with you, petrol-bomb them.

Technically, I'd already killed Stevie Wallace, Meaty Stevie and Fruity Stevie, so murdering seven more Stevies should've been a doddle. However, when I got to the corner of Philip and Arnold, I realised I had nothing to light the cocktails with. I didn't smoke, you see. Smoking is for people who want to commit suicide very slowly, with bad breath. I was after a much quicker, more explosive death.

Fortunately, there were eight or nine off-licences on the way to the Ristorante. I went in the first one to browse their fag-lighters. The shopkeeper had Clippers in all sorts of colours, and I spent ages deciding which would be most symbolic. At long last, I plumped for the red one.

Walking out, my head pounded with blood. In a way, I didn't want to see the Ristorante looming on the horizon – my heart couldn't quite keep up with all the bad ideas my brain kept putting to it. I wished for a second the Ristorante di Fantasia was an actual fantasy restaurant – just a figment of my imagination – and that my weekly exes were imaginary too. I wished I could've made four Cosmopolitans after all, and bitched about the boys with my girlfriends, like those lot in *Sex and the City*, and not have to kill them. But I didn't have any friends.

All I had was fire in a carrier bag. I kept stomping forwards, each step shortening the distance between me and the gloomy restaurant, each step shortening the lifespan of my doomed ex-lovers and me. To get my ears in the mood for a fiery death, I removed the scratched Discman from the bag, and the unscratched *Closer* case. I paused to put in the headphones. I thought it was suitable to be cremated to the sound of Ian's mournful baritone – however, when I opened the CD case, I was surprised to find a folded-up letter in place of the disc. It was handwritten in blue biro, in a childlike scrawl I recognised. As I unfolded the letter, my heart throbbed in my throat. It took two sentences to realise I was holding Stevie's suicide note.

I slipped under the awning of the AUND ETT , protecting myself and the letter from the slight drizzle and the staring eyes of passers-by. I was trembling, fearing the worst. Stevie was finally going to have his revenge. From beyond the grave, Stevie was going to tell me – to my face – I'm the worst thing that ever happened to him.

Sniffling, I began to read, my eyes filling with tears with every passing sentence. The first thing that made me sad about Stevie's letter was his awefull spelling and punctuation. And then, there were more and more things that made me sad:

*dear kimberly. if only i could tell you this in person but my speech is no good is it. i need **You** to know tho that im in an awefull state and that ive got a terribell pain somewere. so im doing it in ~~words~~ wrighting which im sorry is only just a bit better than the speech. first of all my head has been all over the place **R**esently if you have notised. i love you but something awefull and shamfull has happend which i do not **R**eally want to tell you but i ~~think you should will understand~~ want you to understand. i hope that you beleive me. it happend after the party at seal sands. do you remember tel and natalie from the club. well we desided to drive out to the sands after the atheletics*

party with these bottels of wine. we were all of us dead drunk
exseppted tel was driveing.

I had a feeling I knew where his words were going. They've only gone and killed someone on the roads, after too many bottels of wine. I shook my head in disbelief, then shook the paper again, and read on:

so anyway we got to seal sands. natalie had the idea to get in
the water to look for the ~~achewal~~ acthual seals. she wanted to go
*skinniedipping becos we **O**nly had the cloaths we had on. i shouldnt*
of gone in with her. tel stayed in the warm in car while we got in the
*water. it was ~~very~~ completeley freezing. i cant **S**tress that enough.*

I had another feeling I knew where his words were going. He's only gone and had sex with Natalie in the sea, after too many bottels of wine. How dare Stevie cheat on me! Admittedly, while Stevie was cheating on me with a fat pentathlete, that same night I was cheating on him with a square-faced bachelor, but it's not like I slept with him. I clutched the bag of Molotov cocktails tight in my fist, clutched Stevie's letter even tighter, and read on:

it was allrite at first with the seals but so cold. they slide off
the rocks away from us and kept honk honk honking. we went
after them but some seals wernt that happy with us tho. i think
*it mite of been **M**ating season or they were feeling thretened by*
*us. i thought we should just leave them to **I**t but then all off a*
sudden ther was this huge crashing wave and me and natalie
got seperated. anyway the tide thruew me onto the rocks and
suddenley ther was all this wind and the waves really getting
up. i hit the rocks again and ~~hit~~ hurt my back really bad. all off
*a sudden natali**E** was yelling she couldnt see me and ther was*
this repliy from tel saying he couldnt see me nither. i started to
*panick and had all this water **I**n my mouth and was overwelmed*

by the waves that carried on coming. i couldnt shout nothing
becos of my stammer. it was Like i was paraliezed ther from
the shock of the cold. i was scaired i was going to pass out with
hyperthermier. then all off a sudden ther was this Allmighty
honking behind me and then a great heavy wieght suddenley on
my back. it was one of the seal bulls on top of me. it kept going
honk honk honk and grey and fritening. i tried to fight it off but
it was heavy and had me pinned to the rocks and paraliezed.
it had these claws on its flippers and it kept honking so louwd.
i was scaired and panicking and thats when the Truly awefull
thing happend. it must of been mating season after all becos the
seal kept pushing and pushing me up Against the rocks and then
trying to ~~fuck~~ insert itself into me. to my horrorr i couldnt move
and the seal it was very powerfull. it kept honk honk honking
and kept trying to ~~insert itself wher~~. the seal must of pushed me
so hard against the rocks becos i must of past out. if only i had
died. when i woke up the seal was gone but ther was all this
blood and pain down bellow. tel and natalie were gone aswell
but i maneged to stagger and find my cloaths and fone for taxi.
i am embaresed to even say now but i still have a pain down
bellow and am bleeding a lot out of ~~my~~ ther. i think i must of
contracted something off the seal. i am sorry ~~i have to go~~ but i
can Not tell a doctor and i do not want to ~~you to catch to~~ give
you a disese. ~~when~~ if they see the ortopsey results with std or
gonorreorr do not tell them about the seal. please for my dignitie.
i am so sorry but trust me you do not want to live with me like
this. ~~it is not the first time i have suffered fr~~ i know what i am
doing. im so sorry. this has nothing to do with you. goodbye my
love. i will hopfully meet you again ~~somewere~~ some time. i loved
you. stevie x x x x x x x ps i made a will so you can have my
money. please do not tell ~~anythi~~ anyone about any of this but x x
x x x x ~~and hope your happy~~ be happy x x x x x x x pps the c

145

One by one, I dropped tears onto the paper, making the blue ink smudge. I folded up the spoiled letter and posted it into my pocket. Then I cried and cried and cried, challenging the clouds to see who could make the pavement the wettest.

All at once there was grief, relief and disbelief. Disbelief, mainly. I wasn't sure if Stevie was pulling my leg, though the tone of the note seemed serious, and he was never one for black comedy. I shook my head slightly, and I dropped the Molotov cocktails. Fortunately, they didn't go off. Fortunately, I hadn't lit them yet.

I made my way back home, with my shoulders hunched. Despite everything, I was relieved it wasn't my fault Stevie died. Maybe he didn't go to the grave hating me. I wanted to jump for joy, and blow my own brains out. I just wished he knew it's natural to bleed out of your arsehole, should you get something untoward forced up there – and that, in time, it would've healed. And everything could've been alright.

I crept along the rest of Philip Lane, avoiding eye contact with myself in the silver-screen paving slabs. I never realised seals were capable of such cruelty. There I was, thinking a photograph of my tongue in a square-faced person's mouth was enough to sentence Stevie to death, when, by the sound of it, the culprit was a sexually aggressive bull seal. It was laughable, but I didn't laugh. I just carried on walking, shaking my head, shaking my arms and legs, shaking all of Tottenham's houses out of their foundations.

⊙

And now for a short lesson on seals:

Strangely, the common seal, *Phoca vitulina*, is not as common as the grey seal, *Halichoerus grypus*, at Seal Sands. I'm not sure which species is more likely to sexually harass a human being (if either) – however, the male seal is a polygynous mammal, renowned for breeding with a whole slew of different partners. While it's not uncommon for a seal to mate with a seal of a different species, it's largely unheard of for a mammal to try it on with a completely different class of vertebrate – for instance, a 200m sprinter. The more I mulled over Stevie's encounter with the bull, the more I thought Stevie had lost his mind. However, as I paced solemnly down Philip Lane, my thoughts kept wandering to this story I'd seen in the tabloids, a year or so ago. The article reported a sighting of a fur seal 'raping' a king penguin close to the Antarctic Ocean: the first example of a mammal shagging outside its class. Perhaps seals are the sex pests of the sea. Apparently, the young bulls are the worst, them being pumped full of hormones, and yet last in line to mate with the best broody females. They get what they can.

The thought of it made me feel ill. For weeks afterwards, I tried to block out the image of Stevie and the bull. I preferred the idea he'd just gone mad. However, one midsummer night I was listlessly flicking through the TV channels when I came across a sorry sight. Channel 5 were broadcasting an hour-long programme about an American girl who was born with a sort of mermaid tail instead of two legs, and I nearly choked on my Somerfield's Worst™ lasagne. I wondered to myself: what if the girl's mother had been through the same ordeal as Stevie?

How many poor victims had that seal had its flippers on?

⊙

When I got back from Philip Lane, the first thing I did was cancel my direct debit to the anti-sealing charity. It was a painful phone call. The woman on the other end clearly had qualifications in making folk feel guilty, and she scolded, 'But you do realise over 500,000 innocent seals are clubbed to death every year?'

I stared blankly at the plastic handset.

'Aye, but you do realise at least one innocent human being got inhumanely bummed to death by a seal this year?' I considered replying. I looked at the ground, scratching my neck.

'To cancel your *much appreciated* charitable donation would be to side with the hunters,' the woman went on, in that machine-like monotone you get from working in a call centre. 'Can you imagine yourself going out and butchering the seals yourself?'

I poked my lips out. As she continued reeling off horrific seal statistics, a plan hatched in my head. With the phone nestled under my chin, I slipped through to the bedroom and began fashioning a selection of harpoons from a pair of knitting needles, a bread knife and a bent javelin Stevie had stashed behind his ex-sock drawer.

⊙

Dressed in full Arctic clobber, I bounded across the dunes, sniffing up the fresh ozone. It was around nine when I got to Seal Sands, the oil refineries and chemical plants just beginning to go to sleep under their purple, dusky duvets. There were still a few birdwatchers, sealwatchers and petrochemicalplantwatchers out in the nature reserve, but soon enough a dark shroud would descend on their binoculars and camera lenses, and they'd have to head home for their teas.

I jog-hopped down towards the mudflats, my makeshift harpoons hidden in a black binliner, fraying the polythene. My feet felt like they had weights attached, dragging me down to the shore. I yawned. I didn't have enough money for the train, so I was suffering the morbid, false tiredness and deep-vein thrombosis you get from sitting on the National Express for six hours; not to mention the thigh-cramps from my journey to Seal Sands on the back of a stranger's motorbike. It took a good half an hour before someone stopped for my Burger King napkin with SEAL

SANDS PLEASE? scrawled in Cheery Cherry lipstick, and it felt strange cuddling a masked stranger as we hurtled at top speed towards the nature reserve. I hummed to myself, transfixed by the chimneys belching and breathing fire in a series of industrial processes as mysterious as the chemical processes that go on in your heart when you fall in and out of love. I sighed into the stranger's back, wondering what his face looked like, underneath the helmet.

Seal Sands is, hands down, the most beautiful place on this planet. The sands themselves are a mixture of black and white crushed glass, surrounded on all sides by the elegant Etch-A-Sketch outlines of chemical works. Rather than being put off by the pollution, the wildlife has grown to love the industry, nesting in its myriad metal nooks and crannies, plus the artificial moonlight emitted after dark provides an extra hour or two of playtime.

As I strode along the edge of the shore, it felt like the insoles of my boots had turned to sandpaper. I cringed, wiggling my toes. Round about, the birds were having a good gossip before bedtime and, over on the foggy horizon, matchstick sailors were no doubt staring at matchstick factories, in their matchstick ships and tankers.

I pressed onwards. It was a surprise to feel such a gale against my face, giving me a complimentary temporary face lift. The Capital never experiences this kind of weather, thanks to its monumental, skyscraping windbreakers, which also double up as offices, Monday–Friday.

I gasped, almost forgetting how to walk and breathe. The industry was glowing so much you couldn't see the sky, but I followed the North Star-like beacon on the top of INEOS along the mudflats, to where a group of blubbery dots were basking on the rocks.

I took out my harpoons, which had various messages attached to them, for the seals:

149

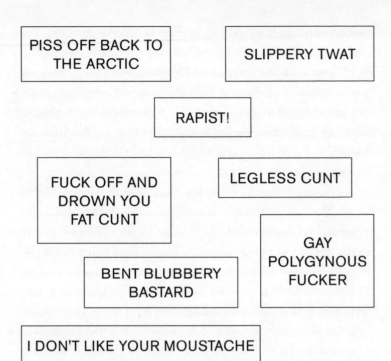

PISS OFF BACK TO THE ARCTIC

SLIPPERY TWAT

RAPIST!

FUCK OFF AND DROWN YOU FAT CUNT

LEGLESS CUNT

GAY POLYGYNOUS FUCKER

BENT BLUBBERY BASTARD

I DON'T LIKE YOUR MOUSTACHE

I smirked, enjoying the witticisms again. As I raised the harpoons aloft in a bundle, the laminated cards hung like paper Stevies in my peripheral vision. I scanned the area for spying sealhunterwatchers, then crept towards the seals, along the wet leopardskin sand. I could hear my breath going wild in the surround-sound of the hood.

Before long, the blubbery dots in the distance became blubbery dots with flippers and whiskers, then fully formed blubbery grey seals. I paused for a moment, glaring at them in the fake, fluorescent moonlight. Then, I made my attack. The hum of the power plants masked my crunching footsteps as I charged full-pelt towards the seals; however, perhaps I shouldn't have let out the screech.

As I skidded across the slick sand, I accidentally made a breathy 'Eeee!' sound. As soon as the first 'E' left my lips, the seals turned their heads at me, then nonchalantly slipped off the rocks, back into the safety of the sea. Unfazed, I carried on striding towards the water, aimlessly firing harpoons at its silver surface. Each impact with the water created a vast, transparent, oscillating dartboard, with the harpoon disappearing into the bullseye. Sadly, though, I didn't manage to pierce any real seal bulls' eyes.

Exasperated, I carried on launching harpoons at the shadows of the bastards beneath the surface, growling at them, 'Die!'

All the roosting birds scattered, thinking I'd lost my mind. Even the light on the lighthouse turned away from me, pretending to beckon in one of the matchstick ships, which had since turned into more of a cigar shape. Meanwhile, I continued gritting my teeth, blindly firing the PISS OFF BACK TO THE ARCTIC knitting needle, then the SLIPPERY TWAT javelin into the low tide. Now and then, a seal popped its head out of the water to spite me, honk honk honking, and I felt my temperature rising. I carried on squealing 'Die!' at the nature reserve, and the distant metal factories sang 'Die' back to me, the word pinging off their shining surfaces.

I crouched in the sand and sighed. My collection of harpoons was spent already – without them, I suddenly felt cold and pathetic. Off in the North Sea, the sardonic honking of the seals had faded to muted trumpets, leaving me with just the swishing sound of the sea, and a distant police siren. I watched the smoky waste products of the industry twist and pirouette in the night air, like ghost ballerinas. I had no idea what I was going to do with myself, so I just squatted and listened as the distant police siren got more and more pronounced on the wind. At first it was just a whisper, then, suddenly, it was roaring at me from the nature reserve car park, and a man in a CLEVELAND POLICE outfit was striding over the hillock.

151

It was time to leave. I shot up from the sand, thrust my hands in my pockets and, Plasticine-legged, hiked back up the sand dunes. I figured one of the birdspotters, or sealspotters, or petro-chemicalplantspotters must've spotted me harassing the seals – or heard me crying 'Die!' and reported me to the authorities. Choking on the breeze, I sped into the marram grass, kicking empty winkle shells and rusted pebbles. The word 'Stop!' rang out behind me, but I didn't stop. Apparently, Stevie used to come running on the dunes here when he was younger, long before he was tormented here. Gritting my teeth, I imagined myself as a young, strapping Stevie, egging myself along the egglike dunes.

Two minutes later, I was exhausted. The Arctic gear had turned into a sort of paddling pool, and my nose stung. I couldn't hear the policeman behind me, so I decided to take a breather, hiding myself in the long, tickly marram grass. I sat there pondering my situation, in the cool of the moon. How had all the raggy threads of my life led me to this? How had I ended up being so nasty, hunting for seals and hiding from the authorities, when all I wanted was to be nice?

I slurped back snot, feeling wrong in the head, like I couldn't quite make sense of reality any more. I scanned the dunes for the soft pitter-patter of footsteps, or the twinkle of a CID badge. The whole place was still and silent, though, apart from the cooling towers still steaming away in the distance, like huge grey cups of cream tea.

In a way, I almost wanted the policeman to come back. Not only would the company be nice, but I might need someone to save me from myself. It was almost tempting to feign madness, to get in the warm of a padded cell for the night – which might well be a sign of madness itself.

Staying in an insane asylum would at least be like a cheaper, more secure version of living in a flat in the Capital. Plus, I'd be presented with a platter of magical mood stabilisers every day and, with minimal effort, I could keep up the nutty act as long as I fancied. All I had to do was shriek 'Die' at people for the rest of my life, with a glazed look in one eye, and I'd be granted free access to a squeaky clean, padded hotel room, with all mad cons.

I brushed the sweat from my forehead. It did worry me, though, that the men in white coats might expose me as a fraud, after a few prods and probings of my grey matter. Perhaps I was better off disappearing altogether – on a plane to Japan, or encased in cement on the bed of the Thames, or in a battleship-grey unit in South Tottenham – and never bothering anyone again. Either option was preferable to taking the long walk of shame to Stevie's mam's in Marton-in-Middlesbrough, and asking for his bed for the night. And having to explain what had gone wrong with my life.

I slipped out from behind the dunes and stamped back down to the shore. There wasn't a seal in sight – just the green, swaying marram grass, dancing to the beat of the factories' off-kilter techno. I pushed onwards, keeping my hood up with one hand as the coat turned from a kind of paddling pool into a kind of kite.

I wondered if there were many dead bodies lying undiscovered in the depths of the North Sea, gathering seaweed in their ribcages; growing coral on their back molars. I wondered if I should add mine to the collection, and be done with it, once and for all. Just as Mother Nature chose not to strike me down with lightning in the internet caff, I decided to put my fate in the hands of the elements again. I kicked off my boots and waded into the water. I figured I'd either drown, die of hypothermia, or be rescued by lifeguards/policemen/mermen, and get a bed for the night. There wasn't another National Express back to the Capital for seven hours – so something had to give.

My feet killed in the surf. I tried to imagine Stevie skinny-dipping in such icy waters – the pain was unbelievable. As I waded through the shallows, I kept stealing glances behind me, praying for that policeman to come back and *Baywatch* me to safety. After a bit, it was obvious no one was going to come. I walked onwards; my eyes fixed on a wishy-washy horizon I'd never reach. Impromptu Suicide Attempt #7 looked to be a winner. I only wished my heart was in it.

As the tide crept up to my kneecaps I squawked 'Die' again, in a spazzy sort of accent. I felt like the anti-Venus, retreating back to the black murk, all life coming to an end around me. I was ready to drop to my knees when, suddenly, I found myself spasming uncontrollably. I was vibrating. I wondered if I'd gone mad after all, or if it was shock setting in. Of course, it was just my phone going off in one of the Arctic pockets. It was a number I didn't recognise. My hands carried on vibrating long after I'd pressed ANSWER. I prayed for the Teesside Mental Health Action Unit.

'Hello?' I groaned, in the spazz accent.

'Hello,' the phone said back. It turned out to be Malcolm's dad, calling from the Wethouse in Shepherd's Bush. I dropped the accent – I didn't want him to think I was taking the mick out of his boy.

'Kimberly,' he carried on, 'how are you, love? So sorry to hear about the restaurant thing. The job. Malc told me. I just thought I'd check in, see how you're doing and all. Are you looking for work? See, we're up to our necks in it over here. There's a bit of a job going, if you want it? Half-decent wage, and all . . .'

I blinked, staring out across the cold, hollow void of the sea.

'Er, yeah, go on then,' I replied.

☉

Walking into the Wethouse was like dropping a pint of strong lager over a first edition of Charles Dickens's *Oliver Twist*, and then slamming it shut on your own face. My belly was twisted with nerves as I pushed open the front door. The exterior of the building was sooty and imposing, like a Victorian poorhouse or haunted castle, set against the bright fabric shops and the chiffon sky. Inside, the place was much lighter and sterile – more like a school canteen or gymnasium. The walls were plastered with adverts for day centres, addiction clinics and MISSING PERSONS posters; then, further down, the walls were bare where some of the MISSING PERSONS posters must've gone missing.

I smiled as wide and cheery as possible at the man with pink eyeballs peeping out from behind the front desk. He seemed weary from too many years dealing with unbearable drunks and overzealous volunteers, and he told me to sign my name, then pushed me off to a small office down a tangerine corridor.

In the office, I found Malcolm's dad balling up a pair of dirty Marigolds. It turned out he'd been clearing up excrement all morning, because I was late. I apologised, with another wide and cheery smile. My lateness was down to me pacing round the green three or four times – plucking up the courage to enter the place – though I blamed it on the Ghost Train: that perfect, catch-all excuse for Capital lateness and laziness. I even went so far as to call it 'the bloody Ghost Train'.

'No worries, love,' Malcolm's dad mumbled, rinsing his hands. It was strange, seeing him outside the Ristorante, on his home turf. At Paolo's, Malcolm's dad came across as a gloomy, antisocial chap; here, he was in his element: rushing about, fingering paperwork, slanging down the telephone, scratching his head.

'Right, love, shall I show you round?' he asked, leading me back out into the corridor. 'Nice easy start today, eh? Introduce

155

you to a few of our residents. But then tomorrow it'll be your call to clean the dorms . . . you know, er, keep the communal areas tidy, housekeeping, take the gang out on the odd day trip, et cetera et cetera . . .'

As Malcolm's dad led me around the Wethouse, he kept confusing me with his jargon. For the whole length of the tangerine corridor, he babbled about 'key working' and 'life mapping', which I think had something to do with making the residents feel happy, and making sure they didn't die. I couldn't imagine the 'gang' took kindly to the jargon – the last thing you want when you're tanked up is a bald, righteous person patronising you.

The idea of it being a wet hostel was daunting, although it made sense not to force the residents to go cold turkey in exchange for a bed. Instead, the idea was to wean them off the stronger gut-rot ales and ciders, and help them realise they've got a boundless, precious life ahead, and 'give the gang their dignity back', Malcolm's dad added.

I wondered where Malcolm was. In the doorways of the dormitories, strange eyes peeked at me. The male eyes seemed to roll excitedly at the prospect of a new female volunteer, while the female eyes squinted at me suspiciously. I was glad I'd worn my most unflattering rollneck.

'The gang have the opportunity to earn a bit of moolah while they're here, through odd jobs and the like – washing windows, et cetera et cetera . . . although it usually gets spent down the off-licence,' Malcolm's dad explained, with a face like a pained mother. 'But we're not here to judge.'

As he led me further down the corridor, Malcolm's dad introduced me to some members of 'the gang'. They didn't seem like a bad bunch: Exclamation Mark was a youngish bloke from the West Country who had a habit of stating the obvious. As I brushed past him he exclaimed, 'You've got a straight old fringe!' then

156

burst into hysterics and fell against the wall. I smirked politely. Lurking by the ladies, the Moaner Lisa was grumbling into a can of Strongbow. From twenty yards away, Malcolm's dad called at her, 'How you diddling, Lisa, love? Chin up, dear.' That just set her off even more, though.

The Wethouse was a lot different to the Ristorante di Fantasia. Instead of fresh ciabatta and balsamic vinegar, wafts of disinfectant and sock-vinegar came sailing round the corridors with us. The Wethouse wasn't bad, though – it was more like a cheap, eccentric hotel than a prison. The residents were free to wander about the place as they pleased, and they could even go out strolling the Bush, providing they were back by 9 p.m.

'They forfeit their bed if they're not back in time,' Malcolm's dad explained solemnly.

'Die!' one of the female slatherers hissed at us, as we slipped past the last dormitory. My heart pounded. For a second, a sharp sense of déjà vu flashed in my head, like a comet appearing and disappearing in one millisecond, just before you've had time to grab for your telescope.

'Now, now, Kimberley,' Malcolm's dad hushed, referring to the slatherer, not me. I stiffened, glancing through the gap in the door at my namesake. It was like looking into a dirty mirror. Kimberley Clarke was a similar build to me but, instead of a Guillotine, she had a ponytail that looked more like a noose. Instead of turquoise eyeshadow, she had black and blue bags under her eyes. And, in place of the rollneck, she had on a baggy blue Nike sweater, and scuffed jeans. I smiled sweetly at her, despite having just been told to die.

'Die,' Kimberley grunted again, leering at me.

'Now, now, Kimberley. Look, meet Kimberly. She's going to be working here from tomorrow . . .' Malcolm's dad announced, then he whispered in my ear, 'Don't worry, love, she says "Die"

157

to everyone. She's a bit . . . *wrong in the head*. Don't take it personal.'

I smiled, but it was hard keeping the smile fixed, what with my cheeks twitching so much.

'Good to meet you,' I ventured, clinging to the doorframe. I didn't think a handshake or an air-kiss was appropriate.

'Good to meet you,' Kimberley spat, wriggling on her bedcovers.

Malcolm's dad brought his prickly lips to my ear again and sighed, 'Oh, Kimberley does have a habit of repeating everything. Just, er . . . ignore it, if you can.'

I nodded.

'Alright, well, cheerio, Kimberley,' I said, walking backwards.

'Alright, well, cheerio,' Kimberley hissed. 'Has anyone ever told you, love, you look like the spawn of a necrophiliac?'

'Er, no,' I replied.

'Behave, Kimberley. We'll see you in a bit,' Malcolm's dad said, closing her door gently behind us.

'Die,' Kimberley muttered as it creaked shut.

I felt sick as we traipsed off towards the communal area, or 'TV lounge', as it liked to be called. Malcolm's dad touched my back as we sat down at one of the plastic tables by the window. He seemed impressed with my handling of Kimberley, and I wondered if she was just an actress, put there to test me on my first day. Her skin was so pale, she seemed almost like an apparition.

'Why does she say "Die" all the time, then?' I asked Malcolm's dad later on, over a polystyrene cup of Nescafé.

'Oh,' he laughed, 'she's alright, that Kimberley. She doesn't mean nothing. She's just a bit, well, she's depressed. She got diagnosed with this DID, dissociative identity disorder thing. Like a multiple personality disorder. Sometimes she calls herself Anastasia. I don't know – I think she's had a tough life: she was adopted, bad parenting, etcetera. We don't like to ask, though –

we just like to . . . try and give answers. Hope, and solutions. I think, well, I think she just wants someone to put her out of her misery . . . but it's our job to put Kimberley's *misery* out of its misery . . . ha ha.'

I nodded, burning my top lip on the edge of the cup. I stared out of the window, at next door's red brick wall, turning redder and redder as the sun came out.

'See, Kimberley can be a handful,' Malcolm's dad said, bringing his face closer to mine again. 'She can be nasty, suicidal, she can be murderous, she'll push you to the edge . . . but she's still one of us. Remember that.'

I nodded again, my face also reddening. I knew Malcolm's dad was saying the word 'Kimberley', but he could've just as well been saying 'Kimberly'. I sucked out the last of the muddy coffee, wondering what the hell I was letting myself in for.

'Let's just make sure Kimberley doesn't die, eh?' Malcolm's dad added with a smirk.

I couldn't agree more.

⊙

For the next few weeks, I suffered from a terminal illness: the Cockfosters blues. The sky-blue line was off for planned engineering works, so I had to suffer the slower dark blue line to get home each night from the Wethouse, breathing in all the germs and seminal fluids of the Love Train for three minutes and three stops more than necessary.

I spent most mornings with my head down the Wethouse toilets, continually throwing up and cleaning up after the gang. I felt like my skull had been replaced with a pillowcase full of cymbals, clashing about every time I moved. My nose dripped green mucus while the Kimberly-Clarks dripped pink handwash, in a never-ending battle to rid my body of bacteria.

159

Despite all the new illnesses, the job was going alright. It was harder work than the Ristorante, even though a lot of it involved sitting in the TV lounge with the residents, or making cups of tea, or sailing down the Thames with them in a catamaran. I'd made a few friends already – Exclamation Mark was already exclaiming his love for me, and the Moaner Lisa regularly used my shoulder to cry, or nod off, on – but I'd made a few enemies as well. Kimberley Clarke, notably, or the fiery fellows who appear to have finished their drinks, then kick off at me for putting them in the bin for them. It was difficult managing a hotel full of drunks – all of them in different stages of inebriation, tetchiness, horn, and nausea. Again, the trick was to be as nice as humanly possible; trying to earn the respect of the residents; all the while, not letting them walk all over me.

On the last Monday in August – a Bank Holiday – I wasted the afternoon sheltering under an Out of Service bus stop, staring at myself in the puddles. I thought I was safe leaving the flat without the scarlet raincoat, but no sooner had I reached the peak of Stamford Hill than the heavens tore open. I was still suffering from city malaise, so I snuck under the first suitable shelter, waiting for an imaginary bus, or for the rain to stop – whichever came first.

I hardly recognised myself in the wobbling water. Flu has a habit of making you feel detached and unattractive – so too does no make-up. In fact, everything around me looked grey and miserable that afternoon – from the crooked paving slabs in front of me to the glistening wet, phallic skyscrapers of the City-within-a-city, way out east.

I wanted the imaginary bus to turn up and take me away from the Capital. I watched planes sail through the puddles, and I wished I was on them.

Many people come to the Capital to 'find themselves' but, in fact, the Capital steals your identity, over time: first, it messes

160

with your dress sense, then it softens your accent, then it sours your sense of humour, then, before you know it, your whole personality's been pulverised. In the reflections, the ripples made me look elderly. I let more planes, birds, clouds and cars become intermingled with my fluctuating facial features until, suddenly, a Hi-Tech trainer and snakeskin loafer stamped me out completely.

'Hello, missus, my name is Donald. I'm not on drugs, I don't drink – I just need one ninety-nine for a cheeseburger and chips,' said a voice.

I hoped Donald wouldn't recognise me without my make-up on. For the first time since meeting him, I didn't have any money for him. Unlike the Ristorante di Fantasia, the wage at the Wethouse was barely enough to pay my rent and travel, and the only tips I got were 'get your rat out', 'sort your hair out', or 'get off the cans'. Not only that, but the six direct debits I still had set up to charities were taking their toll on my savings, and I didn't fancy cancelling them and facing another call-centre jobsworth/eternal damnation.

'Angel!' Donald spluttered, recognising me anyway.

'Donald. How are you?' I asked, more nasal than usual.

'Dying, dying, dying for a drink. Know what I mean?'

I knew what he meant. Donald wanted me to spoil him with Warzones again, but I had to muster up apologetic eyes, and say, 'Ahh, Don. I'm skint myself.'

'Just some cans?'

'I'm dead sorry. I lost that job, at the Italian place,' I said, patting where my pockets would've been, had I been wearing the raincoat.

'Just one can?'

'I'm sorry. I just . . . I've got nowt on me . . . and the banks aren't open, and . . .' I trailed off, feeling terrible. I wondered if my powers as a nice human being were faltering, or whether the people

161

around me were just getting greedier and needier, and asking too much of me. The curse of the financially unsound philanthropist.

Donald looked to the ground. I felt the Devil whipping me invisibly from across the street. I had my Maestro card in my purse and £1,245.93 in my account, but I also had several bills magnetised to my fridge, and not much food inside it. I could've snuck into an off-licence and slipped a case of Warzone under my raincoat, but I didn't think that'd be very nice on the shop-keeper. And I wasn't wearing the raincoat.

'If there's anything else I can do, I'll help,' I said, shivering, despite the humidity. 'Anything you want.'

In the puddles, I saw fifteen thousand twitching Donalds.

'There is one thing,' he mumbled.

⊙

While Donald was in the shower, I made a cup of Best-in and stared at the carpet. As the coffee hit the bottom of my belly, I suffered convulsions. I could hear Donald humming while he cleaned himself, with the faulty showerhead penny-whistling in accompaniment. I could also hear him squirting out all my magic bottles of gel, shampoo and the Japanese Spa shower cream. I imagined fifty-odd years of dirt running off his body like black tar. I imagined myself scrubbing away his scum-line.

When I heard the taps go off, I kneeled back on the bed and took off my clothes. It was warm in the bedroom, but I still looked like a frozen prawn in a wig. I waited silently for Donald.

It was a relief to hear him brushing his teeth, though I made a mental note to buy a new toothbrush once the ordeal was over. After three minutes of brushing, I heard Donald rubbing himself dry with the Tigger towel, which I'd been planning on chucking out anyway. I unsnapped my bra and pulled down my knickers.

162

I was hiding under the gingham bedcovers when Donald finally emerged, sporting a semi-erect penis. He must've been fluffing himself in the bathroom. I smiled halfheartedly. Donald's naked body looked like two pairs of crutches and a xylophone wrapped in cellophane. Despite all the scrubbing in the shower, he still looked filthy, as if the grime of the Capital had congealed over his flesh, creating a brand-new, greyish/yellowish skin. When Donald came over to sit on the bed, I noticed his permablack fingertips and toetips, and the red and white smegma wounds round his foreskin. A spoonful of vomit leapt up and down my throat.

'And we definitely can't kiss?' Donald enquired, showing off his scurvy.

'Aw, sorry, no. And, like, I was going to say . . .' I started, desperately racking my brains for a get-out clause, 'it might sound weird, but I've got this fetish thing. If we're going to have . . . *sex* . . . we've got to do it through plastic. It's like a hygiene thing. Like a fetish.'

Donald's heart and semi-on shrivelled slightly, although he still seemed up for it. Beggars cannot be choosers.

I switched off the lamp, then hopped self-consciously out of bed and scampered to the bathroom. I unclipped the wet, still bubbling shower curtain from the rail, gave it a shake and dragged it back through to the dark bedroom. Two bloodshot eyeballs followed me as I rummaged, flustered, round the flat for a pair of Marigolds, and scissors. I cut a hole in the middle of the shower curtain, with a diameter of about three inches. Then, I pulled on the yellow Marigolds and threw Donald a blue, hypochondriac-proof 'extra safe' condom.

At first, Donald had trouble rolling the johnny onto his dangling member, so I lathered up the Marigolds with Vaseline, and mechanically wanked him for a minute or so. As he got stiff, I could feel the skin cracking round the smegma wounds. Never-

163

theless, he seemed to be having a good time, blowing out hot, pungent 'Uh, uh, uh's.

Once Donald was fully erect, I lay back on the bedcovers and laid the shower curtain over myself from head to toe, lining the hole up with my terrified vagina. The poor thing looked startled, as Donald inserted himself hastily through both holes, without even pausing to unstick my lips. I grunted. On my side of the curtain, I tried to work a bit of Vaseline into the danger area, but it just ended up getting matted in our hairs.

For a while, Donald kept his eyes shut, now and then pressing his face where the sheet was stuck to my lips and tits. Soon, the shower curtain was coated on both sides with sweat and saliva, sliding this way and that while Donald thrusted clumsily. I tried to anaesthetise myself, counting the swirls of Artex on the ceiling, but they were blurry swirls. Whenever I inhaled, I caught a whiff of the Japanese Spa shower cream – I tried to focus on that sweet stench, again imagining myself as a high-class Japanese geisha, rather than a rubber-gloved tramp-skank. But it didn't last.

Another sickly sense of déjà vu flashed in my head. Pressed against the oversized piece of plastic, with all his facial wounds and rotten meat, Donald reminded me of Meaty Stevie. I swallowed down another spoonful of vomit, then spun myself onto my haunches, and buried my head into the pillows. I couldn't watch. I shuddered while he kept bucking me, repeating to myself, silently, 'I'm a wonderful, selfless human . . . I'm a wonderful, selfless human . . .'

'Stop wriggling,' Donald urged. It was hard to hear through the sheet, but I could've sworn he said next, 'I wish you were dead.'

It turned out Donald had a fetish, too. But no talent in pillow talk.

I made a wet circle in the centre of my pillow, drooling, desperate for it to end. I tried to count the individual stitches in the blue and white fabric, while Donald carried on carving holes through me. At one point, he accidentally-on-purpose drilled through my arsehole.

I got to fifty-seven stitches by the time Donald reached climax. Veins bulged in my forehead, as Donald's Jap's-eye bulged open in the condom. Once he'd let go of me, the wet curtain stayed scrunched around my back, like he'd shed his skin and left it as a memento. I peeled it away from my cold, clammy flesh, then balled it up and stuffed it into a binbag. I grimaced as I plodded across the carpet, noticing the tiny specks of red and brown which had collected in the Vaseline.

I swayed about awkwardly on the spot as Donald pulled off the condom. There was a small stool sample attached to the reservoir end. Donald looked unfazed as he lobbed it towards the binbag, though it took him three attempts to get it in.

Satisfied and shattered, Donald laid back down on my bed, leaving a stain. I kept my eyes to the ground.

'Ehm,' he mumbled, after a long, dismal silence, 'so you definitely can't get me a drink?'

Kimberly Clark in . . . the Return of Two Characters You Thought She'd Forgotten About*

To wee or not to wee, that is the question.

Donald had given me cystitis. For the next couple of weeks, every time I went to the toilet my vagina burned, like I was pissing out turpentine and someone was setting fire to it. On top of that, I had periods coming out of my bottom. No matter how soft or slender my turds, without fail they split open my anus, producing the most vivid, scarlet toilet water.

* Or: 'Kimberly Clark in . . . the Return of the Chapter Titles You Thought She'd Forgotten About'.

Donald hadn't half given me rough sex. My cervix felt like an over-twanged elastic band. I don't think he meant to be so violent with me – I think he just hadn't had sex in a very, very long time.

I felt crummy all through summer. I whiled away the journey to the Wethouse each morning with a carton of cranberry juice: every housewife's favourite cure for cystitis. My rectum had prolapsed, so I tended to stand all the way to the Bush, much to the delight of the pregnant and elderly ladies of the Subterranean Love Train. I smiled tight, bright red cranberry lips at them.

Despite being a regular at Wood Green Boots, I wouldn't be seen dead buying Anusol. At the Wethouse, Malcolm's dad couldn't understand why I was walking like Charlie Chaplin all of a sudden. He just frowned at me each morning, instead of saying 'Hello', while I grabbed the mop and laundry trolley from the store cupboard. It was my job to change the sheets and clean out the dorms that week, trundling systematically up and down the corridors to the sound of groaning bedframes and groaning old men.

Occasionally, the gang left me presents in their dorms, such as boiled sweets, unfinished cans of Super Skol or strange notes in strange handwriting. That morning, I found one which said CAN YOU CLEAN MY RINGPULLS, while another read BE WARE THE PASTA MEN ARE COMING, in a childish, spasmodic scrawl.

Occasionally, the gang left me diarrhoea in their beds. If one of the residents happened to soil themselves the night before, it was my job to clean them up and sort out new bedclothes. Fortunately, the week had gone by so far without any upsets. I was almost having a nice time, turning each floor from matt tan to glossy mahogany with my mop, until, that is, I came to Kimberley's dormitory.

I knocked once, bracing myself. There was a shuffling sound behind the door, then a bloodcurdling squeal as I pushed it softly open. Kimberley was standing on her bed, dressed head to toe in

166

black and white, with four pairs of shoelaces tied round her neck and strung to the curtain-rail. I made a choking, gasping sound, banging out pulses in places I never knew I had them. I wondered if she'd been waiting for me. On cue, as soon as we made eye contact, Kimberley leapt off the bed, grinning for a few seconds in defiance of the Earth's gravitational pull. Gradually, though, the smile faded as Kimberley's face went red, then purple, then blue. I shrieked, lunging at her with my arms outstretched.

'Diee! Diiee! Diiii!' Kimberley screeched at me, hardly able to talk, with the noose wrapped so tight around her voice box. In a moment of inspiration, I clambered onto Kimberley's bed, and pulled with all my girly might at the curtain-rail. The plastic was flimsy and the screws were a bit rusty and, after a couple of hefty tugs, the whole rail came loose from the wall. Me, Kimberley and the curtains came crashing to the ground, with a horrid thud.

'What are you doing?!' I yelled, in a whisper. 'You don't want to kill yourself.'

'What the fuck are *you* doing?' Kimberley groaned back.

I grabbed at the shoelaces round her neck, loosened the noose and pulled her to her feet again. I shook my head. To make a point, I was about to set to work on Kimberley's bedsheets when, suddenly, she ripped open one of her empty cans of cider and began going at her jugular with the serrated edge. I grabbed her arms, then, for five minutes, we tug-of-warred with the can: Kimberley trying to pierce both our throats with it; Kimberly trying to save us.

I hated that woman. In the pocked mirror, we looked like twins; a pair of conjoined dogs, chasing our own tails.

Eventually, the serrated can fell out of Kimberley's hand and I managed to punt it out of her dormitory and halfway down the corridor.

'Why can't you just be nice?' I gasped.

167

Kimberley cackled – a spine-twisting cackle that made even the crumpled curtains quiver.

'Why can't *you* just be nice?' she jeered. 'You're not fucking superior.'

I decided there and then I was going to quit the job. I slung the mop against Kimberley's bedhead, then charged off down the corridor to the sound of fading, reverberating laughter. I used to think it was strenuous working at the Ristorante di Fantasia, holding cups and plates and stroking men's necks with my bosoms. At the Wethouse, I was a slave to my own worst nightmare: myself.

As I marched down the square-spiral staircase, I had all these overblown, romantic ideas of leaving the Capital for good. There was no need to stay, after all – I'd only come to keep Stevie company while he ran round his racetracks. However, a move back to Teesside was daunting, too. At least, in the Capital, the anonymity allows all your shameful personality traits to go more or less unnoticed. Elsewhere, in the smaller, more tightly knit towns of Britain, it would be all too easy for people to realise I was a miserable, malingering battleaxe.

Then again, there was always the lure of abroad. Tears hid in my throat as I wondered what I was going to say to Malcolm's dad:

'I've just been offered a better job, in a better hostel!'

'I'm a fucky prostitute!'

'Stick your job up your arse, you big daft twat!'

All I knew was I had to get out of the Wethouse. The reception was unusually busy that afternoon, and I glanced heavy-lidded at all the roaming beasts: louts with gaunt cheeks and distended beer bellies; Father Christmas-a-likes with sacks full of Super Skol; skeletal ladies; a shrieking dwarf wearing nothing but Bermuda shorts; a human swearbox; a wolf threatening to huff and puff and blow the TV lounge down; and a two-headed monster with hair like Hitler and a rather tight T-shirt.

168

'Kk,' the monster spouted in disbelief.

I hardly recognised the two of them, so downtrodden were they, with downturned mouths and faces the colour of old bedsheets. We shared a hug, lurching awkwardly in the packed corridor.

At first I thought there'd been a death at the Wethouse, and Shaun and Sean had come to sweep the body off to their new-fangled funeral parlour but, instead of a black body-bag, they both had blue sleeping bags, and one grubby rucksack between them.

SHAUN	KIMBERLY	SEAN
Kk		
		Ey up, Kimberly
	As if, lads! What youse doing here?*	
		Aw, sort . . . long story
	How's the funeral business coming on?	
It went a bit tits-up		
		Fucking understatement
Fuck off, it's bad enough as—		
		Tit
See, it turned out we—		
		We needed more than five grand to set it up
And the bank wouldn't help us out		
		Bad credit
But it's more than that		
		Aye
We blew the money		
		We're really sorry, Kim
At the bookies		
		Boro were meant to win
Fucking knob		
		Fuck off
I bet even Kim knows never to bet on the Boro		
	Not really	

* Note my accent magically reappearing in the presence of fellow Teessiders.

169

At this point, the two-headed monster started fighting with itself, throwing fists around, growling and cursing. I tried to break them up, but it was difficult, what with them being twice my size and joined at the hip.

Lads, lads

You fucking prick

Look, Kimberly, we're
dead sorry

We can't really pay it
back

We're fucked

Cos, we lost the house
and everything

And, like, the Court's
after us

Unpaid whatnots

You lost *everything*?

We know we've got a
problem, like

Fucking, it's an
addiction

But not our fault, like

Yes, the first step to getting rid of your problem is admitting you've got a problem. I wondered if they wanted me to cheer and pat them on the back. I just stared at them. The four eyes stared back. I felt terrible. It wasn't just that they'd lost all of Stevie's money – it was the crushing realisation that another of my good deeds had turned sour. Before Stevie died, I was a relatively happy housewife, and Shaun and Sean had comfortable jobs in the lifeguard and cocktail industries. Now, we were three sorry souls in a homeless hostel, with two sleeping bags, bad credit, and a prolapsed arsehole between us.

I had to leave. I gave Shaun and Sean a slight thump on each shoulder, then stormed out of the Wethouse with eyes like kitchen sinks. I bawled as I trawled down Uxbridge Road. I wanted to jump under the Ghost Train but, instead, I jumped onto an empty carriage and rode it back, wet-nosed, to Seven Sisters.

By the time I reached the top of the escalator, I realised I'd been so annoyed with Shaun and Sean, I'd forgotten to quit the job.

Kimberly Clark Finds (and Loses) . . . the Secret to Eternal Youth

If it wasn't for the Halloween decorations in the windows of Tesco, I might've made it through October without even realising my birthday had come, or gone. I could've side-stepped it, staying blissfully unaware and blissfully twenty-three years old until next year. Once you hit adulthood, birthdays are a nuisance. They're like an obnoxious, loudmouthed infant who says to you 'God, you're old' once a year, in front of all your friends.

It snowed the day before my birthday, catching me off-guard when I dragged open the curtains to find the world had turned white. I blinked wildly, half-asleep, half-blind. Everything seemed to be in slow motion: cars edging nervously in single file down the High Road; pedestrians hobbling, flat-footed, with their arms outstretched. It made me sad to see a few young and old folk slip over on the ice, bashing their bottoms and elbows; their hands red raw. In Britain, snow is a horrendous natural disaster. I felt a bit selfish, sipping coffee in the safety of the flat, while everyone outside struggled valiantly against the half-inch of snow. I considered going out to buy some industrial-strength antifreeze, to cure the pavements, but I didn't have the pennies for it.

Halloween has always been a strange time for me. Not only does it herald my birthday, it also heralds the evening all the local ghosts and ghouls come round to my house, demanding my sweets and birthday money. I wasn't looking forward to the next day's festivities. With Stevie gone, I had no expectations of

171

receiving any cards, let alone any birthday money.

Nevertheless, I didn't fancy getting my windows egged. To be on the safe side, I wrapped myself in the Arctic gear and grudgingly trudged up the High Road, to stock up on pick-n-mix from big Sainsbury's. It was treacherous out. It took me almost five minutes to travel the first 200 metres, compared to Stevie's personal best of 20.97 seconds, albeit in much better conditions.

In Sainsbury's, I filled my basket with chewable Vitamin C tablets as well as the sweets, then clodhopped back down the hill, with a lemon-sharp facial expression. The snow seemed less slippery down the back alleys, but I still took a few dives as I skated between the wheelie-bins. I hoped no one was sitting by their windows, sipping coffee and watching. Halfway down the first alley, I came across a couple of youngish lads, struggling to unload some electrical gear from their lime green Fiat Punto. They must've been moving house, or else they'd bought all their Christmas presents early. I offered to help, since one of them was good-looking, and their trainers didn't seem to have much grip.

At first, they seemed suspicious, when I dropped my Sainsbury's bag and grabbed hold of one of the tellies, but I wasn't going to run off with their fancy goods – not in this weather. I flashed a smile, breathing heavily as we hoisted a Hitachi hi-fi, Acer laptop, Bush hi-fi, Panasonic TV, iBook, Epson Stylus printer, and another Panasonic hi-fi out of the fuzzy boot, like deconstructing a very expensive game of Jenga.

'You must like music, then,' I said to the good-looking one. He just laughed, slamming the boot shut with his elbow. I laughed back, possibly too loudly.

Once we got all the gear in through the back door, I half expected the lads to give me a hug, or offer me a cuppa. In the end, they just nodded and gave me a halfhearted 'Cheers'. I hobbled back to my Sainsbury's bag. I wiped my nose. I watched the back gate squeak shut and, with it, my one and only chance of spending my birthday with a man with nice facial features.

I tugged at my coat toggles and toddled onwards. Going back to the flat seemed unappealing now – I didn't want to spend my birthday weekend sitting in silence, accidentally eating all those sweets, and calling myself fat in the mirror. After all, Malcolm's dad had forced me into taking three days off, so I felt obliged to at least try and make the most of it. I was almost tempted to tart myself up and head down to China White that evening, to find the Square-Faced Bachelor, or any other suitable polygon-faced stranger. However, deep down, I knew my destiny was just to get drunk with the old duffers down the Dutch Pub, before dithering back to the flat at daft o'clock, eating all those sweets anyway, and still calling myself fat in the mirror.

Onwards, then, to the Dutch Pub. While birthdays can be like an obnoxious, loudmouthed infant, they can also be like a precocious, foulmouthed student, pressurising you into having fun against your will. Surely the anniversary of your sloppy, traumatic extraction from a human's womb should be spent sedately sipping coffee and staring out of the window at snowflakes, not getting slaughtered. Nevertheless, I had my heart set on finding a new man, and I certainly wouldn't find him amongst the rubble of the flat.

The Dutch Pub was more or less empty when I got there. I plonked myself down in the corner with an extra-large Smirnoff Ice, feeling embarrassed. The whole point of having friends is so you don't look awkward in pubs and nightclubs. Luckily, the speakers were screaming Europop at an ungodly volume, so the barman or the fellow with the *Mirror* couldn't hear me shuffling about and sniffing. After a few more Smirnoffs, the place began to fill up, and I fooled myself into thinking Mr Sunday might turn up with someone else's nan (or, better still, on his own, with a red rose between his teeth), and sweep me off my feet. In the dream, I wore easy-on clogs and an easy-off dirndl.

After another lonely hour or so, with slushy self-hatred setting in, I peeled myself off the leatherette stool and decided to call it a night. The sun had won its staring-out competition with the snow, melting a path for the pedestrians, though I still took a few more dives on my way home. That could've just been the drinks, though.

The combination of crisp, Christmassy air, streaky headlights and snowfall kept me from crying as I tottered up the last stretch of the High Road. Before I got to the flat, it took six or seven rummages in my handbag to find my keys and, when I lunged blindly for my front door, I was surprised to find it was already open. The hallway was crammed with sour-faced residents, and two men in black outfits with NECROPOLITAN POLICE badges. A rush of blood flushed my cheeks.

It turned out we'd been burgled. My stomach tightened – I hoped they hadn't taken Lucifer.

I wobbled on the soft concrete, drunk and dumbstruck. There was a lot of damage and mess up the stairway, and all the surfaces were dusted in silver, like a greasy robot had been rubbing himself up against the furnishings. My voice sounded distant and rodent-like as I gave the police my name and details, such as which flat I lived in, and what I'd been up to that afternoon. I didn't mention the dream about the dirndl.

My neighbours appeared to be full-time workers, which meant the best time to burgle them was between the hours of 9 a.m. and 5 p.m., Monday–Friday. They looked shattered, but smartly dressed.

I took a few deep breaths, trying to sober up. As it turned out, Lucifer was alright. In fact, they hadn't stolen anything from my flat (D), since it was on the third floor, and burglars aren't

174

keen on long, creaking stairwells. Even so, it made you shudder, the thought of someone having so much disrespect for your one and only home in the world, barging in, smashing up your fixtures and fittings, then taking off, like magpies, with your hard-earned trinkets. By the looks on my neighbours' faces, a lot of trinkets had disappeared that afternoon. They'd written out a list for the Necropolice. Underneath the police address and incident number, I saw written:

HITACHI HI-FI
ACER LAPTOP
BUSH HI-FI
PANASONIC TV
iBOOK
EPSON STYLUS PRINTER
PANASONIC HI-FI

My skull split open, and four-and-twenty blackbirds flew out.

I wanted to sneak off to my room, wash away the robot fingerprints and smother my head in a pillow, but the policemen wanted us to stay a bit longer, for an uneasy chat. They'd found a wood plane amongst our shoes in the hallway, and they pointed out the door had been easily kicked in because some idiot had made it so good and loose. Had it been flush, the burglars might not have been able to do the trick with the door, let alone kick it through. My cheeks twitched. I could feel my neighbours' eyes drilling holes through me. I decided to admit the plane was mine – the seven Smirnoff Ices forced me into it.

'I was just trying to be nice,' I murmured. I considered offering my neighbours some sweets, but I guessed no amount of rhubarb-and-custards could bring back their electrical goods. They carried on scowling as I shifted from foot to foot. Strangely, it seemed the only thing that might've made them a bit happier was if I'd lost all my trinkets too.

In the end, I sloped off silently, up the stairwell, trying to avoid an argument. Behind me, I could hear the policemen's pens tutting as they scratched more notes into their pads. I couldn't bring myself to mention the two youngish lads and the lime green Punto – I felt bad enough causing the burglary, let alone helping with the getaway and putting my fingerprints all over the stolen goods.

That night I went about scrubbing the silver dust from everyone's doorways, although it meant waking some of them up and being scolded again. I felt pathetic. When I finally got tucked up in bed, I tossed and turned on the lumpy mattress, wishing the good-looking one's badly behaved fingerprints weren't soaking away in the corner of my bedroom, in a bucket. In a way, I wished they were all over my body, attached to the rest of him.

Kimberly Clark in . . . Halloween XXIV

There's nothing like a good burglary to make you feel uneasy in your own home. As predicted, I woke up alone on my birthday morning, with hair like snakes and ladders in my tights. I rose just before 9 a.m., to the sound of my neighbours' grumpy footsteps, thumping around the building.

I hoped they all had insurance.

I re-straightened the bedcovers, then re-straightened the Guillotine. In the fridge there were a couple of crusts, which I turned into toast, and, as I sat crunching them on the windowsill, I knew I had to get out of the flat. By the sound of those thumping footsteps, none of my neighbours had insurance. I finished the crusts and set my compass for my last remaining friend in the Capital. I slithered down the stairs on tiptoes, hoping to avoid contact with Mrs A or Mr B or Mr and Mrs C. I had to do a new trick with the door: gently unbolting the brand-new

Yale lock, and closing it as quietly as possible behind me. On my way out, I checked the WELCOME mat for birthday cards, but nobody loved me.

I was frozen by the time I got to Tooting. My Promiscuous Pal Polly from Southampton opened one of the many front doors in Tooting, and I stepped through it and smiled. Her house was a cross between your grandma's sitting room and an old brothel. She'd left the paisley wallpaper and faded pouffe, and she'd also left skimpy underwear and fishnet tights round the radiators and round the carpet. The fishnets were giving off a weird smell – either she'd been catching mackerel in them, or they hadn't been washed for a while. I sat as far away from them as possible, on the counter in the kitchen.

Polly was cooking an assortment of Mexican food – she'd decided to celebrate my birthday by seeing in the Dia de los Muertos with burritos, tacos, chicken fajitas and enchiladas. And tequila.

We were smashed by the time it got dark, rummaging sloppy-fingered through her dressing-up box for suitable Halloween costumes. Polly was a sceptic when it came to three things: celibacy, teetotalism, and ghosts. Her issue with ghosts stemmed from her stepfather's seasonal seances, conducted in his shed with like-minded phasmophiles from Hampshire. In seven years, not once did Polly see or sense a phantom; all she could see in that shed was mid-life madness. Nevertheless, Polly was happy to make herself look ghoulish for the night. She was always willing to become someone else, in the name of entertainment and/or escapism.

Polly covered her thick, cream foundation with thick, green Frankenstein make-up, and we tried to screw a bolt into the side of her head, but she reckoned it was hurting her too much. I tugged the off-white mattress-cover off her mattress, and Polly let me pierce two eye-holes in it, to create a reasonable ghost outfit. It might've been more convincing if the sheet hadn't been patterned with semen streaks, period blobs and thousands of unidentifiable pieces of fluff. After five minutes of laughing at ourselves, we headed over to the shop in the monster clobber, to stock up on more sweets and turn our pound coins into ten- and twenty-pence pieces, for the kids. I doubted Polly wanted her windows egging, either.

I was having a whale of a time under that sheet. I wasn't sure if it was the costumes, or the tequila – or both – but, before long, I managed to forget about the burglary, and the rest of my bad fortune. I understood now why Donald and the folk at the Wet-house enjoyed drinking so much: it gives your shit life soft edges. While we walked, I wanted to grab Polly and cling on to this precious moment for ever, but it was difficult getting my arms out from under the mattress-cover.

'BOO!' we howled at passers-by, but they ignored us. They were ghosts and zombies too, except without the fabulous sense of humour or the costumes. Or the alcohol.

Back in Polly's pad, we polished off the first Cuervo bottle and a few Doritos, then tried to make a dent on the sweets, for our afters. The kids started coming around five – some of them with their mams and dads, but mostly dragging along sulking older brothers or sisters. Depending on the mood, me and Polly pretended to be terrified of the costumes; or we put on a kind of pantomime, which involved Polly's arm being chopped off with a meat cleaver, and the walls of her hallway being splattered with tomato sauce. The kids loved it, screaming and running away as fast as their legs could carry them.

We must've dished out about twenty or thirty quid by the time the last tiny terror toddled off down Welham Road, rolypolying full of sweets. Me and Polly swaggered back through to the sit-

178

ting room, dancing to no music. The tequila was beginning to taste like salty bathwater, so we cracked open a bottle of Bianco Bianco BIANCO BIANCO BIANCO, then carried on tossing ourselves around the room. We felt like poltergeists, making the furniture topple over, or launching Doritos through the air into each other's mouths.

Later, Polly left me revolving in the mattress-cover to busy herself with something in the kitchen. I felt gloriously nauseous. When Polly returned, she had a large washing-up bowl of liquid, with fruit floating in it.

'Punch!' I yelped.

'No, no – *apple bobbing*,' Polly snickered. We placed the bowl on the dining room table, although technically it wasn't a dining room – it was just a slightly different part of her sitting room. Technically it wasn't a table, either – more just a cabinet with a chair next to it.

I volunteered to go first, quickly yanking off the sheet and throwing my head into the bowl. The cold water was refreshing at first – until my brain got starved of oxygen, and the Granny Smiths turned into bright pink sea anemones.

'How is it?' Polly giggled, kindly holding my hair back, like a half-arsed torturer/interrogator.

I gurgled wordless bubbles. It took three or four plunges to finally get my teeth round one of the apples.

'Not bad,' I answered, pulling it out of my gob on a long leash of saliva. We laughed.

Polly tied her hair back with a bobble, then gingerly lowered her head into the soupy froth. I smirked as she writhed helplessly in the shallows, green buoys swirling around her. She wasn't very talented at it. She kept making seal honks whenever she came up for air, and I shuddered, mopping my face with the mattress-cover. The fourth time Polly came up for air, the Frankenstein

179

make-up had more or less dissolved. By the seventh gasp, her thick foundation had disappeared, too. She plunged her pasty face back into the water for another twenty seconds, at which point ('Thank fuck,' I mouthed) she finally got her teeth round one of the apples.

I cheeeeeeered, just to be nice, then I fell silent. I stared at Polly, put off by something. With all her make-up gone, I could see a plum-coloured patch of bruises round her left eye-socket, like a cheap Phantom of the Opera mask.

'Are you alright?' I asked.

'Yeah. Just soaking,' Polly slurred, smiling.

'Naw, I mean the bruises . . .' I said, gesturing at my own face, though I was referring to hers.

'Shit,' Polly said, running off to look at herself in the mirror. While she was in the bathroom, I heard her say again, 'Shit.'

'Are you alright?' I called out, again. I could hear her heavy breaths clanging off the sharp porcelain walls. I didn't want her to cry.

'Not really. It's that . . . fucking Persian again,' Polly eventually replied, referring to Mr No Tomorrow.

My eyes dipped. I knew there was something sinister about him. Anyone who takes a girl bungee-jumping on a first date must have some problems with their brain cells.

I went through to the bathroom, as white as a sheet, even without the sheet. I put my cold, damp hands around Polly and squeezed her. She wasn't one to roll tears, but her face looked pained, as she explained what had been going on between her and Mr No Tomorrow. It sounded fairytale-ish at first: Polly liked the Persian's pretty cheekbones, and Mr No Tomorrow liked her contraceptive microchip. Apparently, though, he fooled her into saying she loved him, after three free dinners and some expert lovemaking, then quickly began pressurising her into the idea of

180

'quick marriage'. Despite harking on about this 'quick, romantic marriage', it soon transpired that Mr No Tomorrow wasn't interested in love at all – he was only interested in British citizenship. He must've been an illegal citizen after all, and, the way Polly described it, he hadn't taken kindly to rejection. After turning him down for the thirteenth time, Mr No Tomorrow had turned on Polly, and turned her face inside-out.

I carried on holding Polly, feeling awful. For a bit, we stared at the two girls in the mirror, secretly wishing they had much happier lives than the two girls staring back at them.

Polly was desperate to go and put on more make-up, but I said not to bother. It was getting late, after all, and the double bed in the other room was screaming out our names.

'Polly!'

'Kimly!'

I scratched my earhole.

'So, what are you gonna do about him?' I asked as we sloped back through to the sitting room, dodging the patches of splashed water, smashed Bianco Bianco BIANCO BIANCO BIANCO bottles, chewed apples and strung-out monsters.

'Well, obviously I told him it was over, but he wouldn't have it. And now he keeps coming round unexpectedly all the time,' Polly said glumly, at which point the front door burst open, and in stormed Mr No Tomorrow. We froze. His face looked red and devilish, and he wasn't even wearing a mask.

It turned out Mr No Tomorrow was furious, thanks to this text sent at precisely 6.66 p.m. (or 7.06 p.m., to you and me), from Polly's pink Nokia: FUCK OFF STOP PHONING ME I DONT EVER WANT TO SEE YOU AGAIN

Mr No Tomorrow wasn't very good at taking orders. For starters, he was standing on her WELCOME mat, despite being unwelcome. He'd clearly spruced himself up to stalk Polly for the night

181

(gel in his hair, lashings of aftershave), but the grooming was spoiled by his gruesome facial expression. He spouted, 'Polly, we are need to talk.'

Mr No Tomorrow was the type of man who liked to talk with his hands. However, he hadn't accounted for all the water on the carpet and, as he stepped forwards with a look of pure malice, suddenly the look turned to fear as he slipped and clattered into the banister rungs. Me and Polly leapt to attention. We scoffed at first, but were quick to react to Mr No Tomorrow's misfortune, chucking the off-white mattress-cover over his head and shoulders and bundling him back out of the front door. He made an almighty racket as he struggled to break free, but me and Polly weren't daft. We kneed him frantically in the general direction of his testes, then slammed the door shut, remembering to lock it this time.

Panting, me and Polly slumped with our backs to the ketchup stains, rattled but relieved. We were shaking so much, we gave the whole building a pulse.

'I'm sorry about that,' Polly murmured into her chest.

'Don't worry, don't worry,' I said, feeling a bit dismal now, and sober. Technically, it was my fault for bringing Mr No Tomorrow into Polly's life, but I didn't feel up to talking any more.

We made the short walk of shame to Polly's bedroom. It was only half ten, but drinking more Bianco Bianco BIANCO BIANCO BIANCO somehow didn't seem so funny now and, in any case, it'd just become a very, very long night. We got changed into sleeping outfits (Forever Friends T-shirt for me, SEXY BEAST for her), then tucked ourselves into the double bed, like two gloomy tax bills posted in the same envelope.

As soon as we shut our eyes, that's when the excessive banging started. Not banging in the sexual sense, you understand, but banging as in loud, spine-chilling BANGBANGBANGing on the front door. Polly recognised the unmistakable din of Mr No

Tomorrow's fists – after all, she'd been banged by them herself many times before. We cringed in silence. There was nothing we could do to stop it – unfortunately, Mr No Tomorrow wasn't bright enough to realise we weren't going to open the door. For about half an hour he didn't let up with the banging, like he was trying to bludgeon his way into the house with his knuckles.

Me and Polly groaned now and then, desperately trying to drift off to sleep, but our dreams kept getting punctured every time Mr No Tomorrow punched the door. My heavy eyelids flickered. Polly had some ear-muffs amongst the erotic lingerie in her closet, and they worked quite well, getting rid of Mr No Tomorrow. That is, until he started screaming:

'Polly!'

'Open door!'

'Kimly!'

We fell asleep with ears burning.

⊙

As I slept, the cheese from the burritos and enchiladas gave me odd dreams. First of all, I found myself hovering over the Pacific Ocean in a large off-white hot-air balloon, in search of the mythical Great Southern Continent. I saw a tiger shark sinking its jagged jaws into a man dressed like John Travolta. I threw down a lifebelt, to no avail. There was a freak storm, and I got swept off course, crashlanding on what seemed to be my old school playing field. The balloon popped, covering me in milk. I sustained no apparent injuries. Later, I saw me and Stevie skipping away from the wreckage, hand in hand. We were skipping along the Applegarth in Guisborough except, instead of tarmac, it was paved with what looked like bottletops. Stevie had a bottle containing a green, foaming elixir, which he'd decanted into two gigantic champagne flutes. In the dream, we were both very drunk. When we got to the end of the lane we came across a vast comic-book graveyard; all overgrown, with gnarled trees, and Halloween pumpkin lanterns. At this point, the colours in the dream became suddenly vibrant, like someone had turned up the lucidity knob. A long-forgotten memory flashed before me: I saw myself and Stevie as twenty-year-olds, supping Pulse cider in the graveyard. It was early in our relationship – I remember we kissed excessively. We perched on the wall skirting the cemetery, giggling at nothing. Stevie had an idea: he wanted to dance on the Black Monk's grave. He was being uncharacteristically daring – I think he was trying to impress me. I wasn't impressed. I'd already warned him about my schoolfriend, Daniel Brady, who'd treated the Black Monk to a fine bit of Saturday Night Fever, and met a watery death off the coast of West Australia. Nevertheless, I whooped as Stevie clambered over the overgrown fence, and onto the ancient, mossy monument. I cackled as he sexy-danced on the podium. I fired Pulse cider out of my nose. I figured he'd be alright. But then, the colours in the dream became dull again: I saw Stevie, stark naked, splashing helplessly in the North Sea. A whisker. A black, hooded figure. A seal. A wooden box. A Marks & Spencer suit with a puddle where the person should be.

⊙

I woke up with scruffy hair. And the flu. And heartburn. And creased legs. And sweaty armpits. And a brain tumour.

Or perhaps it was just a hangover.

I grunted, realising me and Polly were stuck to each other like a pair of balled-up paper dolls. I prised myself off her, then prised off the ear-muffs. My ears felt red hot. As far as I could tell, Mr No Tomorrow had stopped banging on the door. It was about nine o'clock in the morning, I think. Scraps of daylight highlighted the windowsills.

Polly rolled out of the double bed, mumbling something about tea. I coughed in the affirmative. My throat was so clogged with mucus, I could hardly get any words out.

I coughed again. My feet felt hot and sticky, so I kicked back some of the bedcovers and hung my toes out to dry. Polly laughed. At first I thought she was going to comment on the smell but, instead, she pointed and said, 'God, have you lost weight? Have you seen how much your anklebones stick out, love?'

Kimberly Clark and Her . . . Identity Crisis of Many Colours

I wish I'd never clapped eyes on the *Tibetan Book of the Dead*. Just like the *Barbie* annual inspired me to wear a pink tutu and roller-skates on the Dia de los Muertos 1989, this year the Tibetan book forced me to defecate behind a bush in Polly's back garden, with a dog's tail stuck between my legs. Polly wasn't aware I'd used her mink fur stole as the tail. She wasn't aware I was having a crap amongst her rhododendrons, either.

'Bark!' I barked, self-consciously.

I squeezed out a rock-hard shard of shit – the type that typically marks a terrible hangover. It had a beautiful red marble effect to it, from where my anus was still bleeding. I wiped myself on a handful of dock leaves, then stared at my faeces, still pinching the tail between my cheeks. On page 190, the *Tibetan Book of the Dead* said the only chance a sticky-out-ankled person has of side-stepping death is to eat three mouthfuls of their own dogdirt. Surely, though, it couldn't be good for you.

I grimaced, sweating profusely. I could hear Polly upstairs running the shower, and I thought to myself how lucky she was to be cleansing her body, as opposed to force-feeding it faeces.

'Bark!' I barked again, telling myself, 'It's just a brown sausage, it's just a brown banana, it's just a brown carrot, it's just a brown Mini Milk . . .'

As I bent closer to my humandirt, I felt my stomach muscles quivering. The stench was unbelievable. I got my face about a metre from the muck when, suddenly, my hangover came back with a vengeance. I coughed, and accidentally fired a flume of sick at Polly's flowerbed. Conveniently, the brown lollipop got covered with vomit. It looked bloody inedible now. I decided to leave it be. I sent Polly's soiled mink stole flying over next-door's fence, and covered up my mess with a few more handfuls of dock leaves. Then, I pulled my knickers up.

Moping back inside the house, I was glad I'd avoided eating shit for breakfast, and yet I was aware that – as far as the *Tibetan Book of the Dead* was concerned – my death was imminent. I scampered nervously around the sitting room like a shaky finger running rings round and round a Ouija board, desperately racking my brains for a better way to cheat death.

On the Dia de los Muertos, apparently, all the lost souls and spirits come back to Earth for their annual ghoul reunion, and I imagined the Grim Reaper as a macabre master of ceremonies, roping as many mere mortals as possible into his giant, conga-like dance of death before the end of the day. I chewed my lips, glancing at the crumpled ghost and Frankenstein outfits on the mushy carpet. My head was still clanging, partly because of the hangover and partly because I couldn't resist imagining my own horrific death.

As I sat there sulking in Polly's armchair, I could've sworn a black, hooded figure swept past the front window. I bit my tongue and threw myself to the ground. I hid my face in the carpet.

The Grim Reaper was a sneaky bastard. He didn't need a disguise in a city crawling with shady characters in hooded tops.

I, on the other hand, had been daft enough to fashion one of the most distinctive hairdos in the Capital, making me easily identifiable to potential psychopomps. I scruffed up the Guillotine with trembling fingers. If I was to have any chance of avoiding the Grim Reaper, I'd have to spend the day in hiding. Or, better still, in disguise.

When I thought about it, that black, hooded figure could've just been Polly's next-door neighbour, Lamont. Nevertheless, I remained hidden – after all, Lamont might've been angry about the soiled mink stole that just flew into his back garden.

Once the coast was clear, I clambered back into the armchair and pondered my change of appearance. Fortunately, my Promiscuous Pal Polly had a whole array of different outfits in her dressing-up box. I snuck upstairs for a peek, to the sound of crashing waterfalls, squeaking enamel and out-of-tune singing.

Polly's dressing-up box was full of good disguises. Quite a few had an erotic slant – for instance, nursewear, policewear, full bondage gear – but I wanted to hide from Mr Death, not be chased by him like a malnourished Benny Hill. I searched a bit deeper. I guessed the best way to fool the Grim Reaper would be to imitate someone dead already – like an ex-celebrity, or an ex-relative – since Death was only interested in killing the living, not re-killing the deceased.

I gathered up a red T-shirt, some shorts, a fancy white evening dress, tongs, long red socks, red lipstick, brown eyeliner, a Beatles wig and a pair of white very-high heels, then set about stripping off my bland, incriminating, mortal clothes.

Part 1a) 'Marilyn Monroe'

Prancing out of Seven Sisters station, I had to be careful of whooshing air coming out of the grilles so my dress didn't fly up. I also had to be careful not to break my neck in the stilettos.

At first, the idea was to dress as Marilyn and laze about the house with Polly all day, but then a far better idea came into my ditzy blonde head. I remembered Paolo's fixation with that photograph of Marilyn; him always taking it into the lav and coming back out red-faced and sheepish. He was a dirty dog, but I still wanted to make it up to him, for all the trouble I'd caused. And what better way to appease the near-destruction of his restaurant than appearing before him as his favourite wet-dream celebrity, and grovelling for my job back!

I still hadn't put my notice in at the Wethouse. I figured I'd best secure a new job before I walked out on Malcolm's dad, or booked a frivolous flight abroad. The thought of going back to the Bush on Monday made me itch. At least, for the time being, I felt womanly and graceful again, marching over the junction in the white evening dress. As I breezed past Tesco, the one-legged lad selling pirate DVDs stared up at me, all doe-eyed and enlightened. I was such a beautiful spectacle, his left leg miraculously grew back before our very eyes – unless he'd just been sitting on it all along.

I felt like a swan, tottering over the High Road with the white fabric flapping elegantly behind me. The other Swan – the pub – leered at me from across the street, its black mouth full of sloshed black patrons, cackling and cat-calling.

As the smell of garlic gradually overpowered the other aromas of Philip Lane (fried chicken, decomposing leaves, soap suds from the AUND ETT), I wondered what I was going to say to Paolo. Providing he didn't think I was soliciting myself again, I expected he'd enjoy the outfit. I, for one, was enjoying it immensely, especially the new ringlets and lippy.

I twizzled my hair as I swept through the door of the Ristorante. The place looked the same as always except, instead of Kimberly Clark darting around the tables, there was a new girl darting around. She was like a new, improved version of myself; carrying twice as many plates at once, with bigger tits, smoother skin, and straighter teeth. I asked her, through pursed red lips, 'Hi, is Paolo around?'

I attempted a Yank accent, but mimicry has never been one of my talents, unless you count the time I went to Topshop to get the same vest-top as Marie O'Shea. Raising a finely tweezed eyebrow, the New, Improved Kimberly Clark just laughed, then shouted 'Paolo!' in a much better, bona fide Yank accent, and pointed towards the kitchens. I nodded, smoothing my dress shyly.

I swung my hips as I waltzed between the tables, feeling all the diners' eyes on me. I wanted Marilyn Monroe to appear before Paolo as if in a Vaseline-lensed, Technicolor dream sequence, but I felt more like a cut-price strippergram. And, to make matters worse, Paolo knew instantly who was hiding under the Hollywood veneer.

He wasn't pleased to see me.

'Kimmy,' he snarled, 'what the hell you do here?'

I wobbled slightly in the stilettos, but disguised it as a half-twirl, fanning the dress out. I said, 'What do you think?'

Paolo erupted. He slammed down the saucepan he'd been drying and grabbed me roughly by the shoulder. He hissed at me, 'I think you are disgusting.'

Paolo was acting very strange for someone who liked Marilyn Monroe. My pout dropped. Maybe he thought I was soliciting. I made a sharp, squeaking sound and protested, 'No, no . . . it's only a bit of fun. Er . . . what can I pu-pu-pi-do to get my job back?'

The line had sounded better in my head. As soon as it left my lips, Paolo dug his fingers harder into my shoulder, and spat, 'Get out.'

'Do you get it, though?' I asked, as he frogmarched me out of the kitchens. 'I'm her: Marilyn. From that photo of yours.'

Paolo went bright red, which he tried to pass off as anger, roaring in my face, 'You stupid little bitch.'

The words hit me in a fine drizzle. It was then I realised some people don't deserve to be treated nicely. Some people are bastards. Some people deserve to be carpet-bombed with Molotov cocktails, or reported to the Health and Safety Executive for their lacklustre hand-hygiene.

Just to keep face, I yelled into the Ristorante: 'Paolo's been *pleasuring himself* over Marilyn Monroe, you know! In the back!' I accompanied my scathing speech with the relevant hand gesture.

The diners stared back at me, in silence. Paolo looked to the ground. He finally let go of my shoulder and gestured for me to come back into the kitchens. I followed him cautiously, leaving the door ajar, in case I needed witnesses for the forthcoming assault charge. As it happened, though, Paolo didn't lay another finger on me. Still shaking, he took his wallet from his coat pocket and removed the photo from amongst his cards and banknotes. He unfolded it and turned it over, for me to see.

'It is not Marilyn Monroe,' Paolo stated glumly. 'It is my wife. She dressed up as Marilyn for my thirty birthday.'

I swallowed, gently pushing the door to. I didn't realise Paolo was married. Looking down at my very-high heels, I sniffed, and ventured, 'She's pretty.'

190

Paolo said, 'She died in two thousand six.'

While we stood there in the quiet hubble and bubble of the kitchens, Paolo began to cry. It wasn't just the odd sniffle, either – it was full-blown, red-faced howling. And with that, I realised he'd been crying over that photo all along, not fucking wanking over it.

Part 1b) 'Clark Kent/Superman' for a bit

As I walked Marilyn miserably down West Green Road, the very-high heels were killing, pinching at my protruding anklebones. Perhaps I deserved to die, after what I'd done to Paolo. In my defence, though, his wife didn't half look like Marilyn Monroe. Next to her, I felt more like Nora Batty than Norma Jean.

About halfway down the road, I came across a BT phone box, wallpapered with the reflections of the buildings round about it. I didn't fancy being whooped at in the Fountain – going into the ladies as a lady, and coming back out as a gentleman – so I tottered inside the booth, and started stripping off the foolish Marilyn costume. There was only a Domino's pizza advert to hide my modesty, but years of insecure adolescence had helped me perfect getting changed without baring any flesh. I tugged the tight red T-shirt on over the dress; pulled the shorts up underneath it; wriggled out of the shoulder-straps; whipped the dress off, from under the T-shirt; then slung on the long red socks, Beatles wig and, with the brown eyeliner, I

Part 1c) 'George Best'

scribbled some stubble on my cheeks and chin. Annoyingly, I'd forgotten to bring any trainers, so I squeezed on the very-high heels again and limped out of the phone box, like a crusty, unshaven drag queen. I got a few weird glances and honk honk honks from passing cars, as I crossed over to the corner shop. I wasn't sure what let the disguise down the most: the stilettos, the red lipstick, or the 36Bs under my T-shirt.

In the corner shop, I tried to peruse the aisles with a straight face, but the Cypriot owners kept sniggering, running back and forth to the storeroom to gather more family and friends to come and laugh at me. At the counter, I couldn't help creasing up too, as they scanned my six-pack of Polish Warzone lager, Hall's Soothers, and two boxes of Rodine Mouse & Rat Killer.

'Party time, hm?' the owner asked, doing a joke.

'Something like that,' I replied. I didn't bother with the Belfast accent.

I felt simultaneously self-conscious and detached, stepping back out onto the pavement. If I couldn't fool the Cypriot folk, how could I fool the Grim Reaper? I guessed the only thing for it was to get into the spirit of Bestie and crack open a can. I took a few girlish sips as I trotted up West Green Road. The Warzone lager was disgusting, like six parts Stella to one part turps. By the fifth sip, I had to cough some back into the can. I wondered if George would've been impressed with my dribbling skills. The folk passing by me certainly weren't.

I had a long, hard think as I marched up the pavement. It didn't seem to matter if I was nice or nasty – I always seemed to make people unhappy. After the mishaps of the last few months (stoking Shaun and Sean's gambling addiction, introducing Polly to a British-citizenship-mad stalker, more or less burgling my own building, mocking Paolo's dead wife), I could feel my time in the Capital coming to an end. The place would probably get on alright without me.

I checked my balance at the next cashpoint. Surely £993.89 was enough to cover a long-haul flight, a tent, a rucksack, and a sleeping bag. Somehow, the idea of going missing in the Scottish Highlands or the Norfolk Broads just wasn't as appealing as trying to find myself in South-East Asia or North Africa or South America. So, it had to be long haul. And it had to be today.

Japan seemed like a safe bet. Not only did they have the sweetest-smelling spas, the cleanest cities and the most impeccable manners, I also liked the idea of flying east through the time zones, away from Greenwich Mean Time, the Dia de los Muertos and the Grim Reaper. As far as I was aware, they didn't even have Grim Reapers in Japan.

I figured I'd head over to Heathrow, and see if I could afford a last-minute flight into the sunset – the actual sunset as well, not a slushy, metaphorical one. It was probably getting on for about 8 p.m. in Japan. My mood lifted as I imagined all the neon, the nodding and the bowing, the tuna sashimi, the symmetrical hairdos, the giggling schoolgirls.

First of all, though, I had some unfinished business to attend to. I couldn't leave the Capital without one last, lasting act of kindness.

As I approached Donald's battleship-grey building, I looked for his face in the tracing-paper windows, but autumn had misted them all up. I wasn't Donald's biggest fan any more, after he'd given me cystitis and a prolapsed arsehole, but I still felt sorry for him. I shivered as I went through the entrance – either the Reaper was close by, or it was down to me wearing a T-shirt and shorts in the height of autumn. Knowing my luck, I'd catch my

194

death of cold, regardless. I coughed violently, keeping my head down, taking my time up the uneven, death-trap stairway.

The Wethouse had been leaving me messages all morning, wondering why I hadn't turned up for work, what I was playing at, etc., etc. I just couldn't bring myself to give them 'imminent death' as an excuse, though.

While the Wethouse wasn't the finest hostel in the Capital (it probably wasn't even the finest homeless hostel), I wanted Donald to know there was a clean bed there, if he wanted it. There might even be a job there for him – after all, someone would have to fill my boots once I jetted off to Japan.

I attempted more Warzone, bauked, then walked up up up up up up to floor 6, with the rickety horrible elevator lagging behind me. Once I got to the top, I pulled the neck of the T-shirt over my nose and mouth to keep me from inhaling the mould spores.

I followed a trail of wild mushrooms to Donald's door and gently pushed it open. There were more rats in Donald's pad than I'd remembered. They were a brazen lot – staring me out as I hopped across the exposed floorboards. A few Ecstasy pills crunched under my stilettos as I made my way round the old sewing machines with my arms outstretched. Round the back of the third Brother machine, I was met with a sorry sight. Donald was lying face-down on his 'new' sofa, in a puddle of strange liquid. My lungs collapsed like two houses of cards. I pulled the T-shirt down from my face and coughed into my hand. Had the Grim Reaper got him first? Did his anklebones stick out even more than mine?

I gave him a nudge. No reaction. I gave him a frantic shake. Still no reaction. Panicking, I gently pressed my fingers against the pulse in his neck, at which point Donald sprung to attention, spluttering, and then nearly suffering a cardiac arrest, to see his hero standing over him.

195

'Wh . . .' he mumbled, rubbing his head. Although Donald was mortalled, it didn't take long for him to come to his senses, rising from the sofa and saying, 'Aw, it's you.'

'Naw, naw, I'm Georgie Bestie,' I said, slapping the hand-drawn Man Utd crest on my breast.

Donald just laughed. I shuffled from heel to heel while he coughed violently for a good thirty seconds; then he rubbed his head again and asked, 'Well, have you . . . what are you after? Still no money?'

I thought of my £993.89, converted into yen. While it'd be nice to empty my bank account into Donald's pockets, I had to look out for myself now. I scratched under the Beatles wig and explained. 'Ah, sorry, I'm still skint. But I had this thought. I don't know if you're up for it, but . . . well, you know I lost the job at the restaurant? Well, I started working at this homeless hostel down Shepherd's Bush . . . and it's sound . . . dead clean . . . and I could definitely get you a bed there. See, cos you can't stay here, Don. It's full of mould. You'll die here.'

'I'm not scared of dying. I fuck death up the arse, me!' Donald gurgled, shifting on the sofa.

'Howay, you'd like it . . . and you can drink there. The Wet-house, they call it,' I went on, feeling sad that Donald would rather live in squalor. It's true the human body can get used to just about anything (bar molten lava, shark attacks, machine guns, heart-break, etc.), but it made me depressed, imagining Donald dying here alone, and the rats feeding off his bones until he disappeared completely, and no one would even know he'd been here, or gone.

Donald's left foot (the one with the snakeskin loafer) tapped the floor frantically, as if independent from the rest of his body.

'The Wethouse?' he said. 'Down Shepherd's Bush?'

'Yeah.'

'I can't go there.'

'Why not?'

'Cos . . . Kimberly's there,' Donald mumbled.

'Naw, I know. *I'm* Kimberly,' I said, taking the wig off, to show him. Did he recognise me or not?

'No, no,' he carried on, 'not shower-curtain Kimberly, *my* Kimberley. My little one. My daughter. She's down there. In Shepherd's Bush Wethouse. She's not . . . she won't want to see me.'

I shook my head in shock. I needed a sit down to take it all in, but nowhere looked suitable for sitting.

'Never,' I murmured, though my mind kept flashing back to the first time I met Donald, when he told me he had a daughter called Kimberl(e)y. All this time, I thought he was just saying that to butter me up. Then again, it did make sense they were related – two lost souls, sailing along on an old drunken boat with no oars. I squinted, looking for her face in his, but the scars were too distracting.

'That's mad,' I added. 'I mean, that's more reason to come down, though, isn't it? When did you last see her?'

Donald kept his eyes to the ground as he answered. 'I've hardly seen her. My second wife, she . . . we gave her away. Young Kimberley. We gave her and her twin sister away for adoption. She stays in touch – the wife – but I fucked everything up. We won't get along.'

'Well,' I said, 'I don't think she gets on with *anyone*, like. But you might as well come and see the rooms? Please?'

'I don't know. I won't even recognise her.'

'Please, Donald.'

'No. No.'

'Well, I've brought drinks for you,' I said, swishing the carrier bag. 'Why don't we just go down there for a drink? Have a look at the rooms? I've got plenty of drink.'

Donald looked at the carrier.

'Well . . . I . . . oh, aye . . . go on, then,' he replied, sitting up straighter.

Once the Warzones got going, Donald slowly warmed to the idea of seeing his daughter again. He offered me a coat that smelled of vinegar, which I politely declined, then we set off. By the time we got down to West Green Road, Donald was in much higher spirits, yelling Kimberley's life story at me, as well as the life stories of her six sisters: Nicola, Stacey, Rose, Mary-Ann, Joanne, and Anastasia. When we finally got to Seven Sisters, my brain was overflowing with strange women.

It sounded like Donald's family had endured a horrible run of luck over the years. His first wife died aged thirty-two, from an undetected brain haemorrhage, leaving Donald to run their struggling sugar-beet farm into the ground. Donald knew only two of his four daughters from his next marriage, having given the twins, Kimberley and Anastasia, up for adoption as soon as they were born. Being Irish Catholics, him and his second wife had trouble keeping a lid on their baby production – and they also had trouble with their finances. Shortly after giving up the twins, Donald's second wife turned against him, when he lost his job as a gravedigger, under what he described as 'terrible circumstances'. His ex-wife stayed in touch with the couples from England who took Kimberley and Anastasia under their wings, and occasionally relayed stories to Donald's second cousin Andrea, who passed them on to Donald at her annual Christmas visits to the battleship-grey building. However, both of Kimberley's foster parents tragically passed away when she was in her teens, pushing her into a life of heavy drinking, hopelessness and, before long, homelessness. Apart from the shaky scraps of information he received from Andrea each year, Donald knew very little about young Kimberley. I hoped he wouldn't be disappointed when he met her.

198

'What went wrong with the gravedigging, then?' I asked, as we stepped down into the warm, sweet smell of the station. 'What were these "terrible circumstances"?'

'I got caught play— I got the sack,' Donald stated.

'Why didn't you get a different job? Like, a normal one?' I asked, feeding money into the machine for Donald's Travelcard.

'Well, I'm not exactly normal, love,' he replied, tapping his left foot again. 'Something bad happened. Something I done I shouldn't have done.'

'Ah, you're as normal as anyone,' I said, giving him a nudge. Having said that, some people take 'normal' as a derogatory term, although these are usually people with no personality to speak of – those who wear traffic cones on their heads at the weekend, to make up for wearing a suit the rest of the week.

'What was the bad thing you did?' I asked.

Donald shuddered and laughed, still tapping that foot.

'Ah, I could show you . . . but then I'd have to kill you,' he replied, grinning. He was a strange old fruit.

As me and Donald made our way through the barriers, I got a bit of a start, spotting another black, hooded figure purchasing a Twix from the news stand. My lungs gulped. I snuck in front of Donald, kept my head down and scuttled as quickly as possible onto the escalator.

My heart was still pounding by the time me and Don got sat down on the Ghost Train. For some reason, half the people in the carriage couldn't stop staring at us, while the other half couldn't bear to look at us, keeping their eyes on their laps. In the reflective glass, I couldn't decide who looked weirder: the ladyboy or the tramp.

When we got out at Shepherd's Bush, even the sun couldn't bear to look at us, shamefully shaking its head behind a long cirrus. We crossed over to the green and made a beeline for the

Wethouse. I told Donald to wait on a bench with the Warzones while I went in to talk to Malcolm's dad, and find Kimberley.

As I stepped away from the bench, to the fizzing torpedo sound of a can being opened, I realised I'd forgotten to spike Donald's pad with Rat Killer. Hopefully he wouldn't have to go back there, though.

I licked my fingers and wiped at the stubble. I wasn't looking forward to getting collared by the gang – it was bad enough being teased about the Guillotine. As it turned out, though, the disguise finally worked its magic: dressed like that, I must've seemed like your average drunken jester, and I managed to slip through the foyer unnoticed. Malcolm's dad looked busy in the office, dealing with a bald shouter, so I headed straight for Kimberley's dormitory, down the tangerine corridor. I body-swerved the laundry trolley at the bottom of the square-spiral staircase, then skipped up the steps, selling a strewn Stella can a dummy on my way up.

I stopped to get my breath back outside Kimberley's door, then knocked three times on the chipped paintwork. No reply. I tried the handle, bracing myself for another outburst of 'Die, die', or Impromptu Suicide Attempt #10. However, her room was empty. The broken curtain-rail and the ripped cider can winked, I think, catching the sunlight. I shut the door, then looked up and down the corridor for Kimberley's noose-like ponytail. The whole place seemed eerily quiet, though – just the distant hissing and creaking of lager cans, and the soft yawn of doors gently opening and closing.

I decided to go for a wander. The hostel clock said 11.56 a.m. – the gang were probably out parading the pavements, or tucking into the Halloween leftovers in the mess hall. I marched back down the square-spiral staircase, treating the Stella can to a nifty step-over this time. When I got to the bottom, I spotted my

200

favourite daysnorer standing outside the TV lounge, halfheartedly mopping the lino.

'Malcolm!' I shouted. I hadn't seen Malcolm much since the incident at the Ristorante – he kept himself to himself at work, doing the odd job for the old dears in the kitchens, or hiding away in the office. I don't think he ever asked any of the drunks to squeeze him.

'You're late,' Malcolm stated, handing me the mop. While I wasn't expecting an open-armed embrace, a smile or a nod might've been nice. To be fair, though, I was almost four hours late for work, and Malcolm had been drafted in to cover my shift. And it just so happened I was on toilet and floor duty that morning.

'Ah, sorry, I haven't been feeling that good,' I said. I didn't mention the ankles, humandirt, vomit, Marilyn or Warzones – Malcolm looked constantly confused as it was. He gazed at me with his huge, bottomless eyes and said, 'I done all your mopping.'

'I appreciate it, Malcolm. You're a star,' I said, propping the mop in the wheelie-bucket. 'Why's it so quiet today? Where's the gang?'

'Capital Dungeons. But I had to mop.'

I nodded. It sounded like Malcolm was talking with his mouth full of water, drowning in his own voice. I hoped I hadn't ruined his day, or his week. I asked him, 'Any idea where Kimberley is?'

Malcolm frowned, but said nothing. I glanced through the frosted glass in the door to the TV lounge, but couldn't make out any bodies. Malcolm whispered, 'Don't go in there. There's big dangers.'

'What is it? Wet? I'll only be a sec,' I said, pushing the door open. As I stepped inside, Malcolm made a moaning sound and protested again, 'Don't. Please. The pasta m—'

But it was too late. Taking up one of the sofas in the empty lounge, Mr Wednesday, Friday and Saturday were sitting with crossed arms and legs. They had cans of lager on the go, and *Bargain Hunt* muted on the telly. It didn't look like a party.

'As if! Alright, lads,' I said, trying to stay calm, though I was rattling inside. 'What are you doing here?'

'Graham told us you worked here,' Mr Wednesday said, referring to Malcolm's dad. Mr Wednesday looked strange, wearing sunglasses indoors on an overcast afternoon.

'Can we have a word?' Mr Friday asked, scratching his basketball belly under his sweatsuit.

'What about?' I asked.

'Compensation,' Mr Wednesday replied. 'For that scene in the restaurant.'

Mr Wednesday slammed his can down on the coffee table for dramatic effect. A chill went through me, but I was convinced I could reason with the lads. I said, 'I'm sorry. I was just trying to be nice to you all.'

'You're nice?' Ghanaian Mr Saturday scoffed. 'You are fucky prostitute. Now you do us for free.'

'Just take us in one of the dorms, and we'll forget all about it,' Mr Wednesday reiterated. From his suit pocket, he removed a pack of red Pleasuremax condoms and dropped them onto the coffee table, next to the can.

Oh, the romance. I know George Best got a lot of action in his life, but this was ridiculous. The daftest thing was the look on the men's faces – to them, there wasn't a hint of shame or irony in slamming down a pack of johnnies and demanding a four-way. By being nice to my weekly lovers, and occasionally letting them get their legs over, I'd skewed their grasp of traditional courtship niceties.

'Fuck off,' I snapped, forgetting my niceties, too. Before the

202

men had a chance to grab me and bundle me into one of the bedrooms, I stormed out of the TV lounge, and made a dash for the exit.

'You fuck off!' Mr Saturday shouted after me, ingeniously.

I couldn't believe this was the thanks I got for shagging them (and nearly-but-not-quite murdering them with Molotov cocktails). I kicked off the stilettos and held on to my chest as the dormitory door numbers hurtled past, causing all sorts of blurry, confusing mathematics in my peripheral vision. Behind me, I could hear my weekly exes mumbling and grumbling, no doubt weighing up the pros and cons of chasing after me and gang-raping me. My lungs burned with lactic acid. I was almost free of the Wethouse when, suddenly, door 22 swung open, and a glum two-headed monster appeared.

'Lads! Lads! Help!' I yelped, grabbing Shaun and Sean as they trundled out into the corridor. Unfortunately, the two-headed monster didn't recognise me. Shaun clapped eyes on my fake Manchester football top, saw red, and shoved me to the ground to the sound of

Fucking Man U

Leave it

Fucking

I forgot fucking Man U had been instrumental in losing Shaun and Sean's five grand. I wailed, landing knees-first on the linoleum. Before I could explain myself, I felt a gobful of saliva fly into my hair, and heard more drunken cursing. Sean held his evil twin back, saving me from a pasting, though neither seemed to realise it was their old friend Kimberly, crumpled in the corner. I got up and said nothing. It was time to take my identity crisis elsewhere.

◉

When I got back outside, Shepherd's Bush Green looked more miserable than usual. Not so many years ago, it must've had much lusher, bushier vegetation, with real shepherds and sheep roaming about, rather than plastic ones with kids kicking and screaming on top of them. Over by the playground, I watched a group of schoolboys in emerald uniforms hacking away at a piñata. In a way, I was like that piñata – a soft bag of sweetness, being constantly battered by greedy beggars.

I put back on the Beatles wig, in case my weekly exes were after me with only the famous Guillotine as a reference point to find me amongst the crowds. My feet were killing by the time I got back to the bench. Donald's eyes wobbled when he caught sight of me, having a bit of trouble focusing through the transparent napalm of the Warzones.

'Sorry, Donald, I couldn't sort anything out,' I sniffed. 'And I'm leaving. I've got to get out of here. I'm sorry.'

'Uh, wh-what?' Donald mumbled.

'I'm having a break.'

Living in the Capital was like being in a supercharged, but ultimately doomed, relationship: you get your initial honeymoon period, where your partner tries their best to impress you, then a slow, dismal downward spiral into indifference and niggling frustration. The Capital might have all this magic and romance, but I've got a suspicion it's black magic. Cheap and nasty court entertainment for the gods. Likewise, relationships seemed like cheap entertainment, too: a pointless, beautiful nuisance.

'But what about . . . where's Kimberley?' Donald groaned, sitting up. He inspected one of his empty Warzones for spare drips, then placed it back on the pavement, disheartened.

'I think she's gone, too,' I explained. 'I can't find her.'

I wished I could give Donald some kind of gesture before I left. I wanted to offer him the rest of the Warzones, but it looked like he'd polished them off already. Crushed, in the bottom of the carrier, the Hall's Soothers looked unappealing and unimaginative. So, I rummaged through my handbag, and removed a bronze housekey on a silver AAA athletics keyring.

'Look,' I said, handing Donald the keyring, 'you don't want to stay in the Wethouse anyway. It's full of trouble. Erm, see, cos I've got to say bye now but, if you want, you can stay at my flat. I'm going to pick up some stuff just now, but then it's all yours. There's still five or six months left on the tenancy thing – and all the rent's paid this month, and there's money on the electric . . .'

'What?' Donald mumbled, again.

'Obviously, like, winter's on its way,' I went on, 'and I don't want you freezing to death in that squat. Just, er . . . well, if you promise to feed my hamster, you can stay in the flat till the land-lord chucks you out. But he hardly even comes round . . .'

It felt strange, giving away Stevie's housekey, not that he need-ed it any more. And when I thought about it, there wasn't much in the flat for Donald to break/steal/stain. My worldly possessions boiled down to a hamster, a cupboard full of clothes and a bag full of medicine, and I was taking most of that with me to Japan.

Donald agreed to look after Lucifer – I joked he could let him out of the cage now and then, if he missed having rodents run-ning around his feet, but Donald didn't laugh. In fact, he seemed sad to see me go. I was aware I had plenty of wet-wipes in the Medicine Bag, so I let him shake my hand for a minute or so before I headed off to the Ghost Train station. It didn't seem appropriate to kiss him goodbye, but I managed to rustle up some silver for him, for another can or two of Polish Warzone. I told him the address of the flat, then I walked backwards, away from the bench.

My last memory of Donald was his dull, confused eyes, blink-ing away as I abandoned him. I hoped he'd find the flat alright.

And I hoped he still had his Travelcard.

As I scampered across the grass, I fantasised about stepping off the plane in Japan. I was tempted to buy some sushi for the journey back to Seven Sisters, to double-check I liked the stuff, but the fear and excitement cancelled out the hunger.

While there was a chance I might turn up at Heathrow to find no available flights to Tokyo, I didn't mind camping out at the airport. It was more appealing than staying another night in Flat D, anyhow. The only real fear was losing my bottle at the last minute. It was an extreme step, jetting off to a foreign island on a whim, but I was going on the off-chance life in Japan had more to offer than my half-life in the Capital, or an afterlife six feet underground.

I conveniently ignored the thought of arriving in a city swarming with the Yakuza, motorcycle gangs and *otaku* killer geeks. I focused my mind's eye on all the humble, polite people, the peace-fingers and the pleasant scenery.

Outside the Westfield shopping palace, a pair of Oriental girls were having their photos taken, giggling hysterically in front of H&M. That was good enough for me. As I went over the last zebra crossing, my heart was banging for all the right reasons. I nearly tripped in my socks as I mounted the kerb again, and marched towards the Holy Subterranean station. Its chipped blue signage was like a beautiful azure gateway to happiness. All it took to get through it was a pair of working legs and at least £2.50 on your Oyster card. And then I was free.

Smiling to myself, I was about to duck into the station when something long, blonde and plaited caught my eye. It was Kimberley Clarke's ponytail, swishing about outside Budgens. Kimberley had the same glazed look as her father as she stalked up and down the pavement, eyeing up potential benefactors for brown pennies.

My heart stung in my chest. I wasn't overly keen on going up to her and facing an onslaught of gobbledygook, especially since the weekly exes might still be after me, and Japan was waiting for me on the other side of the world. However, I wondered if fate had placed her in front of Budgens especially, pleading for me to reunite her with her father.

Perhaps it was a test. Perhaps, if I ignored fate, I'd be subjected to a horrific death on the Ghost Train back to Seven Sisters. Or the plane would crash. Or I'd be just as unhappy in the Japanese Capital as I was in the English one.

I pursed my lips and made my way over. Families were invented so lonely, hopeless people could be together, and feel loved. I pictured Donald and Kimberley getting reacquainted over a feast of Polish Warzones and cheeseburgers and chips, and having far more in common with each other than I ever did with either of them. It was to be my final act of kindness, before a move to the Far East to be selfish, normal and happy again.

Once I got through the crowds of schoolkids, litter bins and more black, hooded figures, I caught Kimberley's eye and bellowed, 'Hiya!'

Kimberley flinched. She stared through me for a few seconds, before recognising her doppelgänger and groaning, 'Uhhhhh.'

'How are you doing?' I asked, feeling like her social worker again. 'I've got a bit of news for you.'

I leaned against the shopfront, out of the way of all the charging pedestrians. Kimberley carried on glaring at me, waiting for me to explain myself, or go away.

'Er, you know your dad? Your real dad? He's over there,' I said, gesturing towards the green. 'He wants to see you.'

'My dad's dead,' Kimberley hissed.

'He's not,' I said, with a smile. 'I found him in Tottenham. I found Donald. Your real dad.'

What happened next gave me an almighty chill. As I said the word 'Donald', Kimberley's face turned grey and her eyes bulged slightly. She began to shake, like she was having an epileptic fit.

'Are you alright?' I asked, a bit dumbly.

'He's not m— he's a bad, bad person. I've heard about him. Fuck off,' Kimberley growled, and threw herself into the throng of passers-by. She seemed possessed, or else it was just the booze. She kept punching herself in the temples, grunting and flailing about. As if by magic, all the charging pedestrians instantly cleared a path for her to throw herself about in so they didn't get punched as well. Half of them looked disgusted, while the other half seemed to be enjoying themselves, smirking and getting their camera-phones out.

'Kimberley, calm down,' I pleaded, following her along the pavement. 'I'm just trying to help you.'

'Help *yourself*. Fucking overbearing witch,' she spat.

'I'm trying,' I mumbled.

After a bit more flailing, finally Kimberley sat herself down on the edge of the kerb. She kept shaking her head and twitching, staring at the tarmac. I didn't know whether to touch her, or keep my distance. At any rate, I decided not to push the subject of Donald any more – though I did wonder what this bad, bad secret was.

'Are you alright?' I asked again, struggling to find any better words.

I risked patting her on the shoulder. She tightened up, but didn't make a sound. I checked my Sony Ericsson for the time – the display said 1.43 p.m. Up above us, toy planes waved at me through the clouds. I hoped they weren't going to Japan without me.

I wiped my nose, shuffling from foot to foot. Just when I thought Kimberley had settled down, she made another mournful grunt and launched herself forwards, off the kerb. She rolled across the tarmac and splayed her arms and legs out, like she was sacrificing herself to the traffic of Shepherd's Bush.

My veins tingled painfully. Fortunately, the traffic was still held at the lights by the Empire. I dashed into the road, grabbed Kimberley under her armpits and said, 'Don't be daft, Kim. What's the . . . like, suicide's not going to help anything . . .'

Kimberley grunted again. She was surprisingly light – probably due to her liquid diet – but she was also surprisingly stubborn when it came to remounting the kerb. Round about us, people watched, pretending not to be interested, as we grappled with each other. We must've looked like Siamese wrestlers, or a two-headed monster.

When I finally got Kimberley to her feet there were a few cheers or shrieks from the bystanders, followed by a piercing honk honk honk as a grey Ford Mondeo came hurtling round the corner. The tyres also shrieked, as the car smashed into the back of us. The impact made me swallow my own tongue. We flew over the bonnet, flapping our arms in mid-air for half a second, before coming back down to Earth. We were like bad gymnasts, landing on our skulls instead of the balls of our feet. The crowd cried out again as Kimberley's head fell under the front tyre of the Fiat Punto following behind, and split open. Blood scattered across the asphalt. Honk honk honk, sang the other cars. Despite throwing my hands out in front of me, I landed chin-first on the tarmac, taking a bite out of my brain with my bottom teeth.

The rest is a mystery. One after another, my senses jumped ship. As I lay awkwardly between the white lines, I soon found myself spasming uncontrollably. I was vibrating, but it wasn't a phone call. This time, it was the death rattle.

And then, everything turned black.

Part 2) The Grim Reaper

For God's sake, not more death! If I see one more dead body, I swear I might fuckin kill somebody!

The Gold Telephone screams at me from across the kitchen. I scream back, slamming down my White Russian. I'd only managed half a sip when the thing started going off. I crack my knuckles. Some selfish bastard's only gone and popped their fuckin clogs again . . .

I hate being on call. It's like being in a state of fuckin limbo: stuck between work and play in this sickly no-man's-land, with drink on the one side and tons of dead bodies on the other. My bones groan as I lurch over to the Gold Telephone, creak creak, with my gown dragging behind.

'God Almighty,' I say into the receiver.

'Speaking!' God bellows back. There's no need for him to shout – I think the omnipotent cunt just likes to assert his authority. I clamp the Gold Telephone between my mandible and clavicle and take another gulp of the White Russian. The heavenly cream trickles straight into my spine. I drink White Russians not only to keep the depression at bay, but because they're also a great source of calcium. I've got to look after my bones, me.

I slam the blue-top milk back in the fridge, then hoist myself up onto the polished marble unit. It's a fancy pad, this place. At the moment I'm sharing a penthouse suite with this banker called Bernard, though me and Bernard have never met. He can't see me, you see. It's not his turn to die yet.

I used to have a fancy gaff of my own, back when I was on a bountiful salary, but now the money doesn't come in quite as smoothly as it used to. It's not that there's loads less people dying now, compared to when I started the graft – alright, there's been a few advances in medicine and all that (e.g. my arch adversary, the positive pressure ventilator, replaced the iron lung round the end of the 1950s) but, more than all that, it's the drinking that's been my downfall.

Then again, if it wasn't for the White Russians, I'd be a fuckin miserable bag of bones. It's not a fuckin doss, shepherding round dead bodies all day. And it's one of those occupations – like bailiff, or traffic warden – people love to hate. No one's ever pleased to see me, unless you count those sound suicidal fellows: a good, cooperative bunch, them lot. I met a charming one last February – poor sod had one eye plucked out, but he was dead grateful for me ushering him up the Stepladder.

That's all I am, though: a glorified usher. At first it was satisfying, sending murderous rapists and door-to-door salesmen to Hell, or reincarnating small dog lovers as chihuahuas, but, after fifty years doing any sort of graft, boredom, indifference and dissatisfaction set in.

'What's it thish time?' I slur into the receiver.

'Manners, Reaper! Don't spit!' God scolds; the righteous bastard. I began slurring around the early 1990s, I think, when the drinking and Ecstasy got their claws into me. It doesn't help either, not having a tongue. God, in contrast, has a smashing telephone manner. He explains to me in a warm, assertive tone: 'I'm not quite sure on the details yet, old boy, but there's been a nasty accident in Shepherd's Bush. Car accident. A girl – let's see now; for some reason it's written down twice here – a certain Kimberly Clark has been ploughed down.'

'Nice one,' I drawl sarcastically, imagining the blood. 'So where'sh she going, then? Where do you want her?'

'Up here, please! Heaven. She was a fine specimen. A very nice young lady. A true inspiration. You could take a leaf out of her book, eh? What goes around comes around and all that?'

212

'When do you want her?' I grumble, spinning the cool white glass. 'I'm, er, a bit busy and all . . .'

'Now!' God bellows. 'She's in such a sorry mess, poor girl.'

'But I've jusht set Ludo up,' I whinge.

I love board games. Whether it's a gruelling game of chess with Max von Sydow, or a daft round of Battleships with Bill and Ted, I'm always up for a competition. It's just a shame there's no one to play with up in the penthouse suite. Bernard's boring because he can't see me – and it doesn't look like he's going to bow out any time soon. He's one of those sad, straight-laced creatures, with his sensible job, sensible diet and sensible routine, jogging round Holland Park every morning. Saying that, it'd break my heart (or, at least, break the abstract gap in my ribcage where my heart should be) if Bernard contracted cancer, or tripped and snapped his neck while jogging. I've grown quite attached to him, watching him sloping round the suite in the evenings, mopping up mystery milk rings from his mock marble worktops. Bernard usually comes home around nine, since he loves working overtime, and he loves eating organic Taste the Difference ready-meals, which make him fart something terrible once he's crashed out on the moleskin sofa for the night. He makes me laugh. Sometimes he watches chick flicks, with a plate full of carrot sticks and tzatziki. Sometimes he sings Whigfield in the shower.

'Look, you're on thin ice as it is, old boy,' God spouts. Outside, the clouds turn from cheery white to moody grey, marking his displeasure. I grimace back. I was looking forward to getting leathered and playing Ludo against myself (I always win) but, then again, I don't want God firing lightning through Bernard's French windows and scorching his new pine flooring. I've still got the burn scars on my pelvic girdle from the last time I fucked up a job: accidentally reincarnating a paedophile as a kitten in the house of five pre-teen girls.

213

'Just one game of Ludo?' I mumble, fiddling with the six-sided die.

'No! If you're not going to do your job, I'm sure Kensington Borough Council can *quite easily* find another Reaper,' God goes, becoming petty now. Then again, the bastard makes a good point. It's not easy being a skeleton. If I lost the job, I'd have no choice but to bury myself, throw myself to the dogs, or hang, high and dry, in a school classroom.

Supping more bevvy, I cast my hollow mind back to the Reaping interview, all those years ago. It was easy enough getting the job (I scored 38/40 on the multiple choice: mostly daft questions like USING YOUR SKILLS OF 'FIRST IMPRESSIONS', PICK THE IDEAL CANDIDATE FOR HEAVEN. A: MATTHEW MASSMURDERER. B: ROB S. OLDLADIES. C: THE REVEREND JESUS H. DELIGHT. D: JEREMY O'WNSCOUNTLESS-EXAMPLESOFCHILDPORNOGRAPHY), but more difficult was the initiation ceremony, where I had all my flesh ripped off by vultures while I watched a slideshow of the most horrific, unappetising deaths. One involved a woman being put through a giant liquidiser; another featured a man receiving a sensual, sulphuric acid massage from another man wearing chainmail gloves. The idea was to prepare me for the worst sights an eyeless skull can behold, but that night, when I went to bed for the first time with my scythe and gown, I suffered the most sickening nightmares, and wished I'd just kept my day job as a dairy farmer. Ironically, I thought it was depressing, squeezing cow's teats every morning with Mr Atkinson bleating at me. As it turned out, nothing – no slideshows, no sedatives, no red-hot pokers to the eye-sockets – could prepare me for the horrors that were to come.

'Alright, alright,' I say, scratching my humerus. 'Where did you shay again? Shepherd's Bush?'

'Yes, Goldhawk Road,' God replies. 'Near the Subterranean station. Ahem. Right then, old boy, I'd best get my skates on. I've got this here earthquake to cause in Peru, then I'll be saving a few dying babies to balance it out and that, before tea. Speak soon, old chap. Ciao.'

I slam the dead handset back in its golden cradle, watching the sky brighten again through the French windows. I decant the rest of my White Russian into a flask, then pull my hood up and psych myself up, trying to invoke the sinister, self-assured persona instead of the gloomy, pissed, indifferent one. Just as supermarket assistants are taught how to smile, pack people's bags and say 'Hello' correctly, Grim Reapers go through rigorous training to become nasty, frightening pieces of work. Face it, Grim Reader, you'd be disappointed if Death arrived on the toll of your last breath in his flatmate's faded turtleneck and chinos, having forgotten the black gown and scythe.

Speaking of which, I'm always forgetting that fuckin scythe. Spluttering, I snatch it from between Bernard's golf clubs and umbrellas, then drop the latch and storm quickly, creak creak creak, through to the plush lift. Ten seconds and ten storeys later, I'm out in the open air, dodging traffic with my gown flapping in the breeze. I get halfway to the bus stop on Holland Park Avenue when this great, booming voice thunders out of the clouds, 'The Stepladder, you fool! The Godforsaken Stepladder!'

I freeze.

'God, sorry, my mishtake, my mishtake,' I mumble, looking up at the sky. Not only is God the All-Seeing Eye, he's got CCTV all over Kensington nowadays.

'Look, I'm flying to Peru in half an hour,' God yells, while I blunder my way back down the street. 'Don't mess this up. And if I catch you drinking on the job once more, you're fired.'

I nod, sadly, pouring out the flask. By fired, God doesn't mean me claiming benefits next week down the Uxbridge Road Job-centre Plus – I think he means eternal damnation.

With hunched shoulder blades, I nip round the back of Bernard's ivory tower, where all the afterlife equipment's stored. I wheel Bernie's Kona bike round the bins, then jimmy the garage lock with my smallest phalange and pull the musty old tarp off the Stepladder-to-Heaven. When God first entrusted me with the Stepladder, it gleamed silver – now it's gone a bit rusty, with small haloes of mould peppering the edges. I keep meaning to polish it up but, whenever I buy Mr Sheen, I end up condensing it in a carrier bag and huffing it up instead: another surefire way to suspend the sadness.

Struggling with the Stepladder, I lug it back towards Holland Park Avenue, past the White Russian puddle and the cackling kids coming home from school, completely oblivious of Death. When a bus finally turns up, I slip past the driver unnoticed and head to the back of the bottom deck.

Watching the trees streak past, I sit in silence, clamping the scythe and Stepladder between my skinny tibias. At one point, a fat berk sits on my lap obliviously and sprays me with Wheat Crunchie crumbs. When he finally gets off at Notting Hill Gate, I wonder why God chose to murder an innocent, 'very nice young lady' this afternoon, instead of one of the many fat parasites of the world. He's a complex bastard, that God. I think he's got the hump because less and less people believe in him nowadays. You often see him propping up the bar on Cloud 9 with Father Christmas, smashed out of their faces, beards dripping with advocaat, sharing their maudlin sob stories: 'I'm a nobody,' etc., etc.

A couple of stops later, I reach Shepherd's Bush. I get off gingerly, bracing myself for the blood and misery. As I skirt round the fragrant market, the sound of police cars and ambulances and the anti-sound of people in shock pierce the air. I hate

216

ambulances. I much prefer getting my hands on victims of death before the paramedics do. God bless them, they do try their best to resuscitate the poor sods but, if God's decided someone's time is up, I'd rather not spend all afternoon in A&E, arguing with a life-support machine.

Hugging the Stepladder, I charge as quickly as I can towards the carnage, creak creak creak creak. It looks devastating – quite a few cars and car-owners stand about with sick, concerned expressions, transfixed by the bleeding body parts. Thank God I managed to nail half a White Russian before coming across all this.

So far, the day's deaths haven't been all that distressing: I had to send a senile parrot to Hell after it'd learnt to squawk swearwords and I gave an old lady a heart attack, just in time to reincarnate her as a carnation shoot in her new granddaughter's new bedroom. It's not all doom and gloom, you see, being the Spectre of Death. Sometimes it's ever-so-slightly cheering.

Striding between the wooo-ing ambulances, I soon find the Ford Mondeo and Fiat Punto which have collided, and the young woman crushed underneath. The unlucky bugger's got half her head missing, like someone pulled too hard on her ponytail and her whole scalp came off. Likewise, her blue Nike sweater's been ripped to shreds, exposing the pale, bruised flesh underneath.

I put down the Stepladder-to-Heaven, and cast a long, dark shadow over the woman. The shadow always rouses them. And, as per usual, the moment she claps eyes on my scythe and skull, she panics and wriggles frantically on the tarmac.

'Ehm, are you Kimberly?' I ask.

'Yeah,' the woman splutters.

'Ah, no need to panic, then,' I explain, with my jaws set in a permanent grin. 'You've been granted access to Heaven. Er, if you'd just like to shtep this way, I'll—'

As I point towards the Stepladder-to-Heaven, it dawns on me the woman's legs are broken. She tries to slide, slug-like, out from underneath the smouldering chassis, to no avail.

'Don't worry, love, I've got you, I've got you,' I say, leaning the scythe against the bonnet. It's useless in the city, that old scythe. I haven't done any actual reaping since God 'volunteered' me for the Vietnam clean-up in 1969, when a lot of the dead bodies were piled amongst tough vines, mangroves and thick savannah grass, in the heart of darkness. Nowadays, the scythe's more of a fear-inducing showpiece, or a very elaborate toothpick.

Grabbing the woman under her Nike armpits, I grit my gnash-ers and drag her onto the pavement, trailing her entrails. Then, being careful not to aggravate her smashed-up legs, I walk her up the Stepladder-to-Heaven, puppetmaster-like, still holding her armpits. When she reaches the top, the woman suddenly disap-pears in a puff of pink smoke, and a slight 'Ping!' can be heard in the clouds.

'Ta-ra, then,' I sigh to the empty ladder. Taking down the black hood, I scan the length of Uxbridge Road for a decent boozer, desperate now for a celebratory White Russian and a sit down. I crack my knuckles and pick up the scythe. Belushi's looks bear-able, on the other side of the green, its innards not yet slurried with the rowdy, dowdy after-work crowd. I'm about to head off, when something very red and white on the ground catches my eye-socket. Despite being mangled, with its jaw missing and spine bent out of place, the thing appears to be George Best circa 1971.

'Alright?' I ask.

'Alright,' says George, yanking his jaw back into place.

I stroke the back of my cranium. What's George Best doing underneath a Fiat Punto, in the Capital, in the year 2008? The last time I saw George was in Cromwell Hospital in 2005, shortly after his 'Don't Die Like Me' photo shoot – bearded, jaundiced, and hooked up helplessly to a ventilator.

I decide it must be a ghost. After all, it is the Dia de los Muertos – the spirit equivalent of Christmas. Maybe George came back to Earth for one last pint in his favourite Capital watering hole. Maybe one pint led to another, as it does, and George ended up so trolleyed he couldn't help being run over on his way back to Heaven, despite technically being made up of only transparent ectoplasm.

'Do you need a hand, mate?' I ask.

'Er . . .' says George.

'Actually, do you fancy a pint?' I add. 'I'll pay, like, if you've gone and, er, if you've gone and shquandered all your money on booze, birds and fasht cars again . . .'

George says nothing. He must be smashed, after all – unless I got his quote wrong.

Rolling up the gown sleeves, I use my scythe to fish-slice George off the pavement, then carefully rearrange his limbs and features until he looks more or less human again. Luckily, the blood blends into his Man U top quite well. Brushing him down, I can't help but notice George is wearing a bra, but maybe it's just some daft, kinky game he's been playing with one of his many fancy-ladies. I grin, a bit starstruck. Despite the dodgy jaw and mangled left foot, George looks almost as handsome and healthy as the photo of him on the side of my Subbuteo box.

As we stand there amidst the rushing and wailing of policemen and ambulancemen, and the eerie silence of the onlookers, suddenly a grand idea strikes me.

Instead of taking George for a bev, then flinging him back up to Heaven, I grab his arm and drag him out of the crowds, back towards the bus stop. George looks confused, but it's probably down to all that drinking he's been doing. Or the car crash. He sits silently as we rumble back towards Holland Park on the 94, all the sirens fading to mere whispers behind us.

Back at Bernard's, me and Bestie stand awkwardly in the lift, twiddling our thumbs and phalanges as we zip up to P. He's not very talkative for a ghost that's been on tons of chat shows and quoted in loads of books. The last ghost I came across was William Shakespeare last month down the Shakespeare's Head in Holborn, and you couldn't fuckin shut him up. Fuckin sonnet this, soliloquy that; fuckin prick. It's all me me me with some of these celebrity spirits, like all they're bothered about is their own immortality.

'Thish way,' I say to George, when the lift doors finally break the silence, shunting open. George follows me, with his head down, into Bernard's apartment. I chuck the scythe back in with his golf clubs, then point at the table I want George to sit at. As he takes his place on one of the high-stools, I shake up another carton of milk and crack open the vodka. I ask him, 'Do you want one?'

George looks up with eyes like size-5 Mitre Deltas.

'Naw, naw, you're alright,' he replies, a bit more high-pitched and a bit less Irish than I remember.

'Don't be shy,' I say, but George just shakes his head and looks down again.

After glugging down a good bit of the cocktail, I march across the laminate flooring, creak creak, and stick my skull and shoulders into Bernie's broom cupboard. There aren't any brooms in here now – not since all the witches were evicted in 2006, and Bernard moved in. Now there's just a pile of board games – everything from Mousetrap to Guess Who? – stacked behind Bernie's plastic macs and ironing board. I remove Subbuteo with Jenga-like dexterity from the bottom of the pile, then dust off the box and turn to George and smile.

220

'Look, there'sh your ugly mug on the side!' I jest, bringing it over. George doesn't laugh. He just sits there with his arms crossed, munching on his bottom lip.

I slide the White Russian to the edge of the table, then lay the green felt pitch down and remove the little blokes, corner flags, goalies-impaled-on-sticks, and the plastic balls.

At last, a worthy competitor! I feel almost like an infant skeleton again, back when I had skin around me, long before I lost touch with the living. The last time I played Subbuteo, against myself, it went to penalties and, since my left hand (holding the goalies) was psychic as to where my right hand was going to flick the balls, the shootout lasted more than four fuckin hours. 'Sudden death' was more like a slow, agonising death, until I threw the pitch earthquake-like against Bernard's bookcase, just to get it over with.

'Go on, George mate, kick off,' I say, knees knocking together with excitement.

George just sits there dumbly, staring at the plastic statuettes. He raises a hand, puts it back down, puffs his cheeks out, then goes back to staring at the players with a queer expression.

'Alright, you can be reds, if you musht,' I sigh, shovelling up the blues I'd set up in perfect 4–3–1–2 formation in front of George.

'It's not that,' he says, playing with his lace-up collar. 'You see, ehm . . . you see, I'm not actually George Best, you know. My name's Kimberly. Kimberly Clark, sir.'

A line of cream dribbles down my mandible.

'You what?' I snap. 'Who have I just sent up the Shtepladder-to-Heaven, then? And why are you dresshed like fuckin George Besht?'

Kimberly/George keeps her eyes on the pitch. She sniffs, and replies, 'It might sound daft but, er, I was trying to fool you, sir. Disguise myself, I mean. Like, I had this feeling I was going to

221

die today. A premonition, sort of, so . . . I disguised myself. See, er, that girl you sent to Heaven, ehm, she's not Kimberly Clark, she's . . . well, naw, she *is* Kimberley Clarke, but it's Kimberley with an "e". Er, two "e"s, I mean. Kimberley with two "e"s and Clarke with one "e" on the end. I think you sent her when you should have sent me.'

This is doing my fuckin skull in. I take another sour gulp of milk, straining my eye-sockets, trying to see past the disguise. Looks like God's not so omniscient after all, the supercilious shit. The name wasn't written down twice; it was two different people.

'But how do I know you're the good one? The "nice young lady" one?' I ask, feeling foolish. 'You've got evil eyesh, you know.'

'Ask anyone,' Kimberly/George replies, blushing.

Suddenly, the booze casts bad spells over me: anxiety, paranoia, potential unemployment, eternal damnation, etc. Through the French windows, all the black clouds seem to be glaring at me with fluffy, knitted eyebrows.

'Wait here,' I say, slamming the glass on the imitation oak. I stride over to the Gold Telephone, and my shoulder blades drop. 2 MESSAGES, it blinks on the interface. My phalanges tremble over the PLAY button for a few seconds before pressing it. And with that, God's voice bellows through the penthouse suite, rattling the mock Ming vases. The first message is pleasant enough:

MESSAGE #1: *Hello Reaper, old boy. Just a quicky, er . . . it turns out there's been a further fatality at this here car accident in Shepherd's Bush. Another* Kimberley Clarke, *no less. But with an "e". Er, two "e"s, I mean. Kimberley with two "e"s and Clarke with one "e" on the end. Well now, this particular Kimberley is a nasty piece of work. Drunkard. Loudmouth. Suicidal. Murderous. Split personality. Drunkard. Did I just say that? Complete and utter bitch. Pardon my French. Just to let*

you know, you'd better bring Hell's Bells with you, along with the
Stepladder-to-Heaven. Hope you get this. Sorry. Cheers. Ciao.

The second message is less pleasant:

MESSAGE #2: *Reaper! God! Are you there? Pick up! Pick*
up, you old fool! What the heck! You've sent the wrong effing
Kimberley up here! You drunken fool. Did you not get my
message? I've had it, Reaper – you're effing finished. You're fired.
You're going to Hell. Call me when you get this. Effing idiot.
Ciao.

An image flickers in my skull: all my bones turning to charcoal. I shudder. In times of crisis, when your cards are up and
you're down on your luck, all you can do is drink and disappear.
Like a soldier falling on his own sword, I crack open another bottle of Absolut and a two-pinter of milk, and pour them double-
barrelled down my neck. Kimberly/George carries on contemplating the tabletop, glumly wiping away the rest of her stubble
with the back of her hand. Thinking about it, she looks nothing
like George Best – especially when she takes the fuckin wig off.
    Once I'm halfway through the vodka, Kimberly coughs into
her palm and asks quietly, 'Erm, Mr Death, sir, what's going to
happen to me? Do you think you'd better phone God back?'
    'Fuck that!' I screech. 'Thish is bad enough already . . . in any
case, he's in Peru now. The shignal'sh shit, and it's like fuckin
35p a minute.'
    Kimberly's eyes drift down to the table again.
    'Well, what's the chance of just bringing me back to life, and,
like . . . forgetting all this happened?' she asks hopefully.
    'Ha. Nay. It was your own daft fault getting squashed, washn't
it? And your own daft fault trying to fuck about with fate. Fuckin
dishguises!' I scoff, feeling victimised.

223

Kimberly fiddles nervously with one of the Subbuteo men, twirling him like a tiny dance partner. The one with the George Best beard, it looks like – but I could be mistaken.

'Well, what's going to happen to me?' she whimpers.

'What do you *think* happensh when you die?' I ask.

'I don't know. That's the worst thing about it, isn't it: the unknown,' Kimberly replies. 'But I thought you, er, of all people, might know.'

'Fuck off. I don't decide your fate, do I?' I explain. 'I'm just a glorified usher, me. God makes all the deshishionsh. I do all the fuckin legwork, mind . . . get paid fuck-all for it as well, the tight sod. He fuckin getsh the hump and all he d—'

'That message he left, though,' she interrupts. 'It sounded like you've got all the gear. Why can't we decide this one? Please? Like, er, you've lost your job anyway, haven't you?'

'Cheeky shit,' I say. The cheeky shit scratches the back of her neck. To be fair, the cheeky shit makes a good point. I've got all the afterlife equipment downstairs, in Bernard's garage, gathering dust. God forbid the Grim Reaper – the man on the street – should make the odd decision now and then. After all, I'm the one break-ing my backbone, meeting and greeting the corpses, while His Holiness fannies about all day with his head in the fuckin clouds.

'Alright, then,' I give in, after another slug of vodka, 'but I suppose Kimberly with one "e" wantsh to go to Heaven as well, does she?'

Her face lights up, and she breathes, 'Please.'

I laugh: one of those booming, spine-chilling laughs we're famous for here in Limbo.

'Who'sh to say you don't deserve to go to Hell, though?' I ask, wishing I could stop grinning at her. I'm trying to be fuckin fearsome here. I continue, 'After all, you've made me loosh my fuckin job.'

224

Kimberly's shoulders sink. She glances up at me with her best helpless-woolly-monkey expression and suggests, 'Well, maybe you or me shouldn't choose. Maybe we should get someone . . . impartial.'

'Who like?' I ask. Bernard doesn't get back from work till nine, and I doubt he'd be up for deciding the fate of a young dead lady after a full day's slog in the office.

'Well, do you know any other gods who might want to step in?' Kimberly enquires. 'The Hindus and Buddhists have some spare, don't they? And I've been rea—'

'Bah! No chance!' I spit. 'I'll have nothing to do with other gods.'

Kimberly plays with her hands again, anxiously. Whether authentic or not, it looks like she might roll a tear.

'Well, let's shee now . . . I can think of one person who might be able to help,' I offer, feeling unusually sorry for the girl. I must be going soft in the fuckin bone marrow. I add, 'You see, we're not the only ones here, are we?'

'Who do you mean?' Kimberly asks, looking about herself. The Subbuteo players stare back at her with glazed faces.

'Well, what about the Reader?' I suggest, nodding up at you; yes, YOU, the one holding the book. You stare down at the page, reading this sentence, wondering what you've got to do with it.

'Maybe I shouldn't be telling you thish, but there's someone else watching over us, as we shpeak. A kind of transcendental peeping tom, if you will,' I explain, pointing out your eyeballs, swinging from side to side on the ceiling. 'The Reader'sh here with us, in Limbo – that strange shtate between life and death; fact and fiction; the known and the unknown . . .'

'Oh . . . I . . .' Kimberly mumbles, taken aback. 'I thought they were just over-the-top lampshades.'

'Nay. See the stalks?' I say, pointing to the red cords hanging from the ceiling, holding up your eyeballs. 'They're not connected to the electric supply. They're plugged all the way into the back of the Reader'sh skull.'

'Oh,' Kimberly says again, with glowing cheeks. 'So, what should we do? What do you think? I mean, could the Reader play God, do you reckon? Could the Reader decide my fate? Could they throw a coin or something? Or roll that die?'

She gestures at the six-sided die sat minding its own business on the Ludo board, in the kitchen.

'Well, I suppose,' I say, mulling it over, 'but how are they going to roll that die when it'sh all the way over here in a penthouse suite in some book called *Kimberly'sh Capital Punishment*, existing not in the Reader'sh reality but represented through language in the form of mere black symbolsh on a white background?'

'Alright then, smart arse, well maybe they've got dice at home,' Kimberly snaps. I look down, a little shameskulled. She adds, frowning, 'Anyway, what was that . . . *Kimberly's* what?'

'Nowt. Anyway, let's not get ahead of ourshelves. Let's see what the Reader thinksh first, eh?' I say, glancing up at your swinging, twinkling eyeballs again.

'Oi! I mean, er, excuse me, dear Reader,' I say, referring to you; yes, YOU, you nosy bastard bookworm. 'I was wondering if you could do me and Kimberly a favour? If you'd be so kind as to find a six-sided die – a real one, not that one on the Ludo board, shtuck here in Limbo – myshelf and Miss Clark would be ever so grateful. And, if you'd be kind enough to roll it when I say so, I promise I won't appear on your doorshtep waving my scythe for at leasht six months after you finish this here sentence. Cheersh. Ta-ra.'

Kimberly smirks, like she's not bothered about her fate being decided by a complete stranger. Then again, God's a stranger to most folk, and even those who go to church every Sunday aren't automatically invited back to play in Heaven once they've

226

snuffed it. The bouncers run a very strict door policy.

'Are you ready, then?' I ask, referring to both you and young Kimberly. Kimberly nods, becoming solemn again. I watch her bite her bottom lip as she awaits the nerve-wracking result.

'Right then, fair, impartial Reader, ROLL THE DIE!' I yell up at the lampshades/your eyeballs.

You roll the die, doing as you're told.*

If you roll a ONE, Kimberly is sent to Heaven. Turn to page 229.

If you roll a TWO, Kimberly is reincarnated. Turn to page 270.

If you roll a THREE, Kimberly becomes a ghost. Turn to page 317.

If you roll a FOUR, Kimberly is resurrected. Turn to page 339.

If you roll a FIVE, Kimberly rests in peace. Turn to page 371.

If you roll a SIX, Kimberly burns in Hell. Turn to page 413.

Nice one. Have fun. Take care. See you soon.**

* Dearest Grim Reader, if you don't happen to own any dice, simply pull out six of your teeth and number them 1 to 6 with a saliva-resistant marker. Then, pop them back in your mouth, shuffle them with your tongue, and spit one out at random. Failing that, just pick a fuckin number from 1 to 6 then.
** But not *too* soon, I swear.

Part 3) Kimberly in Heaven

Yes yes yes yes yes yes yes! Bright white light! In fact, the brightest, whitest, nicest, lightest light I might've ever seen! And a wondrous, sloppy feeling in my veins, like pharmaceutical heroin, or another drug I've never even done!

The Grim Reaper grumbles into his cloak as he sends me up the Stepladder-to-Heaven, patting my back with the butt of his scythe. Then, all of a sudden, the corrugated metal transforms into a pink marble staircase, and I find myself eight miles high in the sky.

Firstly, there's vertigo. Then, all feelings of altitude sickness, flu, heartburn, brain tumour, hangover and after-effects of the car crash melt away in the sun. I suddenly have the queer, unselfconscious urge to squeal with joy, wobbling all the stars and planets, like toys on a baby's mobile.

I carry on up the staircase, each step giving off a scent more and more lovely than the last. Treacle tarts! Rose petals! Sunday dinner! Autumn leaves! Up ahead, the Gates of Heaven twinkle, ringing with a kind of metallic classical music whenever the soft breeze catches them. They must be about a mile tall and, if you look carefully, there are ex-demons in overalls clinging to the sides, polishing them. I squint, trying to make out the delights waiting for me behind the Gates, but it's far too foggy. Someone's left a dry-ice machine on, I think, to give the impression of general otherworldliness.

The word HEAVEN flashes above the Gates in white gold neon, as if it's not obvious enough. I smirk, absolutely buzzing. Guarding the misty entrance are two burly angels with white bomber jackets, earpieces, and a clipboard each. One of them – your typical meatheaded, neckless bouncer, except with fancy wings and sandals – frogmarches Fred West back down the marble staircase, brushing past me. Fred yells bloody murder as his dark glasses and false beard topple off down the steps. The bouncer grips Fred around the shoulders and stuffs him into a secret, fiery trapdoor at the bottom of the staircase. For a moment, me and the other bouncer watch his colleague, with our arms crossed. After a bit more struggling, Fred and the trapdoor finally disappear, in a puff of odd-sock-scented smoke.

'Name?' the first bouncer pants at me, jogging back up the staircase.

'Er . . . err . . . Kimberly Clark, sir,' I mumble, feeling like a child. The bouncers don't seem all that angelic, what with their regulation haircuts and permafrowns. I rock from one foot to the other while they scan their clipboards, pushing my dimples out, trying my best to appear sweet and saintly. I keep my arms crossed, covering up the Red Devils badge. And I keep my fingers crossed.

'You've already been ticked off, love,' the second bouncer states, with a glare.

'Sorry, love, you'll have to turn back,' the other one adds. 'Trapdoor.'

As I stand there in the golden shadow of the Gates, Heaven feels more and more like an overpriced, overpolished, overprejudiced nightclub, or an overly oppressive immigration office. I flap my eyelashes and explain as best I can, 'Eh . . . there's been a mistake. The Grim Reaper sent me, just now.'

Deadpan, the first bouncer prods his earpiece with a finger, listening.

'See, I think another Kimberley's been sent up when she shouldn't have been,' I add, annoyed at my quivering kid-voice. While I talk, the other bouncer gazes off into the middle distance of the Milky Way, ignoring me, asserting his authority/being a twat.

I decide not to say anything else. After a minute or so of silence, the first bouncer pulls his finger out of his ear and says, suddenly all smiles, 'Right-ho, Kimberly. That's fine. Sorry for the wait. Mr Death gives his regards. 'Ere, Pete, we've got a loose one. You'll have to sift out that other Kimberley, when you get the chance. Get her down the trapdoor. Reaper's in a right old tizzy . . .'

Pete sighs as he stamps the inside of my wrist with an inky crucifix.

'This is so you can get back to Earth, and then get back in,' he explains. 'Just if you fancy doing any miracles and that.'

Then Pete tells me a few house rules – no blasphemy, no Satanism, no complaining, no other gods, no shoes on the carpets – and hands me a luxury silk-lined goodie-bag, which contains:

Stainless-steel halo
100% genuine swan-feather elasticated wings
Map of Heaven
Sandals
Sunglasses
Party Poppers
Crystal Castle Keycard
£∞ Topshop Voucher

I almost bite my own tongue with excitement. Hopping from foot to foot, I kick off my red football socks and slip into the sandals. I ask the first bouncer, 'There's a Topshop in Heaven?'

'Course there is.' He consults his clipboard. 'It's one of your best-loved fashion retailers,' he explains. 'Just turn right once you're past all the dry ice.'

At this point, there's a loud, melodic rumble, and the huge Gates of Heaven slowly, laboriously hinge open, drenching us in more of the brightest, whitest, nicest, lightest light I might've ever seen.

I put the sunglasses on.

'Do you want us to do your halo?' Pete asks. 'They're a bit fiddly, see.'

I nod, face frozen in rapture. I watch Pete uncoil a barbed, semi-transparent wire from the back of the halo, then I hardly get the chance to flinch before he stabs it straight into my cranium. The halo springs to attention above my head, making all my visible and invisible lady-hairs stand on end. I yawn blissfully, feeling a white centipede-like rush of ecstasy tumbling through my veins. As it turns out, the steel halo doubles up as a miniature chemical plant, manufacturing and releasing 120mg of MDMA into your bloodstream every five minutes. Within thirty seconds of the first dose, I'm a gurgling, gurning mess.

'Oh, thanks *loads*, youse are stars, cheerio then, lads,' I coo, suddenly attracted to their muscles, not to mention their tight trousers and bloody sexy plastic earpieces.

The men wave me off as I stumble through the Gates. It's sad to see them go. I purr again, 'Bye, lads! Bye now!'

They just laugh.

It's nerve-wracking stepping off the marble staircase and onto cloud while shivering uncontrollably at each attack of MDMA, but the first fat nimbostratus holds my weight perfectly well. Once I've snapped my wings onto my shoulders, getting about is a breeze. I flap effortlessly through the troposphere, with the mist all warm and gloopy between my toes.

I laugh hysterically when I see the extent of Heaven around me. It's like Disneyland, except at least three times better. According to the map, there are nine major clouds in Heaven, each with its own theme: Cloud 1 is Retail Therapy, Cloud 2 is Food & Drink, Cloud 3 is Sound & Vision, Cloud 4 is Sport, Cloud 5 is Extreme

Relaxation, Cloud 6 is the Animal Kingdom, Cloud 7 is Comedy, Cloud 8 is Sex, and Cloud 9 is Drugs. The clouds are set out in a perfect circle around the Crystal Castle: a huge twelve-star hotel complex containing all the angels' lodgings, lavatories, and a large Get Acquainted Room. The hotel is like a vast, transparent anthill, with angels of all shapes and sizes floating through the corridors, slurping bottomless cups of tea, giggling, receiving free massages and watching one of 19,000 top-class TV channels.

Chewing my own face, I decide to carry on exploring before checking in. I dart this way and that through the condensed water vapour, grinning in everyone's faces. As you're probably aware, I've never taken drugs before – they make you die, etc., etc. However, I've got nothing whatsoever against taking drugs if you're already dead – in fact, I highly recommend it.

The thing that always scared me about Ecstasy (aside from the various possible deaths, for example heart failure, seizures, or the one where you drink too much water and your brain explodes) was its weakening of the immune system, resulting in more colds, flu and sore throats. Not only that but, apparently, one night on Ecstasy results in two or three days of moaning and depression. Fortunately for us angels, the halo keeps firing MDMA into your brain indefinitely, so there's no come-down, and it doesn't even give you cottonmouth.

'Ahhhhhh!' is all I can think to say, as another 120mg spills down my spinal cord.

Glancing about the silky cirruses and strati, every single angel seems to be engaged in some kind of debauchery, but maddest of all are the ones with dog-collars and rosary beads and the like: the Christians. It seems they knew what they were doing all along: living clean, straitjacketed, Christ-like existences to ensure entry into Heaven, then finally making up for lost time, swapping the seven deadly virtues for the seven holy sins.

233

'Good God!' I hear one of them yelp, coming up on his ump-teenth pill.

I smirk into my chest again, and point my wings towards Cloud 1 (Retail Therapy). Wobbling on its misty foundations, the main structure looks like a glorified shopping centre – a cross between The Mall at Wood Green Shopping City and the Acropolis. When the automatic doors open, I'm hit with the overpowering stench of Krispy Kreme, Stilton and Chanel: a queer, cheesy aroma, which makes me feel both cheery and queasy. I cough, wending my way round the aisles, tongue lolling at all the bright shops and boutiques. Despite there being almost two hundred miles of aisles, the £∞ voucher in my goodie-bag seems magnetised towards Topshop, kindly tugging me in the right direction.

I receive a blast of warm, synthetic Polynesian breeze as I step through the entrance. It's weird – for some people (men, in particular), trawling round Topshop all afternoon is their idea of Hell or Purgatory. However, I'm in my element. The Heaven branch is almost twice the size of that five-floor beast on Oxford Circus, with only a fraction of the amount of obnoxious custom-ers getting in your way. The rails are filled with exotic garments of every style imaginable, in a variety of colours: White, Very White, Titanium White, Diamond White, Off-White, Creamy, Creamier, Vanilla, White Lightning, Snow White, White Strike, Dirty White, White Christmas, Skimmed, Semi-Skimmed, Full Fat, etc. Rather than your usual High Street fare, the Heaven branch stocks a few rarities, like dodo-feather dressing gowns and unicornskin trousers. Getting another rush of excitement (or MDMA), I ravenously grab at the rails, giggling like a schoolgirl, until I realise – with momentary dismay and heartbreak – every-thing's in size 8.

The discriminating bastards! I kick the nearest mannequin and let out a whimper, caught between the sludgy caresses of the

MDMA and a sudden hatred for the fashion world. The demons of this world are girls who are skinnier than you. They should be chopped up and twisted into coat stands for healthy-looking size-12 folk like me and you.

With shaking hands, I throw the £∞ voucher to the ground, then spin on my sandals and storm out of the establishment, two inches off the ground. On my way out, I scowl at this stuck-up, stick-thin size-8 superwaif skipping towards me from the opposite end of the shop. She looks so irritating and idealised, with her lollipop physique and only slightly knobbly kneecaps. She scowls back at me. I scowl harder. She scowls harder. I sneer. She sneers. I mouth, 'Fuck off, you gaunt bitch,' not wanting to swear or blaspheme out loud. She mouths, 'Fuck off, you gaunt bitch,' back at me.

Just before I pluck her fucking eyeballs out, I realise I'm actually scowling at my reflection, in a mirror.

'Heeeeeee!' I screech, ecstatically. They've turned me into a beautiful, stick-thin, size-8 superwaif! Cackling, I twizzle my hips in the mirror, admiring myself, then I launch back into the clothes rails. Surreptitiously, I take back the £∞ voucher. And I take back anything I said about size-8 people.

I actually really like them.

⊙

Fifty-two outfit changes later, I waltz out of Topshop wearing the unicornskin trousers and dodo-feather dressing gown. Now I'm a size 8, I can pull off more than just raincoats and dotty cardigans. The only slight downside is my breasts have shrunk, like halved grapefruits. Big boobs, however, have and always will be the last refuge of the unattractive: a booby prize for the fat and ugly. I would not be seen dead with flabby bits.

Sailing through the mist with my hips jutting out at jaunty

angles, I suddenly have the urge to stroke some kittens. It's one of the finer pleasures in life, and becomes quite a habit of mine over the next few weeks, nipping over to Cloud 6 (the Animal Kingdom) to tickle the kittens' fuzzy undersides. The days and nights blend into one seamless silver movie reel, tossing me from one overblown love scene to the next, sprinkled generously with methylenedioxymethamphetamine. Sometimes, I like nothing better than lying supine in a synthetic flowerbed on Cloud 5; other times, you can find me in the comedy club on Cloud 7, spraying Bollinger out of my nostrils. In Heaven, no one has much of an appetite thanks to the constant MDMA (though I still go to Krispy Kreme now and then to sniff the doughnuts), but there's always free drinks on the go. Most pubs and restaurants serve complimentary pints of draught champagne, though most angels prefer it from the bottle, in the correct flute, with gold leaf floating in it.

Usually, this amount of pleasure would make me feel guilty, upset and run-down. However, in Heaven, it seems you have unlimited energy, serotonin and hardy white blood cells, and not even any hangovers! In a way, I wish I'd died sooner. Here's a tip: if you think you're definitely going to Heaven (e.g. good Samaritans, Bible bashers, binmen, etc.), I recommend getting on with it and topping yourself.

Unfortunately, though, the human brain is just as insatiable in Heaven as it is on planet Earth. And what can you possibly give to boys and girls who have everything? After a couple of months with the stainless-steel halo, I start looking for ever more elaborate ways to get off my face. The constant stream of MDMA soon seems monotonous – all it does is make you artificially cheerful, kind and compassionate to your fellow feathered friends. As far as I'm concerned, that's how I acted when I was on Earth, only without the bit of metal stuck in my head.

I decide it's high time for something a bit stronger. Cloud 9 lies somewhere near the bins by the Back Gates of Heaven and, while it's not the prettiest of all the clouds (it's a thick, grey thunderhead, lined with golden, green ganja smoke, like the effect in a mouldy marble cake), the angels sprawled on top of it seem in particularly high spirits. I nervously flitter about the outskirts at first, before plucking up the courage to step onto the heavy foam.

Surveying Cloud 9, it's not obvious at first where they keep the drugs. There are no pharmacies, medicine cabinets, people with dreadlocks, or hash menus. I pick at my thumbnail, feeling foolish. After a long period of indecision, I'm prepared to cut my losses and slink back to the Crystal Castle when something strange catches my eye: all the daisies have pills growing from them, instead of petals; there's a thorny rosebush sprouting syringes; there's a white sandpit, overflowing with coke; and a man licking the acid off a huge, perforated poster of God.

Next to the sandpit sits a hulking, hirsute beast playing an acoustic guitar, sitar and toy drumkit simultaneously. The beast looks like a cross between the Hydra and the Hindu goddess Saraswati, with its many heads, and arms filled with musical instruments, sitting cross-legged in a lotus flower. The heads sprout on stalks from what looks like the body of a leather-clad lizard. As I edge closer, I recognise a few of the faces – Jim Morrison, John Lennon, Elliott Smith, Ian Curtis, Buddy Holly, Brian Jones and Kurt Cobain blink back at me, nestled between twenty less recognisable, but no less rock-and-roll, others. Their presence gives me palpitations. I settle myself down in one of the poppybeds, fifty metres or so from the Many-Headed Musical Misadventurer, and cough into my palms.

'Can we help you?' the beast asks, halting its lovely rendition of Elliott's 'Happiness'.

'Oh, er, sorry, sorry,' I splutter, all stuttery and starstruck. 'I just came to see what the, er, what the craic's like.'

'The crack? Uhm, it's okay . . . I guess,' the heads mumble amongst themselves, misunderstanding.

I shuffle about in the poppies. I feel bad – not only have I disturbed the beast's beautiful playing, I think I might be sat on the opium. Cooling my cheeks with the backs of my hands, I shimmy out of the flowerbed to join the Many-Headed Misadventurer by the sandpit.

'Erm, I mean, well . . . well, can you show me how it's done? The crack?' I ask, looking at no head in particular.

Grudgingly, the Multi-Headed Musician shows me how its works work. The beast picks up this sort of test-tube (the 'crack-pipe'), then stuffs a semi-precious stone in one end (the 'crack'), on a nest of what looks like robot pubes or bits of Brillo (the 'filter'). Then, the beast sets fire to it, and sticks the pipe into one of the musician's mouths, who sucks on it appreciatively. I watch the smoke cascade through the crystal test-tube, and the beast's chest expands. After a bit, all twenty-seven heads let out a self-conscious, yet tuneful, breath.

'My go?' I ask, knees knocking with anticipation. The Misadventurer blinks, bobs its heads to one side, then sets fire to the semi-precious stone again, and places the sickly sweet, hot thermometer between my lips.

I give the pipe a modest suck. Initially, there's disappointment. Then, ten seconds later, there's unbelievable bliss, like my whole body's been cast in the finest warm Belgian chocolate. A friendly tingle wobbles through my veins, like a marching band, stirring the most elaborate forms of happiness and contentment in each and every blood cell. I'm in Heaven! Not just literally, but metaphorically and all!

It's almost too much to bear. Slumped next to me, the Multi-Headed Musician looks comparatively nonchalant about the whole ordeal – then again, some of those heads have been here more than forty years, and even before that they must've had their fair share of terrestrial drugs.

'So, uhm, why are you here?' Jim Morrison asks, as each head slowly comes back to its senses.

'Oh, ssth . . . er . . .' I slur, with a frozen tongue, like I've been swallowing sugar-coated snowballs. 'Er . . . the drugs, the drugs. I'm a bit bored of this old thing.'

I touch the stainless-steel halo, spinning at 45rpm above my cranium, all out of control. Jim's halo looks a bit skew-whiff but, when I go to adjust it for him, the whole beast leans back suddenly, like it doesn't want to be touched.

'No, uhm, we mean, how did you die? If that's not a . . . weird question, or . . .' Kurt Cobain interjects, peering at me through his blond curtains.

'Oh, er,' I stumble, gradually gradually gradually coming down from the crack, like the end of a fantastic, static rollercoaster ride. 'I died from being too nice.'

'Ha!' John Lennon blurts, beaming.

'Yeah,' I add, smiling, wanting them to like me. 'I tried to be dead nice all the time, but I ended up . . . I got taken advantage of and, er, yeah . . . died.'

Some of the heads nod, as they take it in turns to suck on the last embers of the crack-pipe. Patiently waiting his turn, Brian Jones asks me, 'So, have you continued, up here?'

I shrug and shake my head once, not following. Buddy Holly carries on, squinting at me through his specs, 'What he means is: you can create miracles now.'

One of the anonymous heads elaborates: 'For instance, stopping people's debts, or stopping planes from crashing, or, uhm . . . stopping those adorable little twins from fighting . . .'

The Many-Headed Musical Misadventurer points down at two platinum-blonde specks on the surface of Earth, which I presume are two adorable little twins. I chew my bottom lip, mulling it over.

'Hmmmmmmm,' I say, 'maybe, yeah, but . . . let's have another go on that crack-pipe first, eh?'

The beast blows hot dragon-breath out of its nostrils, and each head smirks, one after another. I smile too, feeling lovely. However, way down beneath us, on Earth, two adorable little twins start absolutely bawling their heads off.

⊙

Three months into the crack abuse, I find myself in Topshop again, perusing the kids' section for size 4 dresses. I look like death, all malnourished, with an empty birdcage for a torso, to go with my birds' legs. The crack and MDMA have completely obliterated my appetite, making even my daily jaunts to Krispy Kreme dismal and nauseating. I keep meaning to jack in the crack and hop over to Cloud 2 (Food & Drink) for one of Elvis's calorie-clogged Heart-Attack Sarnies (a hollowed-out loaf filled with peanut butter, normal butter, jam, and a pound of bacon, aka the Fool's Gold Loaf), but the smell of burned coke and Brillo pads emanating from Cloud 9 keeps pulling me back.

Teeth chattering, I grab a Diamond White romper suit from the rails and tug it over my skeleton. It's perfect – quite baggy, with enough give in the elbow department to lift a crack-pipe up to my lips and safely back down again.

Back out in the cool troposphere, the bright lights of Cloud 3 (Sound & Vision) leer at me as I spark up another semi-precious boulder. My legs twitch with pleasure for a moment, as the smoke surfs through my lungs, then the feeling subsides just as quickly. The lights of Cloud 3 dim again. My heart quietens to a mumble. Ever since I got involved with the crack, I haven't been making the most of Heaven's luxury facilities. Every evening I crawl into

240

the same Kimberly-shaped hole in the sandpit of coke on Cloud 9, digging for freebased truffles, before stumbling back to the Crystal-meth Castle, to doze vaguely on my bed.

I feel like a big baby – especially in the romper suit. From time to time I get the slight urge to create a miracle for one or two of you down on Earth, though it seems a bit of a hassle. Crack multiplies your selfishness.

One night, drifting glumly round Cloud 7 (Comedy), it strikes me I haven't laughed in weeks. Crack's a sociable drug, of course, but it has a cruel habit of freezing your tongue and burning your lips.

I need lubricating. Down the stratified sidestreets of Cloud 7 there are countless comedy clubs, as well as a circus, and live, televised funerals (some people can't resist laughing at them). I duck into the first club and order myself a Smirnoff Ice, propping up the bar. I stare at my sour reflection in the glass – the fish-eye effect makes me look even thinner, like the worm trapped in a bottle of tequila.

Round the comedy club, angels have packed out the tables, slurping and shrieking at each other while they wait for the next act. Since there's no smoking ban in Heaven, the angels have blown themselves clouds of Regal and Marlboro to sit on, hovering a good three feet above the booze-soaked carpet. I'm tempted to take the old crack-pipe out for another snog when, suddenly, the lights darken and redden, and the velvet curtains hiding the stage slide open.

I spit a gobful of Smirnoff back into my glass when I see who the next turn is. He's about fifty years old, with a bald spot, glasses, and a mop. He's introduced as 'the funniest school toilet cleaner in the world!' He's Barry Clark. My dead dad.

'Dad!' I yell, but it's lost amongst all the other cheering, frothing mouths. Fighting against the false, plastic contentment of the MDMA and crack, I'm surprised to feel real-life human happiness coursing through my system again. Either that, or it's just the Smirnoff Ice kicking in.

Barry Clark adjusts the SM58 microphone, making the PA squeak, then he clears his throat and begins his set:

'Now then, ladies and gentlemen. What's twelve inches long, stiff, has a purple head, and makes a woman scream at night?' he says, then he pauses, for effect. 'A cot death!'

Everybody bursts out laughing, throwing drinks this way and that. It's a classic! I crease up, like a piece of tracing paper being folded as many times as possible.

Mag Clark used to think Barry would go to Hell for jokes like that, but his good deeds cleaning the kids' classrooms must've outweighed the damage done by the disgusting jokes. Perhaps that's how entry to Heaven and Hell works – it's all in accordance to the ever-seesawing scales of niceness. For instance, if a serial killer goes on to found a children's hospice, does he or she still have to burn in Hell?

I cough up a few more giggles before the hilarity dies down around the club. Barry's beaming, dead chuffed with himself. I feel so much admiration for him, my eyes begin to mist over, as Barry attempts another joke:

'What's twelve inches long, stiff, has a purple head, and makes a woman scream at night?' he says, then he pauses, for effect. 'A cot death!'

The room erupts with laughter again. At first my brow furrows slightly, then I can't help joining in with the re-screeching. I spill a bit of drink down the Diamond White romper suit. It's even better the second time round! A bloody cot death – who would've thought it?!

'What's twelve inches long, stiff, has a purple head, and makes a woman scream at night?' Barry carries on, getting on a roll. 'A cot death!'

Hysterical now, I have to hold on to my sides to stop myself from throwing up. I thought he was going to say a willy!!

'What's twelve inches long, stiff, has a purple head, and makes a woman scream at night?' Barry continues, in his stride now. 'A cot death!'

Perhaps the fourth time round it's not quite so funny. My hysterical laughter softens to heavy panting. I pick at my nails for a moment, a little embarrassed. All around the club, the angels are still in stitches, their faces contorted. I take a long glug of alcopop, trying to get back into the party spirit.

'What's twelve inches long, stiff, has a purple head, and makes a woman scream at night?' Barry goes, then, wait for it: 'A cot death!'

My head sinks towards the bar. Barry doesn't seem to notice the laughter turning sour. The angels' honks and hoots quickly turn to heckles. Before long, they're baying for his blood, launching broken bottles at Barry with baleful expressions.

I feel terrible for him. After all, he's not even a real comedian. He's just my dad.

Maybe my idea of Heaven isn't the same as everyone else's. Some people like to heckle and abuse comedians when they're drunk, while others just want to hear their father's smutty jokes.

But, of course, there's a limit to how much cot death one woman can stand in one night.

I want to storm the stage. Not only would it be nice to meet my dead daddy again, it'd be nice to remove him from the bitter limelight now – before the angelic medics do it first, on a stretcher.

Trembling, I rise from the bar and make a wobbly beeline for the stage. I manage to lift my sunken features into something resembling a smile but, before I reach my dad, an unexpected rush of MDMA turns my face into a churning, gurning mess again.

I turn on my sandals and sprint as fast as I can out of the

comedy club. I don't want my dead dad to see his dead daughter like this. He probably wouldn't even recognise me, what with the size 4 skeleton, and crack sores round my mouth. I don't want to break his heart two times over.

All my life, I stayed away from drugs (unless you count Smirnoff Ice, ibuprofen, Strepsils, antihistamines, multivits, medicated plasters, etc.), and I used to scratch my head at ridiculous drug-taking divs in the street, only to become one myself.

Fluttering about aimlessly – like a drunken, dirty moth, as opposed to a crisp, white butterfly – I want to commit suicide off the edge of one of the clouds but, unhelpfully, I'm already dead. Instead, I make the crack-pipes commit suicide for me, launching them one by one off the nimbostratus. Some lucky scallywag down there (it looks like Peterlee to me) will have a field day, finding my works in a field somewhere, stuffed with heavenly freebase.

I sigh through my nostrils. I wish I could stop the disgusting, delicious MDMA dribbling into my spine. Dithering from cloud to cloud, all around me the angels look like manic, malnourished mannequins. I've come to realise Heaven's just one big pantomime, or puppet show. The haloes only ply you with MDMA so you're compliant and can't stomach any of the expensive, luxury foods. In fact, I've got a suspicion half the foodstuffs are merely plastic display models, arranged to give the impression of luxury, without all the hassle of mould or stocktaking. When I pass by the mammoth greengrocers on Cloud 2, it takes a few minutes of scrabbling through the orange ping-pong balls before I come across a genuine satsuma. Sinking my teeth into it, the flesh tastes unbelievably fizzy and refreshing, like a citrus firework going off in my gob. The effect is almost comparable to the first time I did crack cocaine: mindbendingly blissful.

From here on in, I'm substituting C for Vitamin C.

Sucking up the sweet juice, I sidle past the vast Olympic

Stadium, held up by brushed-aluminium abutments, with rainbow floodlights, a 25ct-gold clocktower, and specks of Olympic sweat fountaining over the sides like salted confetti. Cloud 4 (Sport) caters for that strange breed of folk who gain pleasure from non-sexual physical exertion, for example badminton, 3,000m steeplechase, tiddlywinks. Some scientists believe exercise increases people's happiness levels (through the release of endorphins), despite it usually involving jogging in treacherous drizzly conditions and coming home with dogmuck on your trainers, absolutely knackered, with a stitch.

Just thinking about athletics tires me out. I sit down with my back to one of the aluminium abutments, listening to the distant echo of shotputs landing; javelins injecting the soil; the soft applause of running shoes; and the odd, gravelly warcry of exertion. Opposite me, there's a digital chalkboard which reads:

THIS EVENING AT THE OLYMPIC STADIUM

17.00 FOOTBALL (DEAD NAGOYA GRAMPUS EIGHT vs
DEAD BORUSSIA MÖNCHENGLADBACH)
19.15 TRACK AND FIELD (INCLUDING 100m, 200m, 400m,
800m, 1,500m,
LONG JUMP, TRIPLE JUMP)
21.30 CABER TOSS
22.00 SYNCHRONISED SWIMMING
23.30 MUD WRESTLING/WET T-SHIRT COMPETITION

I glance up at the 25ct-gold clocktower, just as it chimes half seven. The chalkboard turns my thoughts to Stevie. I haven't seen him since arriving in Heaven, but he must be here somewhere – he was a good sort, after all (providing he hasn't gone to Valhalla instead, thanks to his Scandinavian melanin). The corners of my mouth prick up as I double-check that mention of the 200m.

245

Brushing myself down, I try to sort out my appearance in one of the steel cylinders, then stride gracefully through the entrance of the stadium, taking a ticket from the dour ex-demon at the box office. A wave of tropical perspiration hits me as I enter the arena. With a helping hand from the MDMA, I make it up the steep terrace to the back row, and sit down with the whole Angel Gabriel Memorial Stand to myself.

I stretch my legs out across Row ZZ, seeing stars at first, before my eyes adjust and I see sportstars instead. They've designed the Olympic Stadium well, stuffing all possible facilities (running track, air-conditioned luge, swimming pool, table-tennis tables, wrestling ring . . .) in the open-plan basin. Some of the competitors even manage to do two sports at once – for instance, the chap over there doing underwater archery, or the girl doing equestrian pole-vault.

I decide to buy a hot dog from the lone vendor zig-zagging through the Gabriel Memorial Stand. While my appetite's still suppressed by the evil MDMA, I'm desperate to plumpen myself back to a healthyish size 6, or 8. I need to get back into those unicornskin trousers, and I need to get my old, beloved boyfriend back, I think.

My heart expands when the 200m competitors emerge from the tunnel, with their wings poking proudly out of their tracksuits. I shift on the velvet cushion, listlessly chewing the first bite of frankfurter. It doesn't want to go down, so I end up just licking it instead, like a pink, meaty Mini Milk.

When the sprinters are introduced over the tannoy, my heart shrinks again. There's no mention of Stevie. This afternoon, the track and field programme is a historic reenactment of the 1936 Berlin Olympics, with black beauty Jesse Owens claiming his four golds in the face of Nazi adversity. The only difference is the distinct lack of Nazis, since they all happen to be roasting in Hell.

I leave the half-licked hot dog under my seat and slump back down the terrace. I feel sticky, sickly, and unattractive. I wonder

if Stevie made it to Heaven after all – what if he was a secret paedophile, or an ex-traffic warden, or a part-time racist, and ended
up boiling with Hitler and the gang? The more I think about him,
the more I miss him. I've been to a lot of funerals in my life,
so I'm sure there are a lot of my long-lost friends and relatives
floating around here, but there's no one I want to see more than
my Stevie. I owe him a huge kiss and a cuddle, and I owe him
an apology for being horrid. I also probably owe him £7,777.77.

Floating aimlessly between the Crystal Castle and the bubble-
gum sunset, I feel the £∞ voucher being magnetised to Topshop
again as I pass Cloud 1. I take the escalator up to the second
floor, then I shed my skin, tearing off the mucky romper suit
and jumping into a fresh pair of White Strike tights and a size 6
Titanium White shift-dress. The shift looks daft, hanging off me
like an extra-large lampshade, but it's meant to be an incentive
to put on a few pounds.

After Topshop, I hop over to Cloud 2 for some full-fat Italian
gelato. Annoyingly, most of the flavours are made of Plasticine
instead of ice cream – the only edible ones are chocolate, orange,
and chocolate orange. I plump for all three, taking my bowl to
sit by the busy window, in full view of the twinkling castle. One
hundred thousand pink sunsets wink at me, reflected in its tur-
rets, as I whizz the three flavours together with my spoon, and
shovel them down the hatch. After the first few mouthfuls, I let
out a slight grunt, suffering an almighty brain-freeze.

Across the room, another ice-cream enthusiast grunts as
it struggles to wrench its huge, hirsute frame out of one of the
sunken armchairs. I grin chocolate-coated canines as the beast
shuffles past, between the tables. It's the Many-Headed Musical
Misadventurer again.

'Hi!' I say, causing the beast some unnecessary whiplash, as
its twenty-seven heads turn in unison.

'Hey. Hi. How are you?' the heads chorus, crowding around me. 'How've you been? What have you been up to? What's up?' etc., etc.

'Ah, nothing, not much,' I reply, timidly twizzling my spoon in my bowl. 'I've just been looking for someone. But, like, I don't even know if he's here or not. You know?'

'A friend?' Brian Jones enquires, just to be polite.

'Mm. My boyfriend. Well, like, my ex-boyfriend,' I say. After another mouthful of ice cream, a second electric shock fires into my brain but, rather than Es or a brain-freeze, it's a cold, sharp flash of inspiration. I dig my spoon back into the bowl, and ask the Multi-Headed Musician, 'Actually, you lot might've seen him. Stevie Wallace, he's called. He's, like, he's a big fan of most of your music.'

Some of the heads seem to blush, causing an iridescent effect, like a scarlet peacock displaying.

'He's about this tall, with like white-gold hair, muscly, with freckles, and like a small scar on his cheek,' I explain.

The beast performs a Mexican wave of shaken heads and shrugged shoulders, muttering apologies.

'Oh, and he's probably got one eye missing,' I add, at which point the heads perk up, and they babble, 'Yeah. Uhm, Steve? Stevie? We know a guy who we call, uhm, One-Eye Steve. Sure. The sprinter? Stevie? Do you mean Stevie?'

The backlog of MDMA suddenly breaks open the mental dam I'd been beavering away at with my gloom. I give the Misadventurer another brown and orange grin.

'God, as if he's alive!' I say, before rethinking. 'Well, naw, he's dead, but . . . you know . . . that's amazing . . .'

Jim Morrison smiles and says, 'Uhm, we can take you to him, if you'd like?'

'Aw, yeah, yeah!' I yelp, then after a short silence: 'Please.'

◉

It turns out the Many-Headed Musical Misadventurer has known Stevie for quite some time. Their friendship blossomed after the beast played a one-off gig on Cloud 4 back in February, round about the time Stevie hung himself. Stevie, being a fan of many of the Many-Headed Musician's heads, waited backstage for the beast, gurning and stuttering uncontrollably, having just arrived in the dizzy heights of Heaven. While the conversation was strained at first, Stevie and the beast shared a strange sort of affinity, mumbling tales of music, heartbreak and happiness, over a 6l bottle of Johnnie Walker Red (the Misadventurer) and a Mixed Berry Lucozade (Stevie).

The Multi-Headed Musician doesn't perform many concerts here nowadays – due to stage fright, 'exhaustion' and, more than anything, extreme creative differences – but the beast still meets up with Stevie now and then for a natter, or a nose about the record shops.

As the Misadventurer leads me round the outer limits of Heaven, where the clouds are ever so delicate and wispy, I wonder how Stevie'll react when he sees me. I wonder what he looks like now, in his white angel gear, with a halo and one eye plucked out. The way I remember him, he was blue and limp, like a Finnish flag flying at half-mast.

Glugging a little Scotch from an inside-wing pocket, the beast kicks through the patchy strati as we hop, skip and flutter our way to Cloud 8 (Sex). While Cloud 9 is dark and rich, with the earthy tang of cannabis, Cloud 8 looks like a gigantic, pink bouncy castle; slick, with the sour-milk stink of shagging. I wonder why the Misadventurer's taking me here.

I flick my wings harder, trying to keep up as the beast clambers on top of the candy-coloured cumulonimbus. It's quite an experience, seeing Cloud 8 for the first time. After all that bad love with Donald and my weekly exes, my sex drive's been more

249

or less non-existent since I arrived in Heaven. My holes feel like clammed-up clamshells, and it'll take more than just prodding and probing with the right implements to shuck them open again.

Having said that, the place does look intriguing. The Misadventurer leads me down the main 'strip', which is lined with large, private 'sex sheds'; wipe-clean public beds and sofas; toyboxes brimming with disinfected sex-aids; and tight staircases leading down to dingy dominatrix dungeons. Some of the sex sheds are locked, with the sound of squealing just about audible under the doorways, while others are wide open – exposing everything from orang-utan gangbangs to masochistic midget self-humiliation to a lost bridge club of old-age pensioners, accidentally 69ing sixteen-year-old glamour models. Coming from Shed 8 I hear the shriek of a businessman being fellated by a Humboldt squid. In Shed 57 there are more saucy goings-on: I see a woman covered in tomato ketchup writhing against a man covered in mayonnaise. The door to Shed 101 is locked, and the lights are off. Through the keyhole, a man and wife appear to be conducting the missionary position, underneath the covers. My stomach turns over.

The Many-Headed Misadventurer hardly bats an eyelid as we manoeuvre through the orgy, where all manner of men and women and whites and blacks and inbetweens and carnivores and crustaceans and dairy products are indulging in every sex act imaginable – as well as a few sex acts you couldn't imagine even if I had the words for them.

'Uhm, here,' the beast mumbles, stopping outside Shed 4123. 'Uhm, you should knock.'

The door – painted fluorescent lavender, with a large gold letterbox and doorhandle – is shut. As the Multi-Headed Misadventurer slopes off, I place my ear against the gloss finish, but the noise of the orgy out here far exceeds the faint mumbling within. I decide to give it a knock.

'Clang clang clang!' the door says first, then from behind it: 'H-h-howay in, my l-lovely!'

It certainly sounds like my Stevie. I'm not sure what he means by 'my lovely', though – perhaps it's the MDMA talking.

I twist the gold handle and swing the door open. Bright, white, nice light spews from the shed, along with the choking stench of angel sweat. I cover my mouth. Through the fluorescence, the first thing I see is Stevie Wallace – stark naked except for an eye-patch – laid on a pink, quilted four-poster bed. I step into the blinding light, ready to swing my arms around him, when I realise he's got eight female arms around him already.

I freeze.

The four girls look up at me in various states of undress, with perfectly raised eyebrows and breasts. They carry on clutching Stevie, stroking him here and there with the delicacy of professional kitten-groomers. The girls are impeccable: 25ct-gold skin, beautifully sculpted hairdos, legs like buffed banister rungs. I think one of them might even be Marilyn Monroe – unless it's Paolo's dead wife.

I feel sick. At first, Stevie doesn't seem to recognise me, thanks to my size 6 skeleton and cracked crack-lips. However, even in Heaven I've managed to retain those pesky evil eyes, and they narrow as I watch Stevie shuffle awkwardly, before the penny finally drops.

'K-K-Kimberly?' he mutters. 'Wh-what are you you doing here?'

'What do you think I'm doing?' I snap, feeling defensive in front of those delectable bints. 'I died.'

Stevie's cock and balls shrink and his cheeks glow red. Nevertheless, the ladies carry on pawing him, like begging dogs. Just looking at them, I can tell they've all got crap personalities.

'So, er, hm, how have you been?' I ask, trying to ignore their pouting glares.

'Oh, er, f-fine,' Stevie stumbles.

'I found the note. About the seal,' I say, glad in a way he seems to be over his trauma, although I wish he wasn't getting over it quite like this.

When I mention the seal, Stevie's chest seems to crumple. I imagine there aren't any seals swimming on Stevie's version of Cloud 6 (the Animal Kingdom). You see, each angel's Heaven differs slightly from the next angel's, since some people like sugar, while others prefer spice; some people like coffee, while others prefer tea; some people find blubbery sea mammals ador-able, while others are allergic. The only problems arise when two angels' dreams overlap, and begin to override each other's; for example, right now.

'L-l-look, Kim, er, can you give give give me fifteen m-minutes with the g-g-g-g-girls?' Stevie says. 'Then I'll c-c-c-*come* out and talk.'

I make a sound halfway between a sigh and a scream, then storm out of the shed, slamming the door behind me. All around, the cavorting couples and animals mock me, enjoying their no-strings sex far too loudly. I perch myself on a slightly clammy sofa and cover my ears. I want Stevie to be happy now he's dead, but somehow I feel a bit used. If your boyfriend dies while you're still going out with him, is he technically still your boyfriend if you bump into him in Heaven? Is he cheating on me in there?

Admittedly, I've had my fair share of sexual encounters since Stevie tied himself to the climbing frame but – don't forget – my escapades were purely selfless acts of kindness. Four gorgeous pinups on one Stevie, on the other hand, does seem a little selfish.

I press my chin against my chest. Maybe if I focus my mind hard enough, those four beautiful bimbos might disappear in a puff of odd-sock-scented smoke. Perhaps I can override Stevie's sordid idea of Heaven with some careful meditation.

Concentrating, I imagine the girls suddenly coming down with appendicitis, or leprosy. I imagine their breasts and fingers falling off. I imagine their mouths, vaginas and bumholes becoming filled with cement and hardening in seconds, refusing entry to Stevie's knob, or any of his other appendages. I sigh. I'm just adding colour to an image of their make-up and collagen implants spontaneously combusting, when the fluorescent lavender door swings open again and Stevie storms out, panting.

'Will you st-stop imagining all th-those bad things?!' he yells. 'The g-girls are in a r-right state!'

I smile, but keep my chin down. Absolutely shattered, Stevie collapses next to me on the sofa. He's got his clothes back on now – a creased Dirty White Hugo Boss suit, with all the pinstripes going in different directions down his arms and legs.

'You f-found my note, then?' Stevie asks, getting his breath back. I nod, gently placing my hand on his, despite where his hands have been.

'You've settled in here alright,' I say, not meaning to sound so catty.

Stevie smiles shyly, then scratches the back of his neck and says, 'Yeah, s-sorry about . . . the g-g-g-girls . . . it's just just just been hard g-getting my senses back after the s-s-s-s- . . . after the s-s-s- . . . the s-s- . . .'

'Don't worry,' I whisper. 'I understand.'

S-S-Suddenly the boy s-s-seems so fragile, it's impossible not to wrap him up in my arms and wings. It's just a shame he smells of bottomless ladies.

'I feel like I was bad to you before you died, though,' I say to his neck. 'I thought it was my fault.'

'N-noo,' Stevie coos.

Lips pressed against him, it's tempting to say 'I love you', but I'm worried I won't hear it back.

'So,' I start, releasing the grip slightly, 'tell me about all these vixens you've been seeing.'

Stevie looks me in the eyes with just the one of his, and sighs, 'Ah, the-the-they're nothing. I couldn't even g-get it up, when I first g-got here. Because of the s-s-s- . . .'

'Yeah,' I say, still understanding.

'I I I was dead sad when I got here, just c-c-comfort eating and that,' Stevie explains. 'But but then then I found this cl-cloud. I was afraid to take my cl-clothes off at first, still w-wound up about the s-s-s- . . .'

'Seriously, Stevie, I understand, love.'

'B-bu-but then then I found those g-girls,' Stevie continues. 'They c-came up to me with all these l-lines about w-w-w-w-one-eyed men being irrerrerrerrerrerresistible. I couldn't stop myself. I'm so sorry. I d-didn't think I'd see you again. Or, not yet.'

I chew my lips, a little ashamed to be dead so soon after my boyfriend. In a way, me and Stevie have been fairly useless human beings, not even managing to make it into our thirties. I touch his hand again, watching the tops of the clouds turn from lilac to bright magenta to moody blue, as the sun slides slowly off their sides.

'But don't you find it all a bit, like, unfulfilling?' I venture. 'All the endless debauchery?'

Stevie shuffles on the sofa, feathers all ruffled.

'See, cos I've been a bit poorly,' I carry on. 'I went and over-indulged myself on Cloud 9 – you know they've got crack and all that, over there? And now look at me. I mean, it was alright at first, but soon I realised I was missing out on all the other good stuff – like, you know . . . being with someone you actually love, or loved, or whatever. And that's why I came looking for you.'

254

Stevie's cheeks pulse red again, as he scans the shenanigans of Cloud 8. He sighs. Nearby, a girl with a mouth as wide as the Tyne Tunnel is giving head to sixty-odd men simultaneously. Stevie wipes his nose. I can tell he's been brainwashed by the bawdy goings-on of the cloud, but surely the love of one person is worth more than the cold, lusty, flippant dribblings of the masses?

'So you're off the dr-drugs?' Stevie asks.

'Yeah. I'm quite buzzing off fruit now, actually.'

Stevie smiles. For the first time in almost a year, he slips an arm round my waist. He tries to kiss me on the lips, but he has a bit of trouble judging distance with only one eye, and he ends up kissing my nose instead. Nevertheless, it does the trick.

I whisper in his ear, 'Might you want to get back together?'

Stevie gazes blankly over my shoulder. His grip round my waist slackens as I become aware of a menacing presence towering over us. It's a 6ft, leggy presence, with an hourglass figure and at least DD breasts. I think it's a woman.

'Stevie, darling,' it says, 'it's time for your nine o'clock, my little love pup. Whenever you're ready, darl. I'll be in the shed.'

It smiles, swinging a pair of leather trusses, pink fluffy handcuffs, and a 2l bottle of transparent Harmony lubrication. I scowl at it, grinding my teeth.

'O-o-o-o-o-okey . . . okay,' Stevie splurts. The menacing presence waltzes off, wiggling its perfect bottom.

'L-look, Kim,' Stevie says, flustered now, 'I'd better go. I'm s-s-s-sorry. I'll see you s-soon. S-Sometime. Soon.'

And then in a flash he's gone, stumbling through the fog, back into Shed 4123. The lavender door goes clunk. Locked.

I pick the skin out from under my fingernails, rocking back and forth on the sofa. I feel utterly useless and unattractive. Stevie didn't seem to appreciate my slender size 6 skeleton – then again, I probably looked like a Holocaust victim, next to his juicy pinup ladies.

I feel the halo trying its best to sedate me with MDMA, but it does nothing to combat the crush of rejection. Unpeeling my legs from the sofa, I hide my snivelling face with my hands, then begin the slow trek back to the Crystal Castle.

Despite all the free cake, cock and crack, Heaven's not all it's cracked up to be. Those of you who read page 236 and are now desperately trying to paper-cut your radial arteries in an attempt to join me up here – don't bother. You're better off where you are, with your books and your own beautiful, banal, bewildering existence on Earth.

I try not to think about Stevie in the leather trusses, as I hover in front of the Crystal Castle, searching for my keycard. I just want to get my head down.

On my way up the glass staircase, I feel like everyone's eyes are on me. I swear all the angels keep nudging each other and pointing at me, unless it's just paranoid backlash from the MDMA and heartbreak. As I slope through Methuselah Block B, the bastards' faces leer at me, reflected millions of times over in the prisms and rhinestones. If it wasn't illegal to swear or vandalise in Heaven, I'd scream obscenities at them and smash all their windows through, from Magnum Block to Nebuchadnezzar.

Once I'm safely inside my dorm (a 50m² dwelling, with all mod cons, and a double bed which doubles up as a Jacuzzi, with optional running hot water, champagne, or melted chocolate), I rip the halo out of my skull. The barbed spike gets snagged on my scalp at first, making my eyes water, before finally coming loose and landing with a clang on the mother-of-pearl linoleum. I fall onto the bed in a sudden spasm of exhaustion. I detach my feather wings, then pull my Titanium White shift over my head and yank the White Strike tights down. As the tights land

256

in a snaked pile between my legs, I realise why everyone's been pointing and laughing at me. My heart sinks. Stuck to the gusset of the tights is an elephant's-trunk-sized condom, smeared with spunk. I must've sat down on it by mistake, while I was waiting for my ex-boyfriend.

⊙

The first thing that strikes me when I wake up is the hangover and heart-wrenching depression. My head kills, like someone's been practising brain surgery on it with a pickaxe, and my white sheets are soaking wet with sweat. The reflective crystals sting my eyeballs. I let out a groan.

Once the initial suicidal sensation passes, I roll out of the bed, grabbing blindly, manically, for the dented stainless-steel halo. Clumsily reattaching it, the MDMA softly trickles back into my nervous system. The relief is sublime. I literally make the sound 'Aaahh', like someone forced into an orgasm.

Pulling the wings on again, I stare at my ugly features in the stretch mirror, bordered with many smaller, sparklier mirrors. For now the hangover and heart-wrenching depression have been replaced by a soothing, nondescript contentment, although I'm aware the contentment's a con. Karl Marx was right: religion is the opiate for the masses. Outside the Crystal Castle, I watch the other angels dithering about in a vaguely happy trance, gurning a lot, but I don't believe their hearts are in it.

I decide to go out for some breakfast. As I flap hard against the breeze, with my nose aimed towards the greasier end of Cloud 2, I try to think up ways to steal back Stevie's heart. It seems to be a strange sort of beast, that boy's ticker – not susceptible to ordinary coaxing such as flattery, cuddling, or desperate begging for forgiveness. It only seems interested in people with bigger breasts than me.

I order a Full English 'Belly Buster' breakfast and a triple-chocolate milkshake, hoping to quickly put on weight and grow my curves back. I yank the steel halo out of my head again to conjure up an appetite, then I get stuck in. I haven't eaten meat in months – the sausages and bacon are indescribably delicious, sailing around the beans, two eggs, chips, hash browns and black pudding in a shallow pond of grease. As I slurp up the last of the milkshake, making the glass burp, I surreptitiously rub my waistline, feeling for expansion. I wonder if there are any plastic surgeons in Heaven willing to give me a free boob-job. Having said that, surely there must be a less superficial way to win Stevie over? After all, I was with him for four years – I must have some insight into the boy, to help me steal control of his heartstrings. Apart from sticking his penis into perky, personalityless pinups, what are Stevie's interests?

Fourteen sips into another triple-chocolate milkshake, the idea finally surfaces. On a white napkin, I scribble in lipstick:

WEIGHT
SUNGLASSES
BEARD
CLEARASIL
FOOTBALL (CHEESE ETC.)

Two months and two larger dress sizes later, I find myself back on the sex cloud. In sunglasses, an overcoat, and Fred West's false beard (robbed from the edge of the Stairway-to-Heaven, under the cover of darkness), I breast-stroke round the back of the Crystal Castle and emerge Ursula Andress-like on the pink fluff of Cloud 8. There's a lot of breast stroking going on here as well, not to mention penis stroking, bottom stroking and puppy stroking. It's a wonder the place isn't just a sad A&E full of STD and carpet burns.

It hasn't been easy putting the weight back on. Underneath the Guillotine, my scalp's in tatters, thanks to the constant removing and reattaching of the halo. While the MDMA's been useful in keeping my spirits up, it's impossible leaving it inserted when you're trying to chow down an extra-large McDonald's. Overchewed chips are spat out. Juicy burgers turn stale and dehydrated.

Throughout spring, the ex-demons working at McDonald's watch me balloon to a size 10. Once my hips and tits are sufficiently rerounded, I flutter over to Cloud 1 to buy a long overcoat in Vanilla, some scanty Semi-Skimmed Ann Summers lingerie and a canister of Jacob's cheese footballs from Cloud 2.

Back on Cloud 8, with the beard and overcoat on, and the fancy lingerie underneath, I creep furtively past the spooning seahorses, 69ing giraffes and housewives having their clitorises bashed with vibrating Newton's cradles. I wince, trying to keep focused on Shed 4123, approaching just as furtively in the distance.

Apparently, the best route to a man's heart is through his stomach. So, ignoring the muffled moans and groans of Stevie and co. behind the fluorescent lavender door, I lay out a Hansel and Gretel trail of cheese footballs from Shed 4123, all the way to my glass doormat at the Crystal Castle. Fortunately, the horny creatures nearby are too busy nibbling each other's flapping genitals to be interested in nibbling my cheesy breadcrumb trail.

Back in the safety of Methuselah Block B, I throw off the beard and overcoat, then lie in wait for Stevie with a sultry expression and the Jacuzzi taps set to CHAMPAGNE. The silky Semi-Skimmed underwear shimmers in anticipation.

Six hours later, the sultry expression has sagged. The bows on the underwear look like angry, crossed arms. Stevie hasn't shown up.

Despite the MDMA trying to reassure me I'm not completely pathetic, I can't help ruining my make-up with tears. Once my mascara's run all the way down my chin, I almost don't want Stevie to appear. Just as baby tapirs are born with stripes, to camouflage them from prowling lionesses, I want to bury my daft, black-striped face in the pillows, and never be seen again.

⊙

The next day, I work my way through the wasted cheese snacks and champagne, plotting new ways to woo Stevie. Aside from eating and drinking, apparently men's favourite pastimes are sex, sports, and driving fast cars. There's no use for any cars in Heaven (although there's a racing-track round the back of the Olympic Stadium, where James Dean, Grace Kelly and Ayrton Senna regularly battle it out), and Stevie seems to have had his fill of sex already, so I flap over to Cloud 4 (Sport) to see what's on offer at the old Wembley Empire Stadium. (In Heaven, even the football stadiums are dead.)

For a female angel in Heaven, it's incredibly difficult to find tickets to a game of football. Not only do most female angels prefer to banish matches to the belching depths of Hell, most male angels prefer to banish females from football matches, since they tend to spoil them by talking, or not understanding. However, this morning, I cunningly reattached Fred West's false beard, and I've stuffed napkins from the greasy spoon into my overcoat shoulders, to bulk them up.

The ex-demon at the Twin Towers box office eyes me suspiciously as I say through the beard, in a gruff voice, 'Er, ahem, can I have two tickets to Dead England veez Dead Hungary, please?'

I think it's a safe bet buying England tickets – there's nothing better to get a man's testosterone flowing than patriotism and balls. After a slightly awkward conversation with the ex-demon

260

about seating plans, I take the tickets and scuttle away from the Empire Stadium, towards the pink sex cloud, made even pinker by the perky sunrise.

The sweet-and-sour stench of Cloud 8 gets into my lungs as I slip through the crowds of copulating acrobats. Keeping my hand pressed to my mouth – to keep the beard from falling off, and to keep my breakfast down – I follow the trail of uneaten cheese footballs back to Shed 4123. As per usual, the door's locked. I decide not to knock. Instead, I push one of the tickets through the large gold letterbox, which doubles up as a peephole for passing perverts. I keep my eyes shut tight, until the letterbox shuts again with a heavenly clunk.

Jittery and excited, I hop back towards Cloud 4, using the small altocumulus clouds as stepping-stones. The football doesn't start for another couple of hours, but I want to get seated, and psyched up for Stevie's arrival. I hope he turns up. I hope he can sacrifice sex for ninety minutes, to see his beloved Dead England demolish Dead Hungary, and unwittingly bump into his beloved ex-girlfriend again.

Stomach knotted, I trek round the periphery of the Empire Stadium until I come to Turnstiles 1100–1125, then hand my ticket to the ex-demon at the window. The red-headed beast frowns, letting me into the empty 82,000-capacity stadium almost two hours before kick-off. The pitch is still tucked under its protective plastic sheets, though rain seems unlikely – doesn't the groundsman realise we're above the clouds?

I skip up the thirty-nine steps to the Royal Box, and take my seat directly in line with the centre spot. With one of my shoulder-pad napkins I buff the scarlet seat next to me, ready for Stevie. Then, I rip off the false beard and undo the Vanilla overcoat, revealing my Very White polyester halterneck to the empty stadium. The wind whistles.

I spend the next hour shaking the royal row, bouncing up and down on my seat as the stadium slowly fills up. Dead Hungary play in a green and white striped uniform – their fans make the south stand look like it's sprouting mould, as the clock ticks. I take a Matchday Programme from one of the wandering vendors and bury my head in it, killing time.

There's still no sign of Stevie when the corpses start warming up, half an hour before kick-off. The stadium cheers and swoons when Dead Hungary's handsome centre-forward, Miklós Fehér, jogs onto the turf, freshly hallowed by Pope John Paul II. Apparently Miki died of a heart attack aged just twenty-four – hence, he's left behind a beautiful cadaver. In contrast, most of the other players are decrepit old codgers: Stanley Matthews has to play with a cane; scrawny Wilf Mannion looks like a dithering goalpost; Ferenc Puskás has to be pushed out in a wheelchair.

I keep an eye on Miklós as the teams mumble their way through the national anthems, then line up in formation at opposite ends of the pitch. The game's just about to get under way when I'm choked by the sweet-and-sour stench of sex again. I cover my nose and mouth with my hands – at first in disgust, then in delight when I see Stevie slowly making his way towards the Royal Box.

'Stevie!' I say, not sure whether to wrap my arms around him. Instead, I just touch his elbow politely.

'I I th-thought I'd find you here,' Stevie says, sitting down on the gleaming seat next to mine. As his bum hits the ruby velvet, the whistle goes. Dead Hungary start out by passing the ball amongst themselves, drawing out a huge dot-to-dot puzzle in the grass.

I've been gazing at Miki so much, Stevie seems somehow plain in comparison. But maybe that's the point – in Heaven, you can lust after as many beautiful, imaginary bastards as you like, but nothing beats rediscovering the one long-lost love of your life. And it's good to see Stevie with clothes on again.

'What have you been up to?' I ask, smiling away inanely.

'Erm, n-not much. Just just just the shed,' he replies.

My smile falters. Heaven knows where he gets the stamina to please these multifarious slappers. I stare at the pitch again in a mild huff. For a bit, I watch Jackie Milburn dribbling near the corner-flag, and he hasn't even got the ball. What a mess.

'Have you missed me?' I ask, still looking the other way.

'Y-yeah,' Stevie mumbles.

'You know, I felt awful when you died. Like, I was . . . thinking of going the same way, you know. I thought it was all my fault.'

'W-why?'

I bite down on a hangnail. While I'd rather Stevie didn't know I was intentionally nasty to him in the delicate days leading up to his death, I think it's high time I told the truth. More than anything, I want him to know I'm not a cruel person, deep down – it was all just amateur dramatics. All just an act that backfired.

'Er,' I start, finding it difficult to breathe, 'well, first I want to say I'm sorry. See, I think I was horrible to you, before you died. I don't know why. I ruined your athletics kit. And I made Lucifer bite through the telly cable, so we didn't have to watch the Boro.'

Stevie looks down and smirks bashfully. He whispers, 'Don't worry.'

'Naw, but it gets worse,' I explain. 'I . . . like, it didn't mean anything or anything, but I accidentally had a kiss with someone, when me and Polly went to China White that time.'

I feel about five centimetres tall, shuffling my sandals on the cold concrete. Stevie blows out a gust of air. A dark gloom descends on us. He wriggles uncomfortably on his seat while I keep my eyes down, bracing myself for a slap across the chin, or an earful of abuse. And I deserve it.

'S-seriously, don't don't don't worry,' he says eventually, scratching himself. He looks out across the grass before taking another sharp breath and adding, 'Well, I I I I feel bad now. Er, see . . . there's s-something I've got to tell you . . . I, well, I I don't know how to s-say this . . . but, I'd been s-sort of seeing s-someone else before I died.'

A force like a huge red cannonball grinds at my chest.

'Who?' I snap.

Stevie makes a slight gagging sound, and says, 'This N-N-Natalie . . . she's this p-pentath-thlete . . . from the club . . .'

'Never,' I grumble, feeling even smaller.

'I felt awful. I w-wanted to tell you, but I di-di-didn't want to hurt you. I d-didn't know how to break up with you.' Stevie takes a breath. 'I'm s-sorry about that note. I di-didn't get raped by a s-s-s-seal. We went to S-Seal Sands, but but but that painful growth I told you about . . . it wasn't from a s-s-seal.' He takes another breath. 'It was from N-Natalie. She d-didn't know she'd been c-carrying g-gonorrhoea. And I d-didn't want to give it to you . . . and I di-didn't know what to do . . .'

Despite being surrounded by 81,998 noisy football fans, somehow me and Stevie manage to sit in awkward silence for a minute. Eventually – whether genuine or not – Stevie starts to cry from his one good eye.

'And I I I think I got her pr-pregnant,' he adds, between sniffs.

I shake my head, remembering Natalie's bump at his funeral. And her tears.

I want to strike him across the face, but I'm rendered useless by the shock. I ask him, solemnly, 'Why did you cheat on me? What did I do?'

'I I I'm sorry, I d-don't know. C-complacency, or something,' Stevie offers.

'But I was just pretending to be nasty. Just *pretending*.'

'It's n-not that. P-p-people just get bored.'

I feel like an idiot. If only we'd known we were tired of each other, we might've made it into our thirties. As it turned out, we were both too timid for our own good. We were so frightened to break each other's hearts, we ended up breaking everything else in sight instead. All it would've taken was something along the lines of, 'It's not you, it's me,' or, 'You're a boring bastard – I'm leaving.' Any of those words could've saved us.

I bite down on my nail again and draw blood. I think about the common seals, basking on the rocks at the Sands. I wonder why Stevie chose such an absurd lie. Then again, if you're planning on being unfaithful, you've got to be prepared to come up with some far-flung, pathetic excuses for it.

'B-but, I dunno, I I think you're right, you know,' Stevie says. 'It's a bit unfulfulfulfilling, b-being with all them weird women.'

I look up at him. Despite everything, it feels like as good a time as any to touch his arm again. In life, as in death, we've both cheated on each other numerous times. We've both been timid, and we've both been terrible people. And, weirdly, we seem to have more in common now than ever before.

'I've missed you,' I say. 'A lot. And, I dunno, it seems like those girls are just using you. I reckon, anyway. And I bet they've got crap personalities . . .'

Stevie says nothing. He glances at the football, then back at me, then back at the football. He keeps shuffling from side to side, making it difficult for the angels behind us to see Alan Ball sky one over Dead Hungary's crossbar. Half the stadium goes, 'Ooooohhhh!' while the other half goads, 'Aaarrrrhh!'

'I wish we'd just stuck together . . .' I say, once the crowds calm down again.

'Mm, I I I know. I m-meant it, in that note, when I said I l-loved you.'

A smile tugs at my lips. Despite our behaviour, I still think we've got a chance of happiness. While the match carries on beneath us, I can feel the north stand shaking, as the cheering builds to an almighty crescendo. I'm not sure if it's me who's just scored, or one of the players. Just to make certain, I ask, 'See, you could always move into mine? I've got space – it's in Methuselah Block.'

'Mm . . .' Stevie hums, mulling it over. I hope he's thinking about me, more than the girls in Shed 4123.

'You reckon we might make a go of it again, you and me?' I ask.

I feel like a junior schoolgirl. Stevie scratches his neck, then rubs his lips and replies, 'I d-d-d-d—'

I wonder if it's actually a stammer, or if he's trying to answer my question in Morse code. I cross my arms, concentrating on the 'd' (the one coming from Stevie's mouth; not the 'D' at the edge of the penalty area, where Dead Hungary have a free kick). Does he or doesn't he want to be my boyfriend?

'I d-d-d—' Stevie carries on, red-faced, until finally: 'I d-d-*do*.'

Dead Hungary smash the free kick into the back of Dead England's net, but I still clap my hands on my thighs and grin. Everyone groans as I wrap my arms around Stevie's neck and give him a long, overexcited kiss. Stevie's a little taken aback, but he returns the kiss with a satisfying amount of passion. I cling to him gleefully for the remainder of the match (which ends up 6–3 to Dead England, but it's of no interest to me), then we battle through the angelic, antagonistic crowd, down the terraces and back onto mushy cloud matter. As we float by, everything looks beautiful around us: the police unicorns, the floodlights, the litter bins, the embracing hooligans.

Holding hands, me and Stevie fly at top speed towards the Crystal Castle, trying to keep a conversation going, but the g-force does nothing for his stammer. He seems in good spirits, though, and I can't wait to get him back to Methuselah Block B, to hug the hell out of him under my glass bedcovers, and start our relationship afresh. He might need a shower first, mind you. All those sluts need to go down the plughole.

'Do you fancy something to eat?' I ask, once we're up in my dormitory.

Stevie perches on the edge of the bed, wearing a wide grin which makes his eye-patch crinkle. He says, 'Er, y-yeah. Wh-what've you got?'

I flutter-hop into the kitchenette. In the fridge there's half a Big Mac and a bar of Galaxy. I feel uncivilised, like a bachelorette bringing a boy back for a one-night stand, not a long-term relationship. I wriggle awkwardly on the mother-of-pearl lino, umming and aahing, trying to be cute.

'Umm, aah,' I say, 'tell you what: you make yourself at home, love. Have a shower, or whatever. I'll nip over to Cloud 2 and get us something special. Maybe some Doritos and cheese footballs? And a can of cold Carlsberg?'

'Y-yeah, alright,' Stevie sniggers.

As Stevie strips off (something he's got used to recently), I coyly avert my eyes and slip back out of the dorm. I whizz down the banister, grinning indiscriminately at all the angels that mocked me only two months before.

Back out in the open air, I feel light as a feather, bounding from one cumulus to the next. It feels amazing to have Stevie back, especially knowing that daft, mortal cow Natalie's still toiling down on Earth, out of Stevie's reach. I hope she's suffering from post-natal depression.

As I dash into Somerfield, my heart pounds with joy and lack of exercise. I fill up a basket with Jacob's cheese footballs and Doritos, then waltz merrily out the back exit, taking the long-cut back to the Crystal Castle. Stevie's well known for taking ages in the shower (he shaves his legs and chest), so I take my time, tiptoeing from one wispy stepping-stone to the next. I'm so famished, I crack open the Jacob's canister right away, and kick cheese football after football into my goalmouth. I look out across the Earth's curved, blue horizon, thinking of all the lovely miracles me and Stevie might be able to conjure up for the folk down there. I could introduce him to my new friends: we could help Donald win the Lottery, clean the faeces and vomit out of Polly's back garden, and earn the Ristorante di Fantasia a few extra Food Hygiene Stars.

All in all, though, there'll be no bigger, better miracle than me and Stevie being back together, in Heaven.

I can't stop laughing, darting around the clouds in a daze. On my ascent back up to the Castle grounds, I accidentally bump haloes with a fellow daydreaming angel – this youngish man with blond curtains and a green and white kitbag.

'Oh, sorry,' he says, with an accent.

When I look up, my heart suddenly pounds in a different direction. I drop the Jacob's canister, and all the cheese footballs fall to Earth like yellow hailstones. And all thoughts of Stevie fly away on the next gust of wind.

'Fucking *hell* . . .' I breathe, far too overexcited, 'er, you're Miklós Fehér, aren't you?'

Miki smiles, peering at me through his blond curtains. His mouth opens, but no words come out of it. All of a sudden, the altocumulus beneath my sandals evaporates, and a bright red, open trapdoor appears. I don't even have time to scream. As I fall, Miklós watches me, astonished, his beautiful eyes becoming smaller and smaller and smaller and smaller. When I'm at least 666 metres into the abyss, a self-righteous voice booms at me, 'Kimberly Clark! You have been warned! You've just committed blasphemy. And swearing, too! And you had your mouth full! Off to Hell! Off to Hell!'

'No!' I scream, but it comes out soundless.

I desperately try to grab on to something, but by this time Heaven's a mere cheese football-sized speck above my head, and the abyss appears to be bottomless, and without a fire exit. It's no use. Hell's Bells cry out all around me, nearly-but-not-quite drowning out that self-satisfied, self-righteous voice: 'And as for you, poor Reader, you're going with her! Off to Hell! Off to Hell! Off to page 413! Now!!'

NOT THE END

Part 3) Karma Kimberly

Samsara – the constant cycle of suffering (also known as every-day life, death and rebirth) in Buddhism – is like being on a not-very-merry-go-round with all sorts of wild animals and lost souls, spinning spinning spinning so fast, it's near enough impossible to get off. The Tibetan Buddhists think of it more like a 'swamp' or a 'dark prison'.

At first, I think the Grim Reaper wants to play ring-a-ring-a-roses with me. He takes my hands and spins me in circles: not the nicest thing to do when someone's just been in a car accident.

As we spin, the penthouse suite gradually becomes formless and furnitureless, leaving just a bright, white void where the bright, white, minimalist kitchen-diner used to be. I wish I had a pair of sunglasses. It's like being in the centre of a slow-motion nuclear explosion.

'OM ĀH HŪM! OM ĀH HŪM!' I whisper, desperately wanting to please the deities and not be reincarnated as a muddy puddle, or a piece of cat litter.

I wish I'd paid more attention to the *Tibetan Book of the Dead*. Or, at least, I wish I'd paid less attention to the gruesome, turd-guzzling bits and more attention to the bits about improving my karma. After all, the only way to escape the spinning, suffersome *Samsara* – and attain enlightenment – is by devoting yourself to the mantras, not snacking on your own humandirt.

The Grim Reaper lets go of my hands and I fly into the void. I shriek, clenching my eyes shut, feeling my flesh and bones turning to kaleidoscopic, metamorphic magic dust. When I was young, I often wondered if I'd grow up to be a pop star, or a famous female astronaut, or a good mother, but now all those hopes are dashed. When you find yourself accidentally pushed into Buddhism by the Grim Reaper and a dice-wielding book-worm, suddenly your hopes are different: I wonder if I'll grow into a flower, or a giraffe, or a wave in the ocean, or a tuna fish, or a cucumber.

A loud, high-pitched purr emits from the Bardo sunburst, like somebody rubbing my head around a giant Day-Glo Tibetan prayer bowl. Soon I feel my DNA gently remoulding itself, stretching me into a scaly sausage shape. When I reopen my eyelids, I'm pleased to see I'm not a muddy puddle, or a piece of cat litter. Instead, I've got fangs and sour saliva, and even eviler eyes than last time. And I don't know if that means I've been a good girl or a bad girl.

Part 3a) Kimberly the Snake

I have a hissy fit when I spot my tangerine stripes in the glass. I look like a fake snake – like I've been peeled straight off a Snakes & Ladders board – but, in fact, I'm just your average okeetee corn snake. I slither round the artificial desert scene, kindly installed in the tank by JG Thomas & Sons, the owners of the pet shop. Using my forked tongue for guidance, I run rings round the plastic cactus, making sine waves in the sand. By the taste of the air, the last folks to rent the tank were lizards.

My sight's poor, but I can smell all the colours of the rainbow. It's like I've developed synaesthesia. With just the odd lick here and there, I soon build up a huge olfactory map of the pet shop: it looks like a gourmet taster menu to me, with all the warm-blooded dishes highlighted, in boxes. Scurrying about.

I hiss wearily. It's a bit disheartening, waking up in a 3 × 2 × 2ft tank, after having the boundless, bountiful Capital at my disposal. Three sides of the tank look out onto the shop floor, while the other side's meant to be a paradise vision of Arizona or New Mexico: a beatific panorama of the desert, where it's always sunset, and there's always a lonesome cowboy in the distance, like a star-spangled scarecrow.

I'm so hungry, I could eat a child's face. In my first year as a corn snake, I'm only entitled to one 'pinkie' (a bald baby mouse, not your little finger), every five or so days. I feel like a leper or a victim of war, having the pinkies winched into my tank by a helicopter that smells suspiciously like JG Thomas's hairy-backed hand. It doesn't help being surrounded by the all-squeaking, all-squawking menu of critters, just out of reach. I'd gladly pay the '£7!' price tag to get my constricting muscles around that albino hamster there, if only I could get out of the tank and get into my old bank savings.

272

This is the skinniest I've been in twenty-four years. During opening hours, I fantasise about a family saving me from the artificial desert, and feeding me up on a delicious rainfall of rodents, pet budgies, frogs' legs, snails, and quails' eggs. Then again, they could just as easily starve me to death, if they haven't got the funds, or the dedication, or done their homework.

Almost eight months to the day after my encounter with Mr Death, I find myself hiding from the Goth Family Robinson, in the shadow of my favourite rock. Despite always being sunset in Arizona/New Mexico, it always seems to be midday in the tank, with the sun constantly beaming at me like a 60-watt ultraviolet lightbulb. Corn snakes can cope perfectly well in cooler weather, so I prefer basking under the rock in the afternoons, only popping out to top up my tan, or shed my skin, or strangle a pinkie.

This particular afternoon, my favourite rock hides me from three squinting human faces. Two of them are ugly child-faces, while the other bears a striking resemblance to the child-faces, only with more nostril hair, more forehead, and wilder eyebrows.

'I can't see him, I can't see him,' one of the child-faces whines.

'Where is he?' moans the other one.

I'm a fucking sssssshe, you cheeky ssssssshit, I hiss. A second later, four oily hands are all over my front window, pressing and prodding and knocking. To shut them up, I glumly slither out from underneath the rock, yawning. The child-faces yelp when they see my tiny fangs, scuttling behind their dad, leaving behind twenty-odd sticky handprints. By the look on JG's face, he's wondering where he's left the Mr Sheen. I can smell it – it's over by the till, next to the dog toys.

'That's the one. We'll take it, yeah,' the dad laughs. Judging by his Cradle of Filth T-shirt, Daddy's a sadist. He waggles his fingers at me like I'm a bunny rabbit or a kitten, then he asks JG Thomas, 'What does it eat?'

I'm not a fucking it, neither, you tit, I hiss. I'm surprised by my unpleasantness. Where's all this venom come from?

JG Thomas carefully lifts the clear plastic sky off the desert and explains to Mr Robinson: 'At the moment: baby mice. But she doesn't need many. The common corn snake can go for days without feeding.'

You're fucking joking me, I hiss, as JG lowers his hand into the tank. I could bite off his hairy pinky for that last comment. The cunt knows nothing about reptiles – all JG knows is how to sweep sawdust into a corner, and how to annoy his wife by tramping it upstairs. And how to wrongly label the bowlcut birds 'NORWICH CANARYS'.

And who are you calling common, you cheeky pleb? I hiss again, eyeballing him. *I'll digesssssst your head and ssssssshit out your hair and teeth in a minute.*

I wriggle about, watching Arizona/New Mexico disappear into the sunset, as I'm airlifted out of my desert paradise.

'There, there,' JG whispers. He clearly doesn't want me to show him up and ruin his chances of getting thirty-five quid off the Goth Family Robinson. The kids seem to have calmed down, though, despite my best efforts to come across as a child-biter. Letting go of Daddy's thighs, they creep round his DMs to have another look at me.

'Do you want to hold her?' JG asks the children, as I cling for dear life to his wobbling, DT-riddled digits. The child-faces nod nervously.

With my smell-o-vision, I quickly plot the dimensions of the shop again, paying particular attention to the distance between me and the floor, and me and the door. Then, I narrow my evil eyes, and loosen my grip around JG Thomas's fingers as he passes me gently to the smallest of the kids.

'She's very friendly,' he adds, which is as good a cue as any to

274

lunge fangs-first at the child's face. The child shrieks and throws itself behind Daddy again, leaving me space to crashland safely on the sawdusted parquet, and slalom out of the pet shop. Before hurdling through the cat-flap, I can feel the BOM BOM BOM BOM of JG's scampering Hush Puppies behind me, but I'm far too nimble to be caught. As I spring up his neighbour's drain-pipe, I can just make out JG Thomas catching his breath down below, gasping at the Goth Family Robinson, 'Ehm, phew. Ha. Hmm. Bugger. I'm sorry about that. I can't interest you in a gerbil, can I? Or a budgie? We've got tons of budgies.'

◉

Squawk! Squeak! Splutter! Sssssss!

At first, it's a nuisance roaming around the Capital at ground level. According to Genesis 3:14, snakes are the lowest form of all creatures, forced by God to slither about on their bellies and eat dust all day. By the time I get halfway down Holloway Road, I'm already missing JG Thomas's timetabled titbits. It's not easy fending for yourself in the city, when chicken-shop counters are 4ft high and the binbags have already been ransacked by foxes. I should've eaten that child's face when I had the chance.

It's sad to think I've been reincarnated as the lowest scum on Earth. I thought my karma would've been in fairly good shape, what with all my good deeds (ignoring the sadism towards Stevie, Molotov cocktails, occasional foul language, etc.). Just like mixing alcoholic drinks, perhaps this is the trouble you get when you start mixing your religions.

Hare Krissssssshna, Hare Hare, I hiss, halfheartedly.

Once I'm past the Nag's Head, I slide behind a phone box, out of the way of the rushing shoes and giant dogs. My bright orange camouflage isn't best suited to city strolling, I don't think. I should be frolicking in red clay soil, or a South Carolina

275

cornfield, or an artificial desert utopia, where the temperature's constantly moderated, and you don't run the risk of being split in two by a stray cyclist.

I curl into a croissant shape. I miss my favourite rock, and my favourite lonesome cowboy, and my favourite measly pinkies. In days of yore, apparently the Capital used to teem with delicious, disease-riddled rats, but this afternoon they're elusive. I keep flapping my tongue, fantasising about a juicy 4oz rat steak, smothered in a creamy Black Death peppercorn sauce, with extra scabs. Even a sooty, subterranean mouse would do, if only I could get down the escalators without causing unnecessary panic and uproar.

I set off again, feeling weak, like a piece of ragged string pulled along by an invisible turtle. Heading north, I stick to the back alleys parallel to Seven Sisters Road, sniffing out the dustbins and guttering for signs of life. Nothing seems that appetising, though.

Where are all the pigeons? Where are all the rats?

I keep wriggling onwards, listlessly licking at the wind until, finally, the penny drops.

⊙

It takes twenty minutes to work my way up Donald's stairs, lifting and twisting my abdomen like a frenzied male adder on heat. Fortunately, the free bus ride to Tottenham helped me conserve energy for it and, miraculously, I had stored from a past life the knowledge that a 259 goes from Holloway to Seven Sisters, Monday to Friday, every eight to ten minutes at off-peak hours.

Lubricated by axle grease (I had to wrap myself around the chassis, like a legless immigrant stowaway), I slide down Donald's waterlogged corridor, guided by my smell-o-vision. I follow a clumsy breadcrumb trail of Ecstasy pills into the darkest corner of Donald's pad, and slip underneath one of the industrial sewing machines. Over on the sofa, Donald lies on his back, in a drunken stupor. I wonder what he's done with Stevie's housekey, and why he hasn't moved into Flat D. It saddens me to think he might've been over to the halal butcher's to look at my flat, but found it unlivable, what with the hamster, the depressing CDs and all the feminine articles strewn about. Or perhaps Mr Henry already kicked him out.

Through the dark, twelve marble eyes flicker. For now, the rats seem unaware of my presence. In fact, I think a few of them are gurning, off their heads on the Ecstasy tablets. Now and then I catch a flash of their goofy, grinding gnashers, with globs of cottonmouth matted into their lip-fur. I lie in wait, with my head to the ground, silently keeping track of them racing round and round the floorboards. Occasionally, a thermographic blob comes close to my flickering tongue, but then the bastard's off again, round the back of the sofa.

If only the rats weren't on pills, I might be able to catch one. I'm not used to hunting, especially when your prey's doing St Vitus's dance. After a few more minutes, I just think, *fuck thissssss* – I throw myself lasso-like at one of the dirty-dancing rats, and knot myself around his midriff. The rat shrieks, prompting his friends to scuttle off the dancefloor, causing one hundred sudden pawprints in the dust. Donald stirs on the settee.

As my muscles constrict, my first victim lets out a shrill wheeze, with stiff legs splayed. I squeeze the living daylights out of him, then go after the other five. Now their party's been rumbled, the rodents are easier to catch, believe it or not. The five of them huddle together, rather than finding separate hiding places, trembling under the canopy of Donald's settee. For the fun of it, I weave in and out of the sofa legs, herding them into a corner before pouncing at them quickfire, one by one.

I feel supercharged with bliss. Compared to the sick, crushing guilt I felt after Stevie died, killing things is one of life's greatest pleasures, when you're a snake. Once the six rats have stopped writhing around with their internal organs in disarray, I lump them together into a kind of Big Mac tower and devour them whole. Rat's rump is a fine meat. It's hard to believe I was a vegetarian eight months ago. I gobble the critters in double-quick time, coughing out the odd hairball and spitting out the odd goofy tooth. Donald coughs along with me, violently, in his sleep.

By the third rodent, I'm feeling a little green. I might've eaten too much. I lurch heavy-bellied back out into the corridor, trying not to rouse Donald. After all, he might not recognise me now my evil eyes are stuck in a serpent's head – and he might take a spade to my throat.

I feel like an imbecile. I always thought snakes were these ruthless, bottomless killing machines, but I feel more like an odd sock stuffed with snooker balls. My body's too bloated to manoeuvre down the stairs, so I curl up in the rickety horrible elevator, cursing myself. *Sssssshit*, I hiss. The rats must've been carrying medieval diseases, after all – I feel so sick. I wish I had some stomach-pumping apparatus, or at least a pair of fingers to stick down my throat. I manage to regurgitate the first two rat steaks, but the last one seems to get stuck in my gullet. For a bit, I stumble-slither round in circles, trying to dislodge the rodent with the tip of my tail but, as it turns out, snakes are all throat and no uvula. Before I know it, I'm inadvertently digesting my own tail. And then, digesting the rest of me.

Trance-like, I carry on spinning on the corrugated metal floor, sucking myself into my belly. By the time one of those 'fucking artists' from downstairs calls the lift, I look like a leopard-print bracelet, or a marmalade bagel. I *hissssss* my last breath. If Donald could see me now, I wonder if he'd be sickened by the sight of his old friend. Then again, you never know – he might be able to make some nice new snakeskin loafers out of me. He does live in an old sewing factory, after all.

278

Part 3b) Kimberly the Monkey, aka Nails, the Smallest Dogfighter in the South East

Oo oo aa aa argh! Three months after being reborn, I'm taken to a patch of scrubland near IKEA to watch my mother get her neck snapped in half by a Staffordshire bull terrier. Perhaps it's karmic retribution for accidentally committing gluttony, or perhaps it's punishment for purposefully murdering six loved-up rodents. I whimper, covering my big eyes with tiny fingers.

While I'm not connected to my mother by the umbilical cord any more, someone's connected me to the caravan towbar with a metal umbilical cord instead. My first instinct is to flee from the vicious scene of rabid Staffies, monkeys, and travellers, but I can only get as far as Mr Smith's wellies, propped up against the back of the van. Mother screams as the terrier swings her this way and that like a drunken dance partner, rinsing every last drop of life out of her. Monkeys usually enjoy swinging, but not from their bloody necks. I whimper again, plugging my big ears with tiny fingers. Eventually, mother drops dead, causing a halo of dust where her head hits the ground.

Yet again, I've been born in captivity. Round the scrubby pit, half the gypsies are in happy raptures while the other half curse and grumble. My master, Mr Smith of Smith Fairytale Funland fame, looks devastated, handing over reams of banknotes to the owner of the panting bull terrier. It looks like nearly two grand.

The overexcited terrier carries on lunging at my dead mother, despite the best efforts of the crowd to grab her collar. Eventually, Mr Smith puts Mother out of her misery, gathering her in a large Netto bag and tying a double knot in the end.

'Patty spanked your fecking monkey,' snorts the owner of the terrier, patting it. The other travellers mumble laughter, in agreement.

'You fecking grandmotherfecker,' Mr Smith says, sadly chucking the bag to one side.

Averting my eyes from the squashed Netto bag, I occupy myself with the vivid magenta sunset drawing a curtain over the wasteland. On the first Thursday of each month, the travellers come to this patch of land behind IKEA to partake in dog-fighting, cock-fighting, bare-knuckle brawling and monkey-baiting – in fact, any animals with nails, teeth and a violent temperament are welcome to have a scrap.

'What am I gonna do?' Mr Smith grumbles rhetorically as the travellers retire to their transport.

'You'll have to beef that one up, eh,' says The Other Mr Smith, manager of Smith & Co. Resurfacing, gesturing at me. My heart bashes painfully in my chest.

The dog on the front of Mother's Netto bag sneers at me, with gritted teeth. I whimper yet again, filling my big mouth with tiny fingers.

⊙

That night, once the 4 × 4 and caravan are stationed back at Smith's Fairytale Funland (on Clapham Common this weekend), Mr Smith starts beefing me up. I grudgingly choke down a man-sized fruit salad, and bottle after bottle of cow's milk, while the Junior Smiths give my mother a ramshackle funeral, round the back of the Mad Mouse. Tomorrow evening there'll be all sorts of squealing kids and parents tramping over her grave, leaving her wreaths of candyfloss sticks and sick. I hope the screws pop out of the Mad Mouse tomorrow. And I hope the screws pop out of my leash.

Mr Smith is a bad old man. I think he gets his wickedness from all the Ritalin he munches, and from all the rowdy kids he's fathered. His wife, on the other hand, seems constantly sedated when she's looking after the Pluck-a-Duck, on her own cocktail of prescription drugs.

While it might seem like a kind thing to do, feeding me healthy portions of fruit and nuts, I've got a sneaky suspicion the Smiths are infringing on some basic animal rights. Monkeys haven't been used to fight dogs since the 1800s – back when Jacco Macacco was the simian king of the ring – but the Smiths are a strange bunch. Never content to simply run a legitimate family funfair, the Smiths have a history of breeding animals for fighting, and breeding trouble. Rumour has it Great-Grandfather Smith's in prison, after being caught running an underground freakshow in a derelict cake factory in Hackney. The freakshow was making good money in the sixties, despite being cobbled together: as legend has it, Great-Grandfather Smith amputated the Human Torso's arms and legs on the promise of 'infinite riches'; nailed stilts to the Gentle Giant's shins to improve his frankly ungiantlike 6ft 3in; shaved a squirrel monkey and docked its tail to create the Smallest Man in the World; and glue-gunned his granddaughters together to make temporary Siamese Twins. Apparently, his Elephant Man was a perfectly good-looking man before Great-Grandfather Smith smashed his face in with a lump hammer.

While I'm glad I'm not a squirrel monkey, the thought of getting in the pit with a pit bull makes my fur stand on end. I don't feel like a fighter – I come from woolly monkey stock, a famously timid breed of primate. I should be in Ecuador, foraging for berries and sniffing out females.

Forcing down the last of the fruit salad, I watch Mr Smith methodically counting his riches on the breakfast bar. Despite losing nearly two grand and his prize-fighting primate, Mr Smith has a lot more money hiding around the caravan. The double mattress is stuffed with ten-pound notes; the sofa sits on the fivers; and the tin marked TEA contains the coins. (The tin marked COFFEE contains Mrs Smith's Valium.)

After Mother's funeral, the brats come back in to annoy their father. It's difficult squeezing the twelve of them into the caravan, despite it being designed by space-efficient Germans. There's a whole convoy of VW caravans parked around the Funland, doubling up as kids' bedrooms, cupboards-on-wheels or car-alarmed bank safes.

'Get the feck out of here, or I'll turn youse into Human Torsos!' Mr Smith yells, reaching for a butter knife. Mr Smith doesn't like humans being in the same room as his riches. He finds humans untrustworthy – especially his own kids.

The Smith spawn scatters, charging back out of the van to play on the rides. I wouldn't mind having a wander about myself but, so far, I've had no respite from the leash. My left leg aches under the steel anklet. I can see the oscillating lights of the rides through a small crack in the door, but the lead only stretches as far as the Pluck-a-Duck, just eight metres from Mr Smith's van.

I clamber along the top of the settee to get a better view of the Ferris wheel. Once Mr Smith finishes counting his riches, he pours his coins and notes back into their hiding places and pops a couple of Ritalin in his mouth. He goes for a piss in the shower/toilet cubicle, humming a tuneless Celtic carny song. While he's away, I pick furiously at the screws in the anklet, though my baby teeth hardly leave a mark on the metal.

When Mr Smith comes back, I try to look nonchalant, like I haven't been fiddling with the leash. I try out a passive facial expression, gazing out at the twelve shadow-faces stuck to the Ferris wheel.

'You're gonna be my star fighter, aren't you, Nails?' Mr Smith says, slumping beside me on the settee. I squeak in the negative, but he doesn't understand monkey.

282

Mr Smith and the lads have taken to calling me Nails in anticipation of me being a ruthless dog-murderer. Despite me being born male this time, I've been trying to come across as an effeminate pansy – picking daisies, throwing the girls' make-up about, wearing Miss Smith Number 5's dresses – but they still seem convinced I'll be a bloodthirsty barbarian in the pit.

Drunk on pills, Mr Smith puts his fists up, throwing the odd pretend punch at my face. I hoot, 'Yook yook yook,' hiding behind the curtains, acting like a wet nelly.

'It's time to beef you up again, matey,' Mr Smith slurs, rummaging through one of the drawers. I quiver behind the floral fabric. I can't stomach another man-sized fruit salad. Whining, all I can think to do is cack in my hand and throw it at Mr Smith in protest. Unfortunately, his back's turned, and my shit just bounces silently off his checked shirt, wasted.

I cower in the corner of the windowsill, dreading more rotten melon and bruised banana. However, instead of fruit, Mr Smith has something far less appetising up his sleeve. In one swift motion, the gypsy grabs my feeble right leg and stabs into it with a syringe. My head feels faint as he pushes the plunger, firing fiery ice into my thigh. I screech, eyes wider than ever. I want to lash out at Mr Smith with my baby-nails, but I don't want to break the illusion of weakness and cowardice. Instead, I leap jelly-legged behind the opposite curtain, 'yook yook yook'ing and shaking with confusion. I feel like a red ghost's running wild in my veins.

Mr Smith coughs, putting the empty syringe back in the drawer. Then, he starts chopping up fruit again.

⊙

I wish the Smiths wanted me to wear a fez and juggle peanuts, rather than pump me full of anabolic steroids. For the next couple of years, I undergo a punishing fortnightly routine of muscle injections and sparring sessions with Master Smith Number 4, the Smiths' six-year-old boxing enthusiast. At first, I carry on the pansy act, refusing to scratch Master Smith while he jigs around me with oversized boxing gloves. However, after a few months on the juice, my haywire hormones cause me to see red on a regular basis. I become partial to clawing and biting people. Before long, I'm enjoying causing damage.

Partly, the angst comes from sexual frustration – I never realised just how rampant males can get. It makes sense now, all those weekly lovers fighting over me when I was a human. The combination of roid rage, sexual awakening and a lack of primates to groom causes havoc with my brainwaves. I keep having dreams about juicy, red, distended arses. I keep rubbing my groin against the Smiths' furniture, howling, and throwing around heavy objects. On the one hand, Mr Smith's frightened of me now, putting on an old welding mask before giving me my injections. On the other hand, he seems more loving towards me too, convinced I'm going to win him lots of filthy lucre in the pit.

Despite wanting to either rip the head off or shag the arse off anything that moves, the idea of facing a snaggle-toothed pit bull terrier still worries me. I don't mind sparring with Master Smith Number 4, since he doesn't have a nasty bite, or long nails. Out on the lawn, me and Master Smith are fairly evenly matched, provided I'm not let off the leash. As yet, I've only given him a few superficial facial wounds.

While the Smiths do have their own terrier, I'm banned from fighting it, for fear of giving it a heart attack. The terrier, Max, is elderly now, though he used to be a champion ratter back in the nineties. I wish I'd been introduced to Max two years ago – he might've saved me the hassle of swallowing all those rodents, and I might've been reincarnated as a cheery, beach-dwelling, crab-catching capuchin monkey instead.

On the first of June, after a slow springtime trawling the Smith Fairytale Funland around the gloomy seaside resorts of Great Britain, we return to the Capital to set up in Finsbury Park. Much to the Smiths' delight, the sun comes out the day we land the vans and caravans. Mr Smith takes the credit for the good weather – apparently, he used to promote himself as a mystic or magician, but nowadays his superpowers come in pill form.

While the Ferris wheel goes up, I'm let out of the van to spar with Master Smith Number 4. Number 4's the fifth-youngest of the clan – he's one of nine currently suffering from head lice, hence his skull's shaved bare beneath the red headguard. He's improving as a boxer, though his knuckles show through the front of his gloves, where I've been biting and lashing out with my nails. I'm not on good form this afternoon – I can sense the Capital Zoo is nearby, and I can't stop thinking about bulbous red bottoms. In a way, Master Smith Number 4's scarlet gloves look like a female baboon presenting herself. I wank into my hand and chuck it at Master Smith, forfeiting the sparring session.

Oo oo aa aa ahhhhh, the relief!

Later in the evening, I skulk around the caravan with a few of the youngsters, listening to the fair fill up. As the sunlight turns from pink to navy blue, the neon lights turn from pink to vivid crimson, burning holes through the sky. I force down another man-sized fruit salad, then sit grooming myself halfheartedly, thinking of mandrills. I wish I had a mate to pick the lice from my fur – I don't want the Smiths to shave me, or waste the special shampoo on me. From across the caravan, Master Smith Number 4 plays cards with Number 3, glaring at me now and then, between hands. He didn't appreciate the monkey spunk. Apparently, it took three goes in the toilet/shower to wash the taste away.

I spend the rest of the night dozing under the settee/folding bed, amongst the legs of the Smith girls. I'm halfway through a dream where I'm a dominant male in the jungle, with a harem of lusty females and a tray full of Pina Coladas, when Mr Smith bursts into the caravan, making us all jump. I bomp my head off the bottom of the settee/bed. Mr Smith seems in high spirits, drunk on his Ritalin, slurring, 'Oh, my lovelies! My lovelies! Look at you, look at you . . .'

Glancing up from the cards, Master Smith Number 3 asks his dad/uncle, 'What's up with you?'

'Good news!' Mr Smith announces, squeezing in between the girls. 'I've scored an opponent for Nails. That Staffy from Smith's Used Cars. The one wot got his mother. Grudge match. Tuesday week. Fecking hell, get in there, Nails!'

In my dream, the arses turn back into scarlet boxing gloves, and pummel me senseless.

⊙

The night before the big fight, it pisses it down. Mr Smith's in a foul mood, pacing around the half-empty Funland with a face like thunder and a mouth full of tablets. In a desperate attempt to keep his finances in the black, Mr Smith puts tickets for the monkey-baiting on 'general sale' – in other words, he whispers to suitable folks getting off the teacups, 'Fight tomorrow night. Dogfighting with a twist.' After half an hour of unsuccessful whispering, he comes back into the caravan, scowling, with empty pockets.

The rest of the clan have crammed into the caravan, treating it like a night off, slurping bottles of continental lager instead of manning the rides. With my belly in a twist, I lurk in one of the overhead cabinets, away from the incoherent chatter of the Smiths. The boys keep thumping each other and arguing over the cards, while the girls linger round the kitchenette shyly, topping up the boys' drinks.

As the evening wears on, the booze helps alleviate Mr Smith's foul mood. He makes a string of slurring phone calls to his traveller pals and relatives, taking bets for the bout between 'Nails, the Smallest Dogfighter in the South East' and 'Patty the Staffy'. In between the calls, he throws limp punches at me, ordering me to 'smash shit oyt that fecking mongrel'.

I don't fancy my chances at all, but at least death means I won't have to spend another night with the Smiths. I think the time's come again to zip my consciousness up in a different animal skin.

Over on the double bed, Mrs Smith snoozes in sweet, Valium-spiked slumbers. She looks so peaceful amidst all the chaos of the caravan, snoring now and then when her dreams get exciting. For a moment, my thoughts turn to my own mother. While I'd love to gain vengeance for her death, I can only see one outcome: Patty dining on woolly monkey mincemeat.

To give me some exercise prior to the fight, Mr Smith extends my leash twenty metres, uncoiling the chain from around the towbar. He force-feeds me a chunk of brown apple, then boots me out of the caravan before my diarrhoea sets in. I've had the trots ever since I found out about the fight. The combination of nerves and a fruity diet has resulted in a lot of sloppy droppings cropping up around the caravan, much to the disgust of Mrs Smith and her vacuum cleaner.

It's pleasant out, even when it's raining. The extra twenty metres take me all the way past the Pluck-a-Duck, and up to my favourite tree: this haggard old hawthorn, with plenty of branches to hang from and hollows to hide in. My favourite tree just about makes up for the loss of my favourite rock. Feeling the coolness of the wet grass between my toes, I scamper through the dark, glum Funland. Everything's switched off now the punters have gone home, and I feel free as I speed through the trees, despite that bastard chain clamped to my ankle.

Clambering up the antique trunk, I spray the odd bit of piss here and there, to warn off intruders. If I wasn't so bloated from the fruit salads, I might've been tempted to munch a few of the bugs and spiders marching round the woodwork. Instead, though, I just curl up next to them in a large hollow, once the chain goes taut, three-quarters of the way up the trunk. Hiding my head from the drizzle, I can just about see the Capital twinkling through the thick fluorescent fog of the lampposts. I try waving my arms and legs for help, but the Capital ignores me. No one wants to save me tonight.

Surrounding the Funland, there's a 10ft-high steel fence, erected to keep unpaying customers out, and ungrateful dog-fighters in. If only I had a pair of metal clippers to remove my shackles, I'd easily scale that fence from here. Despite its blurred outlines, the Capital looks beautiful and inviting on the other side, humming with the millions of animal romances, all firing off simultaneously in its many parks, bedrooms and nightspots.

I can almost smell those red, bulbous arses waiting for me in the Capital Zoo. Frustrated, I scratch frantically at my lice and scabby track-marks, then scratch frantically at the anklet. The screws still won't budge. Apparently, Great-Grandfather Smith used this leash in the sixties to restrain the Gentle Giant – 16 stone 2 ounces of man-sized brute force. The Gentle Giant wasn't so gentle after a few weeks of captivity in the cake factory but, nevertheless, he never broke free from the leash.

I meditate for a few minutes, praying for some way to avoid the fight tomorrow night. I rock back and forth in the hollow, visualising my favourite tree collapsing on the Smiths' caravan, killing everyone inside and conveniently snapping off my shackles.

Come midnight, the Smiths are smashed, but not in the sense I was hoping. The youngsters have been knocking back a large bottle of vodka, cackling and gurgling as they charge out of the caravan to get high on the Ferris wheel. Master Smith Number 1 makes a wager with the others, to see who gets sick the quickest on speed 10. Shuddering, I watch the Ferris wheel spark to life, like a huge eyeball winking three or four times before waking up. As the kids spin themselves into distant dots then humans then distant dots then humans then distant dots then humans dots humans dots humans dots, I clamber back down from my favourite tree, to get some peace and warmth in the caravan.

As usual, Mr Smith's still indoors, sitting at the breakfast bar, mumbling to himself, re-counting his pennies. In between gobfuls of ale, he seems to be saying, 'Duck, keep your guard up, loosen him . . . loosen him up with your jab . . .'

I hop quietly onto the curtain-rail, taking care not to disturb Mr Smith, or wake Mrs Smith from her spreadeagled slumbers. To Mr Smith's left there's a lined notepad covered in sums – bets for tomorrow night. It looks like my odds to beat Patty are placed at 10–1, which is odd. The way Mr Smith's been talking, I thought he'd have me down as favourite. I'd gladly take a fall in the first round, if that's what he wants – except that taking a fall in monkey-baiting means certain death.

The blood-red memory of my mother being butchered haunts me again. I pull the closest facial expression I have to a sulk, peering down at the tubs of Mr and Mrs Smith's prescription drugs, lined up on the breakfast bar. Taking care not to make a sound, I lasso the COFFEE tin of Valium with my tail, and lift it to my perch on the curtain-rail. It takes me a while to unscrew, biting and clawing at the fiddly lid, but, fortunately, Mr Smith's too occupied with his pennies to notice the creaking and cracking of plastic. Not only that, but he's too intoxicated to notice me dropping blue capsule after blue capsule into his frothy ale. With the precision and dexterity of a champion darts player, I time the audible PLOPs with the audible CLINKs of pound coins being stacked. I get so engrossed in the game, by the time Mr Smith reaches for a slurp of ale, I've filled his glass with at least eleven Valium, each one in a different stage of dissolution.

Hopping back off the rail, I seek refuge underneath the settee/folding bed, hoping Mr Smith doesn't notice the strange, bluish taste of his ale. I can feel my heart pounding beneath my pecs. Fortunately, Mr Smith's guzzled so much ale and Ritalin, he fails to spot the neon plankton in the bottom of his tankard. I bare my teeth as he takes another big gulp, then another, then another, then another.

Twenty-five minutes later, Mr Smith is comatose, face-down on the breakfast bar, with the glass cradled limply in his right hand. In the distant night air, I can still hear the Ferris wheel cranking and cackling, yet to make any of its victims vomit. Without any further ado I leap onto Mr Smith's worktop and yank the full bags of coins from the TEA pot, as well as the reams of banknotes stuffed in every nook and cranny of the van. In the next ten or so minutes I manage to grab about £4,000 worth of the Smiths' riches. Scampering back and forth from the caravan to the wood, I stash each of the moneybags in the hollow of my favourite tree, while my tail twitches with glee.

A minute later, I'm yanking the last of the tenners out from under the mattress and Mrs Smith's deadweight body when, suddenly, the twelve Junior Smiths come stumbling back into the caravan. One of the lads, Master Smith Number 3, has sick all down him.

At first, the Junior Smiths don't notice the stolen money. First, they notice Mr Smith, not breathing, with no pulse, face-down on the breakfast bar, with the glass cradled limply in his right hand. Then they notice the smashed open tub of Valium/COFFEE on the Formica. Then they notice Nails, the Smallest Dogfighter in the South East, with almost £500 of the Smiths' riches in his mitts.

'YOU FECKING . . .' Master Smith Number 1 screams, not sure what to call me. The five Miss Smiths contort their faces in various states of anguish, gathering round their dead father. Dropping the bag of rolled tenners, I leap out of the caravan, adrenalin kicking me headlong over the moonlit grass. I manage to scrabble twenty-eight metres from the caravan, at which point the leash goes suddenly taut and the seven Master Smiths grab me and start laying into me. I squeal, protesting my innocence in incomprehensible monkey-language.

'Yook yook yook,' I hoot.

'Fecking cont!' Master Smith Number 2 yells, booting me in the head.

My best fear-face does nothing to curb the violence. While the Smith boys carry on strangling me and stamping on me, gradually the leaves of my favourite tree become glittering rhombuses, then oscillating kaleidoscopes, then purple ink blots. I feel myself slipping away.

I don't even have the chance to squeak, 'OM ĀH HŪM, OM ĀH HŪM,' so squashed is my voice box. I'm not sure how it'll affect my karma, accidentally-on-purpose killing an oppressive gypsy and hiding his money up a tree. Surely, though, I can't be dealt worse tarot cards than these.

My eyes roll back into my skull as the bright Dharmic void engulfs me again. Despite me being the so-called Smallest Dog-fighter in the South East, against all the odds I feel myself becoming smaller and smaller and smaller and smaller and smaller, as I'm sucked into the sunkissed portal. When I finally reawaken, I'm greeted by the most godawful stench.

Part 3c) Kimberly the Bacterium

My new mother is a dirty nappy. My new father is a half-eaten meatball. I take it the Buddhist bosses weren't best pleased with my murderous monkey business. I've been reborn a micro-organism.

Once I'm used to my new sensory apparatus (I don't have eyes, just a meagre touchy-feely membrane, hooked up to my nucleus), I take in my surroundings: I seem to be camping in a huge, black polythene tent, with tons of other bacteria, rotten food, nappies, tissues, and torn packaging. I think it's a binbag.

I sail across the putrid pond of milky fish stock, on the back of the meatball. All around me, the litter's stacked high like a dishevelled, dystopian shanty town. The only thing going for the place is the local cuisine. Once I've chowed down one square micrometre of the beef, I feel fit to bursting – in fact, I'm so full, my nucleus has no choice but to split in half, transforming me into a pair of identical twins.

'Ey up,' we say to each other simultaneously. Now we've got twice the appetite, we set to work on the faecal matter in mother's nappy, greedily guzzling the sweet, sticky nectar.

Three hours later, we've got five hundred and ten brothers and sisters, and not much faecal matter or ground beef left. Roundabout the tent, the bacteria and germs soon outnumber the food rations. The pathogens whinge and writhe about like starving refugees, while the flies desperately regurgitate and regobble their breakfasts, over and over again. To make matters worse, a black rat comes along and gnaws a hole in the bag, stealing a hunk of green polka-dotted focaccia and inviting all manner of urban bugs and beasties to gatecrash our paltry banquet.

Before long, there's a power struggle in the tent. As our rations carry on shrinking, the different strains of bacteria cause a bit of a stink, battling each other, trying to seize control of the binbag. Contrary to what scientists believe, pathogens can communicate with each other freely and easily, via telepathy. Soon, each family of germs is reeling off its own propaganda, trying to assert its authority as 'the most harmful bacteria in the binbag'. Over by the broken eggshells, the salmonella and shigella lock horns, spouting tales of upset tummies and vomiting. Elsewhere, the *E. coli* O157:H7 bullies the other, less dangerous strains of *Escherichia coli*, boasting about 'severe bloody diarrhoea', 'mass hysteria' and 'the odd fatality and that'. The most revered and feared of the bacteria, however, is the *Yersinia pestis*, which rides on the back of the black rat, or *Rattus rattus* in Latin (so bad they named it twice!). *Y. pestis* was supposedly responsible for the Black Death in the 1800s, but hasn't been in the limelight much since then. Pushing its luck, the influenza A H1N1 screams from the peak of a scrumpled-up tissue, '*Y. pestis*, go and infect a fucking wild boar and peacock-gizzard pie, you daft old washed-up has-been!'

I think it's a joke of some sort.

As the days wear on, and our families perish, no one's in the mood for jokes any more. The time comes to put our nuclei together and come up with a solution to the starvation. Some of the bacteria swear there's a restaurant merely metres from the ragged binbag, though it could be a mirage brought on by hunger. According to the folklore of the tent, restaurants can be wonderful feeding and breeding grounds, or they can be perilous, squeaky-clean battlegrounds. The fact the binbags haven't left the alleyway for collection in five days suggests the restaurant might fall into the former, but it's a risky business being a bacterium. Land on the wrong work surface and your membrane gets instantly dissolved by citrus-fresh poison. As far as me and my siblings are concerned, we'd rather stay in the warmth of the tent than risk annihilation but, then again, if the food in here dries up completely, we'll die anyway.

There's nothing else for it. Over the next few hours, the pathogens hatch plans to get inside the prophesied restaurant: the shigella wants to travel on the tongue of an alleycat; the salmonella suggests we catapult an eggshell; the *E. coli* fancies waiting for a restaurant worker to turn up; the *Yersinia pestis* wants to Blitzkrieg the kitchens, on the back of a bluebottle.

The discussions divide the binbag, creating a primitive pecking-order of those who want to leave the tent (and how), and those who want to stay put. Me and my siblings position ourselves somewhere on the fence, adopting the role of lookouts. There's not much to see through the torn gap in the liner – only a chipped back door, an air vent, and a handful of other binbags – but at least it keeps us out of the arguments. One evening, conditions in the tent get so severe, the black rat keels over with starvation. It hardly has time to let rigor mortis set in before tens of thousands of bacteria pounce on its corpse, fighting and baying for flesh. Staying put by the lookout, me and my siblings refuse to eat. We're not fucking barbarians and, in any case, we couldn't stomach another rat steak after what happened at Donald's. Instead, we rim the edge of the binbag in quiet protest, sucking the last drops of fatty fish sap, while the greedy bacteria gobble and burp behind us.

While there's some pride in being conscientious objectors – going on hunger strike instead of feasting on our rat friend – there's a good chance we'll be dead before sundown. Forty minutes later, when the back door of the restaurant creaks open – illuminating the binbags with the brightest, whitest, nicest, lightest light we might've ever seen – we're convinced we've died and gone to Heaven. However, when we spot the portly restaurant worker emerging from the light, our nuclei instantly spring back to life.

'Restaurant worker!' we shriek, wobbling the walls of the tent, excitedly. 'Restaurant wor—'

We freeze, mid-sentence, when we see who it is. The restaurant worker appears to be a giant version of Paolo, only with bleached blond highlights and a slightly rounder gut. Of all the binbags outside all the restaurants in all the capital cities of the world, we had to wake up in Paolo's. The thought of rotting osso buco and tofu ravioli flashes through our membranes. Glowing, we watch Paolo tying up the neighbouring binbags, then chucking them one by one down the alley, ready for collection.

Meanwhile, in the belly of the bag, some of the less harmful bacteria are becoming flustered, clamouring for a glimpse of their blond Italian saviour. Others – like the *Y. pestis* and salmonella – look on indignantly, too bloated and knackered from the rat-race to bother moving. To make space for the crowds, me and my siblings shimmy to the very edge of the torn polythene, getting a good whiff of dead meat from the kitchens. You can almost smell table 13 from here!

As Paolo trudges towards us, another wave of bacteria comes rushing to the lookout, pushing and shoving and belching. Everyone leaps kamikaze-like out of the hole as Paolo takes hold of the frayed lips, pulling them together and knotting them in one swift motion. Some of our cells get crushed in the knot, while others are thrown back into the dark depths of the tent. The rest of us have no choice but to leap onto Paolo's fingers. Geronimooooooo! Diving into the greasy trenches of Paolo's fingerprints, me and thirty-one lucky brothers and sisters cling for dear life as Paolo rubs his hands vigorously on his apron. From so high up, it's disheartening to see our friends and family being tossed into the gutter and treated like rubbish, but then there's elation as well, as Paolo carries us onwards, into the Ristorante di Fantasia.

It's strange being back in our old workplace, one micrometre tall. The kitchens look the same as always, only with more pictures of Paolo's wife (dressed as herself now, not Marilyn) Blutacked to the tiles, and fifty perfect squares of ravioli set out on the worktop, ready to be filled with dead reindeer.

As Paolo clomps across the lino, we keep an eye on the handgun loaded with Flash Multi-Purpose by the sink. Fortunately for us (unfortunately for his customers), Paolo ignores the NOW WASH YOUR HANDS sign and the Flash, and gets on with making his ravioli. With a delicate attention to detail, he fills the parcels with a mixture of ground-up venison, chopped onion, mascarpone cheese, garlic, parsley, seasoning, and bacteria. Twenty-four of us are pressed into the first parcel, leaving the rest of us to spread across the plastic chopping board and worktop.

Watched over by Paolo's framed, faded photographs of Rome, we act out a Roman orgy in miniature: writhing against each other; decapitating nuclei; gorging ourselves on the muck down the back of the cooker, where the Flash and J-cloths miss. Soon, there's sixteen of us, then thirty-two again, then sixty-four, all within the space of an hour.

Before long, there's nearly fifteen thousand of us. Like a hard-working, foul-smelling army, we quickly colonise the melamine and surround another batch of defrosting venison in pincer formation. At the end of the night, Paolo chases us halfheartedly round the kitchen with a dirty dishcloth, but it's a feeble counter-attack. Once the lights go out, there's nothing to stop us dominating the dining area next-door. We march across the threshold, some of us doing the goosestep, while others go for more of a jaunty conga-line, shimmying across the mosaic tiles. And, despite Paolo's best efforts with the mop hours earlier, we carry on chewing the fat, squirming, undressing, reproducing, dancing on the tabletops, and sweating out toxins throughout the night – and we keep on multiplying . . .

Two weeks later, the Ristorante di Fantasia has been shut down. The tables and chairs look like tombstones; the cupboards and fridge-freezer have been ransacked; and the Mediterranean curtains are kept permanently shut, leaving me and my 250,000,000 brothers and sisters to run the place in peace.

For some reason, the regulars at the Ristorante weren't impressed with our revolutionary prowess, going back to their homes each night to be sick and shit blood. Their distaste led to a headline in Tuesday's *Tottenham, Wood Green & Edmonton Journal*, which read: FOOD POISONING OUTBREAK IN SOUTH T'HAM RESTAURANT.

We swear it wasn't our intention to poison anyone. We always thought we were friendly bacteria, like the type you find in Müller Vitality yogurts or Actimel, or the type that's crawling around your guts right now.

It seems a bit unfair, two days after the 'outbreak', when five environmental health officials storm the Ristorante di Fantasia armed with facemasks, spacesuits, disinfectant canisters and scouring pads. Rather than bursting in like federal agents or vigilantes, the health and safety warriors plod slowly round the restaurant for twenty minutes, pervily stroking the worktops with cotton buds instead of going at them with sledgehammers. The lucky bacteria are those who manage to grab on to the cotton buds and are rehoused in the safety of a Petri dish, while the rest of us face a deadly thunderstorm of bleach.

Suddenly, it's every bacterium for itself! Starting in the kitchens, the environmental health people smoke us out with a series of disinfectant blasts, quickly finding my hideout in the gap behind the cooker. Then, they pulverise us with scouring pads and mops, causing a fizzy holocaust on the lemon-fresh lino. Just to be on the safe side, the tables and chairs get the same treatment, then get taken outside to be quarantined before incineration.

It's sad to see the fall of the Ristorante di Fantasia. I might not have enjoyed my time there as a human, but the last week or so as bacteria has been euphoric. One of the many good things about bacteria is everyone in your family feels equal, born as they are from each other's split nuclei. While humans tend to argue with people who remind them too much of themselves, there's no point in rivalry when you're an exact replica of your brothers and sisters. There's no hierarchy, and there's no room for betrayal. We're all in it together!

As another wave of Dettol bites into my delicate membrane, I do feel bad about the food poisoning. However, it's not all doom and gloom, as we're splashed with one last blast of disinfectant, turning our insides out. I quite fancy my chances of being reborn as something spectacular. After all, it's not like I've murdered anyone this time.

I cross my flagella, ignoring today's *Journal* headline, just about visible through a crack in the back door: DEADLY E. COLI O157:H7 CLAIMS FIRST VICTIM IN SOUTH T'HAM.

I'm sure it's referring to one of my brothers or sisters, not me.

Part 3d) Kimberly the Common Seal

Is this a fucking joke? Before I have time to develop a fondness for athletes' bottoms, I let go of Mother's full-fat, creamy teat and launch myself off the rocks. I accidentally-on-purpose catch my neck in a ring of four-pack plastic, honking 'OM ĀH HŪM! OM ĀH HŪM!' as my little white face turns blue.

Part 3e) Kimberly the Greyhound

Once again, I wake up in litter. This time, it's in a litter of puppies, in a splendid conservatory in West Hampstead.

It's giving me travel sickness, all these reincarnations. On my soul's arrival into a new species, there's always initial confusion as to what I've turned into, especially since most animal spawn starts out life blind, deaf and dumb. For all I know, I could be a pinky, hanging above the jaws of an okeetee corn snake. For all I know, I could be a decorated demigod, turning the golden key to Nirvana.

As it turns out, I'm a dog. Once I've got fully functioning body parts, I spend my days charging up and down the lawn with my two brothers and two sisters, grinning, growling, being patted, and fed top-of-the-range, organic dog food. For the first time in my lives, I've been born into money.

Household pets are the luckiest folk on the planet. Not only do they have two sets of parents (human and dog, in my case), they have free food, free healthcare, and three-piece suites to sleep on. My human mother, Mrs Claymore, is a soft touch. She made her fortune breeding and training greyhounds for racing, and there's nothing she likes better than pampering new puppies. Even when me and the other pups go out for walkies and I tangle the reins, Mrs Claymore's still patient with me.

I'm not the sharpest greyhound in the pack, and definitely not the fastest. Once Mrs Claymore starts taking us down the training track, I make it clear I want no part of the racing lifestyle. I much prefer prancing leisurely round the local rec, than chasing the clenched arseholes of my brothers and sisters. While my four siblings go on to compete at Wimbledon and Romford, I stay at home most nights, competing with the Claymores' cats for scraps off the dinner table, and pats off our parents. I make friends with a pouffe in Mr Claymore's study, spending hours curled on its plump paisley, contemplating the wallpaper.

After everything I've been through, I think I deserve a few months of decadence. Soon, Mrs Claymore gives up on me completely, leaving me to snooze on the pouffe while the others are slammed in the back of the Land Rover and taken to the training track. I feel more like the Kimberly of days of yore, lounging about the house while my companions charge round a racetrack, although, instead of tuna and cucumber sarnies and Somerfield's Worst™ Lasagnes-for-One, I get my black lips round posh Bakers biscuits and Mr Claymore's Somerfield's Best™ Lasagnes-for-One.

Mr Claymore, like his wife, is a pushover. It only takes half a glance and a slight whine to make him scrape his dinner into my doggy-bowl. I feel like royalty, with a balding, turtle-necked butler and a paisley throne. Soon, I'm hardly even fussed about going for my walkies. The last thing I want is to risk being involved in another car crash, or accidentally behead a bird, and be reborn a muddy puddle or a piece of cat litter.

Mr Claymore doesn't seem to mind leaving me on the pouffe, since he's got a jippy back and hates plastic-bagging dogmuck. Also, both his big toes kill at the moment – I accidentally knocked a paperweight off his desk and onto his slippers, both of which he was wearing at the time. It made him howl at the moon-like lampshades.

Soon, I get the feeling I'm not in the Claymores' good books. I get those slippers slapped round my arse every morning, to wake me up. Despite having a fast greyhound metabolism, I've grown fat around my belly and joints, making me look more like a donkey than a streamlined stallion. Mrs Claymore scolds me, then scolds Mr Claymore (who is also getting fat), and takes matters into her own hands. Each morning, she makes me do laps of the garden, before we power-walk down Sumatra Road to collect *The Times*. I lag behind, purposefully annoying her, sniffing each lamppost for ammonia, imagining Mr Claymore struggling with his fried breakfast back at home.

While my brothers and sisters prance around the house, showing off their ribs and rosettes, I carry on the royalty act without truce. Come January, I've ballooned to the size of a Tibetan mastiff. At a loss, Mrs Claymore tries starving me of the Bakers biscuits, and flogging me down the rec three times a day, but it's no use. With no food in me, I've got no motivation to sprint about – not even when I catch the scent of another dog's bollocks on the breeze. Instead, I just sniff sadly round the wet lampposts, while Mrs Claymore tugs fiercely on the leash, making me strangle-stumble.

One morning, back on the safety of the paisley, I overhear Mr and Mrs Claymore having a dispute:

'She's a waste of space. She needs bloody putting down or something.'

'Ah, she's alright.'

'We could put her up, you know.'

'Hmm?'

'For adoption, I mean.'

'Oh. Well, I don't know if w—'

'The Trust would have her. She doesn't need to be retired.'

'Mm.'

My congested heart sinks. In the other room, I hear Mrs Claymore making a few phone calls, catching the words 'overweight', 'lethargic', 'very affectionate though, oh yes, yes', and that one, 'adoption', again. I lever myself off the pouffe, suddenly inspired to pace about, anxiously. My dogbrain races, wishing I had some say in the matter. I don't want to leave the lap of luxury. I wish there was some way of saying sorry, without resorting to blinking puppy-dog eyes. I wish I could somehow pay them back for all their generosity.

One downside to being a household pet is you don't speak your owners' lingo, and you don't have access to any money. If only I could prove my worth to the Claymores – say, by retrieving a lost World Cup trophy, or unearthing more riches for them – they might want to keep me. I sink back down on the pouffe, racking my brains, desperately trying to think where a hound might come across a handsome sum of money.

⊙

Mrs Claymore stares at me suspiciously when I drop my leash in front of her, panting overenthusiastically. I nudge it closer to her toes, with my nose.

'What do you want?' Mrs Claymore asks, raising her eyebrows. 'Walkies? That's not like you.'

I woof in the affirmative, nudging the leash again. Mrs Claymore, poised halfway through dialling another kennel, replaces the receiver and sighs through her nostrils. She glances at her husband, then breathes, 'Oh, come on, then.'

Half an hour later, we're charging full-pelt towards the green and brown splendour of Finsbury Park. I'm much more animated than usual, leading the way like a puppet dragging its master.

'Oh, honestly!' Mrs Claymore yelps happily, nearly putting her back out.

Once we get through the gates, the park widens in all directions, like a pop-up book being opened, with all the trees and lampposts jumping to attention. It's not the first time I've worn a leash in Finsbury Park, but this time I'm enjoying myself, drooling, pretending to be athletic, snapping at the squirrels and pigeons, growling at other dogs. I sniff a few bums, just to be sociable. I piss against a bin.

302

After a couple of laps of the park, Mrs Claymore gives me what I want. Absolutely shattered, she slumps down on one of the graffiti-glazed benches, and unsnaps my leash 'for two minutes'. As soon as I hear the retractable lead whizz back into the handle, I bark with joy and charge off at top speed, away from her and the bench. Despite looking like a hippo on stilts, I manage to hit 35mph in 1.5 seconds, leaving behind the words 'Oh, oh, no, come back, come back, oh, shoot,' like tiny bells ringing in another town.

Lips flapping, I sprint to the far corner of the park, where the skidmarks and tyre-tracks of the Smith Fairytale Funland are still tangible in the mud, like crudely drawn crop circles. I try not to focus on the bad memories as I slip into the shadows of the wood, keeping my nose to the ground. Fortunately, I had the ingenuity to spatter my favourite tree with monkey piss, so I find the old hawthorn easily enough, standing like a bright green lighthouse in a raging sea of leaf litter. Snuggling up beside the tree, I wait for a few passers-by to finish passing by, then I take a running-jump at the old, gnarled trunk. It takes four attempts to clamber up the bark and squeeze my muzzle into the right hollow. Then, after scaring off a few bugs and rotten berries, I finally find what I'm looking for.

⊙

I feel like gold, marching down the back streets of Kentish Town with almost £4,000 clenched behind my teeth. I wish I could've taken more, but the coin bags proved a bit cumbersome and weighty, so I buried them deep under the leaf litter, in case of emergency.

Thankfully, no one tries to mug me as I head through each estate – only mad people put their hands near strange dogs' mouths. The only trouble is, I can't find my way home again. I've been through so many traumatic reincarnations, I've forgotten

Kimberly the Human's superhuman grasp of the bus routes. Nevertheless, I'm enjoying myself, trotting past the humming bins with the sun as my guide.

I'm not sure if the Claymores are fans of bribery, but hopefully they'll welcome me back into the family if I turn up on their doorstep with £4,000, tax-free. I know for a fact they like money – after all, those Lasagnes-for-One don't buy themselves. You never know – they might even gift me a new pouffe.

Huffing and puffing through my nose, I follow the alleys and pavements this way and that, trying to catch a whiff of the Claymores' legendary corn-fed roast chicken, but all the smells of the Capital crowd in, confusing me with a perfume made up of rubbish, fresh pastry, petrol, hot urine, newspaper, and McDonald's. I end up going round in ever increasing circles, like a dog chasing a huge, invisible tail.

Soon, dusk sets in, casting a dark spell over the city. I carry on marching onwards, though my skinny legs want to buckle under the weight of so much fat and fatigue. After a near-death experience on a busy roundabout, I begin to recognise the odd street name – like Uxbridge Road, or Lime Grove – but they're not the streets of West Hampstead. I'm back in Shepherd's Bush. I must've taken a thousand wrong turns, and I don't have the legs or the motivation to take a thousand more, to get me back to Hampstead. Feeling daft and shattered, I whine at the full moon, in a frequency only me and her understand.

It must be around eleven when I pass out, next to the Wethouse. The front door's locked, and there's no sign of life in the foyer. While latecomers are allowed to ring the bell, I doubt Malcolm's dad'll take kindly to a greyhound disturbing him, and I'm aware the language barrier could prove problematic. I wish I had Lassie-like skills of communication, or at least a dog-tag with my name and address on it.

I whimper aimlessly for a minute, then curl up in the darkest shadow I can find, round the back of the black rails. All around me, the streets are quiet, with only the occasional creak of twisting trees or distant cars. I tuck my tail between my legs and close my heavy eyelids, keeping my jaw clamped tight around the moneybags. Tomorrow, I'll pay more attention to the roadsigns. Tonight, I'll play dead.

As I sleep, the faint smell of cat urine and burned rubber gives me odd dreams. First of all, I'm sat on a huge white cloud marked '6', being stroked by a lady wearing a dodo-feather dressing gown and unicornskin trousers. Next, I find myself in New York City, in the summer. It's an overblown, comic version of New York: mobsters in spats; kids with Afros, setting off fire hydrants; women with chihuahuas in their handbags; honk honk honking yellow taxis. I'm in Central Park. I break loose from my amateur dogwalker to chase a pair of Siamese cats downtown. We sprint through the twinkling corridors of mirrored skyscrapers: left along East 65th, then right down Madison Avenue. There's a jazz soundtrack. I steal a 10ft-long hotdog from a vendor on the corner of Madison and 57th, and nearly lose sight of the cats. They're nifty bastards, slinking between the streetlights and mailboxes, and fearlessly jaywalking in front of traffic. Finally, I have them cornered in the East Village. I chase them down a dark, Gotham-like alleyway, which ends abruptly at a barbed-wire fence and some bricked-up brownstones. The Siamese cats cower between two trash cans, begging me not to kill them, in an accent I don't understand. They look like a pair of bank robbers, with their black masks and paws, but they're acting like wet blankets. I prepare to pounce. However, as I make my approach, the cats grow suddenly taller, on their hind legs, and they continue to grow and grow and grow, to the size of small skyscrapers. The adjacent buildings crumble to make way for their expanding bodies. I whimper, curling up behind a dumpster. But it's too late. *Hissssssssing*, the cats uproot two wooden slats from the Brooklyn Bridge, and bring them down on my head, battering me to death.

The first impact wakes me up. Jelly-eyed, I wake to find a pair of Siamese humans bringing a wooden slat down on my head, battering me to death. I wheeze, coughing blood across the paving slabs. Through the pain, I can just about see my assailants, dressed in raggy jeans and hooded tops. I can't make out their faces – only a dark shadow in their hoods, and thirty-odd gritted teeth. In desperation, I lunge at one of them. I bite hard into his neck. The bastard squeals, but manages to keep laying into me, until my skull finally caves in and my legs go limp. I hit the pavement hard, with a horrid thud. My last memory is this: a Siamese silhouette scuttling away, with its hoods still up, and nearly £4,000 stuffed in its pockets.

Part 3f) Kimberly the Magpie

Animals. We have so many disgusting habits. Dogs eat dogmuck. *Escherichia coli* thrive in binbags. Cats lick their own genitalia. Humans lick each other's genitalia. Mother birds vomit into their chicks' mouths.

It's not the most pleasant introduction to the world, waking up to find your mother retching and bauking down your throat.

I'm the first of the flock to fly the nest. In magpie terms, my moody teenage phase comes around six weeks into my life, causing me to mope about on my own, dressed in black, bringing sorrow to anyone who believes in nursery rhymes and claps eyes on me. It's nice being able to soar above the rooftops and treetops, or snake-charm worms by dancing on the grass, but I wish I was human again. I miss having friends, and changes of clothes, and opposable thumbs, and a capacity for love.

Animals are self-obsessed, paranoid, and predictable. I feel like I'm only capable of bringing more misery to the world, thanks to the magpie's unevolved altruism gene, and that daft fucking nursery rhyme. Our PR's terrible – in the old days, some smart cunt christened us a 'murder of magpies', like the crows, and it's been impossible to shake off the negative connotations since. If I ever meet the wordy bastard, I'll peck his eyes out.

One evening, more than four years after Kimberly the Human's car crash, I'm contemplating suicide again, perched in the middle of a clearing, in the middle of a common, in the middle of the Capital. For birds, the best way to top yourself is to fly over a motorway and accidentally-on-purpose close your wings. Another is to hop through a cattery cat-flap.

From the uppermost branches of the tree, I can see the full extent of the city, with its pretty lights switching on and off like a sad, muddled Morse code. One thing the Buddhists got right was the realisation that all life is suffering. All across the Capital, I can see folk whingeing about the traffic; or whingeing about the weather; or whingeing about the lack of seats in the pub/on the bus/in their own house. Humans were born to be annoyed, but at least they have all these distractions – like loss, lust, happiness, bills, daydreams, etc. – to keep their minds off the ultimate distraction: death.

Maybe I'd be better off as a muddy puddle or a piece of cat litter after all – at least then I wouldn't have to think any more. Apparently that's what makes Nirvana so blissful: the emptiness.

Before I say farewell to the city, I circle the clearing once or twice. From so high up, the Capital looks like the candle-laden birthday cake of somebody ten billion years old. How are you supposed to find emptiness in a town teeming with so many people?

I glance down at the trees again. In winter, the blossom on trees is replaced with stray carrier bags and chip papers – no wonder the other birds have migrated. They've all gone down south for the winter, and I'm going down, too.

Cawing and clawing at the sky, I'm ready to accidentally-on-purpose close my wings over the Turnpike Lane crossroads, when something round and shiny catches my eye. I love sparkly things. Divebombing back into the clearing, I slalom between the horse chestnut trees and land on the handle of a rusty, three-wheeled pushchair. The round, shiny thing looks like a shrunken glitterball, or a swollen, silver marble. It's very beautiful. I clap my wings together. The silver ball stares at me, then it winks, I think. I squawk back, excitedly.

At first, I'm convinced it's Stevie's silver eyeball. However, eyeballs are generally the first part of a corpse to perish, and it's been years now since his death. On closer inspection, I realise it's just a stray Christmas bauble. Nevertheless, the symbolism still works for me.

Taking care not to drop it or swallow it, I carry the bauble to the top of the tallest plane tree, and take shelter in an abandoned doves' nest. Without too much difficulty, I hang the bauble on the highest branch of the tree, then we spend the rest of the evening together, watching the lightbulbs of the city switching on and off, revealing ten million tiny soap operas behind ten billion tiny windows.

And this is what we see:

On the south side of West Green Road in South Tottenham, two officers of the Necropolitan Police are hammering on the door of Flat 6B. After banging twenty-five times with their fists, the officers ready themselves to bang on the door with a battering-ram. A few worried neighbours and nonchalant passers-by stare as the policemen count to three, then blast the slab of white hardwood off its hinges. Everybody gasps in fright, covering their mouths. The foul stench, which has been growing steadily for months on West Green Road, suddenly belches from 6B's open doorway, hitting the backs of the bystanders' throats. A few dry-retch into their sleeves; others scuttle off with grim expressions and their evenings ruined. The smell is a mixture of binbags, rotting fish, sour milk, and faeces. The police officers give each other a hairy look, before striding into the property.

From our safe, sweet-smelling vantage point, me and the crystal ball watch the policemen's heads bob past the stairwell windows, on their way up to the flat. They check the living room and bedroom with grave expressions, noses and mouths pressed into their shoulders. When they reach the bathroom, they freeze, gag rude words, then charge back out of the property at top speed. On the way down the stairway, they radio for backup, trying not to be sick on their uniforms.

Through a gap in the door, we can just about see into the bathroom. Mr No Tomorrow sits on the toilet, with his flesh dripping off his skeleton. He's been sat on the toilet for seventeen months. His abdomen burst long ago, after being a nest for flies and maggots. His hair has grown into a greasy Beatles mop around his skull. His pretty, Persian cheekbones look more prominent than ever, without any flesh on them. Yellow custard leaks from his midriff and trouser legs, mixing in with the dry, crusted vomit on the lino and the severe bloody diarrhoea in the toilet bowl.

Mr No Tomorrow has shat himself to death.

Although dying from food poisoning is rare, sometimes the extreme loss of water and sustenance through diarrhoea and vomiting can cause shock to set in. While this tends to happen only in the very young or very old, if your symptoms are severe and left untreated – like in Mr No Tomorrow's case – the Grim Reaper may well be watching your every bowel movement.

On the bathroom windowsill, someone's left a milk ring.

I can't think how Mr No Tomorrow got in such a state. I've never seen anyone leak so much bodily fluid. Perhaps his guts packed in after one too many bungee jumps; or perhaps he went the Elvis way, suffering a major cardiac arrest; or perhaps he contracted *E. coli* poisoning, after eating the venison ravioli at the Ristorante di Fantasia. It was his favourite dish, after all – his 'usual'. And I guess he couldn't get any medical care, because of his illegal immigrant status. And I guess that's why no one even knew he was here, until the stench got this bad.

I blush into my wing.

I feel awful now, for contaminating Paolo's restaurant. However, in the front room of 5 Welham Road in Tooting, my Promiscuous Pal Polly is opening her curtains for the first time in years. After we threw him onto the street on Halloween night, Mr No Tomorrow began harassing Polly something rotten. Obsessive, angry and lonely, Mr No Tomorrow developed a strange courtship ritual which involved posting cheap chocolate through Polly's letterbox and battering on her door at the most unreasonable, unpredictable hours, demanding love. Some men are bizarre, desperately trying to break into your heart, like a burglar trying to break into a bright red, bulletproof safe with a toothpick.

The more Polly rejected him, the more effort Mr No Tomorrow put into the stalking. He even broke into her house one afternoon, gaining entry through her bathroom window and changing the locks. Polly returned from a friend's funeral to find Mr No Tomorrow in her best silk dressing gown, with a stew in the oven, acting like a good husband. Despite an afternoon's worth of fighting and arguing, Mr No Tomorrow wouldn't leave, until Polly feigned unconsciousness after she fell/was pushed down the staircase. She figured Mr No Tomorrow wouldn't phone for an ambulance (he was afraid of the authorities – and he rarely had battery), so she played dead on the carpet, waiting for him to say one last 'I love you' and scuttle off into the night.

A day later, he posted her his dead mother's engagement ring, with a heartwrenching, apologetic, badly spelt message attached, signed 'YOUR HUSBAND TOO BE'.

Polly was scared. Instead of putting a hex or restraining order on Mr No Tomorrow, Polly took evasive action. She shut her curtains, rechanged the locks, blocked the stained glass in the front door with newspaper and only left the house when it was absolutely necessary, in disguise. She installed a peephole, opening the door only to the Royal Mail, or the bloke from Tesco Online with her groceries. She found work selling fancy dress and sex aids over the internet. She ate in darkness every day, surrounded by her stock.

Despite barricading herself into number 5, still every fortnight the house came under fire from Mr No Tomorrow's fists.

Sometimes her letterbox screamed, 'Let me in, you fucky bitch! I love you!' at her. Sometimes she heard heavy breathing in her sleep.

Polly became jaundiced and depressed. However, not long afterwards, Mr No Tomorrow became ill with *E. coli* poisoning, finding himself bed-ridden, then toilet-ridden; unable to bash his fists on her door any more. Even though the house has remained silent for almost a year and a half now, Polly still kept her curtains shut, haunted by the thought of his face reappearing during *Neighbours* or *Holby City*.

Today, though, she dares herself to take a peek. After months of anxiety and Vitamin D deficiency, Polly opens her curtains again. Outside, the clouds look like cotton pads loaded with pink blusher. Polly can't see the magpie or the bauble staring at her from the top of the tallest plane tree in the Capital, and she certainly can't see into the bathroom of 6B West Green Road. However, in the last of the day's rays, her hazel eyes are twinkling. She already looks less yellow. It's time to remove the mountain of melted chocolate from her UNWELCOME mat, and rip the newspaper from the stained glass. It's time to put on attractive, provocative clothing again, and it's time to get out of the house.

I feel good now, for contaminating Paolo's restaurant. As I dance from branch to branch, another light catches my eye, to the west of the city. In a small flat on Wormholt Road, Shaun and Sean have just returned from an evening of leisure, slurping noodles and cocktails under the cold, garish blaze of the South Bank. For the first time since Stevie's funeral, the boys look well adjusted; almost handsome. Sean is wearing a well-fitting Burton shirt and Shaun has combed his hair the other way. Shaun sits down to watch *Sky Sports News* while Sean shakes up a couple of Long Island Iced Teas in the kitchen. While they drink up, sat side by side on the gaudy corduroy sofa, what strikes me as odd is the silence. Shaun and Sean haven't argued once in the last six weeks. They've been getting along famously, taking up their old jobs as bartender and lifeguard, always paying the rent on time, and coming home in the evening to cook each other tea in peace. What's happened to all the bickering? Perhaps the lads have finally matured and seen the errors of their ways, or perhaps the £4,000 they acquired recently helped put an end to their worries, not to mention their homelessness. As it happens, though, the answer lies in Shaun's oesophagus. Six weeks ago, Shaun had his vocal cords severed by a greyhound. After a week of painful, unsuccessful throat surgery, Shaun can now barely raise his voice above a whisper. Sean tried his best to keep up the arguing, but soon realised it was pointless if Shaun wasn't going to return the slaggings. Shaun became an almost monk-like presence in the flat, dressing in a towelling robe each night after washing away the chlorine from Acton Baths. The peace was hard to get used to at first, but the £4,000 filled the silence well enough. The lads said farewell to the Wethouse and never looked back. They bought new shirts, shoes, underwear, and toothpaste. They found a modest flat to rent. They found their old jobs advertised down Acton Jobcentre Plus. Now, if they could only find a pair of impossibly beautiful female Siamese twins and steal their hearts, Shaun and Sean might never have to steal anything ever again.

I feel even better now, for mauling Shaun's throat. Turning my attention north again, on the top floor of a battleship-grey unit on Lawrence Road there's yet more unexpected silence. While it's difficult getting a good view into the sixth floor, thanks to the lack of electricity and abundance of shadows, I can see one of the shadows is Donald-shaped, and it's moving. In fact, it's writhing its pelvis. Donald's been in a great mood since his cough disappeared. Almost four years back, when I gorged myself on the six loved-up rats in Don's squat, little did I know it'd cure Donald's cough as well as my hunger. Little did I know rat urine and droppings can cause respiratory problems. Little did I know it'd save the old sod's life.

Cooing at the moon, I feel humbled by such a strange, serendipitous chain of good fortune. While the Capital can smash your spirit, it can also surprise you with the most fantastic, life-affirming splendour. It's the extremes that keep you entertained.

Stepping into a shard of silky moonflash, Donald carries on swivelling his hips for a bit before putting on his work clothes. His work clothes consist of: black trenchcoat, white shirt, black tie, white underwear, black cap, and white, soil-flecked sports socks. After the death of his daughter Kimberley, and his best friend Kimberly, Donald wandered the cemeteries of the Capital to find not only the grave of his spawn and special friend, but a job as well. Fortunately, he's being paid cash-in-hand by the church, so there's no need for them to find out he's got no fixed address. And no need to worry about tax. And no need to worry about paltry cheeseburgers and chips any more, either. Donald takes the last bite of the Smoked Bacon and Cheddar Double Angus Burger he's been working on for the past half an hour, readying himself for another morning gravedigging. To complete the outfit, Donald slides his soil-flecked sports socks into a pair of new shoes. Sadly, they're not okeetee snakeskin loafers, like I'd hoped. Instead, Donald leaves the building wearing matching, shop-bought black brogues, clacking his heels as he strides into the crisp morning air. I cackle into my wing. It looks as if Donald well and truly fucked death up the arse after all . . .

By the time I lose sight of Donald, it's nearly dawn. The Capital's curtains begin to blink at me, then, over the course of the next hour or so, house after house spits its weary residents out onto the street. In celebration of my bad past actions accidentally causing some good fortune, I go for a victory lap around the common. I leave the Christmas bauble hanging on its branch and hurl myself at the sky. It's strenuous at first, getting my wing muscles going, before the cold airstream catches my sails and sends me soaring towards the clouds. As dawn turns the last of the navy blue gloom into the brightest, whitest, nicest, lightest light I might've ever seen, I feel brand new. I caw 'OM ĀH HŪM' at the dazzling void, just in case the sky's doubling up as an entranceway to Nirvana.

Again, I wish I'd paid more attention to the *Tibetan Book of the Dead*. Is this what enlightenment feels like? All through these reincarnations, I thought I was being a bastard to everyone – murdering, stealing, infecting – but, as it turns out, sometimes the interconnected nature of humanity means you can be a complete twat and still inadvertently help people out. Who knew that gobbling a few rats would cure Donald's cough?! Who thought that mauling a man's vocal cords would solve his problems?!

It's a shame most religions require an intense level of self-control, mind power and disregard for fun in order to reach the golden realms, and not just a bit of good luck. Apparently, at the moment of death, the Buddhist deities weigh up the white and black pebbles (the good and bad deeds) you've accumulated throughout existence, to see if you deserve promotion to demigod or Buddhahood, or relegation to a muddy puddle or helpless pinky.

In fairness, I'm probably riddled with black pebbles. While I tried my best to be nice to everyone after Stevie's death, you can't force-feed people friendliness. It's supposed to come naturally, from your sublime, empty inner radiance, not slapped on like a cheap cologne.

As I soar ever closer to the centre of the whitest part of the white sky, I've got a feeling I'm not heading towards Nirvana, after all. I think I'm flying into Ryanair airspace. All of a sudden, there's a terrifying rumble, as a gust of rocket-powered air sucks me into the path of the 6.05 a.m. FR052 from Stansted to Stockholm Skavsta.

I smash into the aluminium nosecone, leaving behind a red mark. The wind snaps my wings, and I corkscrew back to Earth like a knackered old shuttlecock. I birdcall for help, dreading the oncoming *Samsara* suffering, not to mention the suffering when I hit the M11. It looks like I'm set for another set of rebirths, after all. Next time, I promise I'll try to be selfless, though. And, if I happen to be born a human girl again, I'll make sure I'm nice to my first and last boyfriend, and every single boyfriend in between. And I'll make sure none of them ever go skinnydipping at Seal Sands.

THE END

Part 3) Kimberly the Friendly-ish Ghost

All of a sudden, I can't see my hands. There's a slight crack-ling sound, as my body's solids and liquids turn to gas, and the George Best costume lands in a heap between my feet.

The Grim Reaper wolf-whistles, trying to be funny. My first instinct is to cover my privates, if only I could find them. Instead, I hover six inches above the stool, staring at the space where Kimberly Clark used to be.

'Can you hear me alright?' I ask. My voice sounds soft and reverberant, like someone's built a miniature cathedral around my voice box. I stress, 'Can you hear me?'

'Loud and clear,' replies the Grim Reaper, after another gulp of vodka. With all the enthusiasm of an automated telephone system, he explains, 'When it comes to paranormal communica-tion, love, what you'll find is: those who believe in ghostsh will be able to hear you perfectly well – and those who don't, won't.'

'Right,' I say, still staring at my empty stomach, 'but no one can see me?'

'No.'

'So, er . . . how do I know who's a believer, then, and who's not?'

'You'll shoon work it out,' the Grim Reaper continues. 'As they say: "For the believer no proof is necesshary, for the sceptic no proof is shufficient." It can be a lonely business, like, being a ghosht – but soon enough you'll come acrossh some nut who believes in you. Until then, you're on your own. But if in doubt: howl.'

I glance out of Bernard's French windows, wondering how many lost souls are toiling throughout the Capital right now, wasting their breath.

'So, what now, then?' I ask.

'How do you mean?'

'Well, like, what should we do? Do you still want me to play this Subbuteo thing?'

I levitate the Bestie figurine again, making him float in front of his teammates.

'No chance,' the Reaper snaps. 'You'll jusht cheat, won't you, now you're invisible.'

I lower Bestie down again. I go to rest my forehead on the edge of the table, but my whole transparent skull goes straight through it, painlessly. I sit up again. I wonder if I could stick Bernard's kitchen knives through my chest, and not feel it. Then again, I'm not sure the Reaper would appreciate me levitating sharp objects around Bernard's soft furnishings.

Mr Death raps his phalanges on the work surface restlessly. They say more than fifty per cent of language is body language, so I guess the Reaper's finding me quite hard to read. I swipe my hands back and forth through the table legs, marvelling at my superpowers. However, as far as the Reaper's concerned, I'm doing nothing.

Five minutes later, the Gold Telephone goes off. It cuts through the silence like an infernal fire alarm. The Grim Reaper stiffens and slams the vodka bottle back down on the melamine. It must be God on the other end, the way his bones start rattling.

'Fuck it. You'd better go,' the Reaper says. He must be talking to me, although his eye-sockets are trained on the empty stool next to me. The Grim Reaper yanks open Bernard's French windows, and wafts me through the gap with one flap of his gown. I don't even have time to fold up the George Best gear, or help put away Subbuteo. I don't even get a goodbye.

It's windy out. As I fly over the balcony, a stiff westerly catches me and sends me hurtling across the Capital at about number 6 on the Beaufort scale. From up here, the city looks exactly as it did in my old *A–Z Street Atlas*, although it's difficult to navigate without all the roadnames printed on the tarmac.

When I eventually land on Oxford Circus, no one bats an eyelid. Twenty-odd cars blast through me obliviously as I make my way onto the pavement by Benetton. For the rest of the afternoon, passers-by stare straight through me, occasionally zipping up their collars and complaining of a nasty chill in the air, though none of them respond when I formally attempt conversation. I hover sadly down the backstreets, trying to kick the litter, but it's difficult when you're six inches off the ground.

Despite the sadness, I soon adapt to being a ghost – after all, I've always felt I suffered from invisibility, ever since I was a little girl. That's what an inferiority complex (and ginger hair) does to you.

Supposedly, the Capital's one of the most haunted cities in the world, but it's not easy finding any friendly ghosts when they're all bloody transparent. Then again, ghosts aren't known for their great personalities. From what I've heard, most ghosts are pathetic. They just come round your house and move a few cups and saucers, or force you into turning up your thermostat, resulting in slightly higher gas bills. I, on the other hand, want to have some real fun . . .

Rather than hiding people's car keys, or scaring shoppers in Marks & Spencer's bedsheet department, I spend my first week of ghostliness trying to make people feel happy. Ghosts get a bad press, after all, thanks to horror films and camping stories – no wonder they all shy away in the attics of old, dilapidated houses, moaning to themselves.

We're just the same as any normal human being, only without the perishable packaging. And there's plenty of potential for entertainment, when people can't see you. For instance, here's a few simple ideas for having a gas in the Capital, when you're a gas: apprehend potential burglars/aggressors/jobsworths/charity workers by making their shoelaces tie themselves together; gate-crash a group photograph, in glowing apparition form; penetrate your favourite football team's/actor's/musician's dressing room; air-condition the Love Train; peer through people's flesh, looking for tumours/blocked arteries/swallowed spiders; help crippled old ladies return heavy objects to high places; spoil a seance, by spelling out daft demands on the Ouija board; return to someone who betrayed/badmouthed you (e.g. the owner of an internet caff) and torment them mercilessly (e.g. hide their mousemats, unplug their wireless routers, cause a devastating electrical fire) . . .

⊙

After a few days, the jokes wear thin. Rather than entertaining gormless, oblivious strangers, it strikes me I must've left behind some unfinished mortal business, not to mention a lot of dirty plates and pants in Flat D. It's a shame you can't prepare for the moment of your death. Even if you put on fresh knickers before downing thirteen Panadol and four Smirnoff Ices, there's nothing to say your bowels won't expel an excessive amount of excrement the second your heart stops.

And it's a shame you might not have tidied your flat, the day a grey Ford Mondeo runs you over.

So, instead of drifting about aimlessly, I decide to get my act together, and head back to Tottenham. I jump unseen on the back of the 73, and as the eel-like bus slithers through the city, it occurs to me I must've left all sorts of embarrassing artefacts in that flat (from a bucketful of fingerprints, to a peed-in saucepan, to a shagged-on shower curtain), and I desperately need to feed Lucifer.

The thought that strikes me as I float towards the halal butcher's is: did I buy enough washing powder before I died? I stall for a second outside the building, forgetting I don't have to do the

320

new trick with the door. After hopping safely through the plywood, I pretend to rub my feet on the doormat, then slide up the banister on my backside, defying gravity. I want to say 'Hello' to Mr and Mrs C when they emerge from Flat C, but I doubt they'd be pleased to hear from me. Not only did I ruin one of their evenings, when their Panasonic TV was stolen, but – by the look of his internal organs – Mr C's on the verge of a heart attack, and I don't want to startle him.

Three floors up, I find the door of Flat D unlocked, with the sound of someone banging inside. New tenants already? My molecules grow colder as I remember handing Donald Stevie's spare housekey on Shepherd's Bush Green. I wonder if he's moved in already, only to find I live in a personalised squalor not completely dissimilar to his own rats' nest of mould and mess. After saying farewell to Don, my intention had been to head straight here and spring-clean, before setting sail for Japan – but I hadn't quite got that far.

As I hover over the threshold, the flat looks surprisingly tidy – bare, even. A pair of shiny brown brogues sit by the skirting board – and they're definitely not Donald's. Intrigued, I move further into the flat, gently lift the cloth off the dining table, and whip it over my gaseous form. Then, I creep through the half-empty living space, towards the banging, and into the bedroom.

'Boo!' I shout, causing my old landlord to make one final bang as he turns and catches his kneecap on the side of the dressing table.

'Chaa—' Mr Henry croaks in fright, forgetting his English.

He looks like a mutant magpie, dressed in a black, white, emerald and indigo sports jacket, and tight, flesh-coloured chinos. I laugh at first, until I notice the cardboard boxes filled with my stuff, each labelled AUCHTION. And then I notice my two favourite necklaces – one of which was my last joint birthday present from Mag and Barry – hanging around his neck, like worms in chainmail.

'What are you doing?!' I bellow, lifting my arms, so the white tablecloth appears more menacing, despite the food stains and embroidered flowers around the hem.

'Who are you?' Mr Henry asks, quivering. Ghosts are powerful beings, causing men and women to be scared of thin air. I remember Mr Henry mentioning he was a believer, back when he came to fix my leaking, crying ceiling – hence he's the first mere mortal to hear my words. Apparently he knows everything there is to know about the spirit world – I just hope he doesn't think I'm a member of the Ku Klux Klan, the way I'm dressed.

'Your . . . *dead tenant*, you daft sod,' I spout, needing a pause there to think up the right retort.

'Wh-what?'

'Look,' I say, pointing at the blank space where my feet should be. But he can't see me pointing.

Mr Henry backs, beetle-like, into the corner of the bedroom, shaking his head.

'I'm *Kimberly*,' I stress. 'I haven't been dead a week. What are you doing with my stuff?'

'I-I . . . shit, shit, shit . . . I . . . we could not find her nexts-of-kins,' Mr Henry says, referring to me like I'm not here – although, I guess, in one way or another, I'm not.

'And what have you done with my TV, and all that?' I snap, gesturing at the empty spaces in my living space.

'No, no. There was no TV,' Mr Henry answers. 'I have been trying to do you favour. When I come here, I find homeless bum broken in. So I kick him out. Maybe he steal your TV.'

I shift uneasily underneath the tablecloth. It's upsetting enough, finding my landlord graverobbing my old flat, let alone hearing he's forcibly removed Donald, too. I say to Mr Henry,

'No, that was a friend. He was a friend. I gave him the key. He wouldn't steal anything . . .'

'Well, you don't tell me he was on the contract.'

I can't believe I'm discussing my tenancy agreement in the afterlife. I let out a strong, gusting sigh, and scold, 'Well, you're the one who's been rifling through my necklaces, anyway. And why's all this stuff boxed up?'

I flap my tablecloth in the direction of the AUCHTION boxes. In the nearest one, I recognise my dotty cardigan, my turquoise bustier and an empty photo frame, which me and Stevie used to smile out of.

'I was just trying to help,' Mr Henry insists, with his arms wrapped around himself. 'To help lift money for the funeral. I swear to you.'

When he says the word 'funeral', my molecules ripple uncomfortably again. I realise my corpse must still be above ground, somewhere in the Capital. I hope someone's looking after me. And I hope I've still got my figure.

'When's the funeral?' I ask, softer now.

'It Tuesday.'

'That's ages.'

'No, they try to do sooner, but it been so so hard to find your nexts-of-kins.'

'Yeah, yeah, I know.'

Gingerly, Mr Henry edges towards the door, with a face like a piece of lost property.

'So, I, er . . . are you continue to live here?' he asks, scratching himself. 'Or do you leave?'

'I'll see how I feel,' I reply. I understand now why ghosts are seen as such a nuisance – we're the cheerless chaff left behind when someone dies. No doubt Mr Henry was hoping to have new tenants in Flat D before the end of the week – however, his property has just become a hell of a lot less lettable.

'So, I just leave you to it then, yes?' Mr Henry asks, still side-stepping along the skirting.

'Yeah, go on.'

'So, you be there at the funeral?'

'I reckon I'll have to be, don't you?' I say, on a roll with the existential irony, but it's lost on him. 'Where is it, like?'

'The, what's it now, Catholic's church, down the Shepherd's Bush. It Tuesday, yes? Three o'clock p.m. I see you there?'

'I might be hard to spot.'

Mr Henry lets out a nervous snigger-sniff, then scuttles all the way out of the bedroom with his shoulders hunched. On his way out, he trips over the metal threshold strip, just to make his afternoon worse.

'I swear, I did not take the TV,' Mr Henry adds, almost in a whisper, as he stalls to slip his brown brogues back on. He struggles with the laces, then rushes out of the flat without saying anything more. The air displacement from the slammed door nearly blows me backwards, into the open wardrobe.

Underneath the tablecloth, I'm seething again. Mr Henry might not have stolen my TV, but the bastard still has my best jewellery around his neck. I shout after him, but there's no answer. Grumbling, I quickly rearrange my molecules, then swing the cloth off myself and race after him.

It's still blowing a gale outside. After jumping, feather-light, out of the third-floor window, I quickly catch up with Mr Henry. I remove the necklaces with one smooth levitation, then stalk him down the rest of the High Road, breathing down his neck and whispering demonic tittle-tattle into his earholes. I follow him all the way to the Somerfield at Stamford Hill, and ruin his weekly shop by replacing all his groceries with white 8–9yrs elasticated knickers and beef onions, as he trudges up and down the aisles.

324

The angrier he becomes, the more of a lunatic he seems:

'Stop it, please!' he growls, talking to himself. I cackle quietly, under my breath. In the pets aisle, I try to hook a dog collar and leash around his neck, but my lassoing technique isn't up to much. Instead, I swap his bourbon biscuits for dog biscuits; his porridge oats for sawdust; his Stagg chilli for Pedigree Chum; and I almost swap his Kellogg's for hamster flakes, when a terrible thought hits me:

I've forgotten all about Lucifer.

⊙

I'm not sure what to wear for my funeral. After feeding Lucifer up on luxury flakes and pellets, I try on a few outfits from the AUCHTION boxes, but they all make me look like a spook, what with no face or hands. And Stevie's black balaclava and gloves make me look even worse – like I'm in the IRA. In the end, I plump for my birthday suit.

Come Tuesday, I'm a nervous wreck, shiver-hovering down Uxbridge Road. I wonder if most ghosts go to their own funerals. I've been to more funerals in my lifetime than all my weddings, christenings and pop concerts put together, and I've noticed a theme: the relatives always make a speech about how they're sure [insert dead person's name here] is looking over them, and how [dead person] would be so pleased to see all the people joined together in honour of [dead person's] marvellous life.

Ghosts are insecure. They just want to make sure people cry over them, as if you can measure the importance of your own life in litres. The better the person, the wetter the funeral.

When I finally reach the church, I'm flattered to see an overwhelming congregation, in an ensemble of clashing blacks, huddled around a fresh gravestone. I must've touched a lot of people, after all. Strangely, though, as I edge closer, I only recognise a few faces: my Promiscuous Pal Polly, Shaun and Sean, Mr Thursday and his daughters, Malcolm and his dad, and Donald shiver at the front of a crowd of complete strangers. Maybe these are people I've helped over the course of my life and since forgotten, although it's hard to tell if their faces are grieving, or merely bored. They look almost like cardboard cut-outs, drafted in to pad out the congregation.

I was hoping for a soaking wet, salty funeral. Instead, it's as dry as a Business Maths and Accountancy seminar.

'Kimberly was a well-liked pillar of the community; a woman with a heart of gold. It is with great remorse that we see someone of such a warm, compassionate nature be taken from the Earth under such tragic circumstances,' the priest drawls without any conviction, no doubt inserting [my dead person's name] into the same fluffy template he uses at every funeral.

All around us, the trees are these tall, terrifying things, like old ladies' fingers. I wonder if all clergymen plant sinister vegetation in their graveyards, to add to the effect at funerals. Or is it the fertiliser from rotten corpses that twists the trees into these frightful poses?

I slide closer to the congregation, to double-double-check for tears. Polly's the only one welling up, her eyelids flickering like half-dead moths. Next to her, Shaun and Sean keep their eyes fixed on the cemetery gates, like they don't want to be here. I don't, either.

'Kimberly was an avid fan of . . . music, cuisine, socialising, and she would never be seen without the latest eyeshadow, or the latest handbag,' the priest carries on, with a false smile.

What a load of shite!

'And now, let us join together in a moment of reflection, as we listen to a song of Kimberly's own choosing. It's . . . ahem . . . two seconds, where am . . . oh yeah, Kool & the Gang. Yes.'

326

I shrink back into the shrubbery. Trust the priest to fluff his lines at my funeral. I can hardly watch as 'Celebration' squeaks out of the church's portable ghetto-blaster. When I was alive, I thought Kool & the Gang might help lift the spirits of a genuinely grief-stricken, 100-strong congregation – instead, everyone looks embarrassed. My mourners keep their eyes to the ground, munching their bottom lips, shuffling about uneasily. I feel awful. My funeral congregation wants to go and fucking kill itself.

Clearly, awkward people have awkward friends, and awkward funerals. I wish I had the guts to put on Polly's black cloche hat and tell everyone not to worry; to just throw me in the ground as quickly as possible, and head to the pub. I want to put them out of their put-on misery. I want to scream, 'I'm back!' and dance on my coffin but, then again, I don't want the priest to start quoting lines from *The Exorcist* at me, and banish me altogether from Earth. So, I decide to stay put.

Throughout 'Celebration' the sun thinks about poking her head out from behind the clouds, to help lighten the mood, but it's all too cringeworthy, even for her. She cowers behind the cloud cover, cheeks burning with shame.

And that's when the cassette tape begins to ruckle. As if the song wasn't daft enough, the 4/4 beat speeds up to about 1,000 bpm, unspooling Kool and his gang. The singers sound like tickled guinea pigs. The kick drums sound like steelpans. The bass sounds like birdsong.

My true friends, Polly and Mr Thursday, keep their heads respectfully bowed – however, the hilarity's too much for some of the others: the cardboard cut-outs come to life, guffawing and firing semi-digested buffet pork pies from their nostrils. And funeral laughter's the most contagious laughter of all. Donald gyrates his hips, biting his lips; Mr Thursday has to grasp his daughters' wrists, to stop them from joining in; Shaun's shoulders shake; Sean shakes his head. Only Polly, dressed in a black PVC dress and knee-length fur coat, stays motionless. Her eyes carry on flickering, as some of the 'mourners' break into song, getting all the words wrong: 'Cel-e-brate good times, for all! Cel-e-brate good times, yeah . . . for all!'

I shudder back into the shadows. It makes you think: humans are all pointless, forgettable, ephemeral. Seeing people laugh at my funeral makes me wonder why I bothered toiling and troubling myself for twenty-four years. It makes me wish I'd been a miscarriage, or a cot death.

The congregation carry on prodding each other and masticating and laughing and singing, even when the music stops. And with that, Polly chucks her black dahlias on top of my falling, coffee-coloured coffin, and steps away from the bastards. Mr Thursday tries to touch her arm, but his hands are still full of his children's arms, and she gets away.

I wait for her to reach the furthest weeping willow, then I give chase, tailing my best friend like a second, see-through shadow.

⊙

I follow Polly to the nearest Ghost Train station, and down down down the escalators to the blood red line. At Tottenham Court Road, she changes onto the death black line, and heads south.

As the train sets off, I curl myself around one of the clammy handrails, listening to Polly coughing violently into her mitt. Travelling on the death black line is like having a long fag break. It's the deepest of all the Subterranean train lines and, apparently, a forty-minute journey has the same effect on your lungs as smoking two cigarettes.

I glance about the carriage. Everyone's faces are glazed; lost in fantasy. Due to its library-like silence, the Ghost Train is the perfect place to catch up on your reading, or have a long, hard think. I wonder what's going on in Polly's head. She does look classically depressed when she gets off at Tooting Broadway. She slopes slowly down Mitcham Road, with all the purpose of someone walking down Death Row. I keep on her tail, praying she doesn't do anything daft.

I cringe every time she crosses the road. When you're depressed, the Green Cross Code changes. You don't have to look both ways, and you tend not to bother with the green man. The idea of a Ford Mondeo taking your life away seems strangely appealing.

As Polly slumps past the markets, some of the fat, foreign stallholders whoop at her. Polly's head dips even further. It's bad enough being ogled in your best clobber, let alone when you're feeling despondent, with no make-up, in mourning clothes.

I don't miss the men of the Capital much. One advantage of being invisible is you can walk past groups of randy bastards stark naked, and none of them bat an eyelid. To spite the whooping stallholders, I push over their rails of knock-off basketball tops and school cardigans, and spill their teas. Polly carries on towards Amen Corner, with her head ducked. When we get to Welham Road, we walk four paces apart, dodging the leaves falling like large, rusted teardrops.

I gasp when a lady's pushbike almost collides with Polly, on the corner of Welham and Idlecombe. The lady tuts. It's not even rush-hour yet, and Polly's already got a twisted ankle and a slap on the wrist. Fortunately, she's only a block or two from her house. I keep my eyes peeled for banana peels, or spilt petrol, or anything else that might put her life at risk, until she's safely at the doorstep of number 5.

Polly must've bought a new black handbag for the funeral, because she takes forever fumbling with the fastening before she finds her keys. She slides the bronze Yale one into the slot, and frowns. For some reason, the door won't open. She jiggles the key, but still no joy. Frustrated, she gang-rapes the lock with the rest of her keys, until one of them snaps, embedding itself in the metal slit.

'Shit,' Polly says gruffly, the way men do when they lose a condom in your slit.

Disconcerted, Polly bashes hard six times on the stained glass. She's hardly finished the first couple of bashes, when a dark shape comes to the door. Strange, really, because Polly lives alone, apparently. Surely it's not another intrusive landlord, playing dress-up with her jewellery? Polly sways nervously from foot to foot as the door creaks open. It stops creaking when the new security chain pulls taut, then the handsome/horrifying face of Mr No Tomorrow appears. He's dressed in one of her silk dressing gowns, and his black hair's slicked back, fresh from a shower.

'Honey, you back!' he announces, grinning unconvincingly. Mr No Tomorrow shuts the door again, undoes the chain, then reopens it and kindly welcomes Polly into her own fucking home.

Polly says nothing, like she's completely exhausted with life, and doesn't want to fight any more. She steps inside, slumping sadly along the wall of the small hallway, with her back to the crusted ketchup stains. Mr No Tomorrow tries to slam the door in my face. I flinch, before remembering I'm invincible.

'Where you been, wifey?' he asks in a threatening tone, although he probably thinks he's being friendly. Polly's shoulders crumple.

'Kimberly's funeral,' she mumbles, looking at me but not looking at me. The three of us form a flimsy Mexican stand-off in the tight corridor.

Mr No Tomorrow twists his face into something resembling sympathy. He puts his arm around her shoulder, and attempts to cuddle her. Shrugging him off, Polly snaps, 'How did you get in?'

330

'I . . . we should be more like the old times,' Mr No Tomorrow replies, not sure where to put his hands now. He hangs them awkwardly by his sides, until next time.

'No; *how*? *How* did you get in?'

'Oh. Bathroom window was open.'

The colour drains from Polly's face. Despite being a semi-famous maneater in the Capital, she looks ever so small and feeble now. Then again, just because you sleep with a lot of people, it doesn't mean you're self-confident and secure. Polly shifts about uncomfortably, no doubt racking her brains for the whereabouts of knives, poisons and heavy, blunt instruments dotted about the house. I catch her eyeing up one of her stray stilettos: a six-incher, with a pointed, steel heel.

'You've changed the fucking locks,' she hisses.

'Don't use foul language,' Mr No Tomorrow scolds, trying to be the good guy. 'I just thought that we could try again.'

Polly sighs, nearly gusting me back out through the letterbox.

'Like this?'

'Like this. I thought we could get quick, lavish wedding and be happy together.'

'Fuck off.'

'Please, Pauly, I desperate.'

I remember Mr No Tomorrow saying he was desperate, back when he was trying to woo (solicit) me at the Ristorante di Fantasia. It's mad how some lads think announcing their desperation will endear them to the opposite sex: the last resort for the relentlessly rejected. Lads have never been good at expressing their emotions – especially when they try to spew them all out at once.

'I don't care,' Polly says, backing into the living room. I stand between them, trying to form a protective barrier, but I'm far too faint.

'I'm sorry, I'm sorry,' Mr No Tomorrow whines, changing his

tack. He seems to think simultaneously apologising and squeezing her arm will help win her back.

'Fuck off!' Polly squeals. 'I'm phoning the police!'

'It was not breaking and entering.'

'Fuck off! You're a sick bastard. And you shat in my back garden!'

'No! I shit? No!'

'Don't deny it!'

'I love you,' Mr No Tomorrow states, clutching at straws now. Again, Polly has trouble wrestling with her bag fastening, not to mention wrestling with Mr No Tomorrow. He keeps yanking at her arms, like he's trying to force her into a cuddle, as well as stop her from phoning the police. Polly screams, on the verge of tears again. They cat and mouse through the house, Polly wailing through her teeth as she keeps struggling with her bag. She runs up the stairs, probably with a mind to find a suitable solvent to spray into Mr No Tomorrow's eye-sockets.

'Please,' I hear, from behind us. 'Let us work this out. Please. Please. Please.'

It's true that you never know what you've got until it's gone, but there's no need to break into your ex's house and change the locks, just because she won't open the door to you. And worse still is pretending this behaviour is normal. I've never known what nationality Mr No Tomorrow is, but I'm sure this isn't the traditional courtship ritual over there.

'No,' Polly stresses. 'There's nothing to work out.'

As you'd expect, the relentlessly rejected don't take extra rejection well. Successful, happy people become more or less immune to – or even bored by – extra success and happiness, but the low people just keep getting lower.

'You evil . . . *evil!*' Mr No Tomorrow booms, with venom in his eyes. I've got no choice but to step in. Concentrating hard,

I swiftly tie his shoelaces together in a triple knot. You heard me – a *tripler*. Not only should this save Polly from his clutches, it might also save Mr No Tomorrow from committing suicide the same way as Stevie (if he's that way inclined). He's never going to undo that knot with those nails.

Mr No Tomorrow tumbles forward with his arms outstretched, like an invisible rug's been pulled out from underneath him. Polly squeals as he hits the deck, but it's a relieved squeal. Fortunately, Mr No Tomorrow doesn't break his beautiful cheekbones on the skirting board. As he lies there, contemplating the carpet, I do feel a mixture of aversion and affinity with Mr No Tomorrow – it's not easy being unloved in a city teeming with strangers. But, then again, it's not easy being overloaded with love, either. If you're going to be promiscuous, you've got to be prepared to break some hearts – but you've also got to be aware that some of those hearts might not take no for an answer.

While Mr No Tomorrow works out how to stand up again, Polly charges down the stairs and back out of the house. She probably feels safer in the street – the windows of the other terraces feel like eye-witnesses, even if the folk behind them are just watching their TVs, oblivious.

Without Mr No Tomorrow breathing down her neck, Polly manages to compose herself, and yanks her black bag open once and for all. She finds her phone easily, then dials 999, with shaking sable-polished nails.

She seems far too overdressed to be in such distress. The fur coat and cloche hat give the impression of a glamorous 1920s gangland bust, while the bomping and crashing going on inside 5 Welham Road sounds more like Marxist slapstick. When the Necropolitan Police turn up five minutes later, Mr No Tomorrow still hasn't emerged from the house. Polly must've explained the situation wrong over the phone, because the police turn up with a battering-ram and truncheons unsheathed. She stands stock-still in the gutter, leaving the Nec to storm the house. At long last, her neighbours prise themselves away from their tellies to have a gawp out of their windows. Squinting, self-righteous faces appear, with expressions that seem to say: 'I knew number 5 was a bleeding brothel!' / 'What on Earth is she wearing?' / 'Christ, here comes her pimp!' / 'Ack, another fucking foreigner. Wait till I tell [insert friend/relative/work colleague here] . . .'

Two brickhead policemen emerge from Polly's house, carrying Mr No Tomorrow like a bad-tempered treetrunk. With his shoe-laces still tied together and his wrists cuffed, Mr No Tomorrow can only squirm helplessly as they shove him in the back of the van. Before the cage doors shut, he manages to catch Polly's eye and he screeches, 'I'm desperate!'

But even number 8's cat can see that.

⊙

After giving a statement to the Necropolitan Police, Polly enlists one of her neighbours to help rechange her locks. The bloke from number 3 has a way with women and DIY – he tries a few jokes with her while he works, but I guess Polly's not in the mood to lose anything else in her slit just yet. Give it a week or two, at least.

After a cup of trembling tea, Polly thanks her neighbour, then sits alone in her front room with the curtains shut. The last dregs of daylight claw at her windowsill, through the gap where the curtains don't quite join. I accidentally make her shiver a few times as I tornado across the room, deep in thought. I wish I was better company. I wish she knew she wasn't alone. I want to talk to her, but I'm aware Polly's a sceptic when it comes to three things: celibacy, teetotalism, and ghosts. If only her stepfather and his phasmophile pals were here, I might've been able to make contact.

I waft her curtains – to give her a 'sign' – but she probably just thinks she's got draughty windows. After an hour or so of sitting and shaking, she gets up and slips her shoes back on. It's easy to get sick of your own company when you live alone. So, Polly decides to go for a walk, to be alone outside instead.

I hope she's feeling alright. She doesn't seem to know where she's going, clomping through the estate with her eyes to the ground. She continues crossing roads without looking, and turning corners without looking, weaving an elaborate spiderweb path between the terraced houses. I'm like her clear, ectoplasmic spider thread, following a few steps behind.

After almost thirty minutes of walking, Polly kicks off her black high heels and stamps the rest of the way down Trinity Road, with just a thin layer of tight protecting her feet from the street. I feel bad – she's going to wear holes in the soles, and they look good quality as well. I want to do something. I want to carry her heels for her, but she might feel embarrassed, walking along with a pair of floating stilettos.

A sickly thought strikes me: what if my death marked the moment Polly became utterly alone on the planet? What if Kimberly Clark was her last remaining human friend? After all, Polly never used to talk about her other lady friends – perhaps she didn't have any. All she ever talked about were her latest conquests: a string of seedy lads she'd shag before being thrown back onto the slagheap.

After the ragged common, I follow her down to the river, where Wandsworth Bridge stands paddling, with its blue trouser legs rolled up. Polly narrowly avoids a speeding wing-mirror to the cranium before crossing over to the bridge. She completely ignores the beautiful view stretched out on either side of us: she misses the sky turning from eczema pink to contusion blue as the sun disappears; and she misses the lights of the city reflected millions of times over in the ripples of the Thames, like all the world's Christmas decorations suspended in a fishtank.

Polly just glares at the paving slabs, in a trance. Just now, she reminds me of a slightly less-good-looking Catherine Deneuve in *Repulsion*: that black-and-white Polanski picture about growing gradually insane in the big city. I've seen countless people made sour by the Capital. I don't think humans were ever meant to be alone, nor do I think they were ever meant to be packed into such a small space with tons of strangers. The Capital has that cruel knack of making you feel both pushed into and left out of society, like turning up late to a masquerade ball in your normal clothes.

About two-thirds of the way across Wandsworth Bridge, my Promiscuous Pal Polly from Southampton stops by the railing to have a long, hard stare into the water. The river seems to be flowing much slower than usual, as if it has the consistency of saliva, or gelatin. I grow anxious, praying she doesn't hurl herself in. I don't want to feel culpable for (and completely powerless against) another impromptu suicide.

Surely she's not going to jump. Love might be the *pièce de résistance* in the otherwise mediocre marathon of life – however, one cupid stunt shouldn't be enough to make you end it all.

Look at the evidence, though: she's got no friends; she doesn't feel safe in her own home; she's not bothered about ruining her good-quality tights.

Silently, I stand shoulder to shoulder with Polly as the tide gently rubs against the banks of the Thames. Soon, Polly starts adding to the swell of water, throwing tears at it. She makes disgusting, private sounds: snortling, 'uh-uh'ing, retching, whining, mumbling. Then, she swings her leg over the railing.

Panicking, I scan the bridge for police cars or good Samaritans, but everybody's too busy trying to get somewhere to notice Polly going nowhere.

336

Her bottom lip wobbles while she straddles the bridge, as if she's simultaneously talking herself into and out of jumping. She carries on sobbing, though her face looks strangely sane and composed, as she contemplates the crash of water. Or it could just be vacancy.

I scan the bridge again. Still no heroes.

I've got no choice but to step in, again. I don't want a rusty railing to be the last thing my promiscuous pal gets her leg over – I want her to realise there are good men still out there; men who don't break into your house, or nick your necklaces, or top themselves without saying a proper goodbye. Suicide's a break from sadness, yes, but it's also a break from potential mindblowing bliss.

My only obstacle is Polly's deafness to the spirit world. Before she takes the plunge, I try to talk her out of jumping ('   !') but her face remains unresponsive, eyes still fixed on the grey, building-blocked horizon. I consider levitating her to safety, but her body's surprisingly heavy for someone who claims to be a size 10. I'm thinking about cutting my losses and sloping off before I witness anything too heart-breaking, when I remember the Grim Reaper's advice:

If in doubt: howl.

Taking inspiration from the growling wind, I summon up every last drop of my ectoplasmic energy reserves, and throw my voice right into Polly's right ear. Her hammer and anvil barely twitch, but something causes all the hairs in her cochlea to suddenly stand on end.

'Polly, it's me! It's me! Please don't jump!' I scream.

When she hears my words, Polly's face whitens and tightens – and she jumps anyway. Or, rather, she slips.

Polly seems to fall for an aeon, shedding her fur coat like some sort of regressive beast, before landing in the froth below. She screams, with her arms flailing, choking for her life. By the look in her eyes, she wasn't expecting to hear my voice just then. By the look in her eyes, she wasn't intending to commit suicide, either.

I dive in after her.

I can't believe what I've done.

'HELP! HELP! PLEASE!' Polly screams at the sky, scrabbling in the high tide.

Once I'm in the water, I can't see much hope for her. Not only can Polly not swim, ghosts make terrible lifeguards. As soon as I hit the river, my spirit dissolves, mixing in with the thick, foaming fizz. I try to call out to her again, but that just makes it worse. Polly gurgles blank breaths, in shock, taking on board far too much water. Soon, she's stiff and bloated, bobbing along on her self-made waves. I lose my spirit completely. Perhaps if I'd thrown down a lifebelt instead of jumping in after her, she might've survived. Perhaps if I'd worn her off-white mattress-cover before coming up and harassing her, she might've known who I was.

THE END

Part 3) Kimberly's Second Coming

Some people grind their teeth in their sleep, but it's not every day you wake up to find your bottom jaw lodged in your brain. I roll over, making my spine clunk. The traffic on Shepherd's Bush Green looks the same as it did when we fell over in front of it, only now all the cars are static and silent, with their drivers scuttling out to look at the dead bodies smashed on the asphalt. Living people are strange – given the chance, they love gawping at the dead.

As I roll over, more and more unfamiliar faces come rushing over to stare at me, like I'm some sort of rubbish circus act. Unfortunately for the spectators, I'm not actually dead. Kimberley, however, has her audience absolutely captivated round the front of the Fiat Punto, contorting her limbs into impossible positions and showing off her brains.

Once I get the feeling back in my joints, I lever myself onto my haunches and yank my jaw back into place. I shake a bit of life into my left foot, then I stand up, using the Punto's crushed bonnet for balance.

I feel like a rhino's been tap dancing on my chest. In the reflections of the car windows, my body looks unscathed, though my clothes are in tatters. Despite everything, I feel well enough to head back towards the Subterranean station, but as soon as I remount the pavement the spectators swamp me. Some pat me and laugh in disbelief, like I'm a modern-day messiah; others keep asking me if I'm alright, or if I'm immortal.

'Yeah, not bad,' I reply, hating the attention. All I want is to regather my limbs and thoughts and make a hasty retreat from the Capital, while all the onlookers want is for me to stay put.

'You might have concussion,' one of them suggests.

'Does anyone here know the recovery position?' another asks.

'Naw, naw, you're alright,' I say. 'I'm recovered. Honestly.'

I'm aware how absurd the spectacle must seem to them. Soon, all the folk 'urgh'ing and 'argh'ing over Kimberley come rushing over to 'ooh' and 'aah' over me instead. Half the crowd pool together their scanty first-aid knowledge, offering me tissues and bandages and ambulances, while the other half stand in transcendental paralysis, suddenly believing in miracles, God, and the quality of Ford Mondeo brakes, not to mention the unbumpiness of their bumpers. Across the road, bystanders take photos of me with their camera-phones, squinting at the buttons, while the odd newcomer stands for five seconds, glares, then toddles off back to their errands.

The drivers of the Punto and Mondeo look inconsolably shocked and sheepish. To avoid incriminating themselves, they fail to say 'sorry' to me, though I don't blame them for the carnage. Kimberley had a death wish, and it came true.

I glance behind the pulverised Punto and grimace. Kimberley's isn't the prettiest corpse I've ever seen. Where her face has caved in, you can see her old mercury fillings dancing in the sun. Poor, poor Kimberley. She might've been horrible to me in the past, but it's strange how your feelings change about somebody when, all of a sudden, they're gone. A bit like my dad, who had hundreds of disgraceful jokes about Princess Di, but still cried buckets at her televised funeral.

Then again, it softens the blow slightly, knowing Kimberley's safe and sound in Heaven. In fact, I'm a little bit jealous of her – no doubt she's having a blast up there, while I have to go through the mind-numbing mundanity of mortality all over again. I decide there's no point trying to resuscitate her. Instead, I borrow a camera-phone off one of my followers, and tap in 999. While I wait for the call to connect, I watch more toy planes drifting through the sky, leaving behind their toothpaste trails. I rub the whiplash out of my neck and chew my bottom lip. Against all the odds, I might still get to Japan before sundown.

⊙

Five or ten minutes later, the Necropolitan Police turn up. Or, at least, you can hear their sirens in the distance, but it takes the van another five or ten minutes to squeeze through the traffic piled for miles up Uxbridge Road.

I brush a strand of Guillotine behind my left ear, watching the two officers striding towards the disaster spot. One of them has lots of muscles and a shaved, oblong head, while the other sports a moustache usually found on French folk or homosexuals. The meaty, muscly policeman barges through the diminishing crowd of disciples, while the fruity, mustachioed one weaves in and out with the air and grace of a bow-legged ballerina.

'Clear away! Clear away!' PC Meaty commands. The crowd shrinks back, leaving just me, the Punto, the Mondeo, PC Fruity and Kimberley's corpse.

'What's happened, exactly?' PC Fruity asks in a breathy tone.

'There was this accident,' I explain, putting emphasis on the word 'accident'. 'I mean, this girl Kimberley' – I point to the bit that looks most like her – 'she ran out into the road. And I tried to stop her, but, but we both got hit. And, er, what happened was . . . well, I . . . I'm alright, I suppose . . .'

I feel like I'm in school again. PC Fruity scratches his moustache, and glances at his colleague, who shrugs. PC Meaty takes a step back, and fiddles with his walkie-talkie, but I'm too busy dreaming of kimonos to catch what he says into it. Once he's finished muttering in code, he gives Fruity a special nod, then they both pounce on me, corkscrewing my arms behind my back.

'What are you doing?!' I yell.

'You're under arrest,' PC Meaty states, snapping on a pair of handcuffs. 'Youhavetherighttoremainsilentbutitmayharmyour-defenceifyoudonotmentionwhenquestionedsomethingyoulater-relyonincourtAnythingyoudosaymaybegiveninevidence. Now get in the van.'

As they manhandle me roughly into the back of the vehicle, I glance towards my disciples, although it seems they've all but disappeared, toddling off discreetly, back into the safe recesses of the city.

'What have I done? I haven't . . . done *anything*!' I squeal, in tears now. Over in the Fiat Punto, the old, haggard-looking driver plays dead, avoiding eye contact.

'What are you doing?!' I scream again, as the van door slams behind me.

The policemen say nothing. Police officers must go through strict, rigorous training to master the art of voluntary deafness. If the police think you're wrong, mad, drunk, or all three, there's nothing you can say or do to change their minds. They're power-mad, professional lawbreakers. I slump down on the Naughty Bench in the back of the van, feeling guilty for nothing, scooping my chin into my hands.

In the front, the two coppers hop onto their luxury leather seats, then the van vibrates, before speeding swiftly away from Shepherd's Bush Green. I appear to be in some sort of cage. There aren't any seatbelts in the back, so I have to break the law as we race through the Capital, tossing this way and that at every red light and every sharp corner.

'What have I done?' I whinge, feeling more like the K in that book by Kafka than the K in this one.

The policemen keep quiet, though, watching the road being sucked under the van at seventy-two miles an hour (also against the law). Now and then, they stick the siren on, to both frighten the traffic and drown out my whining.

342

I grab my knees to stop myself shaking so much. I wish I was still dead – it seemed quite civilised in Limbo, playing Subbuteo with a cocktail-quaffing Grim Reaper.

As we zoom gloomily through Shepherd's Bush, I try to calm my breathing, and evaluate the situation. There's always a chance the police are just looking after me, what with the slight similarity between myself and our Lord, Jesus Christ, in the res-urrection stakes at least. It doesn't really explain the cage and the handcuffs, though.

We stop sharply outside Shepherd's Bush police station – this large white box with white windows, on stilts. I go from one white box into another.

'Seriously, what have I done?' I whine again as I'm pulled out of the back of the van. The policemen drag me along the pave-ment, Chinese burning my biceps. For the sake of it, I try to wrestle my way out of the handcuffs, but that only makes the blighters tighter.

Inside, the police station's typically drab and unwelcoming, with chipped sixties décor and poster upon poster of sad faces. Another sad face lurks behind the reception desk, supping a mug of tea. The two bobbies lead me past a door marked LAVA-TORY, down a sweat-scented blue corridor, to a row of holding cells. I dig my heels into the lino, protesting, 'Please! Why am I here? Can you tell me what's going on?!'

When we get to the end of the corridor, PC Meaty finally breaks his vow of silence:

'The Court's issued a warrant for your arrest,' he states, unlock-ing CELL 6, 'on suspicion of murder.'

⊙

There's nothing like being thrown into a police cell to inspire a bout of loathing and self-pity. It's only when they accuse me of being a murderer that I start acting a bit like one. I go at them with my teeth, crying my eyes out, pleading innocence and ignorance and screeching injustice. Maybe if I hadn't lost my temper we might've been able to talk it over there and then but, instead, they toss me into CELL 6 to 'calm down'. In defiance of the professional lawbreakers, I decide not to 'calm down' – instead, I scream bloody murder at the top of my voice for about twenty minutes, like it'll get me anywhere.

The cell's exactly how you'd imagine it, with a crummy school gym mat for a bed, a manky toilet which burps every half an hour, a heavy iron door with a dinner-hatch or cat-flap towards the top, and a CCTV camera watching me, like a mechanical hawk, from one of the ceiling corners. I spend the rest of the day scowling at the camera, once the screaming and tears get too much even for me.

Ironically, they've taken away the laces from my Man Utd collar, as if I'd want to die twice in one day. In any case, by Stevie's standards, I'd need at least four pairs to hang myself successfully.

Along with the self-pity, there's anger, indigestion and confusion. Just because I survived the car crash, it doesn't mean it was my fault. I'm half expecting the Meaty/Fruity double act to swing open the cat-flap and tell me it's all just a silly joke.

Soon, the blubbing and self-hatred give way to a different sort of hatred, focused towards the policemen. I wonder if they're watching my CCTV in a back room, slapping their thighs and cackling. At one point, PC Fruity pokes his nose through the dinner-hatch to offer me a glass of water, or a slice of pizza. Through gritted, chattering teeth I snap, 'Yeah, go on, I'll have artichoke, asparagus, olives, mushrooms, red peppers . . .'

When I reach 'red peppers', the hatch slams shut. The giardiniera pizza never appears. I try to force sleep on the gym mat, but my brain's racing too much. The longer they keep me in the cell, the less likely it seems this is all a practical joke. I wish

I'd befriended millionaire businessmen now, instead of drunken bums, since I might need someone with some disposable income to bail me out. I might need a hero.

At 7 a.m. the next morning, the heavy iron door creaks open. Instead of a knight in shining armour, it's the same two policemen again, in their drab polyester uniforms, with sauce stains around their mouths. They reshackle my wrists, then lead me into a mess hall of sorts. As it turns out, the mess hall's just a slightly larger version of my cell, with the same CCTV camera in one corner, a dinner-hatch, and a single table and plastic chair instead of a gym mat. Through the dinner-hatch, I catch glimpses of other coppers, gorging themselves on hot Full English breakfasts, with tea and all the trimmings.

I slump down at the single table, in front of a bowl of dry oats. The copshop cooks haven't even turned it into porridge for me. I attempt a few mouthfuls, but there's not enough saliva in my cheeks to cement-mixer it into edibility. I sulk instead, sobbing over the bowl, but it still doesn't turn into porridge.

PC Meaty farts, filling the room with a rotten sausage smell.

'Eat,' he commands, watching over me with bulging, crossed arms.

'What's going on?' I groan, pushing the bowl away. It's a shock to hear my own voice again, after all that silent, debilitating deliberating last night. Despite having two bent bobbies to contend with, it seems, in jail, your main adversary is your own thoughts. Especially when you haven't got a clue why you've ended up here, or how you're going to get back out.

After I've choked down a few more porridge oats, the policemen take me through to a different room, to interrogate me. The room looks exactly the same as the last one except, this time, there's a large pane of one-way glass instead of a dinner-hatch and, instead of the oats, there's a selection of gadgets laid out on the Formica table: Dictaphone, inkpad, pen, paper, camera, cotton buds.

Before probing me with their questions, the policemen probe me with their gadgets. PC Meaty takes my fingerprints and swabs the inside of my cheek, while PC Fruity sets up the photo shoot. I straighten the Guillotine and give them my best, saddest pout.

Next comes the questioning. I stare at them, boss-eyed, as they bombard me with riddles:

'Where were you on the night of the thirtieth of May this year?'

'How many sexual partners have you had in the last six months?'

'Do you play sports?'

'Has anyone ever told you, you look like the spawn of a necrophiliac?'

'What presents did you receive on your birthday in 1989?'

I sigh, and say, 'Am I alright to remain silent?'

The policemen give each other a look. Leaning forward, PC Meaty coughs in my face and announces, 'You have the right to remain silent, but it may harm your defence if you do not mention, when questioned—'

'As in, now,' PC Fruity adds, with a smarmy simper.

'—something which you later rely on in court.'

I launch my head into my hands, and whine, 'Are you sure there's not been some mistake?'

'Take it up with the CPS,' PC Meaty states. 'They issued the warrant.'

'Based on what?' I say.

'Take it up with the CPS.'

I growl into my sleeve, leaving behind a wet imprint. I wish I had my laces, after all – it might be wise to excuse myself from the interrogation chamber, and quietly garrotte myself in CELL 6. Thanks to the CCTV, though, I'm constantly on suicide watch. I drop my chin onto the edge of the Formica, praying

346

for the walls of the station to suddenly collapse, like a cheap, cardboard film set.

'Shouldn't I have a lawyer?' I ask, wiping my nose.

'It's up to you. We can arrange for one, free of charge,' says Fruity, with another smirk, 'or you can sort one out yourself.'

'You've got one phone call,' PC Meaty adds generously.

I scratch the back of my neck. I've got no idea who to phone, especially since I don't have any next-of-kin or boyfriends any more. I wonder if they've got a copy of the *Yellow Pages* at the station – it might be worth ringing a locksmith, or a magician, or a bulldozing company, to get me out of this mess. It might even be worth phoning 999, in case these two aren't bona fide policemen. For all I know, they could just be your run-of-the-mill, unprofessional lawbreakers. Sadist bastards in fancy dress.

I pick at a dent in the table, desperately trying to remember all the characters I've come across who haven't died or betrayed me yet: Lucifer the Hamster, my Promiscuous Pal Polly from Southampton, the Square-Faced Bachelor, the Triangle-Faced Bachelor, Mr Henry, Nina, Mr and Mrs Wallace . . .

And then, winking at me on the back of a blinked eyelid, a face comes to me. I lift my head from the Formica, trying in vain to recollect a phone number I've never phoned before in my life. Timidly, I glance at the two coppers, and mumble, 'Ehm . . . am I alright having two calls?'

'What?' PC Fruity spits.

I flex my neck apologetically, and add, 'Might need, ehm, directory enquiries first.'

'Christ, let's get fucking on with it, then,' snaps PC Meaty.

⊙

The next day, a new face peers in at me through the cat-flap. Martin Sawyer, the Wallace family lawyer, must've been practising

347

his smile all the way down from Teesside – it's an absolute beauty; the most comforting smile I've seen in ages.

'Thank God you're here,' I say, even though my faith in God has faltered somewhat recently.

'How are you feeling?' Martin asks, still smiling. PC Meaty allows him into my cell with a slight shove, asserting his authority, then he slams the iron door shut. Even though the cat-flap stays closed throughout our conversation, I'm sure I can hear breathing behind it.

'Not great,' I whisper, shuffling along the gym mat so Martin can sit down. 'Have you got any idea why I'm here?'

Martin picks at a bit of dry skin on his chin, and says, 'I've had a look through the paperwork, but I've got to say it all seems a bit . . . wishy-washy.'

Martin opens his faux-leather briefcase and pulls out a thick wodge of papers. The papers are tattooed front and back with minuscule black courier print. Slipping on a pair of reading glasses, Martin scans a bit of the text, cringes slightly, and says, 'Now, I'm not sure if you're aware or not, but it looks unlikely you'll be granted bail.'

I shake my head, and shiver. Martin's making me feel uneasy, now the smile's gone and he's speaking all business-like. He carries on, 'We'll have it confirmed when we see a magistrate later today, but don't get your hopes up. Because of the severity of the charge, the Court will probably order that you remain in custody. Just in case you try to abscond somewhere. Abroad. The Far East, for example.'

Here Martin glances at me over his lenses. After studying my expression for a second or two, he turns back to his papers. 'Now, you'll be transferred to your local Ladies' Jail maybe later today, or early tomorrow. Hopefully we'll have the charge sheet with us soon but, as you've probably gathered, the police are being a bit, er, reticent about it all.'

'Have you got any idea what I'm meant to have done?' I ask, feeling dumb.

'Murder,' Martin states gravely.

'Naw, naw, yeah, I know. But, I mean, who have I . . . who am I supposed to have killed? Do you know?'

Martin turns to his papers again. Squinting, he skim-reads the odd passage, looks up at me apprehensively, then glances back down at the tiny print. Finally, he clears his throat, and answers, 'Mm, I, erm . . . I don't know.'

I sigh into my fists. Martin lets out a nervous laugh, and shifts his weight on the gym mat. He explains, 'Well, let me tell you what I *do* know. You see, I'm not sure if you're aware or not, but it appears someone's been spying on you.'

I shudder again, thinking of all the possible eyeballs hiding behind the CCTV camera. I hike my knees up to my chest and restraighten the Guillotine self-consciously.

'See, erm, are you aware you're the subject of a book?' Martin adds. 'The leading lady, so to speak?'

Now that I think about it, a lot of strange things have happened since I found myself in Limbo. It's as if I've been allowed a peek behind the final curtain of an epic play, to see all the gubbins going on behind the scenes of reality. Like Dorothy collaring the scrawny Wizard behind all the smoke and mirrors, in the Emerald City.

'Erm, sort of,' I reply. 'Like, I don't know how much you know, but I'm aware there's someone watching over me. The Reader, I mean.'

I point in your general direction, but Martin only seems to see the ceiling when he follows my finger. His brow furrows, and he says, 'Hmm. Well, are you aware there's someone *writing* about you? Writing about you right now, as we speak?'

349

I shake my head, bringing my knees even higher, up to my chin. The breathing behind the iron door seems to grow heavier, and I'm sure the lens of the camera twinkles.

'Well, let's put it this way,' Martin goes on. 'If you're aware someone's *reading* about you, it makes sense someone must've *written* something about you, doesn't it?'

I nod, peering shyly over my kneecaps.

'Right, well here's the thing,' Martin continues. 'The CPS has issued a warrant for your arrest, based on evidence found in a document called' – here, Martin squints at his papers again – 'er, *Kimberly's Capital Punishment*. It's a book about you – apparently written from your point of view.'

I fiddle with my hands, confused.

'Now, here comes the problem. The CPS appears to have taken this, er, document as factual evidence. But I've been through it myself, and I can't make head nor tail of what's true in it or not. There's a lot of death in it, but I can't see any evidence of cold-blooded murder.'

This is all completely puzzling. I play with the Guillotine again and ask, 'Someone's been spying on me?'

'Yes, well, spying on you – or just plain making up lies about you. It's hard to tell, with these novel things. Does the, er . . .' Martin rechecks his papers, 'does the name Milward mean anything to you?'

I shake my head.

'Apparently he's been at it for a while. Watching people. Making up stories about people,' Martin explains.

'And he's been writing things about me?'

'Mm, yes. Don't ask me why, but it seems he's been using you as a puppet. A plaything. Or, rather, as a kind of voodoo doll, to take all his . . . grievances and insecurities out on. But I believe you're innocent, Kimberly. I really do, love.'

I smile halfheartedly. As I sit pondering the name Milward, a few cloudy, conflicting faces and memories hobble about the peripheries of my brainwaves. Images of dinner trays, apples, library books, itchy carpets, and broken dolls creep in and out of the butter-finger grips of my memory banks, before being suddenly illuminated by a single, devastating lightning bolt. Oh Lord. I think I know who this Milward character is. I think he used to be in my English class at secondary school.

'Actually, I do know him,' I grumble. 'He used to sit behind me in English, I think. Are you on about, er . . . who's it? Rrr . . . ichard?'

'That's the bugger.'

I take my knees away from my face, and inhale deeply. I wonder if this whole confusing calamity is a side-effect of my second coming. Maybe I've been imprisoned, simply to honour the fate dished out to me by Mother Nature on Shepherd's Bush Green. I am the Resurrection and the Life, and I am a Slight Nuisance to the Births, Marriages and Deaths indexes. And I need rubbing out.

'So, what are we gonna do?' I ask, shifting in my shallow bum imprint.

'Well,' Martin starts, taking off his glasses and cleaning them, 'I'll go through the novel again, this weekend, with a fine-toothed comb. You try and get some rest. I hope the Ladies' Jail isn't too awful. We'll soon get you out though, love.'

Before Martin leaves, we hug solidly and awkwardly. It worries me, the idea of him analysing my so-called memoirs – not because he might discover I'm guilty of murder (I'm not), but because I've been spending my time shagging homeless men through glory-holed shower curtains, being nasty to my ex-boyfriend/his ex-client, and constantly failing suicide. I hope I didn't say or think anything rude or rotten about Martin Sawyer when I first met him, after Stevie's funeral. I hope my subconscious was well-behaved.

I hope Martin thinks I'm worth saving.

⊙

As expected, the Court doesn't grant me bail. Later that day, PCs Meaty and Fruity take me on another treacherous, rattling day-trip, to HMP Holloway, my local Ladies' Jail. The prison's a red-brick monstrosity with a drab castle wall wiggling around it. As it looms before us, I realise the prison's within spitting distance of that pub, the Copenhagen, where I gave Shaun and Sean my inheritance from Stevie to piss up the wall. My heart feels sore as we drive through the high-security gates.

After signing myself in at reception and undergoing a sickly, semi-erotic (on her side) encounter with a woman wearing plastic gloves, I'm shown to my cell. Inside the Ladies' Jail, parades of dismal dykes and tomboys trudge up and down the flaky, emul-sioned gangways, on their way to take cold showers or queue for the phone or scream into their pillows.

Instead of a WELCOME mat, there's a thick layer of birdshit outside my door. On the upside, my single remand cell's slightly larger than the one at the station, and it even has a bedframe. On the downside, the mattress looks mouldy with yellow sorrow-stains, the chipped desk swears the previous inmates' carved obscenities at you and my new manky toilet burps more often than the last one. Behind my new cat-flap, fearsome female voices grunt and chunter. The only real comfort comes from the lovely shard of light posting itself through a gap in my window. It's only a tiny shard of light, since it's only a tiny, grilled window, but it's a reminder the wonderful, wide world is still out there, waiting for me.

I hope it doesn't have to wait long.

⊙

After a few days in the Ladies' Jail (days which include a lot of wall-staring, nail-biting, tantrums in the TV room, a suicide attempt in C Wing, and seventeen laps of the yard), I'm dragged into the Crown Court to confirm my name and enter my plea. Martin Sawyer's not present amongst the wigs and the robes – he's probably late. I do feel bad forcing him to yo-yo up and down from Teesside to the Capital every five minutes but, thankfully, the day's legalities are fairly straightforward. I proclaim 'Not guilty' with a slight curl of the lips, marking my distaste for this twisted judicial system.

The Ma'am, who seems to be in charge of the whole thing (she's got the best wig), scribbles a few words, then tells my jailers to take me away. I slump out of Court 4 in my ill-fitting eighties power suit, donated by Martin Sawyer's unfeasibly small wife. The dusky blue sleeves end halfway up my forearms and the waistband cuts into my stomach. Messrs Fruity and Meaty – now masquerading as prison officers in crisp white shirts, black chinos and black kicking-boots – handcuff me again and frogmarch me down the mock-oak corridor. As we pass the Gallery Entrance, I spot Martin Sawyer racing towards us from the reception area, with his briefcase and VISITOR badge flapping. He bounds two steps at a time up the Gothic staircase before reaching us and panting, 'Kimberly, love, so sorry I'm late. Train was delayed at Darlo. You haven't made your plea yet, have you?'

'Er. Yeah,' I reply, a bit wary. Visible pain pinches at Martin's red cheeks – I hope it's just exhaustion; lactic acid off the sprint up the staircase.

Getting his breath back, Martin takes me aside for a moment, into one of the empty offices. He sits me down. Then, with cascading syllables, he explains, 'I was looking over the papers again on the way down. You won't believe this. I, er . . . I don't know what to say.'

'Just say,' I urge, resting my hands and steel bracelets on the desktop.

'Right,' Martin goes on, unable to look at me, 'well, if I'm honest, I suspect foul play, but . . . there was a tea stain on one of the Court documents – not my fault, I might add. I thought nothing of it at first but, erm, just about legible under the stain, in tiny print, it says . . .' Here Martin pulls the offending sheet from his briefcase, and continues, 'Under the Court's new, erm, legislation, the maximum punishment for murder, when the accused has pleaded not guilty is . . . is *death*.'

The word *death* makes me convulse, like I want to cough up all my internal organs. Martin pats my hand and carries on. 'See, I *know* you're innocent, but pleading guilty would at least spare your life. Maximum punishment is life imprisonment, tops, if you, er, plead guilty. Maybe there's still time to change your pl—'

'But I'm innocent,' I snap.

'Ah. Yes. Of course,' Martin mumbles unconvincingly. 'Yes. Alright, then. Don't worry. We'll get you out of this. I . . . yeah.'

⊙

I'm starting to wish I'd appointed a better lawyer – not one whose biggest success was sorting out the Wallaces' planning permission for their new conservatory, and not one who relies on the promptness of the East Coast railway line to get to my hearings on time. Then again, despite all the anger and worry, I still wouldn't have pleaded guilty. This isn't Martin Sawyer's fault. Together, we'll sever Milward's twisted puppet strings. Together, we'll set the story straight.

Surely, if the CPS have read this *Kimberly's Capital Punishment* (providing it's based more on fact than fiction), they must know it wasn't my fault Stevie or Kimberley died. And it certainly wasn't my fault Mag and Barry Clark died, I don't think. It wasn't even my fault Meaty Stevie and Fruity Stevie died – farmers and fruit-pickers are to blame for that.

I breathe into my paws. The only way to avoid going nuts in prison is to make friends with whatever inanimate objects you share your cell with. By my fourth week of incarceration, I find myself having in-depth conversations with the lovely shard of light (when she's available, anyway – she tends to come and see me around dawn, and leaves at dusk) and my chipped, scribbled-on desktop. The desktop's a horrible bastard – it says things like FUCK THIS and FUCK THAT and WELCOME TO HELL. In contrast, the lovely shard of light's genuinely lovely. I imagine her speaking with a plum in her mouth.

'Chin up, my little cherub!' the shard of light ding-dongs, interrupting my thoughts.

I force a smile. I haven't been crying all that much recently. After four weeks of imprisonment, a certain level of detachment takes over. Plus, I've been too busy thinking about the court case – or too busy trying not to think about it, depending on the mood – to be whining all the time.

'What do you reckon the jury'll be like?' I ask the white painted bricks, of which there are 752 in this cell.

CUNTS, says the chipped desktop.

'Behave,' I snap.

FUCK YOURSELVE, says the desktop.

I tut, and put my head between my knees. I wish the prison officers would take away that horrid desk, cluttered with decades of ex-cons' bitterness and bad grammar.

I wrench myself from the sagging yellow bed, and execute a few laps of the cell. Despite the cell being only 10ft long, I get tired after just seven circuits, stopping to pant with my hands on my knees.

I haven't been eating well lately. My skeleton has begun to protrude from my flesh, and my gums are coming away from my teeth. I feel like all my skin's about to slide off round my ankles, as if I could just step out of it like a jumpsuit. The meals aren't bad here (instead of dry porridge oats, me and the jailbirds dine on crisps, sarnies, corned-beef hash, shepherd's pie, cake and custard, etc.), but the constant fear and paranoia have shrunk my stomach to the size of a 10p piece. On the upside, I've slimmed from a size 12 to a size 8; on the downside, there aren't any handsome males in the Ladies' Jail to appreciate my new figure.

I sit back down on the gloomy mattress, seeing stars.

'When does the court case start again?' I ask the room. I've lost track of the days passing by, what with the previous inmates cluttering the desktop with their own tallies.

TOMORROW, says the desktop, just below a lump of hardened chewing gum.

'Piss off,' I growl, spitting at the desk.

'Actually, he's not mistaken,' interjects the lovely shard of light, twinkling with sympathy. Behind us, the manky toilet gulps theatrically, relishing my unease.

'Shut up,' I snap at the toilet, getting upset now. What with all the weight loss, I was vaguely hoping to die of starvation and not have to bother with the court case. For some reason, starving to death seems a nobler way to go than being hung up, plugged in or put down with poison.

'What am I gonna do?' I moan, more to myself than my inanimate companions, though the 752 white bricks just echo back, 'We don't know.'

I suppose there's always a chance I'll be proven innocent, but how's Martin supposed to defend my case when we're not even sure what I've done wrong? Maybe all will become clear tomorrow. Maybe the law folk have only read the beginning of *Kimberly's Capital Punishment*, where I'm all weepy, suicidal and pathetic, and where I blame myself for Stevie's death. Maybe it's best to get the whole thing over with. I can't wait to prove the law folk wrong, and finally get myself on that golden plane to Japan.

I can't wait for them to get to the bit in *Kimberly's Capital Punishment* where I'm very, very, very nice.

⊙

It turns out the chipped, scribbled-on desktop was right.

On Monday morning, I'm marched into Court 4 again, to face The Ma'am and a jury of twelve giant, dribbling vaginas. The first thing that strikes me is the stench. Martin Sawyer looks completely stressed and out of his depth, rustling papers with one eye on The Ma'am and the other on the twelve vaginas. Even before I walk in, I can hear the cunts yapping, 'Guilty guilty guilty!' amongst themselves. They don't seem like the most reliable jury, since they don't have ears, but they've definitely, definitely got lips.

'Guilty guilty guilty!' they squeal as I sit down in my shrunken blue suit.

I feel like I'm in a waking nightmare. I shift uneasily on my plastic chair, in the shadow of The Ma'am and her henchmen. I rub my temples. Surely there can't be twelve giant vaginas in the jury box. Are they not just twelve everyday lads and lasses who happen to have quite cuntish-looking faces?

I yawn into my palm. I couldn't get to sleep last night. Not only was the manky toilet burping non-stop, the desktop kept taunting and tormenting me, and the lovely shard of light wasn't around to fight my corner, it being nighttime. The stained mattress felt like a shallow grave, sucking me into its belly of cold, rusted coils.

Before The Ma'am begins proceedings, Martin nudges me and gestures towards the gangly court reporter in front of the dock. It's Richard Milward, my old classmate. He looks hideous, hunched over a typewriter, with his rodent-like features and greasy moptop. Milward appears to be keeping the minutes of the court case, unless he's just making it all up as he goes along. Peering over his shoulder, I catch a glimpse of what he's typing:

Before The Ma'am begins proceedings, Martin nudges me and gestures towards the handsome court reporter in front of the dock. It's Richard Milward, my old classmate. He looks dashing, touchtyping at a rate of 60+ words per minute, with his elegant piano fingers and lustrous sixties bouffant. Milward appears to be keeping the minutes of the court case, unless he's just making it all up as he goes along. Peering over his shoulder, I catch a glimpse of what he's typing:

'Silence in court!' The Ma'am yells, scratching under her wig.

The vaginas shut their traps. Even though Milward must be aware of me and Martin staring at him, he doesn't turn round. He just carries on typing. I wish the keys would turn into shark's teeth and swallow his hands. I still can't believe my old classmate's been spying on me the past few years. I'm sure I would've noticed the lanky streak of piss lurking in the reflections of shops and car windows and frosted shower cubicles. Nevertheless, the case begins with the prosecution, Vincent Williams QC, presenting to the jury a first edition of Milward's *Kimberly's Capital Punishment*. I was half expecting it to be scribbled lazily in biro and badly photocopied; not the fancy-looking tome Williams holds up.

'Here, in my hand, we have evidence of murder,' the lawyer exclaims. 'Cold-blooded murder.'

Getting excited, the jury starts making the odd fanny-fart. One of them even has the audacity to squirt the word 'Guilty!' again. I shake my head softly, scratching myself under the dusky blue power suit. Since being banged up, I've been cultivating stress hives on my neck, back and wrists – unless I'm just allergic to

Mrs Sawyer's washing powder. Either way, it's an uncomfortable moment.

Over the next few days, I listen solemnly as Vincent Williams QC calls forward characters from various corners, cubbyholes and compartments of my life (for instance, Paolo, Nina, Mrs Wallace, my Promiscuous Pal Polly), and tries to pick apart my personality, temperament, background, hobbies, and dress sense. None of them have the foggiest what's going on, though. Each stands apprehensively in the witness box, answering the QC's questions in stumped, stumbling mumbles.

The whole procedure's completely confusing. At one point, my three weekly assailants squeeze into the box, shiftily avoiding eye contact with me. When asked if they think I'm capable of murder, Mr Saturday loses the plot, spurting out, 'Yes. She was quite controlling us. Making us fight for her when she was prostitute.'

'Thank you, that will be all,' Williams announces proudly, enjoying himself. Yes, thank you for that, Mr Saturday.

I pinch myself to double-check it's not a nightmare, though the pinching aggravates the hives. While Vincent Williams QC commands respect in the room, with his plummy, public-school accent and shiny black and white silks, I'm yet to hear him deliver one solid lump of evidence against me. On the fifth day, he tries to catch me out by announcing, 'Murder is a very serious charge, Miss Clark. Punishable by death, as I'm sure you're aware. What the jury needs to understand is: did you do it? Or did you not do it? Or did you not *not* do it? Or *didn't* you not not do it?'

'If it's alright by you,' I venture, feeling completely lost, like Alice in Blunderland, 'I wouldn't like to not not answer that question, for fear of incriminating myself accidentally.'

Williams sits back down with a self-satisfied smile. He leans back in his leather armchair, wafts his magpie silks and kicks his black brogues up onto the oak desktop. Over to his left, the twelve vaginas give each other hairy glances.

'Williams! Feet! Off the table!' The Ma'am squawks, prompting the prosecution to sit sensible again, a bit shamefaced.

After a shaky teabreak, it's Martin's turn to get stuck into the defence case. After such a farcical morning session, Martin seems calmer and more collected, standing up in his pressed pinstripe suit. He begins by waving his own copy of *Kimberly's Capital Punishment* at the judge and jury, and declaring, 'While this may be a 142,000-word novel based around the subject of death – commercial suicide, if you like! – there is not one mention in its pages of cold-blooded murder. My client, Miss Clark, has been duped. I believe she's the victim of a cruel plot. A plot envisioned by one Richard Milward, sitting here today. A plot involving sexually aggressive seals, a heavy-drinking Grim Reaper, a cack-handed Reader and, dare I say it, a jury of genitals.'

The twelve vaginas hiss at Martin, twisting and turning in their seats. Above us, The Ma'am speaks. 'Mr Sawyer! We are not here to pass judgement on the jury.'

To our right, Milward continues bashing away at his typewriter, no doubt relishing this daft scene with the cunts and the inept lawyers. The lanky bastard's probably considering using the term 'fanny batter' in a minute, if things get boring.

'Pardon me, My Lady,' Martin coughs in apology, frantically flicking through his dog-eared copy of the novel. For the last week or so, Martin has spent his waking hours underlining, circling and dissecting the criminal sentences in *Kimberly's Capital Punishment* – anything to help me avoid an actual criminal sentence. Rather than summoning characters from the book to the witness box, Martin draws the judge and jury's attention to the characters already in the book. He reads out passages in past tense, such as:

There I was, thinking a photograph of my tongue in a square-faced person's mouth was enough to sentence Stevie to death, when, by the sound of it, the culprit was a sexually aggressive bull seal.

and:

I dashed into the road, grabbed Kimberley under her armpits and said, 'Don't be daft, Kim.'

as well as Stevie's badly spelt suicide note, gradually building a robust defence. In the jury box, the twelve vaginas listen halfheartedly, with fanny batter gathering in the corners of their mouths.

'Objection, your honour!' Vincent Williams shrieks, clamouring for the limelight. 'This information may well be there in black and white, but it is redundant! Sawyer has failed to read between the lines. He is missing the point completely. He has failed to look *beneath the surface*! This book' – here the QC holds his near-pristine, unmarked copy aloft – 'contains evidence of cold-blooded *murder*!'

'Where?' Martin Sawyer snaps, losing his cool. His lacklustre, bloodshot eyes tell of so many sleepless nights and long, uncomfortable train journeys.

'Ha!' Williams honks, getting overexcited. 'The defence crumbles! He has failed to notice the *glaringly obvious* murderous nature of his client!'

I shuffle in my seat, growing hotter and hotter under the polyester. Martin Sawyer picks awkwardly at his tie. Veins throb in his neck. Eventually, he drops his copy of *Kimberly's Capital Punishment* onto his desk and growls at the QC, 'Well . . . I challenge you to show the jury this so-called murderous nature! Unless we're reading different novels – there's no mention of it in my copy.'

Vincent Williams stalls for a moment, flicking desperately through his version of the paperback, before woofing petulantly, 'Somewhere between pages 101 and 202 . . .'

'Now, now!' The Ma'am shouts. 'It seems we're getting nowhere. Let's put an end to this farce. The summing up, please. One at a time. Let us hear from the defence first, for a change.'

After a fit of the coughs, Martin rises again and faces the jury. He taps the battered book on his desk and states, 'There is no murder in this book. Given my client's misfortune, given that she has witnessed death in her immediate family, and given that she has actually experienced death *first-hand*, being run over mere-ly weeks ago, it's understandable, is it not, that she has a slight preoccupation with death? However, she's not a murderer. In the pages of this book she recognises the preciousness, the *fleeting-ness*, of life. All she wanted was to improve people's lives; not take life away. I believe she's been set up by Milward and the Crown Prosecution Service. She's been framed for murder solely for the benefit of those readers who bought *Kimberly's Capital Punish-ment* in the hope of reading of some juicy execution or other.'

Vincent Williams wafts his silks uneasily. Over in the jury box, the twelve vaginas still look confused, their pubes knitted into eye-brows, and lips pursed. Above us, The Ma'am sits with her hands knotted, quietly mulling over the facts. Unfortunately for all of us, the boundary between fact and fiction has been blurred for quite some time now. Milward carries on recklessly bashing away at his typewriter (which, for one millisecond, transforms into a chocolate crocodile!), oblivious to the increasingly restless courtroom.

'And now for the prosecution,' The Ma'am says, urging Vin-cent Williams to rise and get it all over with. 'Well, is she guilty?'

Williams glances around the courtroom. Flustered, he flicks a few papers in front of himself, doodles on a notepad, tinkers with an abacus, then blows out a sigh and squints at me. At one point he seems set to sit back down without having said anything when, suddenly, a flash of inspiration hits, and he announces, 'Well . . . she does have quite evil-looking eyes.'

Livening up, The Ma'am, then the jury, then the rest of the courtroom focus their attention on my slightly up-turned, cat-like, 'evil' eyes. Being in prison, I haven't had access to my turquoise eyeshadow, let alone any concealer or tweezers. When I catch a glimpse of my peepers in the silver gleam of Milward's ringing typewriter, they do look somewhat sinister and incriminating. One by one the vaginas' lips gape open, then they all scream in unison, at the tops of their vulvas: 'GUILTY! GUILTY! GUILTY! GUILTY! GUILTY! GUILTY! GUILTY! GUILTY! GUILTY! GUILTY! GUILTY! GUILTY!'

⊙

The next day, we return to Court 4 to find out if I've been sentenced to life imprisonment, or death. With moist eyes, all Martin Sawyer can do is hug me awkwardly as we wait for the twelve vaginas to slither back into the jury box with their verdict. I feel sick with nerves. I think my last experience of affection on this planet is a skin-crawling cuddle with an incompetent legal executive. I want my mam and dad. I want my ex-boyfriend.

The world slows down as the foremanwoman readies herself to read the verdict. I have to clutch my thighs to stop myself trembling so much. I dye the dusky blue fabric midnight blue with perspiration.

'Order! Order!' The Ma'am shrieks, glaring at no one in particular. 'This is a matter of life or death. Jury foremanwoman, what is your verdict regarding sentencing?'

The giant vagina avoids my gaze as it announces to the courtroom, 'The sentence shall be death.'

'And this was unanimous?' The Ma'am enquires.

'One million and ten per cent yes,' the vagina replies, curling its lips.

I suffer convulsions, rattling the plastic chair. As the court and gallery erupt, I feel Martin's limp arms go round me again. I can't summon the energy to push him away, or pull him towards me.

'Kimberly Clark, you have been found guilty of murder,' The Ma'am declares, though her words sound distant and muffled, as if spoken down a long cardboard tube. 'I hereby sentence you to the death penalty. You will face execution within seven days. You will be executed in the same fashion as your disgraceful atrocity – perhaps then some light will be shed on your apparent confusion.'

I burst into tears again, hiding my face in my sleeves. Each noisy sob resounds around the – now silent – courtroom, like notes on a black-comedy trombone. Before long, I hear chairs shifting, and Prison Officers Meaty and Fruity prise me from Martin's awkward embrace. I don't bother fighting with them. I want to walk out with dignity, but my legs keep buckling, and I end up being dragged out.

'It'll all be alright,' Martin shouts after me, but he can't mean it.

⊙

In the lead-up to my execution, I'm transferred to a different cell in the Ladies' Jail – a larger affair, with a cleaner mattress and the faint tang of chlorine in the air. I spend my days in an inert state of disbelief – there aren't many tears, once the initial devastation's over. I do feel terrible, though, not being able to say goodbye to the lovely shard of light, and the world outside. There doesn't seem much point befriending the new toilet, or the freshly painted table, or the lonely shard of light that visits me now.

To keep myself occupied, I spend each night rolling this way and that on the single mattress, sopping with sweat. In the daytimes I rock back and forth, silently contemplating my second death in six weeks. As if to compensate for the oncoming ordeal, they've put me up in relative luxury. They offer me one last meal of my choice ('How about death roe and chips?' they quip, the bastards), and a prison chaplain pays me a visit to see if I fancy signing up to Christianity, in a last-ditch attempt to get me into Heaven.

I can hardly stomach the double-decker tuna and cucumber sandwich. It comes served on a clean plate, with extra mayonnaise, as requested, but the knot in my belly won't accept it. After an hour or so, the chaplain gives me a knock, smiling at me in that half-compassionate, half-disturbed manner he has. I don't smile back. I don't see any use in being nice any more – there's nothing to gain from it now.

'How are you feeling?' the chaplain asks me, in his soft, husky lilt.

'Dunno, really. You know I'm innocent?' I say. The chaplain avoids my gaze. He smooths a crease out of his black chinos, waiting for me to carry on. I say, 'Will I see the Grim Reaper again, do you reckon?'

'The Grim Reaper?' the chaplain spurts, halfway through the smoothing.

'Yeah. He was drunk, you know. Do you reckon I could sue him?' I babble. 'He got the wrong Kimberley, you see, so he . . . he let the Grim Reader decide my fate. Do you know what I'm on about?'

The chaplain squirms, creasing his trousers again. He scratches the back of his neck, underneath his dog collar, and says, 'I . . . er . . . this might not be my prerogative, but . . . have you considered an appeal? Are you feeling in stable mind?'

I scoff, 'Aw, yeah. Naw. Don't worry, I'm not mad. I'll . . . he'll be there. Naw, forget anything I said. Next question.'

The chaplain still doesn't know where to look. Clutching at straws, he offers me some religious verse, with his eyes fixed to the ceiling: 'Yea, though I walk through the valley of the shadow of death, I will fear no evil: for thou art with me; thy rod and thy staff they comfort me . . .'

'He's not in the valley of the shadow of the thing, though,' I interrupt. 'He lives in Holland Park. With Bernard.'

I consider bringing up the Subbuteo, but I don't want to ruin his precious belief system. I can tell I'm doing his head in. I clap my heels up and down on the concrete, unsure what to say next. At a loss, the chaplain rises slowly from his seat and edges towards the door.

'Right, well, Kimberly, I'll leave you in peace,' he says. Before he edges all the way out of the cell, he takes a biro and a pad of plain A4 paper from his satchel, and places it on my desk.

'In case you'd like to write a final statement,' he explains. Then, with a sharp clunk of the cell door, he disappears.

I feel bad about fazing him. He could have a point – I might have a good case, to plead insanity and appeal for a less harsh sentence. My mental state hasn't been in good shape since Stevie's suicide, let alone since I suffered that bump on the head on Shepherd's Bush Green. Then again, the folk in the courtroom seemed even more deranged than me. Especially those mad cunts in the jury.

My second coming has been a complete disaster. For the sake of it, I grab the biro and scrawl CAN SOMEBODY PLEASE FEED LUCIFER? as my final statement. I laugh into my knee-caps, listening to the 1,041 bricks playing ping-pong with my giggles, before absorbing them into their white, dusty emulsion, for ever and ever, amen.

⊙

They come for me at 13.00 hours. The last portion of my life is spent trembling on a bare mattress, dreading the arrival of

366

Officer Meaty and Officer Fruity. I wish I could just disappear into thin air, painlessly, or happen upon an escape route under the thick concrete. I claw at it, but nothing gives.

Strangely, when the knock comes, the nerves are replaced with numb acceptance. As it turns out, when you're faced with capital punishment, your body adapts itself – however grudgingly – to the forthcoming slaughter. A sense of dismal detachment enables you to stand without buckling, or fainting, or screaming. You have to accept your lot. After all, we're each of us condemned to death the moment we're born – at least with capital punishment you're given the chance to brace yourself, rather than being suddenly surprised by an unexpected knife, cancer, or speeding Ford Mondeo.

To add to the theatrical atmosphere, Officers Meaty and Fruity are wearing black executioners' masks. Following closely behind is another black, hooded figure, carrying a scythe and a half-empty glass of white, creamy liquid. I give him a nod, but I don't want to talk.

At least one helpful thing about my execution is I'll finally find out what 'disgraceful atrocity' I'm supposed to be guilty of. As Executioners Meaty and Fruity march me down the chlorine-scented corridor, I'm half expecting to face hanging, or another car crash – I've got an inkling the judge and daft-cunt jury think it was Stevie or Kimberley I've knocked off. But, fair Reader, you of all people know I'm not to blame!

Bizarrely, at the end of the corridor there's a door marked KIM-BERLY'S CAPITAL PUNISHMENT, which leads to an Olympic-sized swimming pool. As the door creaks open, the faint whiff of chlorine becomes a sinus-ripping stench. The place is like any normal swimming baths except, instead of the pool being enclosed in a greenhouse, with frosted, perv-proof glass, it's sur-rounded by 30ft-high brick walls, and there's no roof. I stare up at the beautiful rectangle of blue sky, with occasional birds and planes passing through it, embroidering it with cloudy thread.

'Change round here,' Executioner Fruity commands, showing me behind a curtain-on-wheels. He glares at me while I swap my unflattering jail clothes for an unflattering grey swimming costume. I take my time pulling it over my body, savouring every last drop of crap existence. It doesn't bother me, being naked in front of the fruit – it seems, when you're about to be executed, certain useless emotions like embarrassment, resentment and jealousy fade from the brain. Plus, he's homosexual.

Once I'm in the swimming costume, Executioner Fruity pulls me back out from behind the curtain. Meaty looks me up and down and asks, 'Can you tread water?'

'Probably,' I say, in case it's a trick question.

'Get in the pool,' the meathead booms next, peeling back the huge tarpaulin covering the water.

I do as I'm told. I'm almost expecting to find sharks or piranhas lurking underneath the clingfilm covers but, as it turns out, it's just ordinary, shimmering water. It seems they want me to drown to death. As I lower myself into the cool pool, I wonder if this has anything to do with the Black Monk of Guisborough. It wasn't me who danced on his grave, though, and I definitely didn't force Stevie to. If anyone's to blame for that mishap, it's the manufacturers of Pulse cider – or the person who built the anti-dancing fence too low.

Enjoying the soothing weightlessness, I swim out into the centre of the pool and tread water. Executioners Meaty and Fruity watch me closely, through their black, beaky masks, with their arms crossed. Behind them, the Grim Reaper rests his scythe up against the curtain-on-wheels, and takes a long, loud swig of his White Russian.

While I'm not the world's best swimmer, it's easy enough treading water. It's almost pleasurable – every kick and splash creates these lovely zebra-like stripes of light in the water and, all things considered, it's as nice a day as any to die. I spin onto my back, marvelling at the endless blue sky above, while I wait for something to happen.

After five minutes or so, the executioners begin to look impatient. They exchange a few grunts and compare watches, shuffling uneasily on the tiles. I let a slight smile twitch my lips. Maybe I'm not going to die after all! Maybe I've outwitted them! The judge and jury were all too ready to send me to my death; they've overlooked the fact I'm actually innocent!

All I'm guilty of is having slightly up-turned, cat-like, 'evil' eyes!

Over on the poolside, the executioners are looking more and more agitated. They keep scratching themselves and cursing under their breath, completely stumped. I bite my lip. Still treading water, I'm already thinking about getting home, or getting to Japan, or getting swimming membership. I bob on the soft tide, unfazed by the black thunderhead slowly creeping across the azure blue rectangle, like a silent, overweight assassin.

All of a sudden, my thoughts are interrupted by a loud popping sound, way above me. Instead of a lightning bolt, a huge bent javelin fires out of the thunderhead, trained directly on my forehead. Birds scatter as it whooshes through the blue. Before I can get out of the way, the rusty spike pierces my right eyeball, tunnels swiftly through my skull and skewers my brain, making a slushy sound. I shriek silently, conscious for a few seconds of the spike sliding into my face. Flapping my arms, I manage to grab the javelin-grip, but it's stuck fast.

As I wrestle with it, I notice a message attached to the weapon with fishing-wire. Typed onto the laminated card, I read through my good eye: SLIPPERY TWAT. I cough bloody bubbles in disbelief, lungs bloated with chlorine. I carry on flapping my arms and legs for another ten seconds before I roll over and honk my last breath, like a helpless little seal pup off the coast of Seal Sands.

And then, everything turns black again. And, this time, it stays black.

THE END

Part 3) The Illustrious Shaun and Sean in . . . 'All the Fun of the Funeral'*

SHAUN

The twat – Sean doesn't realise there's a slug on that can! Fucking serves him right for twocking it. I'm this close to putting him in a headlock, when the Nokia starts writhing and bleating in my jeans. 'La la la la la bamba,' it screams, like a mechanical cat being strangled. I swish the phone about, grinning at Sean. I wish I still had the original, with Ritchie Valens wailing like he's been left out in the sun too long. Sean doesn't even like 'La Bamba'. The only wailing that gay mong likes doing is the depressing kind, when things go wrong. Across the green, these lads of unknown ethnic origin keep staring at us. They're probably eyeing up the Nokia – it's got a Louis Vuitton fascia, and Snake 2 to boot. I tuck it under my flapping fringe, keeping it well hidden. I couldn't cope being phoneless as well as homeless. They let me keep the Nokia charged up at the Wethouse, on

SEAN

The twat – Shaun doesn't realise I've nicked one of his cans! Fucking serves him right for hiding them. I turn away from him, and launch into a coughing fit, to cover the sound of the ring-pull getting pulled. When the first sip goes down, my brain wakes up, like a gnarled old walnut suddenly germinating. Aahh. The afternoon seems alive with potential, when you've got a can in your hand. I cross my legs, and get back to my favourite daydream: the one with the blank cheque, the weight loss programme, and the platinum-blonde bombshell. I can almost feel the warm, Bahamian breeze in my hair when Shaun's ringtone suddenly slaps me awake. Fucking 'La Bamba'! If we weren't low on cigs, I'd stab my Pall Mall up his nostril. Shaun's my best friend, and the bane of my life. I wonder how long it takes him to clock the stolen Special. I wish I

* To read this section, please remove your eyeballs. Place your left eyeball on the heading SHAUN, your right eyeball on the heading SEAN, and let them roll down the page simultaneously. One-eyed readers can go to page 413.

the off-chance an entrepreneur fancies chucking cash at me, or in case that lass we harassed on the grass last week phones me back. Fuck me; women! I jog my memory back to her prominent nip-ons in the red jogging top, then I cross myself and answer the call. 'Hello?' I sing, going back in the carrier for another can. Then, I freeze. 'Hello there, this is Martin Sawyer,' the phone says. 'I'm a lawyer. I'm ringing on, er, on behalf of the Necropolitan Police. Am I speaking to Shaun or, er . . . who am I speaking to, please?' The phone nearly slips out of my hand, like a bar of soap. 'Er . . . Sean with an "e",' I say, hoping to incriminate my fat companion. I turn to pass the mobile over to my chum, but he's gone and fucked off to the playground, to stretch his legs. My mouth feels dry suddenly. I knew the Necropolice would catch up with us. My arsehole whines, in three-month-old boxers. It hasn't been easy living off an immigrant wage at the Wethouse – getting paid a pittance to scrub sloppy logs out of the bogs, or shine the banisters – so me and Sean have been moonlighting as petty thieves and backstabbers. A shoplifter's salary lets you wine and dine like high society, more or less. Just

hadn't spent my coin on tabs now. At the Wethouse, we get odd bits of money for doing odd jobs, like touching up paintwork, scrubbing the bathrooms, doing the dishes and that. But it always leaves you in the same predicament: whether to spend it on fags, booze, or down the bookies. Kauto Star came through for me the other day at the Down Royal Champion Chase, but Shaun took it on himself to spend my winnings for me. I was looking forward to sleeping off the rest of the week with Wray and his overproof Nephew, but Shaun had other ideas. Once I'd regained consciousness on the first morning, I found out Shaun had paid to get his bell-end polished by one of the local Polish tarts. And he'd polished off the rest of my rum and all. 'Fuckin answer it, then,' I grumble into my sleeve. The only reason I stick by him is the fear of being alone. Plus, I hate making decisions. God knows why I chose fags this morning. Cigs are easy enough to cadge off passers-by without frightening them too much, whereas alcohol's generally kept behind bars. I must've been gasping. Anyway, as luck would have it, Shaun's cack-sighted in one eye, so pilfering a can or two's easy enough, providing you're on

one woman's purse can go on providing you with fags and cans of Special for twenty-four hours or, at least, till the off-licences shut. But all good things come to an end. I think me and daft arse have been rumbled. 'What's this in reference to, please?' I ask the lawyer, putting on an airy-fairy accent. I bite a bit of black out from under my nail. 'I'm contacting you in reference to a Miss Kimberly Clark,' Martin Sawyer replies. My arsehole lets out a sigh of relief. The can of Special also sighs, between my knees, when I crack open the ring-pull. 'Oh?' I say, keeping up the accent. 'Yes, I'm not sure if you're aware or not, but Miss Clark was sadly killed in a car accident two days ago,' the lawyer carries on, 'and, now, I'm not sure if you're aware or not, but she had a card in her purse, with your details on it. A business card, for your funeral home.' I scratch my nose. Some years ago, I lost the ability to be sad or shocked at people's deaths – even people who were close to me, like whatshername. It comes with being an undertaker. You and me, we're just stupid, sentimental lumps of decomposing meat. The words that shocked me most there were 'funeral home'. I suppose one bad thing

his left. He seems oblivious to me stealing sip after sip, while he swishes his phone about, grinning. When he finally answers it, he puts on this daft, pompous accent. I bet it's that Polish tart. I sigh through my nose, wishing the Vodafone satellite would send a shower of sharp knives and forked lightning at his head. I need a good excuse to leave him – for example, his untimely death. As I go for another glug of Special, my stomach suddenly turns, and the nipples in my cheeks leak. There's something disgusting slithering up the can. It's a living cat turd with antennae! No; even worse – it's a slug. All sweaty, I sneak off to the playground railings, to scrape the sloppy beast off the aluminium. It won't budge, though. Just like humans, slugs are attracted to strong lager, even though it kills them. I've almost plucked up the courage to flick the brute off with my finger, when Shaun yells at me from the bench, 'FAT LAD!' I hide the can behind my back again. 'What?' I say, making my way back across the grass. 'FAT LAD! BAD NEWS, MATE!' Shaun shouts, waving, with this look of exaggerated anguish. I'm not in the mood for his childish pranks. I slump back down on the bench. 'What is it?' I

is, thingy gave us all that money to set up SS Funerals (and all we could give her in return was a poxy business card), and we went and blew it all down the bookies. The worst thing of all, though, is Sean thought Boro were a surefire bet against Man Utd, away from home, with fucking Ronaldo back from injury. Never trust a fat cunt when it comes to football – or any sport, for that matter. 'Now, I'm not sure if you're aware or not,' the lawyer carries on, 'but Miss Clark also had a note in her purse, explaining her wishes should she, ehm, pass away. A will, of sorts.' I take a long swig of Special, and say again, 'Oh?' In a way, it was whatsherface's fault the funeral home went tits-up – she should've known not to give money to wastrels. At one point, we were all set to sign the papers for the building where Iceland used to be in Acton – in the hope they'd left the fridges in – but there happened to be a brokeLads next door, and Sean insisted we stick money on the Boro game, as a fucking 'safety net investment'. He's a cunt. 'The note seems straightforward,' Sawyer explains. 'Just that she wanted to be embalmed, open casket, airtight coffin, what song she'd like . . . ehm . . . but I'm getting ahead of

ask, surreptitiously swapping my half-empty, slug-infected can with his half-full, clean one. Shaun shuffles his holey trainers on the tarmac. 'Thingy's dead,' he says, gravely. 'Whatsherface. Kimberly thingy. Clark. And it gets worse . . . cos the police want you to embalm her. For free. It was in her last rites.' My brain shrivels again, and my cheeks burn. Shaun smirks as my eyes begin to glisten. 'What happened to her?' I ask, shakily slugging down the pristine Special. 'Erm, she was . . . raped then murdered,' Shaun explains. I stare out across the green, with all the passers-by and their pets blurring into tear-stained hexagons. The hard snot in my nose turns suddenly liquid. 'Don't cry, you fucking fanny,' Shaun goads. 'You big baby. It's not like you've – anyway, you've twocked one of my fucking cans, haven't you!?' I look up with raw, salty eyes. 'Naw,' I protest, through the sniffles, 'yours is down there. And, look at that – it's got a little friend.'

*

We walk around the green for a bit, me in silent despair while Shaun prattles on, working out the logistics. Poor, poor Kimberly. All around us, Shepherd's Bush

374

myself. Ehm, is the funeral home still going strong?' I place the can between my feet. 'Oh, yes, yes,' I say. Lying is great for business. What my dad used to say, before we embalmed him, was: the customer's always right. Martin Sawyer might not be your typical customer and all, but he must have access to thingymabob's bank account now, to sort me and Sean out some coin for our 'kind, reliable service'. We might even get away with charging him upwards of two grand for what me and Sean call the 'economy funeral'. Rather than using expensive materials and expertise, the 'economy funeral' can be undertaken with just a van, a syringe, a visit to a timber merchant outside normal working hours, a Boots Advantage card, and three bottles of premium vodka. The profit margin more than makes up for the blood on our hands. So, before Martin can say another word about it, I babble, 'Oh, yes, yes, it'd be an honour to take care of it. Give Miss – *ahem* – a bit of dignity back in death. She was a dear friend.' I grin into the handset, with bubbles between my teeth. Ten metres away, it looks like Sean's scaring off the pre-schoolkids, rubbing himself up against the playground railings.

seems so cold and still, like all the trees and buildings have been embalmed as well. While it's touching Kimberly thought of me to replace her blood with preservatives, I don't think I can stomach seeing her corpse. I've never liked working with corpses. It was Shaun's idea for us to apply for the embalming diploma, on account of it being 'dafter' and 'better craic' than doing plumbing. It was also Shaun's idea to start SS Funerals five years back, and Shaun's idea to resurrect it with Kimberly's five grand, after we met her at the Copenhagen. I sabotaged the business on both occasions. The first incarnation of the funeral home went tits-up after I intentionally mixed up two of the corpses, sending Mrs Bramwell to the McGiven funeral, and Grandad McGiven to the Bramwells. We almost went bankrupt after paying the families damages, and I'm not even sure if the £10,000 brought either of them any closer to closure. That's why we had to leave Middlesbrough – no one wanted to give us their dead relatives any more and, with it being a smallish town, we quickly found ourselves at the butt of people's jokes, and had eggs regularly yogged at our windows. When we moved to the

'Grand,' the lawyer carries on, 'I trust she'll be in good hands.' I reply, 'Oh, the best hands. Like I say, it'll be an absolute honour. You'll get your money's worth, definitely.' Here Martin's voice changes. 'Ah, but, ehm,' he goes, 'I'm not sure if you're aware or not, but Miss Clark left very little money behind. She had a number of direct debits which rinsed the money in her account, the day she died. First of the month, you see. And, ehm . . . well, I've been at the end of my tether, trying to get hold of her relatives. But then we found your card. I didn't realise you were so close . . . I mean, I hate to ask and all . . . but perhaps, ehm . . . perhaps you might be able to waive the charges? The girl left behind nothing. And you know what paupers' burials are like, and . . .' My jaw flaps open – finally, I get a pang of true shock and sadness. 'Aw, er,' I start, desperately racking my brains for a get-out clause, but it's like birdspotting through back-to-front binoculars. 'Naw. No probs, mate.' I drop the telephone manner. I hang my head, then I hang up the phone. Why did I have to start fucking babbling? There's no honour in burying someone when you haven't got any fucking embalming fluid. Or a fridge. Or

Capital I was happy at first, serving cocktails on minimum wage for wankstains and nice lasses in negligible negligees, only to find Shaun was desperate to restart the funeral home. Rather than saving and resuscitating kids at Acton Baths, Shaun would've preferred it if they'd all drowned, so he could make more money embalming and burying them. He's got a heart of stone, that fucker. As soon as he mentioned reviving SS Funerals, I knew he'd rope me into it. I've got no backbone. He kept calling me 'the quickest eyelid and arsehole stitcher in the West', complimenting me for the first time in twenty-odd years. I was flattered, but that night at the bar, all the lads and lasses seemed more alive than ever, and it wasn't just because of 2-4-1 Tuesdays. I spun cocktails in a nervy trance, desperately weighing up the pros and cons of starting up the funeral home again. In the death trade, you get to meet a lot of people, but they're not the most talkative lot. I didn't want to force fake eyeballs into sockets the rest of my life – I was happy as I was, forcing Eyeball Martinis down drunk people's throats. But I couldn't say no to Shaun. When Kimberly gave us the five grand, all I wanted was a funeral home. Or any fucking home, for that matter.

*

Aside from thingy giving us that money in the Copenhagen, I blame Sean for the collapse of SS Funerals. Despite getting better marks than me in Biology, Sean's got no passion for the job. He'd rather serve cocktails to cocks in the West End, than wet-wipe corpses' brows. He's good at putting on dead grannies' make-up, though – I'll give him that. I swear, he must be queer. As we pace round the market, Sean's bottom lip keeps wobbling. The soft sod. You can't be sensitive in the funerary business – in fact, I think sensitivity in general is uncalled for. Turtles live for ages because all their soft bits are hidden in a rock-hard shell. Sometimes I think humans purposefully set out to get let down by life. Look at Sean – he'd be a much better person if he wasn't in touch with his feelings. He gets runny eyes and nostrils every time we come into a tiny bit of bother. We hardly even knew thingy. The best way to deal with corpses is to act like a corpse yourself: cold and numb. Sean's going to be a fucking liability today. When I got off the phone

for us to lose it. So, I started taking Shaun with me to the bookies, fooling him into thinking we could quickly turn the five grand into £50,000. Shaun bought into the gambler lifestyle, despite not fully understanding it, gazing for hours at the *Racing Post* Spotlights like a rabbit in headlights. He reckoned it gave him an air of masculinity, even though he whinged like a girl when he lost his first fiver. Meanwhile, I conned Shaun into thinking I was an expert (borderline psychic) statistician – I watched and taped *Channel 4 Racing* one afternoon while Shaun was at the Baths, then replayed it the next day 'as live', miraculously predicting each result before it came through. Shaun was gobsmacked. He didn't cotton on, even when I said, 'Ooh, Haunted House is pulling a bit, like,' two seconds before the commentator. For the next few weeks, Shaun put me in charge of the money, pestering day after day for us to go down brokeLads. I started out making sensible bets – coming home sometimes with a half-decent profit, and slowly luring Shaun into a false sense of financial security. Then, one afternoon in September – let's call it Black Tuesday – I blew all our money

to Martin Sawyer, I figured we'd sack off the 'economy funeral' altogether and chuck doodah into the incinerator, but Sean shrieked and insisted we carry out her last wishes properly, to the letter. He's only in a huff because he spent all his money on fags instead of booze. He's not getting another can off me. The only upside to this whole ordeal is Pat the Priest might give us the winnings from the collection box after the ceremony. I doubt we'll get close to the usual two-grand fee, mind. I lead the way through the market, with a toothache dancing in my back molars. I should be the one fucking complaining, not him. 'Right, let's get grafting, then,' I snap, once we come to the end of the stalls. 'You go and get make-up. I'll sort out the van and the gear. And cheer up, you fucking pansy.' Sean looks up with dribbling eyes. 'Can you sort us out a can?' he whines. I sigh, and reply, 'You're not going on the rob with a fucking can in your hand. It's like you don't want thingy to have her fucking dignity back or owt.' We go our separate ways at the crossroads, without saying 'Ta-ra'. What with the lawyer and the Necropolice on our backs, I can't trust Sean with any fuckupable tasks. Then again, I was

on one outlandish bet. One of the first rules of gambling is never bet on the Boro – those unpredictable underachievers – but we bet on them anyway. I swore to Shaun I thought it said '£200', not '£2,000', on the chip and PIN machine when I pressed ENTER, but it didn't help. In the space of ninety minutes, we'd lost all our riches. In the space of the next two months, we'd lost our electricity, then the water, then the whole flat. Naively, we thought we might suit the free-spirited, homeless lifestyle, with no more rent, bills or work to worry about. As it turned out, though, drifting about brought with it a whole slew of new problems. For starters, it's upsetting that the best places for homeless people to sleep are the best places for non-homeless people to piss. And it's upsetting to suddenly find yourself the lowest-status citizens in a city full of stuck-up, suspicious strangers. 'Can you spare some change, please?' I ask everyone wearing red on Uxbridge Road, but they all turn out to be deaf. So I try the blues. But they all turn out to be blind. We walk in silence through the dark, modern, meandering underpass, which is the best spot in Shepherd's Bush to scare people into sparing you change. After looking forward to an afternoon of al fresco wining and dining, not whining and breaking my back to find medical gear and transport. While it's easy enough procuring premium vodka and make-up for an 'economy funeral', it's a trickier business scoring a syringe, hearse, and fridge when you're homeless. As I walk past Greggs, I take in a lungful of pasty fumes – my first and last meal of the day. My stomach creaks in despair. With the sun behind me, my shadow looks like a pantomime Jack the Ripper, leaking into every nook and cranny of the pavement as I stumble by the shops. I keep my good eye on the Biffas and binbags brimming with cardboard and old cabbages, but I can't spot any syringes. I thought the Capital was supposed to be full of bagheads, chucking their STD-encrusted works all around town. This is pathetic. There's nothing for it but to crack open another Special. My palette's dead nowadays, but the feel of it waterfalling into my belly is pure bliss. I spring onwards, grinning to myself. I've heard there are clinics in the Capital that provide free, clean syringes for smackheads, but they probably come with a mind-numbing anti-drugs lecture. I haven't got time

twenty minutes, begging at opposite ends of the tunnel, we've raised a grand total of £0.00 for the Kimberly Clark Economy Funeral Fund. As usual, society pushes us into going on the rob. After a bit more weary wandering round the market, Shaun comes up with a plan. He tells me to dash and grab some cosmetics from Boots, while he goes after a syringe, thread, transport, etc. 'Can you sort us out a can?' I ask before we part, gazing up at him with half-cut doe eyes. 'You're not going on the rob with a fucking can in your hand. It's like you don't want thingy to have her fucking dignity back or owt,' he spits. He must still be pissed off about the slug. Shaun has a spectacular knack of making people feel miserable. When we finally go our separate ways, it's nice to be rid of him for a bit, though I might have to sniff the ethanol out of the perfumes when I get to Boots, to tide me over. Trundling through the crowds on Goldhawk Road, I can feel my armpits sticking. I've got a big problem with perspiration. Back when we had the funeral home, Shaun used to shout at me if I dripped on the corpses. Despite working in one of the coldest professions (bar Arctic whaling, ice-cream van

for small talk, me. Instead, my first port of call is the Wethouse. I don't want to hang around there too long either, in case I get roped into doing chores, but I manage to nip through the foyer unnoticed, and march down the corridor with my head down. I find the Moaner Lisa in her usual spot, moping about by the ladies. She's called the Moaner Lisa because she's a constantly recovering morphine addict – she's got the best intentions to quit, but none of the willpower to stay off it for good. 'Lisa,' I coo, putting my arm around her. She flinches. 'You haven't got a spare "   ", have you?' I ask, replacing the word 'syringe' with a mime of one going into my left cephalic vein. The Moaner Lisa glances at me with clotted eyelashes. 'No, I need it,' she replies dolefully. She bites her fingernails while she talks, which could be a sign of either anxiety or attraction. She's not that bad-looking under the welts and sores. 'I'm a bit desperate, like,' I explain, playing with her claggy hair. 'It doesn't need to be clean or owt. Anything with a spike and a plunger, love.' I consider turning the words 'spike' and 'plunger' into a kind of sexual innuendo, but I don't need to grovel. The Moaner Lisa looks

man, igloo renovation), in summertime my hands always turned into Jacuzzis when stitching up the cadavers' mouths; or blowing their noses; or barricading their arseholes. Any job that constantly reminds you you're going to die is bound to give you a sweat-on, but there's nothing worse than a corpse with a clammy brow. Moisture breeds decay. Fortunately, the easiest bit of the business is picking up supplies, though I can be indecisive when it comes to choosing lipstick shades and eyeshadows. As I plod down the scented aisles of Boots, I feel far too scruffy to be rubbing shoulders with all the posh toiletries. I feel like I'm drawing attention to myself, like my head's full of magnets, attracting the security guard's steely eyes. I dry-swallow some saliva, trying my best to browse the make-ups in a natural fashion. 'Mm,' I mutter, pretending to be interested in the Fire-Hazard Red Revlon. I try to picture Kimberly's face, but I can't quite grasp it. I wonder if she'd look better with the Black mascara from the Maybelline range, or the Very Black, or the Blackest Black. I think, 'Fuck it', and slip all three into my pocket. My coat's perfect for thievery – it's full of holes. Occasionally, the

up at me again. 'I just put my old works in the sano-pad bin,' she drawls, 'but you know about my thing? My condition?' My face erupts with delight. 'Aw, I'm not arsed about that!' I say, glancing up and down the corridor before darting into the ladies to fish out Lisa's infected syringe. 'The lass I'm using it on's dead already,' I add, with my head in the period-stained bin. Before I steam back out of the Wethouse, I give the Moaner Lisa a peck on the cheek, but the daft cow still doesn't cheer up. In fact, she looks more confused and upset than ever.

*

Lisa's HIV-spiked syringe is a real beauty. The needle's straight and true, and the 2.5ml barrel's in good nick, with only a little rusty residue of haemoglobin round the chamber. I keep it tucked in my breast pocket, with the prick poking out of my buttonhole, like a Remembrance Day pin without the poppy on the end. Good old Lisa. She takes all manner of pills and potions to help with her condition, but everyone reckons the morphine – or the depression, from the lack thereof – will get her first. After a slight detour down the back alleys, I take a breather on the wall skirting the coat's even been known to steal from yours truly, sucking pens, coins and betting slips into its fuzzy lining, as if the coat's cultivating its own private gambling habit. After a couple of minutes in the cosmetics section, the coat's fit to bursting with make-up. I'm about a stone heavier when I leave the shop, but luckily the security staff don't chase after me. They seem more interested in the two young girls in short skirts contemplating the Cystopurin. It's been three weeks now since I last got caught stealing and, to be fair, I did have the Danish pastry in my mouth at the time. The Sainsbury's staff weren't sure whether to make me spit it out or swallow it. I hide a smirk as I slip back out into the speeding human traffic. To stave off the hunger, I light up a Pall Mall. The smoke soothes every alveolus in my air sacs. On my way back through the green, I can see some selfish bint's stolen mine and Shaun's favourite bench, so I stall for a bit, picking Kimberly a wreath from the council flowerbed. Kneeling in the soil, all the lipsticks and eyesticks jingle as I pluck a few fuchsias from the shrubbery. I know lilies are more commonly associated with death, but beggars can't be choosers.

Boots loading bay, watching the goods vans snaking in and out of the car park. It's turning into a smashing afternoon. The late-autumn sun massages the back of my neck while I finish my fourth Special of the day. I wonder how that fat bastard's getting on inside Boots. We might get away with this super-economy funeral, after all. All we're missing now is some transport, and the corpse. Back in the Boro, when we started SS Funerals, me and Sean had a classy pair of hearses. They both got crushed in the end, after the court case, and the compensation and all that, which I won't get into. I press the golden can against my lips, weighing up the options. We can't just turn up to the morgue with a pair of black binliners to store thingy's body in. What we need is a large vehicle – preferably one with air-conditioning, and space in the back for an operating table. Something hefty and professional-looking. Something like a Boots goods van. I take another glug of the amber acid and glance about the loading bay. For the next ten minutes or so, the place is quiet. I pick more black out from under my nails, and squash the empty can. Finally, at 14.23 by the Nokia clock, the late 2 p.m.

While I wait for the old bint to finish her bap and move on, I trim the snaggly bits off the stems with my nails, then I scuttle over, and sit in her bumprint. At long last, I can relax, basking in the firing line of the late-autumn sun. I waft my T-shirt and coat, unpeeling the sticky fabric from my chest and pits. I haven't had a shower at the Wethouse for a week or so – once we've taken care of Kimberly, I plan to take care of myself again. I close my eyes, letting the sun brand itself on my eyelids. I'm moments away from rejoining the platinum-blonde bombshell in my favourite daydream, when a booming foghorn jolts me back to life. My veins turn to icicles, when I spot the Boots goods van beeping at me from across the playground, with the driver inside gesturing at me wildly. Fuck! At first, I can't move. I'm not sure whether to surrender the lippies, plead ignorance, or run. However, the Boots van seems to be stuck in traffic, so I unglue myself from the bench and make a dash for the opposite corner of the green. The Capital, after all, is one of the worst places in the world to conduct a car chase. As I waddle quickly across the threadbare grass, I keep an eye on the goods van gaining on me, at about three

delivery shows up, swaying and shunting down the alleyway. A bit flustered, the driver parks up and jumps out of the cab, leaving the engine running. 'Hmmdllldrrun-nmdrnhdrn,' the driver mutters, scrutinising his Boots clipboard. Taking Lisa's syringe out of my buttonhole, I charge towards the scrawny driver, holding it aloft like a medieval lance. 'I've got AIDS, me!' I shriek, with wild eyes, waving the spike at him. The driver stiffens, splutters a few letters of the alphabet, then stumbles backwards. He turns the colour of a three-hour-old corpse: yellowy grey. There's nothing more frightening than a madman with AIDS, threatening you with a soiled syringe. I learnt that the other day from a friend of mine called Old Joe, a madman with AIDS. Dribbling, I shout 'AIDS!' at the driver again, then clamber clumsily into the van cab. The driver stares with frozen, swollen eyes as I take off the handbrake and rev her up. 'Stop,' he says halfheartedly, keeping his distance. It's probably not worth his while, contracting a debilitating virus for the sake of saving his afternoon delivery of Pantene. I give him a thumbs-up as I reverse out of the bay, safe in the knowledge he'll spend the rest miles an hour. My armpits get soaked again, and my legs soon get stunted by lactic acid. Luckily, the lights keep changing to red in front of the Boots van, so I don't have to break into an embarrassing sprint. Instead, I stroll sharply through the trees, taking care not to crush Kimberly's wreath under my arm. When I get to the corner of Uxbridge Road and Wood Lane, the red man keeps me and the other pedestrians waiting, and my heart twitches despairingly as the Boots van finally catches up with me. 'What?!' I yell at the dark windscreen. 'I only got a daft few bits!' Panicking, I start pulling the cosmetics out of the padded cells of my pockets. 'Have them!' I shout, offering them. Nearly mounting the kerb, the van shouts back, 'Fucking hang on! Sean, it's me!' Somehow, the van knows my name. The passenger window slides down and, through it, a voice says, 'Calm down. It's me: *Shaun.*' Squinting, I can see the van's right – it's him: Shaun. 'Oh, thank fuck,' I say, smiling, climbing into the cab. 'You daft cunt,' Shaun says, shaking his head. I throw myself onto the passenger seat, as the van sets off again. 'Aiyas!' I scream, accidentally sitting on something sharp. Shaun

of the day with a spring in his step and a newfound lust for life. Unless, of course, he's got AIDS already. Craning my head out of the cab window, I struggle a bit, trying to manoeuvre the vehicle through the tight alley, like trying to thread a piece of rope through the eye of a darning needle. I tut, nearly scraping the BOOTS logo off the left side of the van, against the bricks. After a bit of deliberation, I drive forward again into the bay – almost crushing the scrawny driver in the process – then reverse again, changing my trajectory slightly. In my defence, I haven't driven for fucking ages. Once I'm in amongst the traffic of Uxbridge Road, I keep my good eye on the car in front, while the other scours the green for Sean. I wonder how the big gay mong's been getting on with his make-up. I do worry about his sexual orientation sometimes – he wears tight T-shirts; he knows his foundations from his concealers; and he cries when people die. Next, he'll be wearing fucking dresses, or picking flowers! I smirk, keeping my foot poised on the clutch as we crawl between the lights. I squint into the trees. After a few swift, hawk-like glances about the green, I finally pick Sean out, kneeling in one of the council

creases up, as he sticks the van into second. 'You dickhead,' I snap, yanking the hypodermic needle from my backside. 'Fucking . . . should've put it in the glovebox,' I say, chucking it in amongst the tissues and playing cards. 'Where'd you get it?' I ask. Shaun glances at me, still grinning. 'Aw, er, down one of them clinics. This needle-exchange thing.' I wriggle about in my jeans, rubbing my arse against the seat. 'Good work, good work. At least it's fresh,' I remark, as we rejoin the heavy traffic snaking up up up and away from Shepherd's Bush, and onwards to the morgue.

*

When Shaun comes out of the hospital, wheeling the black bodybag, my heart and stomach shrink. I can't go through with it. I drum nervously on the dashboard, as Shaun loads her into the back of the van. Before we set off, I spark up a Pall Mall, and shake ash all over myself. For the past half an hour I've been shadowboxing, bracing myself for this moment, but one glance at the glorified binliner and all my steel turns to blancmange. No amount of mind games can prepare you for stitching your

shrubberies. I pip the horn, waving. Then, I burst out laughing, when I see what the fat fucker's doing.

*

'It's a wreath, for Kimberly,' Sean explains, keeping hold of the fuchsias as we rumble towards the morgue. I bite my lip. What a soft sod! When we get to the hospital, I make Sean stay in the van with his precious ladies' things while I go in to talk to the death staff. I don't want that emotional wreck blowing our cover, bursting into tears as soon as he sees thingymabob's body. In any case, I'm the brains of the business. When me and Sean went bankrupt earlier in the year, I remembered to keep my embalming licence and handling-the-dead certificates – along with my passport, driving licence and birth certificate – in the inside pocket of my bomber jacket. You never know when you might need your debraining papers. Morgues don't hand corpses over to just anyone, you see. Before I head into the building, I spruce myself up with a few toiletries from the back of the van. I shave my beard in the rear-view mirror with a Venus lady-razor, floss, and spray my armpits with two flavours of Sure.

friend's face back together, or rearranging her twisted, post-rape genitalia. 'I can't do it,' I say to Shaun, when he jumps back in the front. 'You're gonna have to help. You're better at it than me. Just make her look normal-ish, and I'll do the rest.' Shaun strokes his chin. 'Mm,' he says, 'I'll do it for the rest of them fags.' My heart and stomach expand again. What a pushover. I toss him the Pall Malls as we crawl out of the hospital car park. Once we're stationed safely in a shady alleyway in White City, I stay in the front while Shaun gets on with the dirty business. I try to ignore the sounds of bones crunching and flesh being sliced, tapping my foot frantically to the hits on Heart FM. I focus my attention on the two pigeon-coloured tower blocks peeking out from behind the flyover, wondering if the folks behind the windows are having a better or worse day than me and Shaun. To be fair, Shaun seems to be enjoying himself, humming along with the radio while he works. At one point, he even lets out a snort. 'How are you getting on?' I ask. Shaun pokes his head into the cab. A string of dead muscle tissue hangs from his chin. 'Er, we might have to put her in a balaclava,' he replies. My

385

As I march steadily down the Day-Glo hospital corridors, I convince myself I'm George Clooney, or Dick Van Dyke, or another fake celebrity doctor. There's a certain amount of pantomime necessary to pull off an 'economy funeral'. When I greet the morgue technicians with my documents and a firm handshake, they take me for a well-heeled, professional chap. Little do they know my worldly possessions have been reduced to a pocketful of papers and a carrier bag of cans back in the van. 'It's sunny, isn't it, today?' I say to the techs, emptily. The lads smile back, emptily. Us lot in the death trade have a habit of making small talk like this; constantly reassuring each other we're not in the worst job in the world, or that we're not twisted fuckers, if we seem like we're enjoying ourselves too much. While the techs go off to get thingy out of the fridge, I have a good look at the fresh fatalities, lifting the white sheets one by one. The first fella's head looks like it's been run over by a lawnmower. Another, a young Paki lass, looks like she's been in the oven on full whack. None of them flinch when I pinch their noses. Dead people are the only people you can trust – they don't complain when you manipu-

heart and stomach shrink again. I feel sick. When I finally muster the courage to glance in the back, I instantly blur her up with tears. At first, I'm convinced Shaun's picked up the wrong corpse, until I spot Kimberly's famous, cat-like eyes, leaking halfway out of her nostrils. I cough a mouthful of bile into a carton of shampoos. 'Urgh, you cunt,' Shaun snaps. I shouldn't have looked. Her face is like a cheap Halloween mask. I wish my own eyes would leak out of my nostrils, taking that image away with them. 'I'm not finished yet, am I,' Shaun spouts, as I clamber back into the front. I slump, trembling, with my knees up to my chest. I feel so sorry for Kimberly, having to spend her last couple of days above ground with a pair of useless bastards. Another angry mob of tears bangs on the backs of my eyelids. 'Make yourself useful,' Shaun yells, getting back to work on Miss Frankenstein. 'Go and get us three bottles of vodka. The good stuff. Smirnoff, if you can get it.' I lift my chin from my chest. Shaun's right – the only way to salvage our sanity is to surrender ourselves to the nondiscriminating, warming embrace of a bottle of booze. A certain level of detachment is required to undertake an 'econo-

late them. Sean's easy to manipulate, but he doesn't half make a song and dance about things, when he's upset. When the morgue technicians come back with doodah, I can see Sean's going to be unbearable tonight. Thingymajig's in a right old mess. I barely recognise her, laid face-down (or is it face-up?) on the wheelie-stretcher, with her fingers twisted into swastika shapes and her spine curved into a question mark. Her bottom jaw arrives separately, on a metal dish. Her left foot's been ground down to chalk dust. And the palms of her hands are bright red. It must've been quite a bad car accident, is my reckoning. 'Was it a bad car accident?' I ask the shorter of the two techs, just to fill the silence. 'Yes,' he answers. 'We had to dislodge her mandible from her brain,' the other one adds. 'Perfect,' I say, for want of a better word. The techs post whatshername into a stay-fresh black sandwich bag, shuffle-shuffling across the squeaky lino. 'Did she leave any personal effects? A phone? Purse, etc.?' I ask, in the hope of landing a few bob. 'Er, actually, yeah,' the taller one says, striding off to a different table, 'we found her mobile phone. It must've, er . . . it

my funeral'. I slide awkwardly out of the cab, droning one dull note while I walk, until the sounds of Kimberly getting recklessly recapitated disappear. All the colour seems to have been sucked from the city. It's early evening already – as I walk, the sky turns from a bright blue billboard to a dull, spilt-soft-drink colour. I wish I had the guts to walk as far as the city limits, and leave Shaun for good. When Kimberly gave us those £2,500 cheques, I should've cashed mine, and made a dash for sunnier climes, rather than squandering it on the funeral home/bookies. But, as much as I hate him, I'm dependent on Shaun. Two heads are better than one, after all. And there's nothing worse than being homeless and friendless in the Capital. I shiver, and hug myself all the way to Morrison's. It's important, if you're planning to steal booze, not to be seduced by the off-licences. Supermarkets might have semi-sophisticated security systems, and tags on their pricier bottles of plonk, but a squealing siren is preferable to reaching behind the back of a burly Balkan booze baron. Besides, supermarket workers don't give a shit about their stock – they're not going to chase you in public, in their

must've got lodged in her abdomen, with the impact. Do you need it?' I nod. I hope they've cleaned it. And I hope whatsit remembered to top up her credit before she died. Since she hasn't got any close relatives to rally the mourners, me and Sean will have to cold-call her CONTACTS list tonight. I wonder if she's got any good-looking friends. Thingy used to be good-looking, before her jaw snapped off. Mind, I'd still shag it like, if it was alive. After sealing up the sandwich bag, I thank the techs for the phone, dead person, and pleasantries, then wheel whatnot out of the unit. It's high time I got out of here. I bet the air's been through at least ten terminally ill patients' bodies already today. At least I can't catch a car crash off thingy. I glance at her again, in the black sandwich bag. With her bottom jaw gone, she's got one hell of an overbite. I wheel the girl's remains out of the back exit, bracing myself for Sean's waterworks. He's not going to like this one bit. 'You know when I said she got raped and then murdered?' I enquire, once I'm back in the driving seat. Sean nods, glumly. 'Well,' I carry on, 'it turns out she got flayed and decapitated a bit, as well.' Sean dry-retches

burgundy blouses, for the sake of three bottles of Smirnoff. Dabbing my eyelids, I walk onwards through the ever-darkening estate, the spilt-soft-drink sky becoming a navy blue sleep mask around the last of the sun. By the time I get to Morrison's, my legs feel heavy. The fluorescent striplights of Market Street make the fruit and veg spin, like a giant one-armed bandit that never pays out. I yawn, plodding onwards, letting my eyes adjust to the rows and rows of tempting foods and elixirs. My stomach heckles the biscuit section. As per usual, the booze aisle is the furthest from the entrance, like a dingy back alley you feel uncomfortable walking down at certain hours. Rubbing a wiggle of dribble off my chin, I can almost feel the alcohol being telepathically transferred to my veins and brain, just by looking at it. With all these flavours to choose from, it's a shame to go for vodka. It's not the tastiest tipple, and Shaun gets lairy after 70cl or so. So, I lift eight cans of Super Skol from the bottom shelf, and post them into the nooks and crannies of my coat. I'm in it for the fizz – not only do the bubbles fill you up; they act like the most beautiful fireworks in your belly, and your brain. On

the last puff of his Pall Mall, on the brink of tears again. He's so easy to wind up – that's why I enjoy spending time with the cunt. He makes me feel 10ft tall – and I'm only 6ft 2in, normally. 'You'll have your fucking work cut out, mate,' I say, turning the ignition. 'I'd help out, but I don't want to disrespect her last wishes and all. You'll be alright though, eh? Her jaw's on a separate dish. And just ignore her foot.' Sean convulses, and the colour in his cheeks leaches out. 'I can't do it,' he mumbles, between sharp, shaky sucks. 'Is she that bad?' Sticking the gears into first, I reply, deadpan, 'Do you remember that last lass we did? Ages ago. The one from the thingy . . . the meatpacking accident? Well, she's like that, but with less meat on her.' I bite my tongue, suppressing the sniggers. Sean stares into space as we crawl out of the parking bay. 'I can't do it,' he repeats. 'You're gonna have to help. You're better at it than me. Just make her look normal-ish, and I'll do the rest.' I scratch my newly smooth chin theatrically. 'Mm, I'll do it for the rest of them fags,' I say. The gay poof hands them over without a second thought. His heart seems to visibly lift, despite the tears misting

my way back out of Morrison's, I stop for a second at the herbs and spices aisle, pretending to be normal. 'Paprika,' I mutter, even though I'm holding the cinnamon. I think about rubbing some on my neck, but I don't want to push my luck. Putting back the shaker, I casually turn on my heels, then stride purposefully through the EXIT – though not so purposefully that people think I've got eight cans of Super Skol tucked in my coat. I leave the supermarket feeling like God. Not only do I have a mad-strength lager to look forward to on the long walk back to the van, but the alarms don't even go off. I suck away the froth, and step sluggishly across the car park, like I'm wearing a coat of bricks. As the sky makes its last transition from navy blue sleep mask to the blackest black bodybag, I start feeling myself again: very, very drunk. I can't wait to see Shaun's face. He's going to love me for this. When I reach the white Boots van, I'm grinning like an idiot. I'm glad I didn't leave him for good. Like I said, there's nothing worse than being homeless and friendless in the Capital. And there's nothing better than getting legless.

*

389

up his eyeballs. To add to the bargain, Sean agrees to fire up and feed me fags while I drive, like a flunky. I soon have us parked in a dark corner of White City, which is an estate full of black people, funnily enough. We squeeze the van between two derelict business blocks, overlooking a weed-ridden petrol station and a few withered streetlights. It's imperative to undertake 'economy embalmment' in privacy. The stench can give you away in built-up areas like Shepherd's Bush Green or Piccadilly Circus. And, since we're working in a freshly stolen vehicle (which the Necropolitan Police are no doubt on the lookout for), the fewer witnesses, the better. Sean keeps watch in the front while I put the human jigsaw puzzle back together. I remember to grab his fags, and the syringe, then I clamber over the seats. Shoving the black sandwich bag to one side, I erect a makeshift lab table out of upturned shampoo boxes and punnets of anti-ageing cream. Then, I tip out the sandwich bag. 'Fuck!' Sean coughs, from inside the cab. He turns on the radio, as if it'll drown out the smell. For the sake of it, I spray round the van with more Sure For Men, making Sean cough again. Then I

'You fuckin twat!' Shaun screams, throwing a bottle of Pantene at my head. I trip over my own ankles and hit the deck. How was I supposed to know we were embalming Kimberly with the alcohol, not drinking it? I should've run off into the sunset with the Super Skol when I had the chance. 'What are we gonna do?' I whimper. It's already gone eleven, which means lockdown for the local off-licences. 'Well, we can't let her fuckin rot,' Shaun spits. I close my eyes, playing dead. My performance isn't so convincing, though, next to Kimberly. Shaun stomps around the makeshift lab table, muttering blue murder, kicking me once every lap. Shaun's only violent towards me on Special occasions. 'We'll have to fucking embalm her with this, then,' he growls, cracking open one of the cans of Super. I bury my head in a box of disposable shower caps. Shaun takes a long gulp of the super-strength lager, then dips the syringe into the liquid and pulls back the plunger. The mucky vessel fills with beige foam. I watch from the ground as Shaun jabs the needle into Kimberly's grey flesh and empties the chamber into her poor, dehydrated arteries. I shake my head. By tomorrow morning, she'll be

rearrange thingy's body, like a butcher turning his cuts of raw meat back into a cow, or pig; or your mam turning Sunday's leftovers into a vaguely appetising bubble and squeak. I use the dental floss to stitch her bits back together; wrapping it round and round the detached needle, then forcing it in and out and in and out of whatsherface's cold, rubbery flesh. If you condition your mind right, playing with a corpse is just like playing with an old stuffed bear. I press cotton wool into her eye-sockets – to fool funeralgoers into thinking her eyeballs haven't dissolved and trickled out of her nostrils – then I glue her lids shut with Garnier Fructis Extreme Hold Gel. After a sticky-fingered fag, I set to work on breaking her arms and fingers back to normal. Sean's not overly impressed with the Goliath knuckle-cracking sounds coming from the makeshift lab – he turns up Heart FM and whimpers into his collar. I roll up my sleeves, working myself into a frenzy. Once thingy's limbs are in order, I take her gooey mandible, and suture it roughly to the bottom of her face. It's a nightmare trying to get her gob to shut – I have to ram the needle and floss into her firm cheekflesh, up through her

honking. There's not much worse than the smell of stale lager, not least when it's injected into a corpse. I can feel another cold sweat coming on. Curled up, I try to occupy myself by staring at the strewn cosmetics, while Shaun alternately slurps the lager and squirts it into Kimberly. I see the Japanese Spa Shower Cream contains linalool. I ponder linalool for a bit. Once Shaun's finished slurping and squirting, I prise myself off the floor and brace myself for more tears. My eyes flick nervously round the walls of the van, before finally settling on Kimberly. Against all the odds, Shaun's done a sterling job. Despite smelling like a brewery, Kimberly's grey flesh looks fuller and more lively, and only just the wrong side of yellow. 'Good work,' I mumble, and add, 'Eh, eh, is there a spare can, then?' Shaun glares at me. 'You can have one after you've done some fucking graft,' he snaps, taking the remaining Skols into the cab with him, like a toddler guarding his toys. I scratch my nose, and take another look at Kimberly. She'll be beautiful again, once I'm finished with her. While Shaun makes gurgling noises in the front – vindictively trying to polish off the cans before I finish Kim's

391

palette, and figure-eight it through her septum. I scoff, wiping my wet brow. She looks like a spatchcocked, patchwork spastic. 'How you getting on?' Sean asks gloomily, turning the music down again. I poke my head into the cab. 'Er, we might have to put her in a balaclava,' I reply.

*

When Sean sees the state of so-and-so, the sod sobs so much, the van shakes. I almost pierce her ears by mistake. What a fucking baby. 'I'm not finished yet, am I,' I snap, as Sean leaps back into the cab, holding his mouth. What was he expecting: fucking Coppélia? I rub my bloody hands on a wet-wipe. Sean could at least give some fucking encouragement – a 'good eyelid-plumping' or 'mighty nice earhole rinse there, matey' wouldn't go amiss. I yawn, then shimmy thingy's floppy, dead-weight legs along the lab table. After unravelling it from the needle, the red floss decides to stick to my fingers, forcing me to do jazz hands for a few seconds. Then, I screw the needle back onto the syringe, and give it a once-over with a Simple cucumber face-wipe. I almost want to let the corpse rot, just to see Sean's face. Then again, if we don't get

make-up – I lay out the Very Black mascara, foundation, eye-shadows, and other cosmetics on the unstable lab table. Before I paint her face, I cover up Kimberly's privates with a couple of Boots' *Look Good . . . Feel Better* magazines. I always wanted to see her naked, but not like this. Corpses aren't half as attractive as living human beings, even when they're fresh off the tarmac. That's part of the futility of being in the funerary business – no matter how hard you try, you can never quite restore the appearance of a dead body to its former glory. But God knows, I'll give this one everything. Chewing my tongue, I start out with the foundation, spreading it liberally across Kimberly's uneven complexion. I'm glad I stole Honey Glow from the L'Oréal range – corpses have a habit of looking on the pasty side. Then, I flutter a brushful of blusher across Kimberly's cheeks – enough to make her look nice and rosy, but not so much she looks like a harlot, or embarrassed about being dead. I don't mind putting make-up on cadavers – it's better than blowing their brains out of their noses, or wiping their backsides. The only downside is it's usually old ladies you're dealing with, unless

on with the embalming, the back of the van'll be swarming with creepy crawlies by morning. Especially if the sun comes out again. Stabbing the syringe into the girl's best artery, I draw out the remainder of her blood (although she must've lost a lot of it to the tarmac of Shepherd's Bush), whistling along to the radio. I've grown quite attached to this van already. I wonder if it'd be much hassle changing the number plates, giving it a respray and turning it into a mobile home. It's not a bad size, for two hot-blooded males and one cold female. Squirting 2.5ml after 2.5ml of thingymajig's blood into a line of upturned lids of deodor-ant and shampoo, I get lost in my thoughts, weighing up the pros and cons of the traveller lifestyle. Me and Sean could slope around Britain like snails, with a huge metal shell on our backs, offering cut-price cosmetics and quickfire funerals to folk along the way. I think of all the fresh widows, as I carry on with doodah's blood extraction. The more I suck out, the more deflated her body becomes, like an old birthday balloon left out on the windowsill. Here's some trivia for you: human flesh works the opposite way to pork-pie flesh. The greyer the

there's been a gas leak at a local beauty contest. Concentrating, I gently smear turquoise eyeshad-ow (Kimberly's favourite) into the shadows hiding under her eye-brows. She doesn't flinch when I pluck them. I blow her hairs off the tweezers, then carefully do her lid-liner and mascara. Now and then, I have to pick Very Black crumbs off her cheeks with a cucumber-flavoured wipe, like tiny coal tears. By the time I get round to her lipstick, I'm dripping my own tears onto her cheeks. Shaun never likes me leaking on the corpses, but this is different. It's all too much. I arch my back, and burst into hystericals, as qui-etly and privately as possible. I glance back at Kimberly; her pink lips almost pursed into a smile, or a heart-shape. I kissed those lips once, four and a half years ago. We were in the Marton Country Club, dancing like idiots at someone's friend's cousin's birthday party, on a wet and windy Wednesday night. We got to know each other after me and Shaun sorted out a 'luxury funer-al' with all the trimmings, for her mam, Mag Clark. We were always too shy to speak to each other in sober hours but, that night in the Country Club, there was an hour or so of free bar. For five minutes,

pork-pie flesh, the fresher the pork pie; the greyer the human flesh, the further it's gone past its best-before date. Thingy's cheeks are the shade of the finest Melton Mowbray. Salivating, I draw the last chamberful of blood from her head, which darkens to a filthy lilac colour. I clean the needle again with another face-wipe, and use two more on my forehead. I'm not sure when to break it to Sean about the shortage of embalming fluid. I catch a glimpse of him, still sulking, in the rear-view mirror. If you ever find yourself pressured into performing a last-minute 'economy funeral', there are tons of household products which can act in the place of embalming fluid, so long as the mourners are partially sighted, with no sense of smell, and no direct relationship to the deceased. One of these household products is known as 'alcohol'. Both a sterilising fluid and commonly used gateway to Heaven, triple-filtered vodka such as Smirnoff can enable any old corpse to look vaguely rosy-cheeked and human for a maximum of forty-eight hours. I wouldn't recommend you use it on your loved ones, but me and Sean are desperate. 'Make yourself useful,' I say to the fat, blub-

we got away from the flashing lights and 'La Bamba', and went out for a breather. It was chilly out. Somehow, we ended up huddling together under the canopy, and our tongues accidentally landed in each other's mouths. And that's when I fell in love with Kimberly Clark: the platinum-blonde bombshell. With each stroke and poke of our tongues, the odds on me finally getting a girlfriend seemed to be shortening. However, as soon as the kiss finished, a heavy cloud of awkwardness hung over us, and we realised we had nothing to say to each other. I had no idea how to make the kiss come back. Two weeks later, I saw the same kiss again, but this time it was Stevie Wallace on the end of Kimberly's lips. I hadn't seen her since the Country Club, but I'd been thinking about her non-stop, trying to recall her face with just the patchiest of drunken memories. When I spotted her again in the Southern Cross on 16 June 2003, my heart erupted with panic and joy. Then, my heart fell sadly out of my trouser leg, when I saw that selfish, stuttering cunt Stevie kissing my Kimberly. I don't know what she saw in him. Me and Shaun were only friends with him because he was a semi-

bering mess in the front. 'Go and get us three bottles of vodka. The good stuff. Smirnoff, if you can get it.' Sparking up another Pall Mall, I watch Sean shift slowly out of his seat, like his body's made of lead. I've never seen him this bad before. There's a Sainsbury's two minutes down the road, but for some reason the daft cunt heads in the opposite direction, towards Morrison's. I roll my eyes at thingy. She rolls a bit of eye at me too, out through her earhole. I leave her to dehydrate while I hop in the front to finish the fag, turning the radio up again. I'm fucking exhausted. The fags are worth the exertion, but there's still a ton to be done before bed. Luckily, Sean won't be able to sleep with a corpse next to him, so I can set him to work on menial tasks through the night, while I get some shut-eye. First, though, we need to secure a venue, and some guests. Sean's telephone manner's like a timid ten-year-old's, whereas I mastered the art of persuasion aged minus three weeks. Apparently, I persuaded my twin brother to hang himself with Mam's umbilical cord, to make sure I'd be well-fed and reach my optimum height through childhood. Resting the fag between my lips, I take whatsherface's phone

famous sprinter, and had money. As a human being, he was a chore to be around, with his speech impediment, and his sobriety. And I'll never understand how anyone with a girlfriend could commit suicide. I'd give my right eyeball to have a woman. Soon after Kimberly and Stevie got together, SS Funerals went downhill. I started making mistakes – like mixing up the McGiven and Bramwell funerals – in the hope of ruining the business, and finding a more savoury occupation. I even borrowed a book from the library, about mixology. I wanted to be like Tom Cruise in *Cocktail*, snaring Kimberly with my flaring and fancy footwork. Soon, though, the mishaps at the funeral home slurried mine and Shaun's reputations as good job material, let alone good marriage material. The widows, widowers and orphans of Middlesbrough fell out of love with us. At first, when Shaun suggested we move to the Capital, I was haunted by stress dreams involving terrorists, illegal immigrants, and £4 pints. But then I found out Kimberly and Stevie were thinking of moving down, too. Shaun liked the idea of desperate Eurotrash lasses looking for thoroughbred British husbands, and I liked the idea of

out of the glovebox, and give the screen a wipe. I flick through my own contacts until I get to PAT THE PRIEST, then ring the old bastard off thingymabob's credit. Pat's a good mate of ours – he looks after an RC church not too far from here, and he shares the same interests as me and Sean: death, Catholicism, food and drink, guilt, and greyhounds. He's a funny old fucker, often turning up to his sermons blind drunk after a religious experience with a 1.5l bottle of Scotch. I clear my throat and take another puff of the fag. Whatnot's Sony Ericsson makes a *bbring-crickle* sound three times before Pat picks up. 'Now then, Pat,' I say, 'it's Shaun. How you diddling?' Pat takes a sharp breath. 'Bloody hell!' the blasphemous bastard bellows. 'Which one is it? Thing One or Thing Two? Boris or Bela? Ho ho.' I've got no idea what he's on about. 'Eh, it's me. Shaun. With an aitch,' I say. Pat cackles, crackling the line. 'Ah, Shaun, matey! You lanky streak of shit! What can I do you for?' Pat the Priest seems to have stolen the accent of a cockney. When we first met, at a funeral in 2005, I could've sworn he was from Lancashire. 'Er, well, see, me and Sean are in a bit of a pickle,' I

Kimberly and Stevie splitting up. I waited for months on end, praying for his demise. On 23 February 2008, my wish came true. Frightened by my psychic, witch-like powers, I couldn't bring myself to ask Kimberly out at the wake. She seemed so distraught, and so drunk. And it's so hard talking to girls when I've got Shaun breathing down my neck. Even in death, with her arteries clotted with Super Skol, Kimberly looks like a goddess. I wish I could keep her in formaldehyde, and put her in a museum. I love her and hate her for kissing me under the canopy of the Country Club. I love her and hate her for dying, for putting an end to all my daft fantasies; for putting an end to the possibility of us ever getting together. Sniffling again, I wish I'd had the wit and wisecracks to sweep her off her feet, on that wet and windy Wednesday night. I dig my nails into my palms. I wish I could've stolen her heart before Stevie. I swallow back some snot and look at her lips again. I might not be able to steal Kimberly's heart, but I can steal one last kiss, at least. I blow my nose, and straighten my collar. I restyle my hair. As I lean over the lab table, I feel prickles in the tips of my fingers. I can't tell if I'm being dis-

explain, 'or, at least, we will be once he comes back with something to embalm her with.' Pat creases up again. He's a big fan of our 'economy funerals'. A fellow alcoholic and wastrel, Pat turned to religion after meeting a pretty, big-titted Bible basher named Lucy, in a teashop in Burnley. At first he started going to church just to stare at the back of her head, and occasionally tell her a bad joke. Before long, though, the hypnotic power of the priests' weekly sermons began to take control of Pat's brain. He stopped coming to church just for the wine and the women; instead, he immersed himself in the magical tales of Job, Solomon and St Peter, and found new meaning to his life. Pat wanted a pure, untainted existence, sunbathing in the Lord's loving rays, plus he heard priests can get free accommodation in pricey parts of the Capital. After five or so years of seminary study, his wish finally came true – he found himself in a modest, mothball-small residence in Hammersmith, living off the church. 'See, don't go mad,' I explain to the old cunt, 'but we need a venue for the funeral pretty sharpish. Like, the next couple of days. Before she goes off.' Pat's loving rays switch off for a

gusting or not, but I don't care. It's not like I can stick my tongue in – her lips are stitched shut. My heart thuds, as I plant one on her. Kimberly's mouth feels cold, and it doesn't kiss back. It was chilly outside the Country Club, but at least her lips were body temperature back then. I could just be kissing a doorhandle, or a piano key, or a chisel, but I keep on kissing. I miss her so much. I want the kiss to last for ever, but it only lasts about ten seconds, thanks to Shaun sticking his big, daft head between the seats and shrieking, 'You fucking . . . you sick bastard!!'

*

I feel dead sheepish at the funeral. Shaun hasn't spoken to me all day. We stand silently in the queue to see the casket, watching people's expressions as they file past. The smell of off-licence hovers around the coffin, like a pissed-up ghost. Nevertheless, the mourners don't seem put off by Kimberly's beery body odour, or the Day-Glo boob-tube and tutu she's wearing. It turned out Kimberly's Promiscuous Pal Polly only owns skimpy, provocative outfits, and the only bits she was willing to part with were the monstrosities Kimberly now has

397

moment. 'Fucking hell, Shauny, I've told you about, you know . . . you've got to give me *notice*,' he scolds. I reply, 'Yeah, I'm sorry, I'm sorry, mate. It's just we're gonna be pickling her with vodka, and she wanted an open casket. Like, so I don't want to bring you a fucking wormery at the end of the week. Health and Safety, and all that.' Lightening up, Pat makes the line crackle again. I think me and Sean have provided a lot of entertainment for him over the years. We always seem to get ourselves into one shitty, sticky situation or another. Just to tip Pat over the edge, I say to him dryly, 'And, er, I don't know if I mentioned, but me and Sean are homeless now.' The phone nearly explodes. 'Christ Almighty, stop, stop!' Pat gags, gasping for breath. The laughter's contagious, making my toothache flare up again. 'Alright, alright,' he says, 'I can do Tuesday arvo. The only thing is, my gravedigger's gone AWOL. So I might need a hand with some digging.' I watch a pigeon limp across the street. 'Nice one, no bother,' I say, 'Sean'll do it. He loves getting his hands dirty.' When I get off the phone, I see the streetlights are all warming up around the van. My belly rumbles. I'm looking

to wear for the rest of her death. Luckily, the guests don't comment on the terrible state of the clothes, let alone the corpse itself. That's because we had to hire most of the mourners. In the eventuality of somebody dying without many friends or family, Pat the Priest has an address-book of people willing to eat a free buffet and pretend to pay respects to a dead stranger. Me and Shaun are on that list, too. My belly's still mumbling with thanks, after Pat's sister's mini Scotch eggs and tuna buns. Glancing about the church, most of the mourners look bored and cold, shuffling in their black Puffa jackets, black evening dresses, black burglar outfits, black pyjamas, and black track-suits. Usually, you'd do the open-casket ceremony in the funeral home, but it didn't seem right inviting people into the Wethouse, or the Boots van. Especially since we haven't scrubbed the blood off the insides yet. Last night, after a groundbreaking argument, Shaun fell asleep in the cab with those four Super Skols singing sour lullabies in his stomach. I stayed in the back with Kimberly. I redid her lipstick, and dabbed concealer on my bruised cheekbone, where Shaun caught me during the scuffle. After lights out, I

forward to a good spread on Tuesday, plus Pat usually lets us have a stoppy-back in his red wine cellar. All we need now are the guests. Before whojimmywhatsit's battery and credit run out for ever, I flick through her CALLS list, figuring the last few people she phoned are probably the first she'd like to invite to her funeral. Dialling the most recent one – PP POLLY – I cough up a bit of phlegm, oiling my vocal cords. I hope thingy's mates don't have a fit when they see she's ringing from beyond the grave. For a laugh, I think about putting on her voice, but I don't want another economy funeral on my hands. After six *bbring-crickles*, PP Polly answers. 'Hello, there,' I say, putting on my most charming, manly telephone manner, 'sorry to phone out of the blue. This is Shaun from SS Funerals. I'm looking after the funeral of Miss . . . hang on . . .' Here I have a slight panic attack, desperately scouring my brain for thingy's name, but it's like searching for someone in a hotel during a power cut. Leaning into the back of the van, I grab the tag hanging off the corpse's big toe, and yell (a bit too enthusiastically), 'CLARK! Ahem, see, I don't know if you've heard, but she sadly passed away

didn't try to kiss her again, but I couldn't resist clipping a lock of her platinum-blonde bob. As the queue snakes slowly slowly towards the casket, I twirl Kimberly's knotted hair in my pocket. Once the funeral's over, I might plant a strand on Shepherd's Bush Green, in the hope of growing a new Kimberly. Then again, we're about to plant an even bigger Kimberly seed in the ground outside the church – and I'm not sure if I could handle two of her. I couldn't even cope with one of her. Up ahead, Polly edges closer to Kimberly's polished, MDF husk, her sob-sob-sobbing echoing throughout the church. Shaun glances at Polly's arse as she leans forward to say farewell to her friend. I stare at the ground. I feel unwell, and not just because of the seventh Scotch egg. Soon, the stench of booze is giving everyone a headache. We shuffle faster along the stone slabs, dying to get the viewing over with, and get out for some fresh air. Pat the Priest looks green, blessing the guests in his best robes. Ahead of us in the queue, a white-haired man we met at the buffet called Charles Thursday joins in with the sniffing and sobbing, clutching his three daughters round the shoulders. Him and Polly do a

two days ago.' I use the word 'sadly' grudgingly – friends and relatives of dead people seem to appreciate it. I bite a bit more black out of my fingernails, waiting for her response. At first there's silence, then the Sony Ericsson begins to cry. Funeral directors are used to waterworks. It usually passes, if you ignore it. Once I've explained thingy's death as thoroughly and tediously as possible, lo and behold PP Polly calms down. When she's not sobbing, she sounds like she might be attractive. Or young, at least. 'Do you need any help with anything?' she asks, with a sniff. I scratch the inside of my leg. 'Actually, yeah,' I reply. 'See, it's going to be an open casket, so we might need to borrow some clothes off you. Would that be a hassle?' PP Polly sniffs again, and says, 'Erm. No, no, I'll find something. Ehm. We're the same size. Yeah. Ehm.' What a saint. We arrange to meet early tomorrow morning, for a cup of tea and the clothes. I hope PP Polly's got enough money for both our teas. I lean my head against the steering wheel and grin into the leather. My cock and balls squirm in my three-month-old boxers, waking from hibernation. Those *Easy Rider* fantasies of me and Sean

hooting duet at the coffin. I clutch Kimberly's hair tighter, getting sweatier and sweatier. I fight the urge to faint. 'Poor girl,' Charles Thursday says, through thin lips. Despite not having much family, Kimberly clearly touched a lot of people. I just wish I could've touched her, too. 'I can't believe it,' Mr Thursday adds, speaking to no one and everyone at the same time. 'Here, I . . . I never tipped you before.' Charles rummages through his moth-eaten suit pockets and removes a few coins and notes. He flutters the notes into Kimberly's casket, while his three daughters hover disinterestedly around his kneecaps. 'Ee, how nice,' Shaun announces flatly, trying to put his arm around Polly. She glances at him anxiously at first, then smiles. The jammy bastard! Why oh why did I have to fall for the dead one? Gingerly, Mr Thursday unpeels his daughters' arms from around his legs and marches them out into the graveyard, where the mourners/ extras are catching their breath, having fags. I finally take my turn to stand by the casket, shuffling along the stone slabs with my head bobbed. It pains me to look at Kimberly again, especially with all the gold and silver shrapnel round her head, like a ramshackle

zipping up and down the country in the Boots mobile home morph into one sweet-and-sour shot of Sean being shot by rednecks, and me and PP Polly swanning off into the sunset. I've never even seen her face, but she can't be that fat or hideous if she wears the same size clothes as thingy-mabob. Chuffed with myself, I scramble into the back of the van again, where whatsit's laid out, stern-faced, causing a Hammer Horror shadow against the wall. I chuck Boots boxes this way and that, searching excitedly through all the toiletries, wipes, and canisters, until I find the box branded DUREX. I claw the seal open, and stuff my right jeans pocket with ten or twelve Pleasuremax johnnies, just as Sean comes clambering back into the cab. 'Got a surprise for you,' he says, grinning. My face drops when I see what the fat fucker's holding.

tiara. I feel bad again, for squandering her money. I wish we could send her off into the afterlife with King Tut's treasures or Cleopatra's crown jewels. Still, I'm touched by Mr Thursday's tips. I wipe my nose, and stare at Kimberly's lips till my eyes start to glisten. Glancing away from her now would be like switching off her life-support machine, because I know it means I'll never ever see her again. I wait till my eyelids are brimming with saltwater, then I splash them closed. As Pat lowers the lid of the casket and locks it shut, Shaun turns to me with a grave expression and says, 'What a waste. What a waste.' I know full well he's talking about the money, but I don't want to argue. I glance back at the coffin, but I can't see a thing for tears now. 'Yes,' I say, as we plod back out into the biting churchyard. 'What a fucking waste.'

HERE LIES KIMBERLY CLARK
31.10.1984 – 1.11.2008
A DEAD NICE PERSON
REST IN PEACE

Part 3b) The Trouble with Maggots

Just when you think things can't get any messier, there's a crack of silver lightning in the MDF sky, and it starts raining soil! We're just minding our own business, finishing our dinners, when the disaster strikes. It's not the usual bogstandard fare this week: we've been blessed with a juicy size-12 steak, marinated in malty alcohol, like a lump of the finest Kobe beef. I'm chomping enthusiastically on Kimberly's rump when the initial bump of thunder catapults me into the small of her back. Like male humans, maggots love a nice bit of thigh, breast, and buttock. Young Kimberly's bottom is particularly delicious – perfectly tenderised, after receiving many playful slaps in its lifetime. I glance worriedly at the sparking night sky which, tonight, is a dark pine colour, with whorly constellations and small, splintered stars. Beneath the sky, there are hills of red cloth. I've often fantasised about flying into that sky, once I get my wings – apparently there are delicacies out there called dogturds: luxurious brown meringues, readily available from any park or pavement. I writhe about, cuddling up to my neighbours. It's freezing down here. Underground, you don't get changing seasons – it's a bit like Greenland in winter, I expect: it's always pitch dark. Surely, over those faux-velvet mountains, there must be sunlight, and a better life. Rumour has it the sun makes dead bodies and perishable foodstuffs decompose twice as quickly! A shard of lightning opens the sky again, like the end of a steel spade digging through wood. I retreat up Kimberly's lovehandles, where my mates are still gnawing away, oblivious to the storm. Beneath the surface of her skin, you can see where Kimberly's good bacteria's turned to bad bacteria, feeding on her like microscopic, legless rats. I think humans would be surprised what goes on inside a coffin –

they're not worth the expense, to be honest with you. You might as well just chuck your dead bodies onto landfill. Humans imagine coffins to be these armour-plated, airtight time capsules, protected by force fields, but what they don't realise is decay starts from within. You've already got all the bacteria you need to wither and rot, surfing in your belly. Likewise, people reckon embalming is like casting your loved one in solid bronze but, in fact, it only holds off decomposition for a few days. It's more like covering up the mould between the tiles in your bathroom with a thin layer of Polyfilla, rather than scraping it off, blasting with bleach, and regrouting. Then again, I'm not sure why humans hold such a grudge against maggots. Humans have no problem killing animals and eating them, but somehow they hate the idea of being eaten themselves. It's not like maggots go around with shotguns or garrottes, picking off helpless humans, with napkins tucked into their tuxedos. We just wait patiently for Mother Nature to serve us a tasty, pickled treat. All over Kimberly's steak, my maggot friends hover around her mouth, eyes, ears, nose, vagina and anus, like diners sensibly queueing to get into a fancy restaurant. At first, *morte-cuisine* is divine – all that fresh flesh, fat and sinew. But, after a couple of days or so, there's pretty much only egg on the menu. Me and the maggots multiply just as fast as the bad bacteria; hatching here, there and everywhere before our eventual, beautiful, butterfly-like metamorphosis into flies. Then, we buzz off without paying the bill! Oh, how we love the smell of putrescine in the morning. I scrabble along Kimberly's exposed hipbone, beating a beetle to a morsel of fatty lovehandle. There's no particular hierarchy in parasite society, although the bad bacteria do seem superior, what with their shape-shifting skills, sparkling nuclei and ability to live on the tiniest scraps of sewage. Maggots, on the other hand, are more like the salt-of-the-earth proletariat: mining the body of its fat, earning cheap thrills

404

off tits and arse, then becoming very fat themselves while dreaming of flying off to a better life. People think vultures, lions and piranhas are at the top of the food chain – they're not. It's the bad bacteria who'll get you in the end. Up above us, the lightning rips another black hole in the sky, causing more muddy comets to drop into the coffin. As the storm carries on, the shards of electricity look more and more like actual spades, smashing through the lid of the casket. An earthquake rocks the red mountains. A huge Fila Classic kicks another piece of sky off. And with that, the coffin's suddenly in disarray, with beetles, bugs and maggots flying everywhere – even the ones that haven't turned into bluebottles yet. In a fit of desperation, we burrow into Kimberly's abdomen, down down down into the safety of her small intestine. Meanwhile, there seem to be voices coming from the hole in the MDF sky. I can just make out a male voice shrieking, 'Fuck, it stinks!' Then, a deeper voice: 'Shut up! Howay. Help get it out.' Me and my pals huddle together as another earthquake shakes us into Kimberly's colon. Our whole world gets turned upside down as the coffin is wrenched out of the grave. The deeper male voice grunts, 'Get the lid off. Quick.' The casket experiences aftershock after aftershock as the MDF sky disappears completely and is replaced by the real-life night sky, miles and miles above our heads. I take a peek out of Kimberly's burst appendix. The real sky looks wonderful, with its own whorly cloud formations and woodworm stars. I'm marvelling over the moon – that giant, indigestible eyeball – when, suddenly, the whole sky is blotted out by a gruesome, two-headed monster. I scramble back into Kimberly's small intestine. 'Fuck,' one of the heads whimpers. I wonder what the monster wants. Perhaps it's an old-fashioned bodysnatcher, or a thrifty fisherman looking to save a few bob on bait. 'Fucking grow up,' the deeper voice snaps. One of the heads keeps crying, while the other looks cross but concentrated, squinting into the coffin. 'I'm gonna be sick,' the crying head gurgles, turning round to be as good as its word on the grass. 'Sshhh!' the other head spits, reaching into the grave with carrier bags on its hands. Poking my head out of a different wormhole, I listen to the crying head whine between retches, 'We shouldn't be here.' The other head scoffs, and scolds, 'You fucking baby. Howay, it'll only take a second.' And with that, he plunges his bagged hands all the way into the coffin, to rummage through Kimberly's rotten human pâté. At first, it's hard to tell what he's looking for. I hope he's not going to steal the steak – I've become quite attached to Kimberly. 'Fuck,' the head mutters, struggling. Even the cross, bossy head can't help re-re-retching as he scoops through the maggots and muddy entrails in the bottom of the casket. After a minute or so of breast-stroke, he strikes gold. He finds approximately £35 in notes and loose change, submerged in the quagmire. As he gathers up the last few coins from Kimberly's skeleton, there's a flurry of polythene above my head, and I accidentally get swept up in one of the carrier bags. I try to wriggle free, but I'm stuck fast to the plastic. 'Argh, shit!' the head squawks, spotting me. He flaps his left hand, like he's furiously waving goodbye to Kimberly. Kimberly doesn't wave back. I'm thrown across the grass, crashlanding behind a grey, weather-beaten gravestone five yards away. Blind with fear, I scrabble back in the direction of Kimberly's putrid perfume, but it's too late. The two-headed monster hastily shovels a mound of soil back on top of her coffin, stamps on it, then stomps off towards the gnarled cemetery gates in silence. I feel like a fat person from America seeing their local Krispy Kreme outlet closed down before their very eyes. As the two-headed monster fades to a mere two-headed speck in the far corner of the graveyard, I wriggle around in circles, at a complete loss. If only I was a real worm, I'd be able to dig back down to Kimberly's coffin. I feel famished already. Up above me, a few early birds dart through the dawn, cackling. I lie prone in the soil, imagining all the happy maggots sucking the succulent steak beneath me. Soon, they'll be having flying lessons. I glance sadly about the graveyard. There's no sign of life or death in any direction – just headstones, and those spindly, sinister trees that enjoy living in cemeteries. After a bit more crawling, I find a few mouldy berries under one of the trees, which tide me over until sunrise. I spend the rest of the next day with indigestion. Curled beneath a rusty leaf, I watch the odd wedding and funeral pass through the churchyard. All sorts of weeping wives and weeping widows slink by the weeping willows, far too wrapped up in their own glee and misery to think to throw me a cocktail sausage or spare animal carcass. By 4 p.m. I'm seriously considering climbing up a bridesmaid's dress, but there's probably no trace of dead skin up there either, after she's been exfoliating all bloody morning. I head back to the trees. If only I was a bit fatter, I might be able to force metamorphosis. As it stands, I might not make it through the night. Feeling weak, I watch the church's new gravedigger readying the plots for tomorrow morning. As the sky presses the sun against the horizon, he hums a Celtic ditty, levering up the turf like a fluffy green sardine can being opened. He looks like a scruffy beggar, with odd shoes and scars scribbled across his face. I wonder if he's on the verge of death himself. I wonder what his liver tastes like. An hour later, the gravedigger's finished his graft, without any handy acts of God or unexpected violence claiming his life. I think of all the selfish bastards having strokes and heart attacks in the privacy of their own homes. I think of all the wasted flesh. Come midnight, I've shrunk to the size of a fingernail clipping. I'm considering autocannibalism, when the sound of crackling foliage and footsteps gives me a start. I take my tail out of my mouth, and dart under the rusty leaves again. I pray up to the beautiful sky: please let it be a fat person from America, on the verge of a cardiac arrest! It's difficult making out a clear silhouette in the dark, especially with my measly maggot-vision. I stick my nose to the wind, lying in wait, like a cross between a tiger and a grain of rice. However, my hopes are dashed when I see the gravedigger's odd shoes again, crunching back through the foggy moonlight. I wonder what he wants this time. Maybe he's come back to commit suicide for me, or perhaps it's just time for work again. I feel sorry for the old fellow as he collects his spade from the tool shed – he's only had a few hours' respite between shifts. I watch the gravedigger panting heavily as he paces across the grass, carrying the spade in one hand, and a Tesco bag in the other. He must be delirious – or else it's just sleep deprivation – because he heads straight for Kimberly's grave and begins digging it up. Surely he's aware there's somebody trying to sleep down there. I creep out from under the leaf litter, looking forward to his reaction when he sees Kimberly's half-eaten body. I might even be able to jump back into bed with her. Then again, all the choice cuts of steak have probably gone by now – plus, she might've exploded down there. Corpses love to explode – it's their last blast of entertainment before surrendering themselves to the soil. The main reason corpses explode is they've lost the will to burp and fart. Above ground, people can be a bit sniffy towards other people who enjoy a good pump – however, farting is humans' natural defence mechanism against exploding. When you die, you no longer have control of your sphincter muscles – hence, you're unable to pump out all the excess methane the bad bacteria's been excreting inside you. After a few days, the gases have built up to such an extent, your abdomen suddenly bursts open, like a disgusting Christmas cracker. However, instead of screaming when he sees Kimberly's rotten body, the gravedigger carries on panting excitedly, hauling her coffin out of the black hole. He

doesn't even flinch at the smell. What's he up to? I hope he real-
ises somebody's already robbed her riches. Prising off the remainder of the MDF lid/sky, the gravedigger unpeels Kimberly from
her faux-velvet bed, yanking her under the armpits. He drags her
along the grass and leans her against her own headstone. Kimberly spits out beetles as she slumps against the polished granite,
staring lazily at one of the many twigs in her eyeline. I crawl
round the front of the gravestone to inspect her meat. It's disap-
pointing. She's hardly got an ounce of fat on her now: her breasts
have withered to pancakes, and her buttocks are like burst bean-
bags. Elsewhere, Kimberly's midriff has been varnished with
mould; her thighs have vanished completely; and her bones look
like badly made papier mâché. Apart from that, the rest of her is
more or less intact, although it's the bland, lean areas such as
chin skin, ankle and wrist skin, finger skin, nose skin. As expected, Kimberly's hair and nails have carried on growing – she looks
like a dog-eared ginger werewolf, with yellow claws and stubble
growing on her tibias. A few maggots fall out of her kneecaps,
joining me on the grass. They look nervous. Meanwhile, the
gravedigger adjusts Kimberly's position, making her sit up
straighter against the headstone, with her legs crossed, ladylike.
He sits down opposite her, on the grass, and removes a bottle of
Babycham and a cracked bone-china teacup from his Tesco carrier. While a lot of men are attracted to bony superwaifs, it still
comes as a shock when the gravedigger pours Kimberly a drink,
and mumbles sweet nothings to her. 'Angel . . . angel . . .' he says,
placing the trillium teacup and saucer between her legs. I can't
watch. I try to focus my attention on the same twig as Kimberly,
while the gravedigger babbles at the corpse, like she's an old
friend. He takes long, frequent slurps from the Babycham bottle,
stopping now and then to blow Kimberly the odd kiss. I'll never
understand people's perversions. Occasionally, the old sod

adjusts himself in his trousers, but I doubt he's here for sexual gratification, with all that putrefaction. Instead, he just carries on slugging from the bottle, urging Kimberly to 'Drink up . . . drink up . . . one for the road . . . one for old times . . .' Kimberly doesn't seem that thirsty, though. It's like an awkward first date – the conversation's somewhat one-sided. Me and Kimberly carry on staring at that twig, pretending to be elsewhere: Heaven, Nirvana, Valhalla, a halal butcher's. I try to think about old offcuts of beef, run-over cats, wheelie-bins, compost, fuzzy sausages, crusty underpants, Best Before Ends, dogdirt – anything to keep my mind off the morbid goings-on next to us. I'm quickly running out of ideas, when a voice screams out from the cemetery gates, 'What the fuck?!' I recognise the voice. Peering round the headstone, I see one half of the two-headed monster (the fat, tearful half) striding towards us with his hood up. He looks distraught. Likewise, the gravedigger panics, standing bolt upright and accidentally kicking over the Babycham bottle. Yellow fizz dribbles across the grass, mixing in with Kimberly's own yellowy secretions. 'What are you doing?!' the hooded lad hisses. 'I fuck death up the arse, me,' the gravedigger protests, slurring his words. The lad isn't impressed. For starters, you can hardly tell Kimberly's arse from her elbow. The lad gags, with a face the same shade as the corpse. 'You what?' he gasps. The gravedigger clenches and unclenches his fists, and explains, 'I just wanted one last night with her. One last drink. For old times.' The lad shakes his head. 'You're fucking *disgusting*,' he snaps, twitching with rage. The gravedigger spits on the ground, and slurs, 'Fuck off. It's alright. Fuck off. I know her. We were lovers. When it was alive. Fuck off.' The lad shakes his head again. He takes another glance at Kimberly, and throws up in his mouth. 'Ggggg . . .' he growls, lost for words. 'I fucked Kimberly up the arse, me,' the gravedigger adds. 'I fuck death up the arse. Just having a teacup with her.

410

Fuck off.' The lad's legs begin to tremble. In a moment of madness (or is it sanity?), he pulls the upright spade out of the soil and lunges at the gravedigger with it. 'Sick bastard!' the lad howls. The gravedigger grunts, trying to block the swift hacks from the spade, but he's too drunk to focus. The corner of the spade catches him on the skull, and his legs give way. He lands face-up in the grass, leaking red liquor. Kimberly can't watch. The fat, hooded lad spasms, gasping for breath, still overcome with rage. He gives the gravedigger a few more hacks with the spade, until the grass turns burgundy. Then, the lad crosses himself. While the fifth commandment might say thou shalt not kill, one of the first rules of survival says thou shalt not trust a pissed-up thanatophile. Gasping for breath, the lad stiffens, realising what he's done. He keeps his hood up and his head down as he hastily returns Kimberly to her grave. He decides not to touch the corpse, instead scoop-rolling her back into the black hole with the bloody spade. As he rolls her, he speaks softly to the dead girl. 'Fuck,' he says, between sniffs. 'I've fucked up, I've fucked up. I came to give back the money. I'm sorry. I'm sorry. I was going to leave Shaun. Shit. Here.' He drops some coins and notes into the grave. The lad wipes his nose with his sleeve, then he whispers, 'I love you.' I give them a little privacy, creeping behind the headstone again. Although the lad says he loves her, you can tell in his eyes he probably doesn't love her quite so much now he's seen her like this. He might not even have known she was a natural ginger. The lad makes an almighty bark when Kimberly crashes in the bottom of her grave. By the sound of it, she breaks a few bones. I wriggle forward again, as the lad scoop-rolls the gravedigger into the same hole as Kimberly. It's a handy piece of kit he's got there. Not only can you kill someone with a spade, you can get rid of the evidence with it, too. And there's no better place to murder someone than a cemetery. The fat lad might not be as daft as he looks – in fact, he's my saviour. As the gravedigger's fresh meat rolls past, I flick my tail and latch myself onto the necrophile's neck. Yet again, it's not the usual bogstandard fare: I've been blessed with a matured medium-sized steak, also marinated in malty alcohol, with a crispy cheese crust. I cling on for dear life as we're chucked into the ground. The lad covers us up with soil, then his footsteps make a mad dash across the grass, away from all this. It shouldn't take long for the gravedigger to decompose. I feel like royalty, having first dibs on his best bits: thighs, buttocks, gut, etc. First, though, I bury down through his belly-button, and into his stomach. It's bad etiquette to chomp on the corpse's flesh before you've even had a look at their last dinner. I hope he's not a vegetarian. It was annoying last week, mistaking Kimberly's semi-digested Quorn for minced beef. As it turns out, the gravedigger's stomach contains the most wondrous, greasy banquet: floating in a pool of gastric fluid, there must be about three or four portions of cheeseburgers and chips, in varying stages of digestion. I soon get myself plumped up again – gorging on the rotting beef and starchy, sugary-sweet bread buns, while the rest of him becomes overrun with beasties. After three days of indulgence, I'm ready for a nice, long nap. Nestled in one of the gravedigger's sideburns, I spin myself a cocoon, and wait for the change. My dreams all consist of one thing: luxurious brown meringues, readily available from any park or pavement. I can't wait to suck on someone's stool, dodge rolled-up newspapers and throw myself at windows. On the twelfth night of metamorphosis, I feel my wings twitching, gently cracking my brittle bedcovers. I blink my big bug-eyes at the brown sky, and sigh. Now all I need is another sick bastard to come and dig up Kimberly's grave, and let me out of this wretched place.

THE END

Part 3) Kimberly in Hell

As Hell's Bells ring out, piercing my ears, suddenly everything turns black. It's only the g-force flapping my face that tells me I'm falling into a bottomless pit. I scream, but it's like screaming in a vacuum: painful silence. I try to grab for a lightswitch, or alarm, or escape ladder, but the formless void doesn't even have a third dimension, I don't think. I cross my arms, legs and fingers, praying for the Devil to go easy on me. But it's probably a bit late for redemption.

Over the next twenty-four hours, I whip off all my clothes as the temperature rises through the Earth's crust. Sweat scribbles all over my body in invisible ink. Before long, I'm choking for air, cooking in my own juices. It's only the bittersweet wind-chill factor that keeps me from burning to a crisp.

After forty days and forty nights of falling, it turns out the pit's not bottomless, after all. I land with an almighty SMASH! in the centre of the Earth. Surprisingly, my skeleton doesn't shatter when I hit the dry concrete. There's a certain sickly immunity you get from being dead, you see – you can hurt yourself as much as you like, without the risk of re-killing yourself. The only problem is your pain receptors still work.

I prise myself off the floor, in agony, and glance cautiously about the place. It turns out Hades is just a collection of cold corridors. I wish I hadn't taken my clothes off now. I feel ashamed, turning up to a stranger's domain in the nude. Getting my breath back, I wait a few minutes in case my outfit reappears, but there's a good chance the 100% polyester fibres have been frazzled during the descent.

I decide to start walking, before I freeze and seize up. Covering my modesty with both hands, I slump through the breezeblock labyrinth, trying not to panic. To be fair, though, Hell doesn't seem so frightening, so far. The only folk I come across in the maze are lazy, crumbled skeletons, and they don't wolf-whistle or pass judgement.

Pacing onwards, every corridor looks identical to the last, only with more skeletons, and more blood caked across the walls. The further I go, the fresher the blood looks. I gag, but my empty stomach's got nothing to give.

The gore looks fake and almost comical, like I'm waltzing through a ten-year-old's rampant fantasy version of Hades. Washing-lines of entrails spin spiderwebs above my head. Several severed legs play footsie with me as I pass. Flowers grow out of cracks in the concrete, with tiny, pointed tongues instead of petals. And the whole place smells of damp carpet.

Before long, my legs grow tired. When I reach the next T-junction I stop for a breather, finding a dry spot to lean against. I try for a little cry, but I don't think it'll get me anywhere. I feel like I should keep walking, but the fear is soon trumped by the fatigue. I consider a quick sleep. I glance up and down the silent corridor, then prop my head up against the breezeblock and let my eyes fall shut. I dream of fluffy clouds, uncut crystal, and bubbling champagne . . .

I'm only out for thirty or so seconds, when a sharp, syringe-like sensation strikes me on the back of the neck, and then WHIP!! I'm wide awake again, stinking of sawdust and ammonia.

At first, Hell's just a collection of cold corridors. Then, it's a hamster cage.

I rub my fringe out of my eyes. I feel shifty and groggy, like I've been under for days. Whoever whipped me unconscious was at least kind enough to tuck me up in a bed of torn tissue, and turn the heating up. I clamber out of the Andrex to survey my new home. I'm trapped in a giant replica of my hamster cage in

414

Tottenham, floating on a gloomy lagoon of molten lava. The lava gurgles and guffs as I look out across Hell, with my face pressed to the bars. All sorts of undignified, disfigured sinners, skeletons and traffic wardens bob about on fire-retardant dinghies, while hundreds of other demons cling to the volcanic mountains jutting out of the Tabasco froth. The mountains all end in pointy peaks, poking at the toxic cyan sky. Up in the sky, Tourette's-afflicted thunderheads throw lightning and abuse at the folk down below. Pterodactyls and magpies slalom between the forks of lightning. And the whole place smells of damp carpet.

In a way, I'm glad to be behind bars, in the relative safety of the CE-certified hamster cage. A few little devils try to prod me with bent javelins and sharpened knitting needles, but they can't quite get close enough in their dinghies. Over in the red swell, I spot a few familiar faces: Fred West surges past in a speedboat, nearly capsizing Meaty and Fruity Stevie's clingfilm canoe. Meaty Stevie glares at me with his one mini-meatball eye, clad in a cloak of maggots. Fruity Stevie's adopted a more sophisticated look: a pistachio green fur coat of mould, and matching slippers.

In one corner of the cage the Death-Cap Mush-Room keeps groaning, full to the brim with penned-in prisoners. Sad, grey faces peer out at me. In the opposite corner, the Wheel of Misfortune has been doused with petrol and set alight, like a giant, deathtrap Catherine Wheel. Glancing over the toiletwaterbowl, I hardly recognise the fat, naked reflection staring back at me. I've ballooned to a size 22, and I'm covered in red whip-welts. The fat reflection gasps when something makes a shuffle-shuffle sound behind me. I shift my titanic frame ninety degrees as a sinister shadow creeps out from under the Mush-Room. Attached to the end of the shadow is Lucifer the Hamster. I'm taken aback by his height, not to mention his three, sneering heads.

'What a

                              naughty girl

                                                  you've been,'

the heads boom, one after another.

Lucifer hobbles forwards on his hind legs, carrying a long, leather whip. The tip of the whip looks brutal: barbed, with a blob of rainbow-coloured serum on each point. It must be the whip's fault I'm a size 22. The serum must fuck with your brain-waves somehow. Or your metabolism.

'I haven't been that bad,' I mumble, dry-mouthed. While I used to natter away to Lucifer in the flat, I never imagined I'd have to explain myself to him in Hell. His six red eyes seem to burn with pure malice, as I stand there sheepishly, in his shadow.

                    'You must

                                        be here

for a reason,'

the Cerberean hamster bellows, causing the cage bars to rattle. Under his pot belly, I see he's wearing a red utility belt, with the following items attached: trident, jumbo 15ml syringe, har-monica, flask, megaphone, pot of wax, pocketwatch, TV remote.

'Might be the, er, Reader's fault,' I suggest, though I swear I'm sorry for bringing you back into this.

I can't stop shaking. There's a major flaw in the human body, in that it begins to shake and malfunction at times when you most need it to be focused. Fear's only useful when you've got the option to flee your foe – it's a fucking nuisance when you're locked in a cage with a gargantuan, fire-breathing rodent.

                    'No

                                        excuses!'

Lucifer roars.

416

The first head scowls at the other two, a bit annoyed not to have a line that time. The other heads scowl back.

'Get on the wheel!'

the first head screams, holding the floor.

'Who? Me?

Us?'

the other heads enquire, confused.

'No, you daft cunts! The girl! You, Kimberly Clark! Get on the fucking wheel! Run! Run! Run!'

the first head squawks, spitting sparks.

Panicking, I stumble towards the flaming Wheel of Misfortune. I wish I'd never bought that daft hamster now. I gave him a good home, and fresh sawdust every week, and only occasionally forgot to feed him – now look how he's repaying me . . .

Cringing, I linger gingerly by the side of the wheel, dreading placing my foot on it. I ask politely, 'Can you switch the flames off? It wasn—'

'Get on

the fucking

wheel!'

Lucifer yells, raising the whip.

I do as I'm told. I slowly edge my big toe towards the whizzing rungs, as if I'm about to step into a scalding bubblebath. As soon as the first flame licks the soft soles of my feet, I squeal, feeling hot electricity jolt up my leg. There's no use crying, though – the trick is to just keep running; hopping from rung to rung, like a Russian bear dancing on hot coals. At least I'm keeping the locals entertained. The devils' dinghies rock

417

with raucous laughter as my screams become more and more outrageous.

'A a a a I a a a want a a a out a a a I a a a a fuck a a a ing a a a a a o o o o o a!' I screech, feeling my feet sizzle. Sweat gushes down my legs, but it's not enough to dampen the flames. I feel hopeless, like that famous Greek fellow, King Ixion, who was condemned to infinite torture on his own fiery wheel in Hell. And all he did was have sex with a cloud.

If I'd known the Underworld was going to be this bad, I might've tried a bit harder to stave off death. Exhausted, I slow my white-hot sprint down to a half-arsed canter. My feet look like elephant hooves already: all swollen, with bits of grilled keratin and callous hanging off. At least the heat doesn't hurt so much, now all my nerve endings have burned and blurred. Limping clumsily from rung to rung, I see someone's strung a huge red banner between the two tallest volcanoes, which reads: WELCOME TO HELL – THE HOME OF POINTLESS VIOLENCE! Underneath the banner, to the left of some neon-jacketed charity workers, there's a ramshackle children's climbing frame. I squint at it between the whirring rungs, and feel my blood run cold. There's a macabre form attached to the top of the climbing frame, with four pairs of shoelaces tied around its neck. Stevie swings softly, with his arms by his sides, like a lonesome, gravity-defying ballroom dancer. I yell breathlessly, losing my footing, 'A a a why's a a a Stevie a a in a a a a Hell a a?'

'To

torment

you!'

Lucifer explains, reapplying a little serum to the whip's barbs, from the pot on his utility belt marked HELLUCINOGENIC WAX: a hellishly bad pun.

Stevie doesn't flinch as a brute of a magpie swoops out of the cyan sky, and lunges for the round, shiny thing lodged in his skull. It's all too much. I scream, choking for breath, 'A a a a get a a me a a out a a a make a a it a a a stop a a I'll a a a do a a anything!'

The magpie flies off with Stevie's bloodied eye-stalk dangling out of its beak, like a sunburned worm. As the black beastie retreats back into the cyan gloom, I feel a swift, sharp crack of a WHIP!! and all the flames disappear from the Wheel of Misfortune. Endorphins and lactic acid instantly kick in, kicking me off the scorched, steaming wheel. I land in a smouldering heap in the sawdust.

'Well, there is

one way out

of Hell,'

Lucifer says, casting a cooling shadow over me again.

Outside the cage, the crowd edges closer, eavesdropping. The Tourette's-afflicted thunderheads stop swearing and sparking for a second. Meaty and Fruity Stevie look about themselves dumbly, wishing they had ears.

'How?' I ask, brushing away the last of the embers.

'We'll let you

work in Heaven,

if you can pass

three simple tasks,'

the Cerberean hamster explains. He takes the TV remote out of his belt and fires it over my head. A fine thread of infra-red lightning shoots out of the end, causing the cyan sky to dim, and a 125ft silver cinema screen rises out of the crater of one of the volcanoes. The crowd 'Oohs' and 'Aahs'.

'What type of work?' I ask, sensing a stitch-up.
'Menial,'

replies Lucifer.

'Cash desks, probably.
                    Reasonable hours, though.'

'Aye, go on then,' I say.

Lucifer's heads curse and cringe, as he struggles to find the right button on the remote. He flicks awkwardly through the AV channels, until the words

TASK ONE
WATCH THE FOLLOWING PROGRAMME
WITHOUT FALLING ASLEEP

appear on the silver screen.

'Make

                              yourself
comfortable,'

he carries on, conjuring up a couple of pillows and a 10-tog duvet out of thin air. He tucks the pillows behind my back and throws the duvet over me, like a tablecloth or napkin. After all the sprinting, it's tempting to stretch my legs out and unwind, although I'd best not get too comfy. Instead, I rub my face vigorously, as the action begins on the silver screen. It starts with two commentators, in grey suits, with grey faces:

Hello, and welcome to the Beelzebub Broadcasting Corporation's coverage of the FA Cup fifth round. We're live from Bramall Lane, in what promises to be a stinker of a match between Sheffield United and Middlesbrough.

420

Oh hell, Hell. Not this. Last time this match was 'live', Lucifer kindly gnawed through the TV cable, so we didn't have to watch it.

On the teamsheet for Sheffield, we have Kenny and Geary and Morgan and Kilgallon and Naysmith and Stead and Tonge and Quinn and Martin and Beattie and Sharp. For Middlesbrough, we've got Schwarzer and Young and Wheater and Pogatetz and Grounds and O'Neil and Rochemback and Arca and Downing and Aliadière and Mido. On the bench for the Blades are Armstrong and Carney and Hulse and Lucketti and Shelton. And on the bench for Boro are Alves and Boateng and Hines and Johnson and Turnbull. The man in the middle is Chris Foy from Merseyside. To recap, for the Blades we've got . . .

I can't for the death of me remember if it was a twenty-goal thriller when me and Stevie trudged over to the Lord Parmo to watch the lowlights. I glance over at Stevie on the climbing frame, but I can't seem to catch his eye.

Southgate looks stern as the teams kick off. Boro pass it about a bit. United pass it about a bit. Geary. To Morgan. Naysmith. Back to Morgan.

The picture flicks to the pitch at Bramall Lane, where the teams are passing it about a bit. The ball's like a pendulum, swinging softly from one side of the silver screen to the other. There's only been one minute of play, and I can feel myself drifting off already . . .

Quinn swings a cross in. Kilgallon gets a volley on it . . . ooh, straight into Schwarzer's paws.

As if Hell isn't warm enough already, Lucifer slips a hot-water bottle under my covers, then skips off to brew me a cup of cocoa. While he's over by the toiletwaterbowl, filling up the kettle, I discreetly nudge the bottle out of the bed with my left hoof.

Some div's chucked a beachball into the penalty area. Ahh, the

421

ref clears it in fine style. Ha, marvellous stuff.

Lucifer hands me the hot cocoa, topped with whipped cream and flambéed Grand Marnier marshmallows. For a second or two, his vast frame obstructs my view of the screen.

'Piss off, I'm trying to watch the footy ball,' I snap, to humour the bastard.

That shot-to-nowt seemed to hit Rochemback on the arm. Hands go up. Blades whinge for a penalty. Referee denies.

In between sips of cocoa, a strange PLOP PLOP PLOP sound catches my attention.

Mido on the break, with Aliadière PLOP in support. It's two-on-one. My word, he's PLOP toe-punted it out of play! Mido seems PLOP to blame a bobble on the pitch. The pitch blushes.

I have a long, delicious yawn. As I carry on gazing at the silver screen, through slitted eyelids, gradually all the players and pixels merge into one big, blurred mess, pulsing in time with the PLOP PLOP PLOP sound. Suddenly, I feel ever so sleepy.

Young clatters into Martin. Quinn clatters PLOP into Young. Free-kick to Boro.

Through sagging lashes I spot something blue and round land in the mug. I swirl the mixture. To my horror, a half-dissolved Valium bobs back up to the surface.

Sharp through on goal, och, dragged down by Wheater. Wheater should be off! Ref goes into his pocket. Ahh, only a crap, boring yellow card.

Panicking, I chuck the mug away from me, showering the spectators with bluey-brown sludge. As the mug smashes against the bars, an infant woolly monkey leaps from the Death-Cap Mush-Room, in fright, with a teapot full of Valium under its left arm. Trembling, the monkey scrambles behind Lucifer's hind legs, 'yook yook yook'ing.

Blades win yet another free-kick.

I force my fingers down my throat and vomit a creamy stream of cocoa all down myself. A dozen regurgitated Valium spatter across the duvet cover.

Bit of amateur dramatics here – if you watch, er . . . watch on the replay: Tonge and Beattie pretend to run into each other. Training-ground antics. Marvellous stuff.

In the corner, the woolly monkey stares glumly into the teapot of Valium with its tail between its legs. Lucifer grabs the monkey and flings it back into the Mush-Room, unimpressed.

Only one minute to be added on, thank fuck . . .

I mop up the puke with one of the pillows, casting evil eyes at Lucifer. While I do feel slightly livelier again in the head, I'm still ever so weak in the stomach – and I'm sure Lucifer has more foul play in store for me.

'Come on, England!' I shout, trying to get back into the game.

Wheater concedes another free-kick. Expertly wasted by Tonge.

I wipe flecks of bile out of my eyes so I can focus on the lads better. One way to keep myself occupied is to judge their legs in terms of handsomeness or hirsuteness, but that only reminds me of all the nice boys I've left behind on the surface of Earth. I'll never take a boyfriend down here. The men in Hell are either hideously disfigured, or only interested in pre-teens.

Finally, the referee puts us out of our misery. Half-time.

'That went quick!' I chirrup, with a smirk. Lucifer triple-sneers.

               'Just carry on
                     making yourself comfortable
now, breathing in
              and out,
                         innnnnnn
and ouuuuuuut,
            as you await the
                    half-time analysis,'

Lucifer coos, attempting some slapdash, amateur hypnosis. He swings his antique pocketwatch in front of my eyes, substituting the commentators' grey faces with clockfaces, one after the other after the other after the other after the other after the other after the other . . .

Unfortunately for Lucifer, the hypnosis fails to take hold. I barricade my brainwaves against his subliminal spiel, filling my head with as much nonsense as possible (like recalling the Boro and Blades teamsheets, counting the shavings of sawdust, praying to God).

Exasperated, Lucifer rummages through his belt of tricks, swapping the watch with a silver harmonica. I bite my lip. Rather than throwing blues into my cocoa, it looks like the hamster's going to sing me some. The middlemost head blows a B for three seconds, then the three of them burst into song, like a demon barbershop trio:

'Rock-a-bye baby, in the treetop,' they chorus, harmonising badly, 'when the wind blows, the cradle will rock, when the bough breaks, the cradle will fall . . .'

This is awkward. It's never nice having someone sing at you. I've spent far too many birthdays staring at the floor with burning cheeks, while people belt the 'Happy Birthday' dirge at me.

With a couple of flicks of the whip, Lucifer commands the crowd to rock the hamster cage back and forth. They heave their oars underneath the plastic, and swish me seasick.

'And down will come baby,' Lucifer's heads carry on, 'cradle and all.'

While the grey-faced commentators carry on discussing the first-half inaction, Lucifer claps his paws together, summoning a queer orchestra from the outer limits of Hell. All sorts of vulpine violinists, bovine bassoonists, serpentine sitar players, asinine

accordionists, noctilionine nose-flautists, proboscine percus-
sionists, tethidine theremin players, and a hippopotamine horn
section turn up, cruising along the lava on separate gondolas.
Sullen-faced, the animals adjust the tuning pegs of their instruments at random, before breaking into an atonal, sickly-sweet
rendition of Brahms's Lullaby.

I feel like I've been painted into the Musical Hell panel of
Bosch's *Garden of Earthly Delights.* The lilting lullaby soon
swells to a death march, with Adolf Hitler conducting from the
mountaintops, throwing Nazi salutes and *Sieg heils* this way and
that.

'GUTEN ABEND! GUT' NACHT!' Hitler croaks, like he's
still at Nuremberg. 'MIT ROSEN BEDACHT! MIT NÄGLEIN
BESTECKT! SCHLUPF UNTER DIE DECK!'

Fortunately or unfortunately, the football begins again on
the silver screen. I stretch my eyelids open, trying to stay alert,
despite the lullaby and lugubrious voices of the commentators
combining to make a kind of aural anaesthetic.

Right, we're under way again, here at Buggerall – pardon –
Bram*all Lane.*

I slap my cheeks.

Martin whips in a cross, oh, oh . . . no. Kilgallon nuts it into
the side-netting.

When Martin whips in the cross, Lucifer WHIP!!s the air, turning the sawdust into some other, green and smelly, substance. At
first, I'm worried he's decked the floor with cannabis buds. A lot
of folk who smoke cannabis suffer from heavy, bloodshot eyes
and lazyitis, but this stuff is even worse: hops. One of the four
major ingredients of lager, hops are what make you fall asleep on
your sofa after a marathon session down the pub. I can feel them
kicking in already, like the Green Man tugging on my eyelashes.

Och, Mido pulls off a bicycle-kick. Straight into Kenny's hands.

'You bastard,' I grumble at Lucifer. The more I writhe about in the hops, the more it ignites their stench. Soon, I'm feeling terribly, terribly drained.

Two substitutions. Hopefully this might liven things up. Boateng comes on for Arca. Martin makes way for Armstrong. Repeat: Boateng comes on for Arca. Martin makes way for Armstrong.

I slap myself across the face again. A hundred half-finished dreams flutter from my brain like swatted flies. I wish I had some smelling salts, or coffee beans, or Pro-Plus. I even start lusting after a goal – anything to keep me occupied for the last twenty-odd minutes.

Boateng's kicked the ball against his hand in the penalty area, trying to spice up proceedings. Ref denies Sheffield the penalty.

Clocking my desperation, Lucifer comes over to ply me with drugs – however, they're not the ones I was hoping for. The hamster detaches the jumbo 15ml syringe from his utility belt, flicks the chamber, and sprays a little of its silvery contents into the air. The spray hits a passing death's-head hawkmoth, which instantly yawns and falls, unconscious, into the hops.

Neither team looks set to clinch the match. In fact, they're all looking a bit spent.

I shriek as Lucifer jabs the needle into my flabby left arm. The sudden pang of pain perks me up for a moment, before the tranquilliser stakes its claim on my veins. My bottom jaw sags. The silver screen blurs again.

Downing launc   wards P gatet   oggin, but Mad D   ecides not to   ore. Bolloc .

'MORGEN FRÜH! WENNS GOTT WILL!' Hitler squawks, whipping the orchestra into a monstrous/monotonous frenzy. 'WIRST DU WEIDER GEWECKT!'

Looks lik   estined fo   replay. Beli   r not, we hav   hrough this all o   ain, next f king Wedn   ay.

426

The tranx sends each of my limbs to sleep, starting first with the arm which has the syringe stuck in it, like a flag marking the territory of the Land of Nod. I feel the evil gel literally creeping through each of the fingers of my left hand, then back up . . . up . . . up . . . to my left shoulder, then back down . . . down . . . down . . . towards my abdomen.

Three minu   dded on. Oh el , no.

The tranx is like a tickly, sickly snake – a horrid, liquid Medusa gently turning me into stone, from the inside. Lucifer watches with glee, kicking hops at my nostrils.

It's all over. It's all over. My plight, that is; not the match.

A bit of a pass. A bit of a kick. A bit of a jump. Ooh, a bit of a kick there by Grounds.

The referee's a wanker! Blow your fucking whistle!

'GUTEN ABEND! GUT' NACHT!' Hitler yodels, egging on the tranquillisers. 'VON ENGLEIN BEWACHT! DIE ZEIGEN IM TRAUM!'

Pass. Kick. Dribble. Dribble. Dribble. Dribble. Dribble. Pass.

If I can . . . just . . . hang . . . on . . .

'Get me

the fucking

chloroform!'

Lucifer roars, his eyes burning redder than ever. He races about the cage, flapping his arms and panting. Perhaps he's given me the wrong dosage of tranx, forgetting to account for my size 22 frame!

There's a rustle of confusion in the crowd. The whole scenario feels like a Vaseline-tinted nightmare. A tank marked CHLORO-FORM is passed from dinghy to dinghy, edging its way towards the hamster cage from a storage unit in the far reaches of Hell. I watch the clock tick to 90:00+1 through sore, slitted eyelids, as Lucifer hauls the tank aboard. The crowd are all in raptures!

They think it's all over!

Dribble. Dribble. Dribble.

It is now.

In a moment of genius inspiration and intense stupidity, I yank the trident out of Lucifer's utility belt and plunge it into my left kneecap. The sharp snap of agony and adrenalin perks me up enough to stay conscious, just as Lucifer comes at me with a chloroform-soaked rag. I scream, blindly pushing his furry wrists away. The hamster spits fire as we wrestle, digging ourselves a shallow grave in the hops. I kick at him helplessly as the rag edges closer to my nose, and the clock ticks to 90:00+2, and the orchestra plays a bum-note, and the crowd all hoot, and then

Toot! Well, you'll be pleased to know it's over. That's all from us here at the BBC. Thanks a lot for watching. See you for the replay. Sorry it's been shit.

I've done it! The silver screen turns black. The orchestra's strings snap. The hops turn back into sawdust. I collapse in a heap of celebratory suffering, clutching my red kneecap.

Pain is a strange experience in Hell. On Earth, when you're hurt, your body sends out quick impulses, telling you whether to fight or take flight – in other words, your brain wants you to stay alive. In Hell, your brain's not that fussed, because you're already dead. Your brain pretends to be elsewhere, while you're tortured beyond belief.

'Ready for

the next

task?'

Lucifer booms, snatching back his blood-pocked trident.

'Urrrrrrrhhhhhhhh,' I whine. 'I'm knackered.'

I sink my head into the pillows, torn between sleep and waking again.

'This next

                 one'll perk

                                you up!'
the hamster explains, summoning Adolf to the cage. The Führer clambers onto a kind of zip-wire, connecting the mountaintops with the cage. I blink sadly, watching his side-parting flapping as he launches himself through the cyan sky, holding tight to the black pole.

                 'You like

                            wearing make-up,
don't you?'

Lucifer asks me, helping Hitler aboard.

'It's alright,' I reply, wondering what the catch is. Toxic face-mask? *Goldfinger* reenactment? Fake tan?

                         'Adolf, mate,
paint her

                 up for

                          Humanseye,'
the hamster says with a smirk, handing the Austrian a small palette of poster paints.

Adolf Hitler, the famous, evil painter of watercolours, slaps back his oil-slick fringe and squints at me, sizing me up.

'What's *Humanseye*?' I ask the ground.

'It's like *Bullseye*,' one of the pterodactyls hisses, landing on top of the cage, 'except instead of Jim Bowen, darts and a dartboard, it's got Lucifer the Cerberean Hamster, Molotov cocktails and your face.'

My fingers and toes tingle with torment. Fortunately, the tranx have long demolished the boundary between dream and reality, so the anxiety has blurry edges.

'Can I sleep on it?' I moan, as Hitler pastes white undercoat on my cheeks.

'*Nein!*' Adolf snaps, glancing proudly at Lucifer with an impish simper. Hitler – the poster boy of terrestrial evil – seems somehow pathetic down here, in the presence of Lucifer. He's clearly worked his way up the Hellish ranks after topping himself in his Berlin Bunker in 1945, but in the netherworld he's more of a glorified flunky than a fully-fledged Führer.

I keep still, while Hitler paints an RAF roundel on my face. The innermost red ring around my nose is apparently worth 25 points, while the middle white ring (which includes my top lip, cheeks, and both eyes) is worth 15, and the outermost blue ring (encompassing my chin, temples, ears, and forehead) is worth 10. In spite of all the tragedy involved, Hitler asks me to smile, so he can etch BONUS 15 POINTS on my front teeth, with a saliva-resistant marker.

My face feels cold and heavy in the warpaint. It takes a bit of strength to wrench my eyes open again, in time to see

TASK TWO
HUMANSEYE™
SCORE 50 POINTS OR HIGHER
WITH 3 THROWS
TO PROCEED

appear on the silver screen. I grimace, wondering if the paint is highly flammable, or water-based.

'No grimacing!

You'll crack

the paint!'

Lucifer screams.

With a swift crack of Lucifer's WHIP!! the cyan sky dims into variety-theatre darkness again. Hitler scuttles up into the safety of the Death-Cap Mush-Room as the crowd edges closer to the cage bars. My stomach shifts.

'Who's throwing the Molotov cocktails?' I ask, as a spotlight suddenly envelops me, like catching a bluebottle in a neon jam-jar.

'Please welcome back
                    to the limelight:
                                        the blindest man
in Hell!'

Lucifer bellows triumphantly, gesturing towards the WELCOME TO HELL banner. By the climbing frame, one of the hamster's minions cuts Stevie down, chainsawing through the four pairs of shoelaces. Stevie hits the hard shards of play bark with a horrid thud, and instantly comes back to life. His blue face gently pink-ens as his lungs ravenously suck up the sparse oxygen.

The bug-eyed minion strongarms my boyfriend into a bright pink gondola, which carries him towards us, through the crowds, like a sacrificial lambkin. I bob from foot to foot, watching the murderers and paedophiles spit at him and jeer as he floats past. In the distance, a giant common seal bull glares at Stevie as it hangs bound to a tree, its belly pierced with bent javelins and knitting needles, like a blubbery St Sebastian. My blood runs cold, despite the choking, tropical heat. I want to be sick.

I'm not sure which is worse – seeing your loved one in pain or being in pain yourself. Stevie looks petrified as the bug-eyed minion posts him through the door of the hamster cage. I can't help focusing on his eye-sockets – the right one dark brown and scabbed over; the left one freshly picked, still glistening and leaking red tears. Welcoming him to the cage, Lucifer gives Ste-vie a firm slap, then explains the 'game' to him:

431

'Get her in
                                    the face, or
I'll show Kimberly
                 the video of
                                    you and Na—'

'No, n-no, no,' Stevie whimpers. I wonder which video they're on about. 'I'm I'm I'm s-so sorry,' my boy carries on, clasping his redblush cheeks. I think he's talking to me, though his dead eye-sockets are pointing towards redneck leatherface Ed Gein when he says it.

I stress, 'Don't worry, it's not y—'

'No speaking!'

Lucifer growls.

                 'There's no place
                                    for sentimentality here!
And you'll crack
                 the *fucking paint*!'

I sigh through my nose, straightfaced. In a way, part of me feels relieved Stevie's blind now – mainly the part with the elephant hoof, and the size 22 belly.

                                    'Right, Stevie,
old boy,'

Lucifer says, handing him the first bottle,

                 'do your worst!'

A second spotlight twitches around Stevie, trying to keep up with his dithering movements. Gritting my teeth, I watch with part terror and part embarrassment as Stevie swivels robotically around the cage, like a drunkard at a Viennese waltz. At one point he trains the bottle on my forehead, but then he spins again, and loses me. He takes a stumbling step backwards, then conducts a sharp whisk to the left, and finally launches the Molotov cocktail – *fzzzzzzzzz* – straight into Lucifer's toiletwaterbowl.

The crowd cheers contemptuously. Despite having no eyes, Stevie clearly looks to the ground in anguish.

'Oh dear, oh dear,'

Lucifer snickers, lighting the second Molotov cocktail. When Stevie takes hold of the bottle, he whisks and spins around again, rejecting skill and spatial awareness in favour of pure chance. Perhaps he's acting imbecilic on purpose, though. Perhaps he doesn't want to hurt me. Perhaps he does still love me. Then again, the fact he doesn't want to fling a flaming petrol bomb at my face means he'd rather see me condemned to infinite, infernal torture in Hell than see me work nine-to-five in the sweet service industries of Heaven. Perhaps he actually hates me.

I raise my eyebrows and flare my nostrils, increasing the surface area of the RAF roundel. However, just as Stevie's about to throw the bottle, an even better idea strikes me. Instead of just standing there on the spot, like a goalpost, I sway in tandem with Stevie, more like an overenthusiastic goalkeeper. They say a moving target is trickier to hit than something stationary – however, when the gunman's blind and the target desperately wants to be shot, the rules of warfare change dramatically.

Fzzzzzzzzz, remarks the Molotov cocktail excitedly.

Stevie twists his hips, and launches the bottle shotput-like into the rafters. Taking a dive in its general direction, I watch the Molotov cocktail ricochet off the side of the Death-Cap Mush-Room (giving Hitler and the prisoners a bit of a start!), then wince as it lands a soft, glancing blow on my right temple.

'Agh!' I grunt, in semi-celebration. Stevie lets out a vague congratulatory cluck, with a dumb, lost expression on his face. Around the cage, the crowd hisses at us, more annoyed about the bottle not exploding than the 10 points gained.

I touch the side of my cheek, stemming a trickle of blood. As I ready myself for the final bottle, I wonder why people thrive so much off watching violence. Everyone hates being on the end of it, after all, and yet there's nothing more entertaining than seeing someone else having their face ripped off.

The spectators are on the edges of their gondolas, as Lucifer sparks up the last Molotov cocktail. He seems annoyed about my lucky 10-pointer, but Heaven knows where I'll get the other 40 from.

'Come on th—' I start, before the hamster interjects:

'DON'T FUCKING
CRACK THE
PAINT!!'

The intention wasn't to crack the paint. The intention was to give Stevie an idea of my whereabouts, subtly disguised as exasperation. Instantly, Stevie's ears prick up. He takes one measured step forward and two steps back, then catapults the last bottle in a beautiful trajectory towards my skull. The cocktail sprinkles sparkles as it spins through the air. I grit my teeth together, just before the bottle crashes neck-first into my gums, then, in a moment of reckless reflex, I headbutt the main body of the bottle into my shoulder. There's a sharp explosion, which takes half my nose off. My two front teeth fall into the sawdust. My face caramelises. I drop to the ground.

The crowd goes silent. For a minute or so, I'm the only one making a sound: a cross between hellish screaming and heavenly cheering. I dunk my head into the toiletwaterbowl, leaving

434

behind chunks of chargrilled flesh. Through molten eyelashes, I see

FOREHEAD + FRONT TEETH BONUS + NOSE =
10 + 15 + 25 =
50 POINTS!!

flash on the silver screen, in a gaudy fluorescent star.

'This

isn't

fair!'

Lucifer screams. Obviously, he's a man who prides himself on his integrity.

The hamster's heads glance at each other with nervous expressions. Meanwhile, Stevie shuffles in the corner, not sure how to celebrate. He starts off by clapping his hands together twice, but then he becomes subdued, in a concerned, boyfriendly manner. I want to tell him I'm alright, but it's difficult getting the words out.

I roll around in the sawdust, weeping at the chilli-pepper sting under my skin. I inadvertently tar-and-feather myself, gluing shavings to my melted cheeks and chin. After a bit more rolling and weeping, I finally wrench myself from the ground, leaving behind a bloody, brown silhouette. I brush myself down gently, and glare at Lucifer through puffed-up eye-slits.

'Ready for

your next

task?'

he drawls, while his minions extinguish the last few flames around the cage.

'Aye,' I answer. I sound like I've got seven golf balls in my mouth.

435

After sitting through a goalless draw and a pyrotechnic facial, nothing scares me now. I can already imagine myself clocking-on at the Pearly Gates in angelic overalls. I might have to wear factor-1000 sunblock now my face has been torn off, but the perks of Heaven should far outweigh the pain. I might find myself a new boyfriend up there. Or, better still, Stevie Wallace might have a doppelgänger in Heaven.

After some hushed deliberation, Lucifer puffs his chest out and barks:

'Alright then, smart

                  arse, give this

                                   one a whirl!'

I want to sneer, but my skin's far too tender. As it turns out, though, the last task's laughably simple. I split myself five new smiles when I see the words

TASK THREE
DON'T MAKE A SOUND
FOR HALF AN HOUR

appear on the screen.

'Are

                  you

                                ready?'

Lucifer snarls, watching me closely.

I say nothing.

On the silver screen, the number 30:00 appears. As it counts down, I clasp my hands over my mouth, silently breathing through my new nostrils. Around the cage, the crowd goes quiet as well, placing their various ears – elfin, pig's, cauliflower – up to the bars. Even the lava outside stops burping, holding its breath.

I pick at my cheek, silently peeling away a dangling, irritating bit. I attempt to look nonchalant, rolling my eyes disinterestedly as the clock ticks past 29:00.

At 28:21, Lucifer announces:

'Now, please welcome
our second
special guest!'

There was bound to be a catch. I stare silently, with lips wobbling, as my dead daddy waddles out of the Death-Cap Mush-Room. Instead of a striped prisoner's uniform, Barry Clark wears a floral pinny and platform heels. The audience makes a loud farting sound, unable to hold back their laughter. Barry carries a feather duster, made from the tickliest tailfeathers of the rare Raggiana bird of paradise. Lucifer claims he made the bird extinct, just so Barry could have that duster.

Barry hardly acknowledges me as he trudges through the singed sawdust. I don't know if he's more ashamed about his cleaning-lady costume, or my obese nakedness. I want to say something. I wish I could blink 'Don't worry' in Morse code, but my pesky, evil eyes have never been good at relaying niceties.

'Take it
away, Mrs
Tickle!'

Lucifer says, giving my dad a WHIP!!

Grudgingly, with his head down, my dad goes at me with the feather duster, tickling me under my armpits and around my midriff. I bite hard into my tongue. After more vicious WHIP!!s from Lucifer, my dad becomes more inventive with the duster, poking me in those famous, nameless places behind my elbows

437

and knees. I lock my molars together, wincing and writhing about in silence. The only way to survive the ticklish torture is to adopt some kind of meditational displacement – for instance, imagining the feathers are in fact maggots, tucking into my corpse above ground. The idea of decomposing is enough to stop anyone giggling. Thousands of other dismal thoughts spiral from the maggot one – for instance, whether the Necropolitan Police found *The Last Will and Testament of Kimberly Clark* in my handbag; whether anyone cried at my funeral; whether anyone still visits my grave to lay flowers.

'USELESS!' Lucifer's three heads chorus, WHIP!!ing my dad again. Barry grunts, stumbling backwards. He picks anxiously at his pinny, and asks, 'You want me to stop?'

'FUCK

HER!'

Lucifer yells. I presume he's being rhetorical.

'Should I go back in the thing?' Barry enquires, edging back towards the groaning Death-Cap Mush-Room.

'You heard

me!

FUCK HER!!'

the hamster booms, much to the delight of the crowd. I feel all my internal organs shrink, sucking the blood from my head. I think I'm going to pass out. Hopefully, I can do it silently.

For all the good it'll do him, Barry squares up to the hamster and spouts, 'You're disgusting. Juvenile and disgusting.'

It's unnerving, seeing your dad in a rage. Barry was never the most authoritative of people but, like any parent, he has a natural knack of sticking up for his spawn in times of crisis. And he's got a natural aversion to shagging his spawn, too.

438

'Fuck her,
or I'll chop

her into a

million pieces!'

Barry shudders, but manages to remain composed. I'm proud of him. For a few seconds, Barry's eyes keep flicking up to the top-left region of his skull, like he's got an excuse not to shag me up there. Finally, he finds it: 'I can't get it up, with her face all . . . like that. I don't do burns victims.'

His dry, deadpan delivery almost makes me splutter. Like most comedians – successful or not – Barry has a quickness of tongue that's helped him out of many sticky situations in the past. It's just a shame it couldn't help him against his heart attack in 2002.

'Very well,'

Lucifer spits.

'Bring on the

back-up head
and Viagra!'

Barry crumbles.

Lucifer yanks open the cage door, where a demonic monk in a black habit is waiting with a silver platter. On the platter, there's a decapitated human head and a syringe filled with blue goo. The head looks freshly plucked, with blood still glistening around the serrated stump. I don't recognise her at first, what with her not squealing abuse at me. However, there's no mistaking her noose ponytail and depressive expression. Kimberley Clarke stares back at me, lazy-eyed and slack-jawed.

Lucifer takes the syringe from the platter and orders more of his minions to pin my father to the floor. I avert my eyes as two turkey-headed henchmen strip the pinny off him and restrain him. I don't see Lucifer stick the spike into my dad, but it sounds like it hits him somewhere sensitive. I've never heard my dad scream before, except during sports events and general elections. I blink away more tears, focusing on an empty section of cyan sky. Barry makes an ashamedly erotic 'Aaah' as the Viagra kicks in, then he screams again, when one of the turkeys comes at his daughter with a machete. I catch a glimpse of my stunned reflection in the blade, microseconds before it swings swiftly through my neck.

It's not the cleanest of cuts. My head dangles for a few seconds, like a heavy medallion, before gravity takes hold and snaps the remaining tendons. Then, I accidentally boot it across the sawdust.

Suddenly, all my senses go haywire. The shock of having my head detached from my body sends me into spasms of panic, existential anguish and skewed perception. I watch in disbelief from the corner of the cage as Lucifer lifts Kimberley's head from the silver platter. As he screws it roughly into the blood-spitting socket where my neck used to be, I feel the room spinning, spinning, spinning, spinning. My decapitated Kimberly head spins in time with Lucifer spinning my Kimberley head, until we both see sparkles, and black out simultaneously.

WHIP!!

When I regain consciousness, I'm upright again, being shagged halfheartedly by my father. Being 25% Kimberley and 75% Kimberly, I have 25% of Kimberley's consciousness interfering with my own thoughts, though it doesn't detract much from the fact I've got my father's cock inside me. FUCKING CUNT! Kimberley screams, subconsciously, stating the obvious.

My new head has bad breath. I plug my mouth with my ponytail, trying not to whimper. Flickering on the silver screen, the clock's only down to 18:22. I must've only been out cold a couple of seconds.

440

I shift my wrists in the shackles. I've been trussed up against the Death-Cap Mush-Room, with two pairs of pink, furry handcuffs. I bite harder into the greasy bit between my teeth. Behind me, my dad pumps away, gasping sadly with every thrust.

FUCKING CHILDCATCHING CUNT! announces Kimberley's subconscious. I'm not sure who it's directed at.

If I shut my eyes, mind-power can help desensitise me. Just as I imagined the Raggiana tailfeathers were maggots, so too I can imagine my dad's cock's merely an indecisive tampon. The only trouble is when Barry repeats, 'I'm sorry, I'm so sorry,' after five minutes of fucking. I'm tempted to look over my shoulder and put a finger to my lips, to silence him, but I don't want to give him the wrong impression.

Watching us closely, Lucifer's having a whale of a time. He juggles my old, charred Kimberly head, before throwing it out of the cage door. It lands with a dull crunch in a dinghy full of gaunt, rabid dogs. Then, it quickly disappears.

After wiping his paws, Lucifer unsnaps the megaphone from his utility belt, switches it on and holds the mouthpiece to my lips. I bite the ponytail even harder. The muffled creak of Barry's penis cranking in and out of my dry fanny is amplified throughout the volcanic amphitheatre. My cheeks wobble, but still no sound comes out of my mouth.

'FUCK

IT!!'

Lucifer squeals, either as encouragement, or in exasperation.

To get Barry more in the mood, Lucifer dabs more 'Hellucinogenic' serum on the barbs of his whip, then goes at him like a rampant jockey, flogging his flabby buttocks. The hamster screams again:

441

'FUCK
IT!!'

Definitely encouragement, that time. Barry ends up deep-
penetrating me; his pelvis jerking forward with every whiplash.
Behind my head, he keeps making a sniffling sound, which can
only be crying. Then, out of the sniffles, come some words: 'If it,
er, if it helps, love, I'm . . . I'm not really your dad.'

The whipcracks fall silent. The crowd edges even closer to the
cage. I turn my face towards Barry, but my lost expression can't
quite express all the questions that need answering when someone says something like that to you.

'I mean, I'm not your biological dad,' Barry carries on. 'If it,
er, helps things, I, er . . . shit. I'm sorry, darling. I shouldn't have
sssssss . . .'

I glare at him, urging him to explain himself. Barry stares back
at me, red-faced and remorseful. Men are never any good at reading women's emotions. Unsure whether to keep shagging me,
Barry leaves his crooked cock inside me as he explains. 'A . . .
well, maybe it's best you c-can't talk. God. I'm so sorry – me and
Mag should've said something. Mag, she lost three kids to cot
death, see. We were at our wits' end. We thought it was something
up with our genes. We were . . . well, there was this awful court
case, which I won't get into, but we were left with a . . . a load of
trouble. Ehm, we d-decided to apply for . . . for an adoption. And
that's where you come in.'

I wonder why Barry thinks this would help me out. Which is
worse: being shagged by your dad, or finding out you're adopted
and being shagged by your foster dad? Either way, it still smells
suspiciously like incest. One more black-comedy clang of a cym-
bal in the cacophonous skronk that is Hell, the home of pointless
violence.

442

'We got you when you were a toddler,' Barry continues. 'You were a blessing, love. See, it took so long for the court case to . . . b-blow over. Ehm, well here's the thing, see: your mam and me were innocent, of course, but we got accused of negligence, because of all the cot deaths.'

Finally, Barry allows his knob to flop out. I wonder if he'd planned to give me this speech when we were all alive, or whether the plan was to keep it a secret for ever.

'You understand we didn't do anything,' Barry stresses. 'It could've been anything. Anyway, the case blew over, but there was still this hassle over our application, for the adoption. Finally, they, er . . . they found us this Irish couple. Apparently, you were one of seven sisters. But the family was so poor. The dad was this old gravedigger. And the mam was unemployed. And so she couldn't cope, with the seven kids. So she started giving them away. And, and we were desperate.'

With a lump in my throat, I'm suddenly hit by a horrible sense of déjà vu. My mind flashes back again, to the first time I met Donald, when he told me he had a daughter called Kimberl(e)y. At first, I thought he was just saying that to butter me up. Then, more recently, I thought he was on about Kimberley.

All this time, was he on about me?

As we stand there, shattered and bent double, Barry goes on to describe the moment he and Mag first saw me, in Belfast City Hospital (not Middlesbrough General, as my mam and him originally made out).

They had a choice between me and my twin sister, Anastasia, but chose me on the strength of my 'darkly intense'* eyes. Anastasia was sent to a couple of postal workers in Dagenham, Mr and Mrs Clarke, who, in a cruel twist of fate, also died when she was

* Evil, as it turned out.

443

in her teens. Following their death, Anastasia – who had always hated the name, and had developed a kind of dissociative identity disorder in her infancy – took to calling herself Kimberley (with two 'e's), in memory of the twin sister she'd never met, or spoken to – until that fated day I stepped into the Wethouse. She always resented being separated from her twin at birth, or so I gleaned, from 25% of my subconscious:

FUCKING SUPERIOR CUNT, Kimberley – or, rather, Anastasia – announces.

I shudder, as my memory creeps back to the time Donald was intimate with me and a bubbling shower curtain. To my left, Lucifer bears a three-way smirk.

'Seriously, though, you were perfect when we saw you,' Barry carries on, half whispering, with his shoulders hunched. 'I . . . I hate to drop this on you, here. I hope me and Mag gave you a better life than what you would've got. I mean, God knows what you would've ended up like, if you'd gone elsewhere.'

FUCK OFF, screams Anastasia/Kimberley, before retreating back into the shadows of my subconscious, for good.

I feel ill. Luckily, it's possible to cry silently, though it means letting your nose drip. I dribble liquid shoelaces from my nostrils, completely worn down by Barry's revelations. I hardly have time to digest all this heartwrecking information before Lucifer pipes up again:

'This is all very interesting, mate,'

he spits at Barry,

'but young Kimberly's

got a task to fail.'

444

I glance baggy-eyed at the clock again, through the tears. 9:57, it says. Five or so seconds later, the clock ticks to 9:56. The bastards – it's a trick clock! Enraged, I point up at the screen, unable to put my point across in words. Lucifer just stares back at me blankly.

'Don't worry, love,

you've got plenty

of time for

more fornication,'

the hamster remarks, before introducing more special guests. He WHIP!!s Barry in the groin, causing him to crumple on the sawdust, then points into the cyan sky, where I can see a small, distant dot growing into a whirlybird seed, then a Frisbee, then a fan, then a helicopter. Pasted on the side of the chopper are huge block capitals, black on red: ON HIRE FROM HELL HOLS AND HOSTELS LTD.

The clock ticks to 9:55 as seven figures descend from the helicopter, on separate winches. Mr Monday, Tuesday, Wednesday, Thursday, Friday, Saturday and Sunday wave at the crowd from their individual ropes, dressed like typical sex tourists: sad old Mr Tuesday wears sandals, with a cardigan flopped around his shoulders, while Mr Wednesday and Mr Friday have plumped for clashing Hawaiian shirts. And all seven of them are severely sunburned.

'Seven bridegrooms

for one of

seven sisters!'

Lucifer quips, thoroughly enjoying himself.

'Unexpected fatal outbreak

of *E. coli* at

445

the Ristorante

di Fantasia!'

he explains.

They look edgy, visiting Hell for the first time. When my weekly exes step aboard the hamster cage, they're told to line up by the still-smoking Wheel of Misfortune, while a gaggle of busty dominatrixes fluff them. The dominatrixes lap-dance awkwardly around the lads, with put-on, pouting expressions. Now and then, they slide their hands up their Bermuda shorts. Now and then, the lads 'Mmmm' self-consciously.

I cringe as my weekly exes disrobe, shifting about, surreptitiously comparing each other's manhoods. Their cocks are in varying states of perkiness, in correlation to their ages. Poor, white-haired Mr Thursday can't seem to get it up at all, although the fact he has three young daughters belies the dangliness. Perhaps his parts want to be no part of this.

One by one, the men shuffle towards me. At first, it looks like they're going to take it in turns to bang me. Technically, I do have seven holes, though.

I glance up at the cyan sky again in desperation. Two bloodshot moons blink back at me, blankly. Dearest Reader – if that's you – now might be a good time to end this. While I'd hate to deprive you of a salacious scene involving a seven-man gangbang, I don't think my body can take it. I might never walk or talk again. And I might be forced to scream out.

If you shut this book now, we can pretend Hell suddenly freezes over, and we all live happily ever after, paused at exactly 9:36 by the silver-screen clock.

Then again, perhaps you're enjoying all this pointless violence. After all, many folk's idea of Heaven is sports, bloodsports, and observing farfetched hardcore sex.

446

Well, it's your choice. But, if I was you, I'd put this book down right now. Shove it down the back of your bookcase, or bury it in the back garden – then we can pretend I'm not going to be ripped to shreds in the grand finale.

Please. I'll give you four blank pages to think it over.

Oh, hell. So, you've decided to read on, have you?

My heart sinks, as my first weekly ex achieves wood. I blink at the clock. The clock blinks back nonchalantly. I've still got 9:29 minutes to hold on. Grudgingly, I take the ponytail from my mouth, relax my pelvic floor muscles and flare my nostrils.

Go on, then, have your kicks, you pricks.

Read how awkwardly they mount me, like seven elephants squeezing into a Mini Cooper.

After a bit of bickering, snooty Mr Wednesday gets dibs on my arsehole, mumbling sinister sweet nothings as he worms his knob in. He cocks his left leg, so basketball-shaped Mr Friday can squeeze in underneath him, turning my labia in on themselves.

Read how I almost bark, when internet-enthusiast Mr Saturday commences the skull-fucking. He plugs my throat, causing a soundless waterfall of saliva to string out the sides of my mouth. Lucifer listens closely for gag sounds. Nothing gives.

As a substitute for Vaseline, Mongoloid Mr Monday and musical Mr Tuesday work some of the Hellucinogenic serum into my earholes, before drilling into them with their dicks. The double-pan tremolo effect of their unsynchronised shagging turns the cacophony of Hell into a kind of reckless rumba: the dance of love.

Meanwhile, the friction between Mr Wednesday and Mr Friday quickly erodes the wall between my anus and vagina, like property developers knocking through the walls of your apartment to create an open-plan shag pad. I hear the elastic of my arsehole snap.

After a WHIP!! or two to their blushing botties, kind-hearted Mr Thursday and Mr Sunday reluctantly stuff their flaccid cocks up my nose. They daren't look at me, averting their eyes to the sky. Perhaps it's remorse – or perhaps it's that I've got a beard and moustache made of hairy testicles, and they don't want to throw up.

452

I think I'm going to pass out. I can't breathe. I can't breathe. While my weekly exes carry on bucking me, the Hellucinogenic serum in my ears reacts with my oxygen-starved brain, transporting me through time and space to a variety of hellish sexual scenarios:

First, I'm basking on chocolate-coloured mudflats, being ravaged by a bunch of butch, honk honk honking bull seals. The common seals are common as muck, fighting each other for the right to rag my arsehole, rejecting any kind of courtship or foreplay, or lubricant.

Next, I'm on my kitchen counter, mummified in clingfilm. Meaty Stevie carves a hole in the plastic with a biscuit-cutter before going at me with his chipolata, squealing, 'Die! Die! Die!'

Next, I'm a corpse. I spit maggots out of my eyeballs, bent over my own headstone, while Donald fucks me in the dog position. He constantly clangs me over the head with his spade.

Then, I'm back in the hamster cage again. As my weekly exes grow closer and closer to climax, the rumba speeds up. I clamp my eyes shut. I can't breathe. I can't breathe. What follows is extremely difficult to describe, not least because my sensory organs are clogged with cocks. I'm vaguely aware of a white explosion, combined with the smell of sour milk, mild bleach and stagnant pondwater. Warm sludge fills my skull and open-plan genitalia, like Polyfilla.

I want to cough. I want to croak. Instead, I throw myself onto the sawdust, exhausted. My seven holes dribble raspberry ripple. Round about me, seven dangly trouser snakes eye me, all abashed. Above the cocks, some of my weekly exes high-five each other, pleased with their performances. I lift myself onto my haunches and peer into the toiletwaterbowl. My reflection has no ears, two red wounds instead of nostrils, a Chelsea smile, and sharp slashes like a Union Jack across my face. The murky

453

water becomes polka-dotted with red. I want everybody dead. But they're dead already.

The only consolation is the quivering, mirror-image clock, ticking away on the surface of the water. I watch it tick from 0:10 to 0:09 to 0:08 to 0:07 to 0:06 to 0:05 to 0:04 to 0:03 to 0:02 to 0:01, while Lucifer desperately tries to smash the screen with firebolts, screaming obscenities. The crowd are up in arms. The silver screen cracks cleanly down the middle, just as the numbers click to 0:00. Then, everything falls silent.

Oh, dear Reader, I couldn't have done it without you!

Hell's Bells toll and tinkle throughout the amphitheatre: a reluctant celebration. Lucifer throws down his fizzing trident. Outside the hamster cage, the crowd carry on kicking up a fuss, demanding a rematch. My weekly exes pull up their Bermuda shorts, nervously avoiding the gaze of Lucifer, their legs pin-striped with semen. I post my prolapsed vagina and dangling rectum back into my body, then hobble through the slurried saw-dust and into the arms of Stevie. It gives him a bit of a start, but I think he recognises the taste of my breath in his mouth. I hope he can't taste the blood, not to mention the rest.

'I love you, I love you,' I whisper in his ear, which is what you tend to say to people after a crisis, and it's what you want to hear back. Stevie smiles, trying to look longingly into my eyes, but his sockets are still focused over my shoulder at Ed Gein.

'S-s-s-s-sorry for everyth-thing,' Stevie mumbles. I silence him with another kiss.

I feel like a low-budget disaster-movie heroine, overcoming all the odds to earn myself a wondrous, slushy, happy ending. After the kissing, I keep my arm around Stevie while I sort out the Heaven-ward travel arrangements with Lucifer. Part of me wants to pick up the trident and jam it into his nostrils but, in the end, I decide to be nice. I ask the hamster, politely, 'So, where do I leave from, then?'

454

With a sour expression, Lucifer WHIP!!s me softly on my left little toe, turning me back into a size 12, with my old, regurgitated Kimberly Clark head and a polyester work uniform. As far as I can tell, under the shimmering skirt and blouse, my hidden holes are in full working order again.

I can't wait to get in the cool of the clouds. It might be better to reign in Hell than to serve in Heaven, but you never know – they might let me sup Krug champagne on the job. I might even be able to wangle a two-hour dinner break. And a bottomless tips jar.

'Hang on,'

Lucifer snaps,

    'I'm afraid there's

           one more twist
to this story.'

The three heads snicker, unable to contain their excitement. Gradually, the sawdust turns into a kind of quicksand or porridge beneath me, sucking my legs under. I shriek, hoarsely, 'What?!'

     'We were only

         joking when we
said we could

    send you to Heaven.'

The hamster pokes its bottom lips out, feigning guilt and pity.

'What the fuck?!' I scream, as I'm pulled slowly into the whirl-pool. Next to me, Stevie sways about, rendered useless again.

          'What do you
think this is?

    Family fucking *Fortunes*?

        You're in Hell.

It's supposed to

be annoying.'

The more I struggle, the quicker I sink. My weekly exes watch uncaring from the sidelines as the porridge gobbles me up. Barry rushes forwards with his arms outstretched, before a feisty barb strikes his balding forehead, and then WHIP!! he disappears, in a puff of odd-sock-scented smoke. I consider grabbing for Stevie's legs, but I don't want to pull him into the maelstrom. I scream, 'Where am I going??'

Lucifer cracks up. Outside, the audience are in stitches too, pressing their hardened, criminal faces up against the bars again. Holding his belly, Lucifer announces:

'You're going back

to Hell! That's

the idea behind

eternal damnation, love.'

'Egh?' I gasp, trying to keep my chin above the surface.

'And that means

you too, Grim

Reader. Turn

back to page 413,

and start fucking

reading again!'

Lucifer stares up at your moon eyes and sneers. I'm so, so sorry, fair, impartial Reader. It was probably bad enough reading Lucifer's excruciating infamy just the once, let alone re-re-re-reading it infinitely. I'm sure you've got better things to do than turn back to page 413, but I still need your help. Don't leave me!

I let out a blood-curdling gurgle, as my whole head is sucked under the swirling sea of sawdust. Then, I find myself falling. As it turns out, the bottomless pit was bottomless, after all. Or, at least, it's bottomless with a short stop-off in Hell every forty days, like being stuck on a Möbius strip with a fag burn in it.

I hope you're not mad at me. Sorry in advance/hindsight for calling you a prick on page 452. You're not a bad sort, and it's not your fault we're in this infernal, infinite predicament. Just remember to shut the fucking book next time I tell you, though, won't you?

WHIP!!

NOT THE END

Acknowledgements

Thank you: family and friends, Leyla Asadi, Will Atkinson, Lisa Baker, *Bare Bones*, Natalie Boxall, Luke Brown, Peter Cleak, Company of Angels, Pia Conaghan, Jona Cox, Crossing Border, Kevin Cummins, Jo Cundall, Rob Dabrowski, Beckie Darlington, Kate Davies/Science Ltd, Beth Davis, Sara Dennis, Greg Eden, everyone at Faber and Faber, Neal Fox/*Le Gun*, Helen Francis, Lizzie Francke, *It's Nice That*, Laurence Johns/Amuti, Tim Jonze, Vinita Joshi, Carrie Kania, Lauren Laverne, Caspar Llewellyn Smith, Claire Malcolm/New Writing North, Philip Maughan, Paul McGee, Jim and Chris McGuinness, the mighty Milwards, mima, Mary Morris, David Mullett, Patrick Neate/Book Slam, Andy Neil, Northern Stage, Stephen Page, Nikki Parrott/Tigerlily Films, Rebecca Pearson, Jo Phillips/.*Cent*, Bradley Quirk, John Retallack, Robin Sheppard, Michael Signorelli, Gavin Smith, Rod Stanley/*Dazed & Confused*, Cathryn Summerhayes/WMA, Tristan Summerscale/*Notes from the Underground*, Becky Thomas, Andy Thompson/Brucey Ripper Band, Annabel Turpin/ARC, Irvine Welsh, Erica Whyman, and sorry to anybody I've forgotten. Thanks also to the cast of the *Apples* play: Jade Byrne, Dylan Edge, Abigail Moffatt, Therase Neve, Louis Roberts, Scott Turnbull.

Special thanks to Lee Brackstone and Trevor Horwood, for whipping this many-headed beast into shape. And thanks to the Reader, for rolling with it.